One Man's Castle

One Man's Castle

J. Michael Major

FIVE STAR
A part of Gale, Cengage Learning

Detroit • New York • San Francisco • New Haven, Conn • Waterville, Maine • London

Major

GALE
CENGAGE Learning·

LIBRARY OF CONGRESS CATALOGING-IN-PUBLICATION DATA

Major, J. Michael.
   One man's castle / J. Michael Major. — First edition.
     pages cm
   ISBN-13: 978-1-4328-2683-3 (hardcover)
   ISBN-10: 1-4328-2683-2 (hardcover)
   1. Widowers—Fiction. 2. Murderers—Fiction. 3. Detectives—Fiction. 4. Murder—Investigation—Fiction. I. Title.
PS3613.A3538O54 2013
813'.6—dc23   2012043428

First Edition. First Printing: March 2013
Find us on Facebook– https://www.facebook.com/FiveStarCengage
Visit our website– http://www.gale.cengage.com/fivestar/
Contact Five Star™ Publishing at FiveStar@cengage.com

Printed in Mexico
1 2 3 4 5 6 7 17 16 15 14 13

For Eileen, Derek, and Colleen
My love, my hopes, my dreams come true
And for Nancy
I miss you so much, Mom

ACKNOWLEDGMENTS

A novel is indeed a long journey of many steps. But contrary to popular belief, the first and last steps are the easiest. It is all the ones in between that are the hardest, and I am forever grateful to the following people for keeping me on the right path:

First and foremost, to my family, Eileen, Derek, and Colleen, who make every day worth living. You make me the proudest husband and father ever. I love you.

To Gordon Aalborg, Deni Dietz, Nivette Jackaway, Tiffany Schofield, Tracey Matthews, Erin Bealmear, and everyone at Five Star Publishing. You're all the best!

To John Helfers, for his interest, encouragement, and incredible patience throughout the writing of this novel.

To Sgt. Michael A. Black (ret.) of the Matteson Police Department for his friendship and terrific writing suggestions and, along with Officer Stephen Shoup (ret.) of the Chicago Police Department, for invaluable help making the police as real as possible.

To Julie Hyzy, another friend and writer who offered great suggestions, who has the cheerful ability to keep me from getting a migraine whenever I have to learn something new on the computer. She also went above and beyond in helping me with promotion. Everyone should be lucky enough to have a friend like her.

To Deborah Morgan, a wonderful writer whom I'm proud to call my friend and ink-sister, thanks for all the encouragement.

Acknowledgments

To Earl A. Peterson, former prosecutor for DeKalb and Ogle counties in Illinois, I send many thanks for helping me with issues related to lawyers and the legal situations involved. You're one of the good guys.

To Carrie Tedore, who graciously answered all my questions about casinos and their security operations.

To Matt and Beth Major, my first readers, for their insightful recommendations (and for being a great brother, Matt).

To Dick and Judy Voegtle, who helped Walter find his way around Minnesota and Iowa.

To Beckie Kendrick, who first suggested that the word *novel* wasn't such a bad thing and the belief that I could write one. Thanks for the confidence, as I send a heartfelt PYUPJ.

And to all those who shared their wisdom and experience but didn't want to be mentioned, I sincerely thank you.

All of the people mentioned above worked tirelessly to help me, and any mistakes are mine alone.

"Behind every great fortune there is a crime."
—Honoré de Balzac

CHAPTER ONE

Walter Buczyno heard the footsteps under his bedroom window even before his wristwatch vibrated.

He froze. His heart pounded as he fought his natural instincts to jump out of bed. He forced himself to remain motionless, lying still under the covers in the darkness of the early morning hours. The element of surprise was his greatest weapon, and any sound might give him away.

Walter could not allow his next victim to know that he was awake.

The watch vibrated then. Silently he slid his right hand from under the pillow and pressed the crystal. A faint red LED seven appeared on the face before blinking out of existence two seconds later. Outside, footsteps crunched the frozen snow as the first flakes of the latest January storm pelted the windowpane. Walter breathed deeply, exhaling slowly through pursed lips, trying to stem his growing anger.

The heavy curtains nearly muffled the sound of a hand slipping on the frosted glass, and his watch vibrated again. Walter allowed the motion to complete its ten-second run, already well aware of the location of the intended invasion. His ears prickled in the expectant silence. He squinted in the darkness. The only light in the tiny room crept in through the doorway from the living room window and the faint glow of the ancient clock-radio on the nightstand beside his lonely bed. As he watched, a panel flipped, the sound like the snapping of a playing card, correcting the time.

Two-nineteen A.M. But this was no game.

Walter heard someone step away from the window and move toward the back of the house.

Flinging aside the faded afghan that Dottie had knitted for their twenty-fifth wedding anniversary, Walter slid to the floor. His movements were practiced and fluid, silent as a spider in its web. He reached under the bed. His threadbare black T-shirt and matching sweatpants stretched tightly over his muscled frame as his fingers skimmed the thick carpet. His hand quickly found the baseball bat and hand-wrapped roll of garrote wire he kept prepared for nights like this. He set them in his lap.

The furnace whooshed. A gush of warm air and the smell of singed metal burst from the nearby radiator vent and blew across his face. Walter tensed. Outside the wind howled, the storm tearing at his brick bungalow, creaking the siding in the back. His ears listened for any unnatural sounds inside the house, unable to hear anything more than the thunderous beating of his own heart. Was it the excitement of the chase, he wondered, or the anger of injustice that drove him to do what he did?

Or was it simply his own form of revenge?

Another clock panel flipped. Walter wiped his sweaty forehead on his shirtsleeve, then draped the afghan over the radio, dousing the light. He curled his fingers through the wire roll, making sure the balled free-end protruded from the side of the wrap just outside his fist. When he squeezed, the thinly insulated wire bit the skin between his forefinger and thumb.

He stood, loosely holding the wooden bat with his other hand. His thumb caressed the gritty medical adhesive tape wrapped around the neck of the bat and found it oddly comforting. Three luckless bastards had already discovered the hard way that Walter Buczyno wasn't going to take their shit any longer, and tonight it appeared his crawlspace would be making room for a fourth. He wanted—no, *needed*—to feel the wire cutting flesh, the bat crushing muscles, shattering bone. Sometimes it was all he had to look forward to, the only thing that kept him going. Served them right for what happened to Dottie.

He shook his head, trying to dislodge the vision of that horrible, painful night. But the excruciating memory had burned so deeply into his soul that it torched his every waking thought and ignited his angry nights. It defined his entire miserable existence, his only reason for not joining Dottie by slitting his own throat or dangling at the end of a rope. Like it or not, they created what he had become. And in doing so, Walter regained control.

The watch vibrated again, switching to an intermittent vibration before he could press the crystal. The special alarm system worked amazingly well, warning him of the immediate danger.

Someone was in the house.

A shiver ran up his spine. He hadn't heard a thing. The others had announced their arrivals with the shattering of glass or a crowbar splintering the backdoor frame. But this one was silent. Did he have something else in mind?

Walter gripped the bat with both hands, the wire roll between pressing into his palm. He crept to the bedroom doorway. The heavily padded carpet absorbed every sound. His eyes scanned the shadows. Nothing moved in the living room or hallway. He nervously licked the salty sweat off his upper lip while he listened.

And then he heard it: a boot faintly scuffing the basement's concrete floor.

The blood drained from his face. Sweat turned cold on his forehead and down the small of his back. Gray flecks sprinkled his vision when he hesitantly pressed the watch's crystal, already fearing the answer he knew he'd receive:

An LED one.

Walter staggered. He leaned heavily against the doorjamb, his knees shaking so fiercely he could barely stand. His breath came in short, ragged gasps; his hearing a buzzing white noise. His mind exploded with memories of a kicked-in screen, muddy footprints, tubes in Dottie's nose and arms, of that man . . . of that man—

How could he know? How could he know? a voice inside his head screamed. The sudden, intense rush of memories hit him like an emotional punch in the gut. Walter doubled over, squeezing his arms around himself, clenching his teeth to keep from vomiting. He swallowed hard, forcing the bile down as his head swam with images he impossibly tried to suppress.

But as footsteps slowly climbed the basement's creaky wooden stairs, a single thought somehow pierced the confused static of his mind: How *could* he know? After the police removed the broken screen, Walter had painted the glass black and boarded up the window from the outside.

So how could a complete stranger know about a window hidden under the back porch for nearly eight years?

How indeed.

Walter heard the basement door open, the rusty hinges screeching in the kitchen. Gray flecks colored to crimson sparks at the corners of his eyes. His breathing grew deep and controlled as the last vestiges of fear oozed from his nerve endings. The churning knot in his stomach condensed into an angry, burning fist.

How dare this man enter the house through the window of his nightmares!

Walter's hands wrung the neck of the bat. His heart pounded as the adrenaline raced through his system. Oh, he'd make this one pay, all right. Even more than the others. He'd show him what it felt like to suffer every goddamned day of his life.

A wet boot squeaked the tiled floor. The intruder hesitated.

Walter lifted the bat over his shoulder, bent slightly at the knees, and readied himself just inside the bedroom doorway. His vision cleared, the shadows becoming sharp and distinct. Across the room another clock panel flipped, the sound muffled by the afghan. His skin prickled like a caffeine rush on a cold morning.

Come on, baby. Come to papa.

The footsteps resumed. He heard the intruder move steadily from the kitchen into the dining room as if he knew the way. Walter rocked back and forth on the balls of his feet while the end of the bat etched tiny circles in the air. His hungry eyes searched the darkness.

Walter waited. Ready. Prepared.

The shadows moved. Around the corner a figure emerged, silhouetted by the living room window. The intruder held a gun in front of him. A semi-automatic, Walter guessed, judging by the short rectangular barrel. The faint light glossed the top of the nickel-plated weapon.

The intruder moved quietly down the hallway toward the bedroom. His thick down jacket made gentle whisking noises when the fabric rubbed against itself. Walter tightened his grip on the bat, knowing he would have to hit this one much harder than he'd hit the boys who visited last summer. His heart pounded with nervous excitement. Another chance to make things right in the world, to correct the mistakes he'd made with Dottie.

The intruder stopped outside the doorway, inches from where Walter stood. Walter could smell the melting snow in the man's greasy hair and the stale beer on his breath. He watched the man's eyes move as the intruder searched the interior of the room while his vision adjusted to the darkness. The gun wavered menacingly in the air between them. Sweat beaded on Walter's balding crown and rolled into his thinning hair along the sides and back like snakes slithering through drought-withered grasses.

He held his breath. Steady. *Steady* . . .

A clock panel flipped. The intruder jerked, dropping into a shooter's stance, aiming his gun at the sound, and Walter swung for the fences. The bat hit under the man's wrist with a reassuring, bone-breaking crack and lifted the gun up into the air as the weapon fired. The shot rang out, blinding in the darkness, deafening in the silence. The force of the blow sent the intruder crashing backwards against the hallway wall as the bullet penetrated the ceiling above Walter's head. He heard the gun clatter into the bathroom, discharging again when it struck the ceramic tiles, the bullet pinging off the chipped, enamel-coated metal tub. The smell of cordite filled the hallway.

Plaster dust rained on Walter's head as he stepped into the hallway and swung again. The bat connected with the man's abdomen hard enough to send a shock wave of pain through Walter's shoulders and to knock the intruder to the floor with a grunted "Oof." Quickly, Walter dropped the bat, grabbed the balled end of the wire, extended an arm's length as the roll spun in his hand, and wrapped it around the man's neck before the intruder had a chance to catch his breath. Walter snapped the wire taut, feeling it bite into the flesh above the man's Adam's apple, and tightened as the rage flooded him again.

The intruder fought wildly. Walter held tight, kneeing the man away whenever he tried to loosen Walter's hands or reached behind to grab his legs. Soon the man's struggles became more violent. He clawed at his neck, desperately trying to loosen the wire. His frantic kicks sent the wooden bat bouncing across the carpet and *thunk*ing against the bed frame. Walter pulled harder, the muscles in his arms quivering with the strain, hearing the intruder's panicked grunts over the ringing in his ears. The man's spine arched, his head tilting backwards as his bulging eyes rolled up into their sockets and his tongue protruded like a surrendered flag. Walter stretched the wire tighter, tighter—

Outside a snowplow rumbled by, the heavy metal plow scraping the storm's first layer off the uneven, poorly patched asphalt. For an instant, its bright headlights lit the darkened hallway like a flashbulb popping in the darkness, illuminating the upturned face.

Franklin Edward Harris. The face of a thousand nightmares.

Walter gasped. Could it really be? His muscles slackened, loosening the wire. Harris's unconscious body slumped to the floor. Walter hesitated, his mind a battlefield of conflicting emotions, unwilling to believe what his eyes had shown him. Before Harris regained consciousness, though, Walter bound his wrists and ankles, then dragged the body down the wooden stairs into the basement.

Walter smiled. He had other plans for this one.

CHAPTER TWO

It was shortly after eleven A.M. when Detective Kevin Riehle arrived at the scene of the accident. A white squad car with Westbrook's black and teal lettering barricaded Blodgett Avenue. A heavily bundled officer, busy detouring traffic onto a side street, stamped his boots in the cold and waved the detective forward. Riehle parked his unmarked Chevy Impala away from the shattered vehicles.

Paul Simmons approached as Riehle slammed his door. "So O'Connell finally retired," the patrolman said, his breath making thick clouds in the crisp, winter air. His eyes blinked rapidly as the biting wind cast a gray pallor over his exposed skin, accenting the dark brown melanin spots on his African American face. "Never thought I'd live to see the day."

"Me either." And that was certainly true enough. Riehle's now-retired partner had hung around longer than most of the current officers could remember. Jack O'Connell's father had been chief of the original two-man police force back in the days when Westbrook, located thirty miles southwest of the Chicago Loop, was little more than a feed store and rural farmhouses. Jack had joined his father after a brief, though somewhat distinguished, stint as an army MP and had stayed ever since, enforcing the law as the urban sprawl expanded beyond their quiet suburban borders.

But while the other officers turned to Jack for guidance, Riehle was silently forced to watch his aging partner slip into lazy habits of shoddy police work and alcoholism. He'd simply been around too long and knew too many people. Riehle lost count of how many times he'd respectfully stood at his partner's side, biting his tongue and shifting anxiously from foot to foot, while Jack shared another over-told anecdote and a toot from behind the local business owner's counter before finally admitting it was time to respond to the dispatcher's call. So when Jack hung up his holster and permanently moved into his fishing cabin in northern Wisconsin, Riehle found himself immensely relieved and more than a little amazed that nothing serious had ever happened in all their late arrivals. O'Connell, it seemed, had truly been born under a lucky star.

"When's the new partner arriving?" Simmons asked.

"Sometime today. The lieutenant will bring him by after all the paperwork is signed. I guess the pension forms and transfer clauses between counties are a real headache."

"Know anything about him?"

"Just that he's transferring out of Chicago for personal reasons." A frigid breeze curled its way inside Riehle's charcoal gray overcoat and scratched the back of his neck like a witch's fingernail. He flipped his collar up, buttoning it against the cold, then nodded toward the wrecks. "What happened? I heard your call on the radio."

Simmons exhaled sharply, the cloud forming tiny ice crystals on his bushy mustache. "Real nasty one. Guy coming home from an all-night poker game hit an ice patch, blew a stop sign, and plowed into a couple bringing their new baby home from the hospital."

"Jesus." It was exactly what he'd always feared O'Connell might do. "Any survivors?"

"Just the husband. And the drunk, of course."

Riehle turned away. Two blocks east of the accident was Middaugh Hospital, and he could easily see the roof of the cylindrical Daisy Pavilion over the bare treetops from where he stood. He tried to block the images of what those last few seconds must have been like as the couple's joy shifted to unimaginable horror. Or how it could have happened to Gwen and him when they brought Karen home from that same hospital seven years earlier. Sometimes his work struck a little too close to home.

"How's the husband doing?"

"Unconscious, thank God. They've already transferred him to the ER. I'd sure hate to be the one that's gotta break the news to him, though."

Glass fragments scraped underfoot as they neared the mangled vehicles. The sky, empty of all the precipitation it had dumped overnight, was a cloudless, azure blue. Riehle pulled his sunglasses from his inner pocket and slipped them on to protect his eyes from the blinding glare. The arctic front off the plains that pushed the storm eastward had dropped the temperature twenty degrees, and the wind whipped the dark brown hair on Riehle's unprotected head and drove the wind chill factor well below zero. The bitter cold pushed through his overcoat and slacks like tacks through gauze, biting his goose-pimpled flesh beneath. Every shallow breath stung his nostrils and sinuses, stiffening his nose hairs, and the frames on his sunglasses burned his skin. He dug his gloved hands into his pockets and wished he'd worn a hat.

The intersection of Cedarcrest and Blodgett was filled with patrol cars and EMS vehicles and their responding personnel. Cedarcrest Drive ended in a T-intersection with Blodgett Avenue, which ran parallel to the southern side of the train line that carried commuters along the many stops through Granger County into Chicago. The embankment between the end of Cedarcrest Avenue and the train tracks was hard-packed with asphalt-peppered snow from last night's plows and trampled with EMT boot prints. A lake of ice from a broken water main filled the intersection, and the cars involved in the accident were smashed against the embankment. The wind whistled around the squawks from the officers' radios, and a horn blared the moment before an express train rumbled past, billowing the powdery snow off the tracks in a ghostly mist.

Simmons pointed to the skid marks on Cedarcrest before they reached the ice patch. "Drunk or not, going too fast for conditions or not, any decent attorney will be able to get the charges reduced. No one could have stopped once they'd hit that patch."

"Don't get me started on lawyers. What's the scoop on this guy?"

He consulted his notebook. "Todd Metcalf, thirty-four, commodities broker at the Exchange. Lives in one of those mini-mansions on Lyman Avenue. Twin daughters enrolled in a private grade school. Wife is unemployed, but spends most of her day helping out at the girls' school and donating her time to local charities." He flipped the notebook closed. "Your basic Yuppie nightmare."

"Oh, you're just making my day."

Riehle spotted Metcalf in the backseat of a squad car. Hands cuffed behind his back, Metcalf wore a slightly bloody bandage over his left eyebrow. His short, blond hair was disheveled, and even at this distance, Riehle could hear him belligerently demanding to speak with his lawyer. A uniformed officer, his armed crossed and wearing a bored look, ignored Metcalf's outbursts by resting his butt against the door. The officer nodded to Riehle, who nodded back, both as a hello and his agreement with the situation: Let the sonofabitch wait until they took him down to the station.

Departmental photographers mulled around the wrecks, taking shots from every angle. Metcalf's black BMW was pushed off to the side, the hood crumpled from its impact with the rusty navy blue Cavalier still embedded in the snow bank. The collision had been directly into the car's backseat and had bent the frame into a *V*, crushing the passengers instantly. Both driver's-side doors had been pried off and set aside, and blood smeared the upholstery and the fractured infant car seat and stained the snow behind the shattered windows on the other side.

"Most of the blood came from the mother," Simmons said. "She was facing the car seat when the collision occurred. Chances are she never knew what hit her." His tone implied *We hope*, the officers not wanting to believe the woman had known what was happening as she desperately tried to protect her child. "They both died instantly, though the mother's body cushioned the impact enough to keep the child's body intact. I don't think our little broker boy would be looking so pretty if we'd found the baby any other way."

Riehle examined the front seat. The blood on the cracked gray dash and steering wheel probably belonged to the father. On the passenger side floor, a few splatters smeared a once-white, plastic string-tied bag that displayed the hospital's yellow and green logo. Looking inside, he found the bag contained wipes, diapers, creams, and other free samples the maternity ward routinely gave new parents. Riehle's temples throbbed as he remembered receiving an identical bag when Karen was born.

"Think the husband will make it?"

"Don't know. The Cavalier's an older model that never had air bags, and his head injuries were substantial." Simmons shrugged. "Me, I'm not so sure I'd want to wake up to the news he's going to get."

Sunlight glinted off an object dangling from the rearview mirror that had somehow remained tied in place through the force of the collision. Riehle cupped the porcelain statuette in his black-gloved hand. A tiny Sleeping Beauty lay on a miniature bed, clutching a long-stemmed rose to her breast.

"Please don't tell me the family's name is Jensen."

"How'd you know?"

"Remember the puppeteer we had at Karen's birthday party last summer?"

It took Simmons only a moment to make the connection. "Oh, shit."

Riehle kneeled beside the open door. He rubbed his gloves together, blew into them, then pressed them against his near-frostbitten ears, desperately trying to keep everything from spinning out of control. Work was something to be kept at work, he felt, as if he could protect his family from what he saw day in and day out by never discussing anything once he got home. But he knew he'd never be able to keep this from Gwen.

He closed his eyes, remembering that hot July day. How Larry Jensen and his puppet show had entertained everyone with Karen's favorite stories from Grimms' Fairy Tales. Amazed, he'd watched as Jensen's hands moved the strings with such deft precision that the marionettes seemed alive on the tiny stage. And how later while the children played in the backyard, the adults—he and Gwen, Paul and Regina Simmons, and the Jensens—sat at their picnic table in the shade under the giant Crimson King maple tree with its maroon-colored leaves. A breeze lifted the corners of the red and white checkered plastic tablecloth as the Jensens excitedly told them they were finally expecting after so many years of trying. Almost unable to contain their joy until after the first trimester had passed and afraid to jinx their good fortune, the Jensens had only told their families the day before and were bursting with the news they shared. Gwen, sunburn just beginning to paint the tip of her nose and shoulders and the breeze feathering her strawberry-blond hair, had passed him a knowing look with her dazzling green eyes, acknowledging the Jensens joining the Parents-To-Be Club. The look had melted his heart and led to their own gentle lovemaking later that night. He remembered how she'd gazed at him afterward, how his fingers had traced the delicate freckles on her face as they whispered their memories of the night they first learned they were expecting Karen. And how she'd recently asked him if the Jensens had had their baby yet so she could buy them a gift . . . and he just didn't know how he'd be able to break the news to her tonight.

Simmons rested a hand on his shoulder. "You going to be okay, Kev?"

"Long as the day doesn't get any worse."

Riehle heard the car approaching before its tires crunched to a stop on the salt-covered street. He pulled his thoughts together while checking the interior once more before brushing off his knees and standing to greet the approaching men. Lieutenant Robert J. Gavin was almost upon him by then. A carryover from the days when barrel-chested meant "Don't fuck with me," Lt. Gavin stood over six foot three and broad shouldered, with a flat-topped gray crew cut and an attitude that always suggested he had something more important to do than the task currently at hand.

Hands buried deep in the pockets of his tan overcoat, Gavin turned sideways and tipped his head toward the new arrival. "Riehle, meet your new partner, Detective Ray Capparelli."

Capparelli was the only one among them who had had the sense to dress appropriately for the weather. Bundled in a heavy down parka, thermally insulated gloves and boots, and a hat with padded earmuffs, the only part of his face that was exposed were his piercing blue eyes, thin, stern lips pressed tightly together within a salt-and-pepper goatee, and a bulbous nose and cheeks that displayed the broken blood vessels of a heavy drinker.

"Ah crap," Riehle muttered under his breath, only realizing too late how the thick cloud in the suddenly still winter air had betrayed him.

Capparelli's expression turned guarded. He hesitated before offering his hand. "How's it going?"

"Not so great." Riehle shook his hand, then looked quickly toward the wrecks as if to indicate the damage done, hoping the flush under his collar would be attributed to the cold instead.

Damn it, how could the lieutenant stick him with another boozer?

Riehle bit the inside of his cheek to hide his anger. The blood tasted bitter in his mouth. "A family was destroyed by a drunk driver."

"Anything I can help with?"

"Already got it covered."

Simmons stepped between them and introduced himself. "Really, we were just wrapping things up."

"Good," said Gavin. "Then Riehle can take his new partner back to the station and get him situated."

"Maybe we can have a little chat later," Riehle said.

"Much later," the lieutenant said firmly. "I've got three more broken pipes and a traffic nightmare to control first." He turned to Capparelli. "Welcome to Westbrook, detective."

Capparelli cleared his throat in the silence after Gavin left. "So, how's the coffee at the station?"

"Terrible."

"Makes me feel at home already."

Don't get too comfortable, Riehle thought.

"I'll catch up with you guys later," Simmons said. "Nice meeting you, Ray."

Riehle shot Simmons a glare. He fished the keys out of his pocket. "Let's head back," he said to Capparelli. He added, "I'll drive," to establish his seniority, then instantly realized how

25

childish he sounded. Of course he'd drive: Capparelli didn't know the way. He slammed the door shut, turned on the ignition, and cranked up the heat. As the defroster cleared the windshield, Riehle's ears started to burn. He wasn't sure if it was the numbness wearing off, his embarrassment at his actions with Capparelli, or his anger at Gavin for sticking him with another alcoholic partner that made them so painful.

"Makes you wonder," Capparelli said.

"What's that?"

Capparelli looked over his shoulder as they drove away. "No matter how many times I see something like this, I always wonder: How's the survivor gonna deal with the loss of his loved ones?"

CHAPTER THREE

Walter had never seen so much blood.

It wasn't the amount that caught his attention. Somewhere in the back of his mind he knew the human body contained about five liters or so. What truly amazed him was how the patterns of splattered blood, bone, teeth, tissue, scalp, hair, and brain matter now covering his basement walls and floor—not to mention what remained of the congealing mass still duct-taped to the splintered wooden chair—gave the *impression* of so much more.

Of course, he hadn't intended it to be that way. But Harris was too cocky and stupid to realize he should have kept his mouth shut, and by the time he understood what was really happening, Walter's rage had passed way beyond any threshold of control.

Not that Harris didn't deserve every bit of it.

Sitting on the floor, legs splayed out in front of him, Walter leaned back against the cold concrete wall, his muscles cramping from the exertion of the last few hours. He ran his shaking hands through blood-matted hair and wondered briefly about AIDS, then realized with a sad laugh that it didn't matter anymore. Nothing did. Eight years of anger burned out so quickly.

He closed his eyes and breathed deeply, willing his heart to stop racing. Now sure as hell wasn't the time to have a heart attack. Just imagine what people would think if they found him this way—as if he really gave a damn what anyone thought of him anymore. He wiped his eyes with the back of his hand and watched a pool of coagulating blood under the broken chair drip slowly into the grate in the floor as the anger drained out of him, leaving behind a feeling of emptiness he hadn't felt since Dottie died.

What was he going to do now? He had dreamed of this, tossing and turning every night for an eternity, waiting, scheming, praying beyond hope he'd be given the chance to inflict the proper judgment that the legal system he'd so blindly put his trust in had been too cowardly to impose. But while Walter had taken care of his own problems for the last few years, learning from his mistakes and perfecting his MO as he went along, he had never truly expected the opportunity to arrive. And now that the moment had come and gone with true justice finally dealt (though far too swiftly for all that he and Dottie had had to suffer through), Walter wondered what—if any—purpose life held for him anymore. Maybe it was time to let go, knowing his absolved soul could at last depart this miserable world in peace.

The wooden chair creaked. The splintered front leg wobbled and snapped under the weight of the settling carcass. The body tipped, barely restrained by the torn duct tape around its chest, wrists, and ankles. Harris's right leg slid forward, bent upward from the floor like a rag doll at its shattered knee, while the left buckled under the tilted chair. His lopsided head lolled, and the smashed, dislocated jaw, held in place by the few shredded muscles remaining at his right temple and ear, swung back and forth, mocking him with a madman's silent cackle.

The hamburger face leered. The light from the blood-speckled overhead fluorescent bulbs cast shadows over the crushed indentations where Harris's eye sockets had been. Soulless animal eyes that taunted Walter in death as they had in the courtroom, in his endless nightmares, and throughout their ordeal last night, denying Walter any satisfaction.

His bile rose, hot and angry, and Walter hawked and spit into the crushed face of the man who had brought so much evil into his life. Why couldn't Harris have shown a little fear? Some remorse? Anything to indicate there was something human inside that monster, a chance for Walter to tap into it to make Harris experience a taste of what he and Dottie had had to suffer through. But no, Harris had returned intending to kill Walter for what he had done, and Harris's smugness never wavered until moments before his own death. It wasn't Walter's fault that everything went out of control. In fact, Walter was amazed he'd been able to keep it together for as long as he did.

The basement was freezing when he had dragged Harris's body down the stairs. The board that previously hid the window on the outside had been pried off and lay flat on the ground, nails pointed upward, farther back under the porch. The wind whipped through the open window, rattling the plastic covers on his woodworking equipment and depositing a layer of snow over the tape-covered broken glass on the floor and in the graveled crawlspace behind the stairs. Walter had dumped Harris's unconscious body, stuffed his coat and boots in a closet, grabbed a chair from his own handcrafted dining room set, and, with duct tape from the green metal tool cabinet in the corner, secured Harris to the chair. Then he donned his own jacket, gloves, and boots and went outside.

The storm was at its height. The wind whistled through the empty trees and blew so fiercely the snow fell sideways, stinging his face like buckshot. Drifts had already begun to collect against the side of his house and the hedges in the neighbor's yard. Walter tightened the drawstrings on his hood and peered out of the fur-lined tunnel. Depressions from boot prints almost obliterated by the wind and snow led from the end of the driveway, past the front door where he stood, and around the side of the house by the bedroom. Across the street a rust-pitted, mustard yellow Camry was parked along the curb, and more than an inch of snow had already accumulated on top. The plow had left a close-shaved path around the car. As his street was a snow route off the expressway, Walter knew a tow truck would be along soon to haul the Camry away, relieving him of the trouble of having to dispose of the car later like he'd had to do for the others last summer.

Walter followed the driveway around to the back of the house. Between the foundation and the four wooden steps leading up to the back porch door, Harris had torn away the decorative latticework and burrowed a path through the snow to the basement window underneath. Behind him, a solitary light burned in the kitchen window next door, highlighting the hanging philodendrons and the African violets on the windowsill and illuminating a faint path across the driveway to where he stood.

A couple of years ago Benito and Mary Salinas had built the addition onto the back of the house, extending the kitchen and adding a TV room for their grandchildren to play in. Walter's house was originally set back a little farther than theirs, and more than once he'd wondered if everything that had happened that fateful evening might have been prevented if they'd built the addition a decade earlier. Would they have been able to see Harris climbing in through the basement window? Would Harris have stopped if he thought he might have been seen? Would Harris have even chosen his house if Walter hadn't cracked open the window to air out the basement after his woodworking that rainy April day or left the house for just those few minutes to run out to rent a movie for them that night? And what if he'd built the screened-in back porch like Dottie had originally wanted instead of the tiny deck between the basement windows . . . and all the other guilty what-ifs he'd driven himself crazy with ever since.

Walter dropped to his knees and crawled under the porch. A roll of duct tape and a crowbar lay discarded by the open window. He wondered why Harris hadn't simply pried open the porch and kitchen doors. It certainly would have been easier, unless Harris had something more sinister in mind than shooting him in his bed. Some place where Harris could take his time to silently break into the house and leave again in a way that would be hidden from obvious discovery until long after he'd disappeared.

Well now, he'd just show *him* a thing or two.

The snow crunched under his knees as Walter leaned inside the window. Overhead, the main water pipes ran under the exposed floorboards and into the crawlspace under the kitchen. Frost painted the sides of the pipes nearest the window. The wind whistled through the burrowed path and dusted the broken glass and floor with snow.

Harris stirred. Goddammit! Walter wanted to be there when he woke, to see the reaction in his eyes when Harris realized how Walter had turned the tables on him, to see the fear deepen when he understood what Walter intended to do. Quickly, Walter grabbed the window cover, aligned the nails with their original holes, and tapped the board back into place with the discarded crowbar, making a mental note to anchor it more solidly later. Then he hurried inside, stopping only to grab the baseball bat on the way.

Harris groaned. Walter slapped him hard across the face. His eyes popped open as a red welt the shape of Walter's hand swelled on his cheek. Angry recognition flared in his eyes. Walter backhanded him as Harris tried to spit, and the saliva dribbled down the side of Harris's mouth and off his chin. He sneered. "Wait'll my lawyer gets hold of you."

Walter grabbed his hair and twisted Harris's head back so hard his chest strained against the duct tape. "This is just between you and me now," he said. "And I've had lots of time to think about it." Then he reached down and bent Harris's pinkie finger backward at the farthest knuckle.

Harris vomited. Walter pushed his head away, and the stale beer and enchiladas spewed into Harris's lap and splattered the concrete floor on the opposite side.

"You motherfucker! I'm gonna—"

Walter snapped another knuckle. Then another. Each one, slowly. One. At. A. Time. Harris convulsed, writhing and retching and swearing louder with every broken digit. Walter savored the sounds of every little snap and Harris's dry heaving, but gradually noticed he was breaking the knuckle joints faster and faster as the anger grew within him. Though his fingers were bent at grotesque, unnatural angles, Harris had yet to show any signs of fear or remorse. The pain seemed to intensify his hatred, and Walter realized that the reform system had turned Harris into even more of an animal than he'd been before. With every painful snap Harris taunted him, telling him what he would do when this was over, what his lawyer would do, how he'd waited a whole year after being released so the cops would never suspect him, and saying things about Dottie until Walter's blood boiled.

Enough of this shit. Time for Harris to understand what suffering was all about. Walter grabbed the baseball bat and did a Willie Stargell warm-up just for the effect it got in Harris's eyes. Then putting eight years of accumulated rage behind it, he shattered Harris's right knee with one mighty swing.

Harris howled. Walter hit him again in the same spot to show he meant business before breaking the other kneecap as well. Harris screamed obscenities as he struggled against his bonds. His eyes blazed with the hatred Walter remembered from the trial, and Walter was thrown back in time: To his anger and astonishment at the fifteen-year-old Harris swearing revenge for

Walter's testifying against him. To the defense attorney who argued the cancer would have killed Dottie anyway, and the judge who sentenced Harris to a measly six years. To the accountants and financial advisors who bankrupted them when they sold Walter's business to pay for her medical treatments, because the insurance company refused any payments and dropped them, even after thirty years of premiums always paid. Faces flashing across his memory, superimposing themselves upon the evil, hideous creature who struggled in the chair before him—but always, *always* coming back to Harris. And Walter swung at every face, his rage exploding in bursts of white-hot light, no longer hearing the dull thuds as the bat sunk deeper and deeper into the pulpy carcass or feeling the blood splattering over him, swinging wildly wildly wildly until the bat broke in two and flew from his blood-slicked hands; and Walter fell back against the concrete wall and slid to the floor, sobbing, his face in his hands as tears streamed between his fingers and ran in rivulets down his blood-soaked arms.

Slowly, Walter opened his eyes. The light spilling down the stairs from the kitchen doorway told him the sun had been up for a while. He wrapped his arms around his legs and rested his weary head on his knees. Every muscle in his body ached, and the weight of exhaustion pressed heavily against his skull. He was so tired. Tired of the anger, the guilt, the frustration. Tired of everything.

He rubbed the dried blood from the corners of his eyes and focused on the broken bat across the room, blood-smeared and dented with bone chips embedded in the wood. What a mess. It was going to take forever to clean this up and he simply didn't care. All of his energy was gone. There was so much to do, and yet, nothing left for him at all.

Walter pushed himself to his feet and staggered to the utility sink in the corner by the washer and dryer, his cramped muscles complaining all the way. He turned on the taps, and as the steam rose and the water splashed around him, he shoved his head and arms under the near-scalding flow. He scrubbed Harris's filth off his wedding band, then rubbed and scraped until his exposed skin was raw and pink and a puddle had collected at his feet. Hanging his head in the swirling steam with the water dripping off his face, Walter rested his forearms on the rim and closed his eyes, breathing deeply, letting go.

And in that moment of relaxation, the first in so very, very long, it occurred to him there was something left to do. A phone call he needed to make. A call that was eight years overdue.

CHAPTER FOUR

"Lieu, how could you do this to me?"

Riehle paced back and forth in the lieutenant's office, ignoring Gavin telling him to sit down. Through the open metal blinds covering the glass office wall, Riehle saw the other officers moving around in the squad room. A few glanced surreptitiously toward him, then looked quickly away when they caught Riehle's angry glare. Capparelli stood with his back to Gavin's office, making small talk with those who came by to introduce themselves while he organized his desk with the few personal items he'd brought in a small cardboard box.

"After all I went through with O'Connell, I just can't believe you would do this." Riehle shoved his hands in and out of his sport coat's pockets as he pinballed around the office. The vents hissed when the furnace kicked on.

Gavin's eyes narrowed. "And what exactly did I do?"

"You stuck me with another drunk!"

"Oh, for Christ's sake, you don't even know the guy." He pointed to one of the worn, imitation-leather chairs parked in front of his desk. "Now sit your ass down or get the hell out of my office."

Riehle sat.

Gavin ran a frustrated hand over his flat-topped gray crew cut. His olive green shirtsleeves were rolled up to his elbows and his brown and white striped tie tilted slightly askew. Behind him, on the walnut bookcase stuffed with procedural manuals, stood a gold-framed eight-by-ten portrait of a smiling Gavin with his wife, Jenny, and their two college-aged sons. His smile in the photo was so unforced, so obviously sincere, the prevailing joke in the department (that no one dared allow him to overhear) was that Jenny must have promised him a wild night of sex in order to produce such a genuine smile. His normal expression was an irritated scowl, which he wore at that very moment.

He exhaled sharply. "Yeah, I know. He's got the look. But his commanding officer said he was never aware of any problems and was sorry to lose him."

"So what's Capparelli's story anyway?" Riehle said.

"He heard about our lateral entry program for experienced personnel and wanted to take advantage of it. For personal reasons."

"What kind of personal reasons?"

"He's *your* partner. Ask him yourself."

Riehle ground his teeth. Knowing he wouldn't get any further this way, he tried a different route. "Why did we have to go outside our department, anyway? Couldn't we have promoted someone from within? Like Simmons? Hell, we'd have made great partners."

"I agree, but Simmons wanted to stay in patrol."

He felt like he'd been sucker-punched. "Seriously?"

"You got it. And no one else has the level of experience we need. Capparelli may be older, but with the transfer, I made sure he understood that you were the senior partner."

"Seems like he's giving up a lot."

"Then that falls under his personal reasons, doesn't it?" The phone rang and Gavin reached for it. "I don't want to hear any more about this. Bring it up again and you're back in uniform." He pointed to the door. "Out."

Riehle left the office. Clenching his fists in his pockets, he watched Capparelli sitting alone at his desk, programming numbers into his cell phone. Without all his winter gear on, he was taller and thinner than Riehle had expected, and he wore a tailored navy blue suit that wasn't out of departmental pay range. His hair, like his goatee, was salt-and-pepperish with the salt winning out, and worn in a style Riehle thought was a bit too long for his age. Riehle started toward him, then spotted Simmons coming in from the back.

"Hey Paul, you got a minute?"

"Just a sec." Simmons hung up his coat and used a handkerchief to wipe the condensation off his eyes and bushy mustache before following Riehle down the hall to the scuffed, off-white cinderblock break room filled with brown metal folding chairs and tables with imitation wood-grain plastic surfaces. Riehle fed a couple dollars into the pop machine and banged a selection with the heel of his palm. But when the can dropped into the dispensing chute, his blood finally boiled over. He punched and kicked the machine like it was the fifteenth round of a kickboxing match.

"You know," Simmons said, his almond eyes crinkling with amusement, "try as I might, I've never been able to get that beast to cough up another can, either. No matter how many times they keep raising the prices."

Riehle gave the machine one last hard kick—and damned if a second can didn't drop down—before turning his anger on Simmons. "You *knew* about this?"

Simmons put his big hands up between them. "Whoa, hang on there, amigo."

"I wondered why you were so friendly with Capparelli this morning." He grabbed a can from the chute and shook it accusingly. "You were in on this from the beginning. You're supposed to be my friend. How could you do this to me?"

"Calm down. I wasn't in on anything. I—here, give me that

before you hurt somebody." Simmons snatched the cola can away from him, popped the top over the sink, and watched the foam spray out. "Damn, this thing's almost empty. Hand me the other one if you're not going to drink it. Thanks. Now grab a seat and chill out a minute." He took a sip. "Man, you've got to learn to lighten up."

They pulled out chairs, the metal rattling as the plastic tips skipped across the tiled floor, and sat down across from each other at the table farthest from the door. Riehle checked to make sure no one was within earshot. With a mixture of anger and disbelief, he said, "Gavin says you turned down the chance to be my partner."

"That's right."

"But why?"

Simmons finished drinking and set the empty can aside with a hollow clank. He leaned forward on his elbows, his huge biceps stretching the sleeves of his uniform tight. Riehle smelled a faint mixture of sweat and cologne. The warmth inside the station had brought back the deep brown color of his skin, but the harsh, buzzing overhead fluorescent lights accented the strands of gray at his temples.

"Just couldn't work it out, man. At least you've got family nearby. With Regina's hours at the library and the kids' school schedules and activities, we couldn't risk the chance of me getting called any time of the day or night and not having a sitter available." He shrugged. "Gavin says the next spot's mine, no question, but I'm thinking about testing for sergeant in the meantime anyway."

"Well, hey, thanks for the warning. I felt like Gavin blindsided me."

"Don't sweat it. Nobody's looking to screw you."

"Sure feels like it. I just can't believe Gavin would stick me with another drunk."

"There's no evidence of that."

Riehle cocked his head. "Know something I don't?"

"You still buying? Maybe something sugar-free this time?"

Riehle scowled, but returned with two new cans and plunked them on the table. "Okay, give."

The can fizzed when Simmons popped the top. "I've got a buddy in Area One who used to work with him. Says Capparelli has a problem with authority—"

"Terrific."

"—but he's a damn good detective. A real hard worker, stays on after his shift is over, though he's not as by-the-book as you are. And he can be a real pain in the ass when something rubs him the wrong way."

Riehle bristled at the by-the-book jab, but let it go. "Anything else? He say anything about his drinking?"

"Only that he stopped going out with the other guys after his divorce. From what I hear, his ex is one fine looker who really took him to the cleaners."

"Nothing new there."

"Except he hasn't been seen in the regular cop bars since."

"So he drinks at home. That's all you've got?"

"I'm lucky I got that much. You know how tight-lipped cops are about one of their own." Simmons glanced over his shoulder, then leaned closer. "Listen. Dixie's brother works there too, and she swears she's heard him mention Capparelli before."

"Oh, great." Plump, with over-teased red hair in shades that varied from week to week, Claudia Dixon, Simmons's partner, was the busybody of the station. During their rides on patrol, Dixie often bombarded Paul with her opinions of everyone around her and their supposedly private secrets. Rumor had it she drank beer while vacuuming her house in the nude, a fact no one was in any great hurry to verify.

"Want me to call her off?"

"Nah, have her go ahead. Can't hurt."

Simmons played with the pop top until it snapped off. He dropped it into the empty can. "Capparelli seems like a decent enough guy. I say give him a chance." He grinned. "Hey, maybe he likes classic rock, too."

Riehle groaned. The night he'd first made detective, Jack O'Connell had invited him to a bar where O'Connell's favorite local band, Swen Fiedler and His Snazzy Jazz Combo, was playing. Thinking it was a chance to get in good with his new partner, he agreed. What followed were four hours of mind-numbingly boring cop stories (the same ones Riehle would hear repeatedly with growing exaggeration until O'Connell retired) and the painful memory of watching sloppy-drunk patrons Chicken Dancing to a polka rendition of "The Ballad of John and Yoko." His biggest mistake, however, was telling Simmons about it the next day, and Paul never missed an opportunity to rub it in.

"Let's hope he likes the original versions, then." Riehle glanced at the wall-mounted clock that always reminded him of his school days. "C'mon, we'd better head back before they think we went AWOL."

They crushed their cans and tossed them in the blue recycling bin. "So have you and Gwen decided what you're doing for your anniversary yet?" Simmons asked.

He shook his head. "She still wants to do the big family vacation thing."

"What's wrong with that?"

"It's our tenth anniversary. I want to spend a quiet, romantic weekend alone with my wife. With her hours at the pharmacy and my shift changes, we don't get to spend much time together, and my mom already said she'd watch Karen."

"Then what's the problem?"

"Gwen says the three of us aren't together very often either."

"Good point."

Riehle sighed. "Yeah, I know. It's just . . . I keep thinking about all the things my parents never got to do. Dad died just before their tenth wedding anniversary, when I was eight years old."

"Well, don't lose sight of the forest for the trees. You get tunnel vision when it comes to your personal life."

Riehle was about to ask what the hell he meant by that when Dixie raced around the corner and barreled into them. Her hair was Lucy-red this week and she reeked of perfume. He wondered how Simmons could stand being trapped in the car with her.

"I just got off the phone with my brother," she said breathlessly. "And, boy, does he have a story about—"

"Got something, Ray?" Riehle asked quickly, when Capparelli suddenly materialized behind her.

His partner's eyes narrowed and the guarded look returned to his face. He glanced suspiciously at Dixie before handing Riehle a radio and a pink memo slip. "A burglary at a computer store on Merrill."

"Let's go, then." Riehle grabbed his coat and hurried out the door, already feeling the cold.

CHAPTER FIVE

"So what did Dixie find out?" Gwen asked him later that evening while they were making dinner. The sounds of Karen and her grandmother laughing at something on TV drifted up from the family room.

Riehle shrugged. "Things got busy afterward and I never got around to asking her." Soft piano music filled the air. On the countertop by the phone, the combination HD radio, CD player, and MP3 dock had been Gwen's favorite Christmas present that year, and was the only visible reminder the holiday had come and gone already. They'd taken down the decorations the previous weekend, and for weeks afterward, he always thought the house looked bare. Plates clacked together when he pulled them from the cupboard. He began setting the table. "I figure if it's anything relevant, Paul will fill me in."

"Well, considering the source, I'd take anything you hear with a grain of salt." Gwen opened the oven and the warmth flooded their tiny kitchen, the aroma of baked breaded chicken and scalloped potatoes mingling with the stovetop smell of steamed broccoli. She wore a green turtleneck and black slacks, and her white lab coat with her nametag pinned to the breast pocket was draped over the back of her chair. Her slender fingers brushed a strand of strawberry-blond hair from her eyes. "You really think Capparelli's an alcoholic?"

"I don't know. No one else seems to think so, and I have to admit, he doesn't exhibit a lot of the signs Jack did. But I also remember how well Jack hid them from everyone, and Capparelli has that same broken capillary look to his face."

"Just keep in mind other medical conditions have that facial appearance, too. I'd reserve judgment until you get to know him better." She closed the oven door and wiped her hands on a flowered dishtowel. "Want a salad?"

"Not tonight." Geez, why was everyone taking Capparelli's side?

"Then pour the milk." Gwen stood at the top of the basement stairs. "Dinner's ready!"

"Coming!"

The first to arrive, however, was their eleven-year-old, brown-and-white spotted beagle, Cinnamon. Her tags tinkled as she laboriously climbed the stairs. Riehle had bought her as a puppy to hide the fact that he was going to propose to Gwen on her birthday, and though Cinnamon had been a part of the family ever since, time hadn't been kind to her. Her hips were obviously bothering her again as she waddled across the floor, and her nails clicked on the linoleum. She pressed her nose against the sliding glass door, wanting to go out, and when the bitter cold hit her as he opened the door, her cataract-filmed eyes pleaded with him.

"Go on," Riehle said.

She hesitated another moment before going outside; then, deciding the snow-covered backyard was too far away, she peed instead on their cedar-stained deck and hurried back inside. She sneezed on his shoe when he closed the door behind her and curled up in her favorite corner by the table, ready to beg for scraps.

"Thanks a hell of a lot."

"You're sure in a grumpy mood," Gwen observed. "Something else happen today?"

Riehle scratched his five o'clock shadow. He'd been dreading

43

this moment all day and he still hadn't been able to come up with any easier way to break it to her.

"The Jensens were in an accident on their way home from the hospital," he said slowly.

The color drained from her face. She sank heavily into a chair. "And?" Her beautiful green eyes searched his for the reassurance he couldn't give her, and his heart ached.

"Larry's in the hospital, but Ann and the baby—" He shook his head.

Her eyes misted with tears, and her hands wrung the dishtowel as she asked: "Did they have a boy or girl?"

"Girl. I don't know what her name was yet. I can find out, but I think the doctors are waiting until after he recovers more before they break the news to him."

She nodded. "If he needs anything while he's in the hospital . . ."

He took her hands in his and kissed her. "Sure."

"Hi, Daddy!" Their seven-year-old daughter bounded up the stairs. Karen was at that awkward age when she was all angles and bones. Pink barrettes held her shoulder-length brown hair behind her ears and her hazel eyes sparkled. She wore a white, long-sleeved T-shirt and blue jeans with rainbows on the pockets, and her smile (though he secretly thought her front teeth looked too big for her tiny mouth right now) guaranteed she had her daddy wrapped around her fingers forever. She gave him a kiss before noticing her mother's expression.

"What's wrong, Mommy?"

Gwen sniffled and wiped her eyes. "Nothing, sweetie. I was just peeling onions."

"I don't smell any onions."

"Go tell Grandma it's time for dinner."

"Too late." Ellen Riehle took a seat at the kitchen table next to Karen. Like Cinnamon, time hadn't been kind to her, either.

Though he could still see the high school homecoming queen beauty in her soft brown eyes, her hair was thin and silver, and the stress of raising him alone since he was eight years old was etched into every line on her face. Osteoporosis and years of gardening had rounded her shoulders to a slight hump, and the sun had dried the skin on her face and arms to leather.

But lately when he saw her, his mind kept flashing back to the guilty memory of her horrified expression when he'd broken his parents' tenth anniversary clock on the day after his father died. It was an image that had always weighed heavily on his conscience, and though he'd suppressed it for many years, it grew sharper and more poignant as the date for his and Gwen's same anniversary drew nearer. Ellen had long since forgiven him, but in his own mind at least, he'd never been able to make it up to her.

"Why the long face?" Ellen said. She picked a stray piece of popcorn off her purple and gray "World's Greatest Grandmother" sweatshirt Karen had given her for Christmas and tossed it to a grateful Cinnamon.

He shrugged. "Just a bad day."

"You both work too hard. You need to get away more often."

"That's what I've been saying." He thought about all the things his parents had never gotten to do, and now everything the Jensens would miss as well. He couldn't bear the thought of something happening to him, and Gwen having to live a life like his mother's. "Today reminded me how much we need to make time for each other," he told his wife.

Gwen spooned some potatoes onto Karen's plate. "Today is exactly why we all need a vacation together."

"What happened today?" Ellen said.

"Vacation? Are we going to Disney World?" Karen asked.

"Not this time, sweetie," he said.

"I can watch Cinnamon, if you need me," said his mother.

45

Karen's eagerness was telling. "Emma's going there on spring break. Can I go on some rides with her?"

"I *said* we're not going."

Karen's face scrunched up and turned red. Tears streamed down her face. She slid off her chair and ran to her room, slamming the door behind her.

Gwen gave him a disgusted look and threw down her napkin. "Nice going, Dad." She chased after Karen.

Riehle buried his face in his hands and sighed. This was exactly why he never brought his work home with him.

"So how's your new partner?" Ellen said, attempting to fill the silence that had descended over the table.

"He's fine, Mom," he said, poking his food with a fork. "Just fine."

CHAPTER SIX

Walter stood frozen in time.

Dottie's younger sister, Helen Markese, had picked him up at the airport and brought him here to the Rostamian household, and Walter huddled in the entry hall of the old St. Paul Victorian home off Summit Avenue, his heart pounding and sweat trickling down under his shirt, afraid to enter the living room where everyone awaited him. Though Dottie's childhood home was filled with loving memories, he found himself unable to move, unable to make that first step forward to bridge the many years lost to the past.

He shifted uncomfortably from foot to foot as the circulation painfully returned. The heater in Helen's car wasn't working, and his toes were nearly frozen. From where he stood he could peer into the living room, and he was surprised to find the house still decorated for Christmas, as if they had purposely extended the holiday in hopes that this year he might finally return. An ancient silver tree decorated with red, blue, and green glass ornaments stood in the far corner, and wooden shoes—not stockings—hung from nails in the mantel. A real log fire popped and crackled in the stone fireplace behind the soot-stained, brass screen, and the room smelled sweetly of burning wood mixed with spices that Eleanor Rostamian, his mother-in-law, sprinkled over fires on special occasions. He could hear hushed voices coming from around the corner just out of sight.

Walter wanted to get the hell out of there.

It was a mistake coming here, he thought, shivering from more than the cold. A mistake bringing them into this. He should have never called. They were better off not knowing what he'd done. He stepped backwards, silently, and turned to leave, figuring he could make up some lame excuse on why he couldn't stay, when Helen, who had deposited his luggage in the guest bedroom, stopped him with a reassuring hand on his arm and tugged him into the living room.

"Everyone, look who's here," she said.

The warmth of the fire enveloped him as soon as he stepped into the room. He shook hands with Dottie's cousin Lorna Boulanger and her husband, Henry, then gave Eleanor a hug as she struggled to rise from her chair.

"Well, aren't you a sight for sore eyes," she said. The thick lenses in her tortoiseshell frames enlarged her watery, blue-gray irises, but the glint behind them when she whispered "We've missed you" made him smile.

Even into her eighties, Eleanor had always been a force to be reckoned with. Survivor of an abusive marriage (the old bastard died of a stroke when Dottie was twelve), she refused to allow arthritis and osteoporosis to control her when they had descended on her later in life. She treated her walker more like a traveling podium than a balancing aid, and with her gnarled, blue-knuckled hands clutching the aluminum rails and her hunched back arched forward, she had always reminded Walter of an after-dinner speaker who was about to deliver her most important message of the evening.

But the woman he held now was worn down by life. Though she wore a thick, beige sweater over a black wool dress printed with faded lilies, Walter felt her ribs protruding when he held her. Her fragile body trembled slightly, and he wondered if she had Parkinson's disease.

"I'm not in a home yet," she protested when he helped her

back into the chair. "Good night." Never having sworn a day in her life, Eleanor always used the phrase "Good night" to express her frustrations, though he could tell she was secretly grateful for his help now. He moved her walker to the side, just within reach, and fluffed the pillows behind her before sitting down with Helen on the davenport that had occupied this same spot for the last thirty years. He spotted nicks in the wooden legs on the couch and coffee table about the height of the lowest screws on Eleanor's walker, and the room smelled of lemon polish and wood smoke and older loved ones who had been shut indoors too long.

And shut out of his life as well, he realized sadly.

"My goodness," Helen said, nervously running her hand through her auburn hair. "It's wonderful to have you with us again."

He could see the earnestness on their faces and how hard they were trying to make him feel at home. The wear around their eyes showed him how much they had suffered over Dottie too. Her memory was like an invisible presence in the room.

Sweat rolled down under his shirt and his skin began to crawl. *They won't be able to handle it*, he thought. *I can't tell them what I've done.*

Instead, he said: "I'm just grateful you'd have me."

That made them laugh. The tension broke and the years seemed to melt away then. They settled more comfortably in their seats, relaxed, each practically stumbling over the other in their haste to share their news, as if by telling Walter everything that had happened since they'd last seen him would mean he'd never been away.

Eleanor apologized that Karl, Dottie's older brother, wasn't able to fly in from Seattle on such short notice. "Robbie—that's his grandson by Kathleen—needs to have seven teeth pulled for his orthodontia." Her shaking fingers played with the blue and white cameo she used to button the top of her sweater. Eleanor's upper denture periodically slipped down while she talked, but with a stretch of her upper lip and a sucking sound when her tongue pushed it back into place, she barreled on as if nothing had interrupted the conversation. "Robbie swore he'd never speak to his grandpa again if Karl didn't go with him to the oral surgeon's." She blinked her rheumy eyes. "Seven teeth. Can you imagine?"

Lorna was still angry about her job loss from a few years ago. Twenty-five years of seniority had gone out the window when the new owners of the grocery chain had refused to deal with unions, fired everyone, and closed all the stores, then reopened them three months later with workers who were desperate enough to take jobs at minimum wage with no benefits, because the parent corporation claimed they couldn't afford the previous wage scale or replenish the depleted pension fund. Within a week after reopening, stock prices soared and all the board members got bonuses in the millions; while six thousand former employees scrambled for jobs because they'd lost their health benefits and pensions and were in danger of losing their homes and cars.

"Those CEOs were nothing but robber barons, and the government didn't give a damn," Lorna said, getting more and more flustered as she talked. Her silver framed glasses slid down her nose and her index finger stabbed them back into place. "In fact, they *encouraged* it."

"Isn't that the truth," Eleanor said, sucking angrily on her denture. "First they send our jobs to other countries. Then they wipe out pension funds. And then executives use bailout money to go to spas. Good night! All to make the rich richer and the poor poorer, eliminating the middle class while encouraging graft and corruption. All the wonderful individual's rights accomplishments of the twentieth century are being wiped out."

She wiped the tears from her eyes. "I remember my grandfather telling me about the early labor riots, like the Pullman Strike in Chicago. The way the current system is taking everything away from the average worker, it's getting to be like that all over again. Only the world is a more violent place now. Thank goodness I won't live long enough to see what's going to happen next."

She leaned forward as if she were on her walker-podium, and shook her head sadly. "How much more can the average person take? Pretty soon they're going to push people into doing things they normally wouldn't do. The rich, the politically connected, and criminals are the only ones who have rights anymore."

Walter tried to hide his surprise. A man being pushed to do something he normally wouldn't do—oh, how he understood that! Maybe he could tell them after all!

But before he could say anything, Helen said, "Speaking of criminals, let me bring you up to speed on the latest crap my ex-husband's been pulling." The line got a round of half-hearted chuckles from the group.

"According to the divorce papers, Roger's supposed to pay the girls' college education, but he hasn't paid a single dime." Helen seemed to try to hide her anger by picking imaginary lint off her forest green turtleneck sweater and brushing her hands against her slacks. "So I have to work two jobs to pay their tuition and hire a lawyer to take him back to court to get what he's supposed to be paying anyway. I've already spent sixty-five hundred dollars on legal fees, and the sonofabitch keeps stalling with continuances. Meanwhile Chloe—the floozy bitch he ran off with—has him convinced I'm only trying to squeeze more money out of him, and that his money was better spent on their Mediterranean cruise they took last summer than on his own daughters' education."

Walter half-expected Eleanor to admonish Helen for her

language, but Eleanor just kept shaking her head throughout the whole thing, sucking her denture back into place and muttering, "Nothing but trash. I warned you about him. Good night."

He listened politely to the conversation around him, nodding his head in sympathy whenever he was supposed to or pretending to remember someone they thought he should know, all the while debating whether or not he should tell them what he had done. His heart raced whenever the memory of beating Harris flashed across his mind; but in the silent gaps between their stories, his tongue grew thick and knotted and he found he was unable to tell them. So instead he stalled by wiping his sweaty palms on his pant legs and filled in their expectant pauses with news about his latest woodworking projects or what his neighbors were doing. He noticed the concerned, secretive glances that passed between them when he abruptly changed subjects, but they patted his hands and continued on with the conversation anyway as if to let him know that they were comfortable with whatever he wanted to talk about. He was surprised to learn that they not only remembered his neighbors, Benito and Mary Salinas, but all of their children and grandchildren as well, and he felt ashamed when he realized that he had never paid as close attention to their previous conversations as they had. Just like he was doing now.

The oven timer saved him. While Helen, Lorna, and Henry brought the serving platters from the kitchen into the dining room, Walter stayed alongside Eleanor as she shuffled forward with her walker. One of its metal legs nicked a corner of the coffee table, and when she muttered, "Oh, good night!" he had to bite the inside of his cheek to keep from laughing at the image of her swearing every time she damaged a piece of furniture.

"The golden years aren't so golden," Eleanor said, as they navigated their way to the dining room. She gave him a couple of half-hearted elbow jabs when he moved a hand up to steady her. "It's hell getting old. Promise me you'll take care of things while you still can."

"I already have," he assured her.

The table was set for a holiday feast. A ham glazed with brown sugar and honey and decorated with pineapple slices, fresh green beans, candied yams, mashed potatoes with gravy, stuffing, fresh baked bread, and a tossed salad with three different dressings in silver serving bowls. The aromas overwhelmed him, and if the family conversation in front of the fireplace hadn't told him how much they'd missed him, the memory of countless holiday dinners at this very table did. Walter realized they must have gone shopping and started cooking as soon as he'd called. He swallowed the lump in his throat. All this to welcome him home.

He broke out in a cold sweat. *Life's been hard enough on them already. I can't burden them more with what I've done.*

Eleanor took her seat at the head of the table. Walter sat to her right, Helen next to him, and Lorna and Henry across from them. The serving platters were passed around with much clattering of silverware on china, then set at the far end of the table, awaiting seconds. Eleanor bowed her head, and they all clasped hands to make a circle around the table while she said grace.

But when they were through, Eleanor held onto his hand. Her skin was dry and chafed where she touched him.

"We've missed you very much," she said, "and it's wonderful to see you again. But you didn't come all this way just to have dinner." Her eyes held him steadily. "What do you want to tell us, Walter?"

He looked around the table. Their eyes were hopeful and expectant, their faces nodding with encouragement, and he suddenly felt ashamed at having shut them out of his life for so long. Believing it would protect them from all the suffering he and Dottie had gone through, he'd erected an invisible barrier around himself, never realizing until tonight how much his isolation had hurt them. But confiding in them now would only bring more pain into their lives. He couldn't do that to them. They were better off not knowing, he decided.

"Actually, I . . ." He wiped a thin film of cold sweat off his upper lip. His heart beat wildly and he had trouble catching his breath. He couldn't think of the right words to say. "What I mean is, I . . ."

"We're your family, Walter," Eleanor said. The others murmured their agreement as Helen slipped her hand into his and their clasped hands formed a circle again. "Whatever you want to tell us, it's okay."

His chin quivered. Tears welled in his eyes as he realized how much his self-imposed isolation had hurt him. They were his family, all he had left, and he understood now how much he needed their love and support, too. And the dam that had held back all the anger and hurt and frustration for so long finally broke within him, and he felt the weight of all he'd carried swept away. He'd found the strength he needed in their circle of clasped hands.

Walter bowed his head. He took a deep breath to steady himself. Then, looking each of them in the eye until their gazes fell away, he told them what he had done.

He told them everything.

CHAPTER SEVEN

"I think I owe you an apology," Riehle said.

The detectives were sitting at a countertop by the glass window of a strip mall deli, their sandwiches and soft drinks on the paper wrappings. It was after the noon hour rush and only a couple of other customers were present: a guy pecking away at his laptop and a homeless man sipping his coffee as slowly as possible to prolong his opportunity to stay indoors. A few salt-smeared cars drove in and out of the parking lot, and a mound of dirty snow sat just outside the window near their feet. Overhead speakers played the music of an alternative rock station.

Shifting slightly on his stool, Capparelli raised an eyebrow as he bit into his turkey sub to let Riehle know he was listening. There had been a lot of unspoken tension between them since that first day, and other than showing him around or chatting with the other officers present, they hadn't really had much of a chance to talk privately. O'Connell might have been a pain in the ass, but he never made their rides uncomfortable. Boring, yes, but not the pins and needles he felt with Capparelli, and Riehle had been looking for a way to break the ice. If it didn't work, well, then at least he would know he'd tried.

"We didn't get off to a great start the other day."

Capparelli nodded. "Yeah, I was trying to figure out in which language 'Ah crap' meant 'Nice to meet you.' "

Ouch. Riehle blew out his breath. "All right, I deserved that.

It's just . . . my former partner—"

"I know all about him. My old station had busybodies, too."
He took a sip, then set the wax-paper cup down heavily. "I'm
not a drunk. A couple of beers or an occasional glass of wine
with dinner, but that's all. Anything more and I either get a
headache or sleepy." Capparelli gave him a level glare. "That
what you wanted to know?"

"Um, yeah. Thanks." Riehle glanced at the broken blood vessels on his cheeks and nose, but Capparelli wasn't about to give
up anything more. He decided not to push it. "So what kind of
music do you like?" he said, aiming for neutral ground.

"The usual. How 'bout you?"

Man, this guy didn't make *anything* easy. Riehle checked the
other customers, but neither was paying them any attention.
"I'm your basic classic rocker," he said. "My favorite periods
were the British Invasion, Sixties Motown, and Eighties New
Wave."

"What? Those people with the purple and green hair?"

Riehle bristled. "At least they weren't all trying to sound like
Led Zeppelin. So, who do you listen to?"

"Led Zeppelin," Capparelli said. "And Springsteen, Clapton,
and Bob Seger. And while I've come to appreciate Seger even
more as I've gotten older, and also enjoy Chicago blues, I'm
actually playing a lot of Fifties jazz lately. You listen to Miles
Davis or John Coltrane? Sonny Rollins?"

"Not really. Though O'Connell took me to see his favorite
group once. Swen Fiedler and His Snazzy Jazz Combo. Ever
hear of them?"

Capparelli grimaced. "No." He gathered up the empty wrappings and cup and tossed them in the trash bin. "And the only
time I want to hear about a snazzy combo is in relation to
something on my plate."

Riehle smiled. Maybe there was hope for them after all.

As things were a little slower that day, Gavin had them driving around to get Capparelli familiar with the area. Riehle hit all the major thoroughfares, as well as the schools, the hospital, and the railroad crossings first before tackling the smaller avenues and suburban side streets of town. Though the sky was overcast, the temperature outside was warmer than the day they'd met, and the roads were wet with melting snow.

"So, you married?" Capparelli asked suddenly.

Riehle's grip tightened on the steering wheel. He hadn't expected him to be so direct. Except for Dixie, who made it her business to nose around in everyone else's, cops usually didn't talk about their personal lives. He tried not to show his surprise, but the tires squished through a mound of slush along the curb. Surely Capparelli's busybody had already told him. Or was this his way of opening their lines of communication?

"Gwen and I have been married almost ten years," he said.

"Gwyneth?"

"Gwendolyn. But don't ever let her hear you call her that." Like that was going to happen anytime soon.

"Kids?"

"Karen's seven and a half." He glanced over at him. "How about you?"

"Divorced, no kids. I'm sure Dixie already told you."

Actually she hadn't, though Paul had mentioned the divorce in the break room on that first day. Either his fretting over what to do about his anniversary or his natural avoidance of Dixie had made him forget about the story she wanted to tell him.

"I've got a nephew, though," Capparelli said. "My brother's kid. Marty started law school this fall."

"Oh, I'm—"

"Sorry? Don't be. He wants to be a prosecutor, so he'll be one of the good guys."

"Good to hear."

"Yeah, his best friend talked him into it. Guy was top of his class, Dean's List all the way through and editor of the Law Review, but he almost didn't make it."

"I've heard the bar exam is tough."

"No, his dean was embarrassed that her valedictorian was graduating without a book deal."

"You know, I've wondered about that . . ."

A light drizzle began to collect on the windshield. Riehle turned the wipers on. Except for the snowstorm and cold snap when he'd first met Capparelli, it was turning out to be another mild Chicago winter. Some snow showers around the holidays with a few nasty frigid days after, then a warm spell in the middle of January followed by a huge snowstorm near the end of the month had become an on and off meteorological pattern in recent years. He remembered the bitterly cold winters of his childhood and wondered if his memory was skewed or if global warming really did have something to do with it.

The radio squawked, and over the sound of the wipers the dispatcher announced a traffic dispute at the intersection of Pinter and Larkspur. A patrol officer responded that he was in the area and was en route. Riehle turned onto Maple Avenue and was driving under the overpass for Route Eighty-three when some black, spray-painted graffiti on the concrete wall caught Capparelli's attention.

" 'Freds Rule.' What the hell is that?"

"Don't know," Riehle admitted. "Some new gang, I suppose. I never saw it before."

"What kind of gang name is that? Fred. Give me a break. At least city gangs have better names."

"You know, you people in the city think you have everything," Riehle said. "Well, I'll have you know we have the same crimes, drugs, and crooked politicians that you do. We're just more, er, spread out."

"I'll tell you one thing we don't have, and that's gangs with stupid names like Fred. Who the hell wants to be known as a Fred?"

"The Flintstones?"

"Not funny." Capparelli shifted in his seat to face him better. "Though I'm surprised you'd try to make any kind of joke. Word I hear is you're a real stuffed shirt."

"Now hold on a minute—"

"Always playing by the book, you must have gone crazy riding around with O'Connell."

Why was Capparelli egging him on? Was this some kind of test? Or was this his way of getting even for the "Ah crap" line?

"National Honor Society in high school and top of your class at the academy," Capparelli continued. "I'll bet you've never done a single rebellious thing in your life."

And why would I? Riehle thought. With everything his mother had had to endure—including the pain he inflicted on her when he broke his father's clock—why would he have ever done anything to add to her grief? Not that it was any of Capparelli's business. "Sure I have," he said, sounding lame even to himself.

"Name one thing. C'mon, I'll bet you can't—"

"My toilet," Riehle said. "There. Are you happy now?"

"Your what?"

Riehle ran a hand through his hair. After the fiasco of trying to get to know O'Connell better, he'd sworn he'd never get personal with another partner. And Capparelli certainly wasn't making things easy for him. But why not give it a shot?

He exhaled. "When I was at the academy, there was this one instructor who rode me all the time. I swear, no matter what I did or how hard I tried, there was nothing I could do to please the guy. It finally drove me so crazy I . . ." He hesitated. "You know how they put pictures on porcelain? Plates, things like that?"

"Sure, but what's . . ." A smile crept onto his face. "You didn't?"

"Oh yes, I did. I put his picture on the bottom of my commode, so I could do to him what he'd been doing to me."

Capparelli actually laughed. "Not bad. Think he ever found out about it?"

"Probably." He was surprised to realize he was feeling more relaxed now that Capparelli was lightening up. "For years afterward, I had guys from other classes asking if they could use my toilet."

"You had it a long time then."

"Until a few months after I started dating Gwen."

"She made you get rid of it, eh?"

Riehle nodded. "Said she felt uncomfortable sitting on someone's face."

"I'll bet."

"Hey, I'm sure your wife would have done the same thing."

Capparelli's eyes widened as if he'd been slapped. A red flush rose up from under his collar and his nostrils flared. His face darkened before he turned away.

"I'm not so sure."

Riehle punched the steering wheel. For Christ's sake, what the hell just happened? Here he'd thought they were starting to get along when Capparelli weirded out on him. He turned down another side street. Well, if that's the way he wanted it, then, fine. His face burned with embarrassment and frustration. Served him right for thinking a partner could be anything more than just someone he worked with.

They drove around in silence a while longer before finally heading back to the station.

CHAPTER EIGHT

Benito Salinas liked rising early. His wife, Mary, preferred staying up late to watch the ten o'clock news, and then, more often than not, falling asleep on the couch watching *The Tonight Show* or some sappy movie on Lifetime. But he always enjoyed the quiet solitude the early morning provided, finding it even more comforting now that he was retired. He could relish the peace in the early, post-dawn hours, knowing the tranquility would no longer be shattered by events later in the day. Having been a structural engineer in a firm that was contracted out to the city of Chicago, there was almost always some sort of calamity or chaos awaiting him (often intensified by the ever-present media), and many times the serenity he'd found in those pre-rush-hour moments had given him the strength he'd needed to make it through the day. But time had taken its toll on his heart and blood pressure, and he didn't think he'd be able to handle stress like that again. Retirement was a blessing, indeed.

Letting Mary sleep in—she seemed to need her rest more and more these days—Benito stood by their family room window and savored his coffee. He watched the rising sun pierce the branches of their Douglas firs and prism through dripping icicles that hung from the gutters or off the remaining patches of ice-encrusted snow in their backyard. A fierce wind rattled the windows and waved the branches on the trees.

Heading back into the kitchen, Benito dumped the cooled remains of his coffee into the sink, his gaze automatically avoiding looking out the window at Walter's back porch and the horrible window hidden beneath. He poured himself a fresh cup. Decaf didn't taste like real coffee to him yet, but his doctor strictly forbade the good stuff, and he had to admit the fresh-ground beans Mary bought him at least removed the oily aftertaste.

He washed his breakfast dishes as the steam from the hot water clouded the glass panes. It was strange, he realized, how they avoided looking out that window. Sure, you couldn't help it sometimes, doing the dishes or waving to Walter if he was out on the driveway, but the ghost of that tragic evening was always there, even so many years later.

Benito sometimes wondered if Walter held it against him that they hadn't built the addition on their house until after that fateful night. But having heard what Harris had done, and watching with his own eyes Harris's remorseless belligerence in the courtroom—especially after being sentenced to only six years—Benito understood that everything that had happened that night was simply a random act of violence perpetrated by a soulless predator. Moving the window back any earlier wouldn't have stopped him at all.

He wiped his hands on a dishtowel and threw it onto the counter. Getting angry about everything that had happened so long ago wasn't doing him any good. But there were times he simply couldn't help it. Like whenever he saw Melissa Thorne, Harris's defense attorney, on TV. Mary literally had to rip the remote out of his hand to keep him from throwing it at the screen. He could still hear Thorne's words in the courtroom, how she argued that Dottie had simply been in the wrong place at the wrong time—as if dying in a hospice bed in her own home made everything Dottie's fault—while Harris's actions were merely "inexcusable." Benito damn near exploded every time she was on the news spouting off about how some new client of hers was only being charged with something because the police had beaten a false confession out of him.

God forbid any of them were actually *guilty* of committing the crimes they were charged with.

He rubbed his chest. There he was getting himself all worked up again. Maybe they needed a vacation. Like Walter. How strange it had seemed when he'd dropped by last week to say he was going to visit Dottie's relatives in St. Paul and could they keep an eye on the place? He and Mary had been surprised to learn that Walter had kept in contact with her relatives because he never mentioned them. But they saw it as a chance that Walter had finally recovered and was moving on.

Go on, they'd said, it'll be the best thing for you.

Was a vacation the magical elixir he and Mary needed? No, that was silly. Why take a vacation when they didn't have anywhere to go? The kids were always over, anyway. It was better to stay home and rest. For Mary's sake.

He took his blood pressure medication, unplugged the coffee maker, and dumped the remains of the pot in the sink. He wondered if it was his anxiety about Mary's tests that was bringing everything back. The doctor assured them that she was fine, but the results wouldn't be back for another week, and the thought that anything might happen to her was making him tense and short-tempered. He remembered how quickly the cancer had eaten through Dottie, how she had gone from a robust, joyful woman who did all the yard work because she wanted it done "her way" to a flesh-covered skeleton fed through a tube less than a year later. He shook his head. And after everything Harris did, he was amazed that Walter hadn't cracked. Benito didn't know how he'd have responded, but he did know the effect her death had had on Walter and their surviving friends, and it infuriated him when the legal system seemed more concerned about the welfare of the criminals than what the victim had had to go through, or the unending suffering their surviving family and friends had to endure.

On the windowsill, a couple of leaves on the African violet had wilted and turned brown where they contacted the glass above the kitchen sink. Benito removed the damaged leaves, set the plant on the countertop, and was wiping away the condensation when some movement outside caught his attention. He squinted through the pane. Something that looked like a sheer lace curtain or a loose piece of paper was flapping behind the latticework under Walter's back porch. Try as he might, though, he couldn't tell exactly what it was. Any other time he'd have ignored it—anything to avoid that horrible window—but Walter had asked him to watch over the house, and that was just what he was going to do. Slipping into his parka and fur-lined boots and gloves, Benito went out the back door as quietly as possible to avoid waking Mary.

Outside, the early morning wind hit him like a freight train. Though they were having a warm spell, it was still January, and the wind burned his exposed cheeks and stung his eyes. He walked across the driveway and dropped to his knees in the patch of snow shaded by Walter's porch—and instantly jumped back up. The front of his pants was soaked from knees to ankles. A thin trickle of water ran down the frozen crust from the window. Bending over, he peered through the latticework and thought: *Oh, dear lord.*

In the dim morning light, Benito saw that the board hiding the window beneath the porch was cracked open about thirty degrees, and the movement he had seen was water from a broken pipe squirting through the opening. Ice had formed on the board, dripping from the edges like gray-white stalactites.

Even with the whistling of the wind, he could hear the sound of water splashing in the basement.

Damn, damn, damn, he thought. *Why did this have to happen while Walter was away?*

Benito called a plumber, but was warned it might be an hour or so before he arrived. While he waited, he stripped off his wet pants and tossed them into the bathroom hamper. Mary must have woken and seen him, because she came in with a fresh pair of pants and thick, woolen socks. He told her what he found at Walter's house while she rubbed lotion on his irritated skin.

"Isn't he coming home tonight?" she asked. Her eyes glanced up at him from their sunken, black sockets.

"We can't let it go until then. Can you imagine what'll happen if we did?" He kissed her on the forehead and ran his fingers through her thinning hair. So much had fallen out already. He tried not to think about what else the chemicals were doing to her system.

She's just tired, he told himself for the thousandth time. *She's just tired.*

When the plumber, Tony Hagan, arrived, Benito led him next door. They were prepared to break down the door, if necessary. But the emergency spare keys he and Walter had traded oh-so-long-ago still fit the lock, and they stepped inside a house Benito had not been inside in nearly a decade.

"I'll shut off the main valve first," Hagan said. The basement door creaked when he opened it. He flicked on the light. "Damn, that's a hell of a lot of water."

Their boots clomped on the wooden stairs. Benito stopped halfway down. Though a chill wind blew in through the open window, he noticed the basement was filled with the pungent, bitter odor of bleach and disinfectant masking decay. He wondered how long the pipe had been broken and what other damage the water had done. Seeing water spraying out of the pipe running closest to the open window, he thought again: *That same damned window.*

Hagan splashed through the ankle-deep water below toward the crawlspace. Benito heard him swear. "What's wrong?"

"The pipe split by the window, all right. But worse, a pipe *fitting* burst in here." Hagan looked up at him. "How long's it been like this?"

"No idea. I just noticed it this morning. I didn't think it got cold enough last night to freeze the pipes."

"It didn't. Pipes don't leak until after the ice inside starts to thaw. Chances are it froze during that frigid spell last week and burst a few days ago when the temperatures rose. The broken pipe fitting is what caused most of the damage. There wouldn't be this much water, otherwise."

Hagan turned the valve and the spraying water ceased. He examined the windowpane, then moved his boot around the floor underneath. "There's broken glass in the frame but it doesn't feel like there's any on the floor. I doubt the water broke the window. Any idea what happened?"

Benito shook his head.

"Well, too late to worry about it now." He rubbed his bleary eyes and scratched his unshaven chin, and Benito wondered how many other calls Hagan had already had this morning. "See the streaks down the wall? I'm betting the water collected in the crawlspace until it overflowed onto the floor. The sump pump probably worked fine until the flow carried something down that jammed the motor and tripped the circuit breaker."

"Like what?"

"Gravel. Wood chips. Strips of cloth—hell, just about anything. You'd be amazed at what you find in people's crawlspaces." He shrugged. "Anyway, it's a good thing you found it before the water level rose above the electric sockets. This way I can just replace the sump pump, toss another into the crawl-space and run the hose out the window, and we'll have this all pumped out in no time."

"All right. Thanks."

Hagan ran out to his truck to get what he needed, leaving the back door wide open. Benito left his coat on to keep warm.

It felt strange being inside Walter's house again, he thought, as he walked around to keep his circulation going. When Dottie was alive, both families were in and out of each other's houses so much they felt like extensions of the same home. The house he remembered always smelled of fresh baked bread and chocolate chip cookies, but now seemed antiseptic and functional. And the odors in the basement filled him with an uneasy feeling he couldn't explain.

Hagan clumped down the basement stairs, and Benito soon heard the sound of the sump pumps starting and water squirt-ing out the back window.

He peered inside the living room and sighed. Ashes in the fireplace and another set of furniture. It amazed him how many times in the last few years Walter had made new living and din-ing room furniture. Maybe it was something that helped him cope with Dottie's loss, but Benito never understood why Wal-ter chopped up the old furniture and burned it in his fireplace instead of donating it to a homeless shelter or charity. This cur-rent set with flowered vinyl cushions looked like something you'd see on someone's patio in the summer. Why would anyone want something like that in his living room? Or for that matter, why did the dining room set have only five chairs instead of six?

And what was that by the front door? When he moved closer, Benito was surprised to discover it was a touchpad for a home security system. Come to think of it, he'd noticed one in the kitchen too. He and Mary had talked to Walter about getting one, but they'd never known he did. A glowing red light in the corner indicated the system was on, but he hadn't heard any chimes or beeps when they'd entered. Nor had there been any inquiring phone calls or police responding to their entry.

Now why on earth would Walter buy a system that didn't alert the authorities?

A scream erupted from the basement, followed quickly by a loud splash. By the time Benito made it back to the kitchen, Hagan, his backside soaking wet, had already run up the stairs and was attempting to use Walter's wall-mounted phone. His hands were shaking so badly his fingers kept hitting the wrong numbers.

"Goddamn! There's a dead body down there!" His lips quivered uncontrollably and it took Benito a moment to realize what he'd said.

A body? In Walter's basement? While Hagan called nine-one-one, Benito headed for the stairs. Surely the guy was just overtired and saw some old clothes floating in the water. A dead body? In this house? No, it couldn't be.

The wooden stairs creaked under his feet. The cold wind whipped through the open window, making the wet steps slippery. Benito gripped the railing with both hands. His breath made foggy clouds in the air. His heart beating wildly, he ducked his head under the ceiling and looked around. The pumps were still running, and the sound of the water splashing outside was louder down here. But he didn't see anything out of the ordinary except a lot of ruined woodworking equipment. Breathing a sigh of relief, he was about to go back up when he heard Hagan say "crawlspace" into the phone.

A body in the crawlspace? Images of Gacy popped into his mind, but Benito quickly pushed them away. Oh lord, no. Not our Walter. Please say it couldn't be. Dropping to his knees, his cold-numbed fingers grasping the splintered-edged boards and his heart pounding against his ribs, he looked under the stairs.

And there, much to his horror, a mangled foot stuck up out of a puddle of water in the loosened gravel.

Benito's chest tightened. A pain like a serrated knife twisted through his heart and raced down his left arm. Sweat beaded on his forehead. He gasped, unable to draw breath against a weight that threatened to crush his rib cage. Staggering to his feet, his hands clutching his chest, he climbed the last few steps and collapsed onto the kitchen floor. White-hot stars swirled around the edges of his vision, and the sound of Hagan's frantic voice talking on the phone was a muffled echo in his ears.

"I'm telling you, I never seen nothing like it. I—Benito? What's wrong? Aw fuck, man, I think he's having a heart attack! Send an ambulance. Quick! Jesus, hang on, Benito! They're sending someone for you. Just hang on, man, just hang on . . ."

The plumber's voice faded to static while the stars blackened, spinning faster and faster as his chest squeezed tighter and tighter. And the last thought Benito had before the pain and darkness engulfed him was that Walter had indeed cracked, after all.

CHAPTER NINE

Riehle stood in the hallway outside Larry Jensen's hospital room. He wanted to check on him before going in to work so he could reassure Gwen that Larry was coming along as well as could be expected. Though it was early, the corridor was alive with nurses scurrying about, bringing patients their morning medications. He heard the sounds of TV programs coming from nearby rooms, and he wondered how anyone was able to get any sleep around here.

Jenny Gavin emerged from Jensen's room, carrying his chart in a metal folding clipboard. She wore green scrubs with her photo ID badge pinned to it. A stethoscope weighed down her right pocket, and the dark circles under her eyes told him she was nearing the end of a long shift.

"How's he doing?" he asked.

"Not so great." She ran a tired hand through her blond hair, and Riehle noticed the gray roots along the part in the middle. A petite, thin woman with a slightly upturned nose, Jenny had the ability to make anyone feel at ease. He and Gwen had even seen her soften the edges of her stoic, no-nonsense lieutenant husband without diminishing his dignity. Likewise, her comforting manner helped grief-stricken families deal with the harsh news the doctors often delivered.

"Physically, he's coming along fine. We'll probably discharge him today or tomorrow. But mentally?" She shook her head. "There isn't a lot of will to recover. He took the news about his family pretty hard. The doctors put him on suicide watch after they talked to him, but he hasn't tried anything."

"Any family members been in to see him yet?"

"He mentioned a sister arriving later today. We'll talk to her first about our concerns before releasing him into her care. Are you sure you need to talk to him? He's still heavily medicated and really needs the rest."

"I'll only be a minute."

She tipped her head by way of permission, and Riehle entered the room. Jensen lay on the bed with the sheets tucked up under his armpits. His left arm was in a cast, and an IV dripped into his right. The TV was off, the curtains closed, and the only light on was the fluorescent tube on the wall above the headboard. The machines beeped with his slow, steady heartbeat, and the green readouts glowed in the dimly lit room. His head was turned away from the door, but Riehle could see the sutured laceration above Jensen's left eyebrow and the severe contusions on his face. It was hard to believe that this broken mass was the same man who'd been able to manipulate his wands with such dexterity at Karen's party that the puppets had seemed almost alive. He wondered if Jensen would ever be able to do so again.

As Riehle looked down on the injured man, the hairs along the back of his neck rose. He hated hospitals. The diseases, the pain, and the suffering all around him made him feel like a claustrophobic locked in a closet. While his "proud" father never made it to the hospital (the bottle of vodka and sleeping tablets had taken care of everything at home), he'd never been able to shake the feeling of loss and sorrow and fear he associated with his worry over his mother's emergency hysterectomy less than a year after his father died. And even though Ellen had recovered fine, and he'd experienced the joy of Karen's birth here, Riehle still believed a hospital was essentially a place people went to die.

"Larry?"

The puppeteer's head turned toward him. His eyes fluttered, and he squinted at Riehle through the right one. The left was almost completely swollen shut, and the tiny bit of exposed cornea looked like a blood bag about to burst. He licked his cracked lips. "Yes?" His voice was a slurred, hoarse whisper from the medication.

"It's Kevin Riehle." He leaned over the bed so Jensen could see him better. "I'm a detective with the Westbrook Police Department, remember? I'm helping with the investigation."

Jensen closed his eyes, and a wave of pain washed across his features. He swallowed hard, then nodded slowly. "Good."

Riehle clasped his hand. "Gwen and I wanted you to know how sorry we are. We know your sister is arriving soon, but if there's anything we can do to help, please let us know."

Larry weakly squeezed his hand. Riehle's phone chirped, but the noise didn't bother Jensen. His muscles had relaxed, and Riehle knew the man was asleep again. Riehle wished him a peaceful, dreamless rest before quietly leaving the room and checking the text at the nurses' station. It was Capparelli's number, with a nine-one-one after it.

"No cell phones allowed," Jenny reminded him, setting their multi-line phone on the counter for him.

"What's up?" Riehle asked when his partner answered.

"A dead body in a crawlspace," Capparelli said.

Located adjacent to an off-ramp for the Tri-State Tollway, the address was the kind of Chicago-style brick bungalow that Riehle fondly remembered from his childhood—the kind currently being obliterated by greedy developers who replaced them with overpriced mini-mansions. A drainage ditch and a grove of trees and bushes within a cyclone fence atop a steep incline buffered the Buczyno property from the road, though the passing cars could still be seen through the winter-bare trees. Riehle wondered how much the leaves in the summer blocked the sounds of the traffic. The smell of exhaust fumes on the chill wind stung his nostrils.

Riehle parked their vehicle on the street behind a squad car. He buttoned his overcoat as he and Capparelli made their way up the driveway. A plumber's van was parked near the back door of the house. The sound of a running pump was louder near the back, and water splashed from a hose that extended out from under the screened-in porch.

Simmons greeted them at the back door. "Ah man, is this gonna be a heater."

Riehle stamped his shoes as he entered. "What have we got, Paul?"

Simmons flipped open his pocket notebook and turned some pages with the eraser end of a heavily chewed yellow pencil. "The house belongs to a Walter Buczyno, age sixty-two, a retired construction engineer. According to Mary Salinas next door, Buczyno is currently visiting his dead wife's relatives in St. Paul and is due home later tonight. He'd asked Mary and her husband to watch the house while he was away, and this morning, Benito Salinas noticed water leaking out of a back window. He figured a frozen pipe had burst and called a plumber."

His eraser flicked to the next page. "The plumber, Tony Hagan, found a pipe fitting had burst in the crawlspace, so he shut off the main line and started pumping water out the basement window. When he climbed into the crawlspace, he found a foot sticking out of the gravel." He lowered his voice. "The guy freaked. I'm surprised he was able to call us."

"Where's he now?" Capparelli said.

"In the living room with Morgan and Kaminsky. He's been getting a lot of calls about other broken pipes, but I said he had to sit tight until after you talked to him."

"What about the Salinases?"

He shook his head. "You just missed them. Benito was having a heart attack when the plumber called in. The ambulance took them to Middaugh. Dixie followed them down to see what else she could find out about Buczyno."

Riehle winced at the image of the heavily perfumed, redheaded officer questioning a woman while she worried about her husband's fate in the ER. But he knew if anyone could get her talking, Dixie could. "Let's have a go at the plumber then."

Simmons stayed at the back door while Riehle and Capparelli went into the living room. Morgan and Kaminsky stood by the front door and nodded to the detectives when they entered. Riehle noticed ashes in the grate of the large stone fireplace, and the room still held the smell of a recent fire. The plumber was sitting forward on a sofa with floral-printed vinyl cushions, elbows on his knees, talking into his cell phone. He wore a gray down jacket, a red flannel work shirt, damp, faded jeans, and dirt-smeared boots. He told whoever was on the other end that he had to go, ended the call, and snapped the phone into the clip on his belt.

The plumber stood and shook their hands. "Tony Hagan. Howya doin'? Listen, how much longer I gotta stick around? I'm losing customers right and left."

"Not much longer," Riehle said. "Tell us what happened."

Hagan rubbed the back of his neck. His face was unshaven and his red eyes looked as if he'd been up all night. "Like I told the other guys, Benito called me this morning saying his neighbor had a broken pipe. Hey, is he gonna be okay?"

"I'm sure," Capparelli said. "Go on."

"Anyway, when we came inside, I shut off the main line, replaced the sump pump in the floor, and put another one in the crawlspace and started pumping water out of the basement. When it started to go down, I saw a sock floating on the surface.

I didn't want it to get stuck in the pump, so I climbed in to grab it. Next thing I know I'm holding a dirty sock and a foot's sticking out of the water."

Hagan glanced over at Morgan and Kaminsky, then moved closer to the detectives and lowered his voice. "Scared the fucking shit outta me. I had a rat jump out of a pipe once, but I never found a dead body before."

"What'd you do when you saw the foot?" Riehle said.

"Whaddaya think? I fell backwards into the water, then ran upstairs and called you guys."

Capparelli gestured toward Hagan's cell phone. "On that?"

The plumber looked down at his belt as if he'd forgotten it was there. "This thing? No, I'd left it in the truck. I used the one in the kitchen." They heard the familiar thump of the sump pump and the splashing sound of water outside stopped. "Sounds like the water's out."

"Let's all go down," Riehle said, "and you can show us where you found everything."

Hagan led them back through the kitchen and down the gray painted wooden stairs into the basement. The steps creaked under the weight of the three men. Riehle saw a furnace and hot water heater off to his left; a washer, dryer, and utility sink in another corner; a workbench, band saw, table saw, router, and other woodworking equipment—probably ruined now— under clear but stained plastic tarps; and a green metal storage cabinet in the far corner. As the window under the porch was still open, the basement was much colder than the upper floor, and the air smelled of mud and sweet-smelling decay.

The plumber wrinkled his nose. "Whoa, that stinks."

"And you'll never forget the smell," Capparelli said.

"I doubt I'll forget any of this."

"So, where is it?" Riehle asked.

Hagan pointed. The crawlspace was located behind a half

wall of concrete under the stairs near the broken window. Hagan said the window was probably already broken as there wasn't any glass on the floor, and Benito had told him he didn't know anything about it. Frost-covered pipes and electrical conduits ran between the floor joists under the kitchen. The churned-up gravel in the crawlspace was wet and muddy, and a foot and part of an ankle protruded from it.

"That how you found it?" Riehle said.

"Hell, yeah. I wasn't gonna touch anything. I've seen those shows on TV."

Riehle smiled in spite of himself. He pulled a pair of latex gloves and a jar of mentholated eucalyptus balm from his overcoat pocket, slipped on the gloves, and wiped a smear of the balm under his nose, then leaned forward to examine the foot closer. Though streaked with mud and already swollen, the tissue was discolored and badly bruised. Riehle began to get an uneasy feeling that if the rest of the body looked this way, the victim had been severely beaten. Knowing the evidence techs would have a shit-fit if he moved anything before they had a chance to photograph the scene, he gently probed the tissue with his index finger and found a tear in the skin at the ankle bone. A large chip of the bone was missing. He carefully tugged on the foot and met with resistance, telling him it wasn't just a severed foot and the rest of the body was still buried.

Hagan's phone rang. He answered it, then asked the detectives, "Can I go now? I got some customers I really gotta take care of."

"Sure."

The plumber nodded gratefully and started pulling in the hose. Riehle looked up at Capparelli to see if he had anything to add, but Capparelli's attention was focused on the wooden floor joists above him and a hanging fluorescent lamp in the middle of the room. When he noticed Riehle was watching him, Capparelli pointed to the ceiling. Riehle moved closer. Though new bulbs were in place, the lamp had reddish-brown smears on it as if it had been hastily wiped down, and the wooden joists and floorboards were crusted with what appeared to be dried blood. Lots of it. Riehle saw other splatter marks as well.

"Mr. Hagan, did you notice anything else while you were down here?" Capparelli said.

The plumber, who had already rolled up the hose and was just starting to carry it and the extra sump pump from the crawlspace up the stairs, stopped short. "No, man. Like I said, I saw that thing and called you right away." His expression seemed both irritated and afraid that they were going to make him stay longer.

Capparelli nodded, and Riehle said, "Thanks for your help. We'll let you know if we need anything else."

Relieved, Hagan smiled and trotted up the stairs. After he was gone, Riehle said, "You don't think he noticed?"

"I doubt it. His attention was on the floor, and he seemed pretty shook up as it was. I didn't want to make it any worse for him."

"Probably a good idea." They stared into the crawlspace. Riehle blew out his breath. "All right. I'll tell Gavin we need more officers to secure the area, then have the coroner and crime scene techs—"

"Hold on a minute." Capparelli leaned over and poked his gloved finger into the wet gravel a couple feet away from the victim's foot. "We'd better get a warrant first."

"Why? We've already got probable cause."

Capparelli flicked some of the gravel away, and a bony fragment became visible.

"Because I think we've got another body."

CHAPTER TEN

The trip to the airport seemed longer in silence.

Helen drove her car with the broken heater. She and Walter were heavily bundled, but their down jackets, gloves, scarves, and wool hats did little to block the cold. A bitter wind and the sounds of the surrounding traffic whipped through the car. Helen had the windows half-open to prevent their breathing and natural body heat from fogging the windshield, but she occasionally had to scrape away some of the frozen condensation with a credit card in order to see the road better. One time, she was so distracted that she drifted into another lane, and after the passing motorist laid on the horn, she practically bit Walter's head off when he offered to clean the windshield for her so she could concentrate more on her driving.

Most of his visit had gone pretty much the same way.

The days after his dinner table confession were filled with forced conversations and uncomfortable silences, and he spent his sleepless nights tossing and turning, fretting over what he'd done to them. They continued being polite and hospitable throughout the remainder of the visit, but no one sat next to him again or came within touching distance at any time. Out of the corner of his eye, he often caught them staring at him, and any sudden movement made them jump. Fascinated and terrified, they'd circled him, watching him as if he were a ferocious zoo animal that had yet to discover its cage was unlocked. Waiting for the beast to emerge and slaughter them all.

Walter was grateful when the time to leave had finally arrived.

"I shouldn't have come," he said.

Helen glanced at him. Her grip on the steering wheel tightened, but the hard lines around her mouth softened.

"Of course you should have. And we're glad you did. It just wasn't what we'd expected, that's all. We thought you were coming to tell us you were getting remarried. Not . . . *that*."

"Are you disappointed in me for what I did?"

She took a long time to answer him, chewing her cheek while she considered her own thoughts and fears. She shivered in the cold.

"I'd be lying if I said I hadn't fantasized about doing the same thing at one time or another to Harris, especially after the way he talked about Dottie in court," she admitted. "Or even, God help me, sometimes to Roger and Chloe. All those sleepless nights with my anger burning inside me and feeling completely helpless because there wasn't anything I could do about it, and knowing the only person I was hurting was myself. But I never gave in to those feelings. Sometimes you have to put your faith in the law and in others to get the job done right."

He turned sharply toward her. "And do you feel it was done right?"

Her eyes avoided his angry glare as if she were afraid his gaze could penetrate her soul into the deepest, most honest feelings she was unwilling to acknowledge even to herself. Almost too softly to hear, she said, "No."

"But that doesn't mean we should *act* on those feelings," she added quickly. "It's one thing to think about it and something completely different to go through with it. We can't exist in a state of total anarchy. That's what laws are for. Couldn't you have just called the police when you heard him breaking in?"

"And what if they got there too late? Then I'd be nothing

more than another statistic, a dead one, while everyone would hurry to make sure Harris's rights weren't violated—if they ever caught him."

"What if they arrived while you were still struggling with him?"

"Then some cop or lawyer would be more upset that I was defending myself, instead of the fact that someone was breaking into my home again. That's if they even knew about the original break-in. Harris's records were sealed, remember? He was a juvenile, which entitled him to special rules, the little bastard. *I* played by the rules when he attacked Dottie and what did calling the police get me then?"

He scowled. "No. You know the old saying: 'Do it to me once, shame on you; do it to me again, shame on me.' The system let me down the first time and I wasn't going to let them do it to me again."

"I understand your anger with Harris," Helen said. "But what about those other boys?"

"What about them? They broke into my home intending to commit a crime. Can you imagine what would have happened if I'd injured one of them instead? Some goddamn lawyer would sue me for damages. Me. The one they were committing the crime against. Well, bullshit. As far as I'm concerned, the minute they entered my house, they lost their rights. Period."

"But their poor families. Their grief—"

"They wouldn't be grieving if their sons hadn't committed the crimes in the first place," Walter said. "Look, this isn't *Death Wish*. I didn't go out looking for victims or revenge. They came into *my* house intending to do *me* harm. Hell, Harris was even trying to shoot me! All I did was take care of the problem. Didn't Eleanor point out that the average man is being forced to do things he wouldn't normally do? So stop feeling sorry for them and put your sympathy with the real victim where it belongs."

Helen angrily scraped the windshield. "But the law is the law. You should respect it."

"Why? What's it done for me? There's no common sense anymore. It's all about money. The law doesn't protect the average person from anything—just look how effective those worthless Orders of Protection are. Nowadays, the only ones the law supports are the ones committing the crimes."

"Now, wait a minute—"

"Think about it. CEOs who get two-hundred-million-dollar severance packages after bankrupting investor and employee funds and ruining the company, and corporations that cancel the pensions of the very people who worked hard all their lives to make that company great. I mean, look how Lorna's grocery chain fired everyone and took away their benefits."

"What's that got to do with—"

"And what about you?"

"What about me?"

"According to your divorce agreement, Roger has to pay the girls' college expenses, right?" Walter said, surprised and pleased to realize he *had* been paying attention to their conversation after all. "You hired a lawyer and took Roger to court. Where are you at now?"

Helen sighed. "The judge and my attorney are pressuring me to garnish his wages. But if I do that, Roger threatened to quit his job, which would leave the girls without medical insurance."

"So let me get this straight: You've paid sixty-five hundred dollars in legal fees to get Roger to do what your divorce agreement—a legal contract—already says he's supposed to do. And now your lawyer and the judge are making you feel like the bad guy because you have to choose between protecting the girls and getting them what is rightfully theirs anyway."

"Are you trying to make me feel worse?" she said, wiping her angry tears away.

"I'm just trying to point out that the law hasn't done anything for you," Walter said. "The lawyer got paid for something that was technically already done—and without getting you the results you hired him for. The judge made you feel like you're making things difficult for *him*. And Roger got away with everything. The law hasn't protected you at all. In fact, it's protecting Roger, and he's the one committing the crime."

Helen shook her head. "No, the law isn't protecting him. His rights are."

"So what are you saying? Laws are for everyone, but rights belong to the criminals?"

"Yes. I mean, no. I mean—Arrruggh! You're twisting everything all around."

"Maybe I should have been a lawyer, then."

"There's no need to get nasty about it," Helen said. "I'm just saying you need to find a way to make the legal system work for you. It's the best system we've got."

"My proctologist says the same thing."

She didn't have an answer for that, so they rode the rest of the way in silence. When they arrived at the Minneapolis-St. Paul International Airport, Helen drove to the Lindbergh Terminal and pulled to a stop in front of the door for his airline. She popped the trunk without getting out of the car, hiding her anger and frustration by scraping the frost off the windshield with her credit card. Ice shavings curled and danced across the dashboard in the wind.

Walter set his garment bag on the sidewalk and walked back to the passenger side window. Shivering, Helen tightened the scarf around her neck, averting her eyes when he leaned on his forearms and stuck his head inside the car.

"I'm sorry," he said. "I never should have brought all of you into this. I've made a lot of mistakes in my life, and somehow I always manage to make things worse when I try to correct them." He reached into his coat pocket and pulled out a roll of bills.

Her eyes widened as if he'd insulted her. "Are you trying to buy our silence?"

Exasperated, Walter hung his head. Unable to hide the sadness in his voice, he said, "It's for a new heater. I can't afford to pay you the money Roger owes you, but I don't want to have to worry about you and the girls getting sick or in an accident driving around in this car. This family's been through enough already." He extended his hand. "Go on. Take it."

A cop whistled behind them, telling them to move it along. Helen stuffed the money in her coat pocket and shifted the car into gear. But as he reached down to grab his luggage, she kept her foot on the brake and leaned across the seat toward him, shouting, "Find some way to make the legal system work for *you.*" Then she merged into traffic, drove around the curve, and was gone.

CHAPTER ELEVEN

By the time Riehle and Capparelli returned to the Buczyno house, the coroner had already begun to exhume the bodies from the crawlspace.

Riehle turned up the collar of his overcoat against the biting, late afternoon wind. The detectives had spent most of the day preparing the affidavit and search warrant forms, finding the state's attorney and making his corrections to the forms, and then waiting until the judge was available to sign them. Riehle had put Dr. Thomas Griskel, the Granger County coroner, on notice, and as soon as the judge gave them permission, Riehle called Griskel and told him to go ahead. His van was parked in the Buczyno driveway, along with the crime scene technicians' SUV and a local funeral home's removal service vehicle.

Three Westbrook patrol cars barricaded the street in front of the house, their bar lights flashing the neighborhood with red and blue. Vans with logos for local and national television stations and additional cars for newspaper journalists were parked farther down the block, as close as the officers allowed. The media never tired of sensational crimes and hungered for every gory detail. The shouting between the reporters and those directed at any officer or gawking neighbor within sight, along with the on and off testing of the minicam lights, had turned the crime scene into a circus.

Nodding to the uniformed officers assigned to hold the media and morbidly curious neighbors at bay, Riehle and Capparelli ducked under the yellow crime scene tape that stretched between the winter-bare trees along the parkway and made their way over the battleground of muddy, slushy footprints in the front yard.

Kaminsky let them in the front door. Their shoes added melted snow and salt and dirt to the heavily trafficked path on the tiled floor leading from the front door to the kitchen. A number of uniformed officers mulled around, and Riehle could hear the sounds of the evidence techs talking in the basement. Simmons grabbed a couple of sheets of paper off the fireplace mantel and came over.

"Was there another body?" Riehle asked.

"Three more, actually. I told Griskel you were here. He'll be up in a few minutes to talk to you."

"*Four*. Jesus." He blew out his breath. "You hear from Dixie yet? How's Benito?"

"They think he'll make it."

"That's good. She find out anything more about Buczyno?"

Simmons shrugged. "The usual: nice guy, real friendly, nobody expected anything like this out of him."

"Aren't they all?" Capparelli said.

Simmons handed them the sheets of paper. "Nielsen sent these over. He pulled up Buczyno's DMV photo, stats, and auto info and printed them up for you."

Riehle and Capparelli studied the photo. The image that stared back at them was hardly what Riehle would have expected. A balding widower with gray-blue eyes and a bulbous nose. But it was the eyes that surprised him the most. They had neither the hard, piercing glare, nor the dead, soulless pupils half-covered by heavy drooping lids, nor the vacant, thousand-yard stare that most killers seemed to possess. Instead, Buczyno's eyes were warm and comforting, if a little tired-looking, but friendly like your best friend's dad; and Riehle realized with a shudder that that was exactly how Buczyno had been able to get away with everything for so long.

"Seems he spent most of his time working around the house and making furniture," Simmons said. "He occasionally helped out with the local neighborhood watch, but mostly kept to himself after his wife died of cancer eight years ago."

"A loner, then," Riehle said.

"That's why this trip seemed so odd to the Salinases. Out of the blue, Buczyno asked them to watch the house while he visited his wife's relatives for the week. Mary said they always thought it would be good for him to get away, but they were surprised to learn that Buczyno had kept in touch with his wife's family since he never mentioned them."

"Stranger things have happened."

Shouting arose outside. The reporters were demanding to know what was going on inside the house, and the officers were having trouble calming them down. Simmons zipped up his coat. "I'd better give them a hand. Oh, wait. Here." He pulled his notebook from his front pocket and tore off a sheet for them. "Dixie got the number for Buczyno's flight to O'Hare and the time of arrival. Nielsen checked. It's still on time and is supposed to come in at Gate E-Thirteen."

Riehle took the sheet. "Thanks. Tell Dixie she did great."

While they waited for Griskel, Riehle took a closer look at the modestly furnished living and dining rooms. He didn't know much about woodworking, but he admired Buczyno's handiwork. The sofa, loveseat, and coffee and end tables in the living room were stained a blond oak and arranged to face the large stone fireplace against the far wall. The cushions of the loveseat and sofa were the flowered, vinyl cushions normally found with a set of patio furniture, which gave the room a rustic feel. The dining room table and five chairs, china cabinet, and corner curio stand, however, were stained a rich, dark mahogany, setting this room off from the other with its own dignified touch. An old-fashioned radiator grill sat under the window in the dining room facing the Salinas home, and the hallway off the other side of the living room led to two bedrooms and a tiny bathroom. Riehle assumed Buczyno slept in the first bedroom because it was the only room with carpeting.

"Sooo . . ." Riehle said. "Think we're handling things like you would in the city?"

Capparelli shrugged. "What's to do differently? Seems like any other murder investigation I've been on."

The sound of heavy footsteps plodded up the basement stairs, and Riehle thought *Maybe not* as Dr. Thomas Griskel, the coroner, stepped into the kitchen.

Dr. Griskel was a short man, five and a half feet tall in dress shoes, though the paunch around his middle had grown over the last few years. He wore a powder blue shirt with the sleeves rolled up to his elbows, and the front of it was streaked with today's excavations. Fifty-three years of hard living were etched into the lines on his pudgy face, and though his large-framed trifocals gave his hazel eyes a watery appearance, Riehle knew they never missed a thing. Today, his long hair was dyed jet black and piled on his head in an Elvis pompadour.

"Man, that's the worst looking rug I've ever seen," Capparelli said.

"It's real."

"You're shittin' me."

"Swear to God. He's been dying his hair and dressing like rock stars for a while now."

"And they let him get away with it?"

"Why the hell not? The guy's a prosecutor's wet dream. A coroner who's an honest-to-God medical examiner, not just another elected official. He's got a photographic memory and can recall any minor detail under pressure of cross-examination without having to consult his notes. So what difference does it make how he dresses?"

Uniformed officers labored up the stairs, grunting as they carried another corpse in a black body bag out the back door. Griskel caught Riehle's eye, nodded, and held up his index finger, telling him he'd be there in a minute.

Capparelli shook his head, seemingly unable to comprehend how anyone dressed like that could be taken seriously. "I thought coroners and medical examiners were supposed to be sullen and morose, weighed down by the burden of their jobs, thinking everyone wanted them fired, and hyper-paranoid that international gangsters were busy plotting their assassinations."

"Get real. Don't you remember the Tamara Larson case? It was all over the media."

"Refresh my memory."

Riehle scratched his head. "That was during his Roger Daltrey phase," he said. "A three-year-old girl had fallen into a well and was wedged upside down in the pipe. The cops lowered down a camera and microphone, but after about fifteen minutes they figured she was dead and called Griskel, because they didn't see any movement and couldn't pick up any sound.

"The mom freaked when the coroner's van showed up— nobody'd warned her. While they were trying to calm her down, Griskel took one look at the video monitor, grabbed somebody's bullhorn, flipped it into the air and caught it, then leaned toward the pipe and yelled: *'Tammy, can you hear me?'* "

"You gotta be fucking kidding me." His eyes darted back and forth between Griskel and Riehle, as if waiting for someone to tell him they were pulling his leg. "So, was the girl saved?" he finally asked.

"Oh yeah. Turns out they didn't see any movement because she'd fallen asleep and was wedged in so tight it was hard to see her breathing. And they didn't get any sound because there was a short in the line. The cops figured she woke up when the mom started screaming and no one but Griskel saw it because they were all looking the other way. Once the mom knew she was okay, though, she spent the rest of the week reminding the media her daughter's name was *Tamara*." Riehle grinned. "Seriously, you don't remember it?"

"If I had, I might not have transferred to this loony bin," Capparelli said. "Ah geez, here he comes."

"Good to see you," Griskel said, shaking Riehle's hand, then Capparelli's when Riehle introduced them.

Capparelli seemed to struggle with what to say. "You're not, like, gonna get all shook up or anything?"

Griskel frowned, delivering a glare that had mown down many a defense attorney in court. "This is a very serious matter, detective. Four young men were murdered in this house and it's my job to handle it properly." He crossed his arms. "We're just taking care of business."

A flush rose up from under Capparelli's collar. But before he could say anything, another car pulled to a stop along the parkway, and the lieutenant stepped out. "I'll get Gavin," he offered quickly, obviously grateful for the chance to get away.

Griskel smiled. "Too much."

"You really enjoy taunting the new guys, don't you?" Riehle said.

"I get a better rise out of them than my regular customers," he admitted. "So that's your new partner, huh? Wound kind of tight, isn't he?"

"Yeah, he's carrying something around with him."

"Well, I hope you figure him out before I have to. So how've you been? Did you and Gwen ever decide what you're doing for your anniversary?"

"Not yet."

Griskel rested a hand on his shoulder. "Whatever you do,

make sure you do *something*. You'll never get back the time you've lost. Trust me."

Riehle understood. Three years earlier, Griskel's wife was killed in a car accident a month after he'd put his mother in a nursing home for Alzheimer's. It came as no surprise to anyone who knew him when Griskel's dressing habits changed shortly afterward. Something had to give.

Gavin strode through the door with Capparelli right behind him. If Capparelli was expecting him to admonish Griskel, he was sorely disappointed when Gavin said, "I wondered when you'd do the King." He unbuttoned the top of his tan overcoat. "Got something for us?"

"Right this way."

Griskel led them down the stairs into the basement. Riehle saw the stains on the concrete walls showing how high the water had been, and the floor was a muddy swirl of footprints. A couple of technicians were labeling evidence bags and vials and storing them in their cases, while another put his digital video and still cameras away. They greeted the lieutenant and detectives. Additional lights were set up in front of the crawlspace, and the sickly sweet smell of decomposition was more pronounced in the warmer air.

Griskel indicated where the basement window had been removed and a new plywood board was nailed in its place. "We're checking the broken window and glass for blood and fibers to make sure Buczyno can't claim someone broke into his home and buried a body while he was away."

"Like Gacy tried," Capparelli said harshly.

"Right. Other than the bodies and what was buried with them under the gravel, I doubt we'll have anything admissible from the floor. Too much water damage." Griskel pointed at the ceiling. "But we sure as hell have enough up there. We also bagged the plastic tarps covering the woodworking equipment because there appeared to be blood stains on them that someone tried to wipe off, and Tadashi found a couple drops on one of the saws."

The young, new technician with black, spiked hair and a diamond stud earring nodded, grateful for the acknowledgement of his work. "The stains look older, but we'll compare them against the other samples we've got. And I'll check the mechanisms in case Buczyno used the saws for something more than woodworking."

"Speaking of which," Gavin said, "did anyone check the refrigerator?"

"No Dahmer souvenirs," Griskel said. "The bodies appeared mostly intact—at least, what remained of them." He pointed at the green metal cabinet. "Tadashi bagged a slightly bloodied roll of insulated wire and an almost empty roll of duct tape he found in there. We'll test the blood and check for any adhesive residue on the victims, see if they match."

Gavin looked down into the crawlspace, his hands buried deep in his overcoat pockets and an angry, troubled expression on his face. "This where you found them?"

Four shallow graves showed where the bodies had been buried. Three were positioned in a column from the back wall to the front, while the latest victim—the one whose foot they had initially discovered—was perpendicular to the others. The lights cast eerie shadows in the graveled indentations.

"The placement of the bony fragment Capparelli found compared to the exposed foot and the amount of space available suggested this kind of burial arrangement," Griskel said. "There's always the possibility there might be additional bodies beneath them, but we haven't found any yet. We'll keep looking, though."

"What kind of condition were the other bodies in?" Riehle said.

"Bones, mostly, and scraps of clothing, but a fair portion had already disintegrated. My guess is they were covered in lime at the time of burial."

"Any idea about the cause of death?"

"Judging by the condition we found him in, I'd say the most recent victim was beaten with some sort of blunt instrument. I'll know better after the autopsy."

"Think the others were beaten too?"

"Hard to say. But I didn't get that impression. At least not compared to the new guy. What was left of him didn't even look human."

"So Buczyno's enjoying what he's doing," Capparelli said. Riehle started at the sharpness in his partner's tone. Capparelli's hands were clenched into tight fists and his jaw muscles were taut from grinding his teeth. His emotions seemed barely held in check. What the hell was wrong with him?

"It's too early to make a speculative leap like that," Griskel said. He shrugged. "Who knows? Maybe this one set off some kind of emotional response."

"Or tried to fight back."

"If so, the beating continued long after the victim was unable to defend himself any longer." Griskel pointed to the stained overhead joists. "Something set him off, that's for sure. There might be blood present from the other victims, but most of that looks relatively new."

"Think he might have killed the others somewhere else and simply buried them here?" Riehle said.

"Could be. Of course at this point, anything's possible."

"How long have the others been here?" Gavin said.

"Best guesstimate? A year or two. Maybe more on the one that was closest to the wall. I'll have a better idea after I examine them."

"What else have you two found out?" Gavin asked the detectives. Riehle told him the information that Simmons and Nielsen had passed along, and mentioned Buczyno's flight was due to arrive shortly. "Anything they can do here?" Gavin said to Griskel.

"Not really. We'll finish checking for more bodies and whatever else we can collect."

Simmons came to the top of the stairs. "Lieutenant, Deputy Chief Volkovitz is here, sir. He wants to speak with you before he talks to the media."

Gavin buttoned the top of his overcoat and put on his gloves. He exhaled sharply. "Time to face the reporters. Jesus. Four bodies in a crawlspace in the Chicago suburbs. That's Gacy all over again. The jackals are gonna have a field day with this."

He turned to the detectives. "Riehle, Capparelli, get your asses out to O'Hare and arrest Buczyno as soon as he steps off that plane. You can do a more thorough search of the house tomorrow after we have him in custody."

"Yes, sir."

"Doc, you keep them up to date on anything else you find tonight." Gavin clapped Capparelli on the shoulder. "And don't be cruel to the new guy."

"You got it," Griskel said.

Though his face turned red, Capparelli didn't say a word. He waited until after Gavin left before mumbling something about how they'd better get going, then hurried up the stairs as if he couldn't get away from the suburban craziness fast enough.

CHAPTER TWELVE

"Ladies and gentlemen," the gate agent announced over the PA system, "Flight Eleven Twenty-three from Minneapolis-St. Paul to Chicago will now begin boarding. Passengers in rows one through twelve and those with special needs may board at this time."

Leaning forward, elbows on his knees, Walter sat at the gate, waiting for his flight home. Other passengers around him gathered their carry-ons and started moving toward the ramp while he remained in his seat. His garment bag rested between his legs and his sweaty hands clutched his boarding pass.

He couldn't get the image of Helen's angry, disappointed face out of his mind. Or any of them, for that matter. His trip to St. Paul hadn't succeeded in anything except alienating his only remaining family completely out of his life. Walter shook his head. He never should have come. He shouldn't have made this mistake. And now he was paying for it. Though the lounge was crowded, he had never felt more empty and lost and alone in his entire life. Even on the day Dottie had died.

"I'm trying my hardest, Mom," insisted a voice behind him. "But the flight's overbooked, and I'm on standby."

Walter checked his watch. He'd be on the plane in the next few minutes and home again a couple hours later. But what was the hurry? His purpose in life was over. Ever since the trial, his whole world had been consumed with hatred and revenge on Harris. But now that that was over, there was nothing left to

look forward to. Sure, he needed to finish cleaning the basement and make a new chair for the dining room, but that was
just busy work, just going through the motions. He no longer
had something to live for. His house had become his prison, an
empty shell of tainted memories.

"All remaining passengers for Flight Eleven Twenty-three
may now board at this time," came the announcement over the
PA system.

"Of course, I want to be there!" The voice behind him carried an edge of frustration and panic in it now. Curious, Walter
twisted in his seat to find a young soldier anxiously pacing in
the aisle around his duffel bag, talking into his cell phone. "I
know Carol's going into labor, but if I don't make this flight,
there won't be another one available until morning."

Walter felt sorry for the guy. And a little envious, too. It
sounded like the start of a whole new life for the young man,
while nothing remained for him.

"Final boarding for Flight Eleven Twenty-three."

"Mom, there's nothing I can do!"

Really, what *did* he have to return to?

Before he realized what he was doing, Walter stood and
extended his boarding pass. "Here. Sounds like you need this
more than I do."

The soldier froze. The expression on his face was one of
gratefulness and relief mixed with guarded hesitation, as if Walter were playing some kind of cruel joke on him.

"You sure?"

"Absolutely," he said, surprised that he really meant it. "Go
on. Take it."

"Last call for Flight Eleven Twenty-three to Chicago." The
gate agent put the microphone down and started closing the
ramp door.

"Hurry!" Walter said.

The soldier snatched the pass out of his hand and waved it at the agent. "Wait! Wait! I'm coming!" He repeated, "I'm coming!" into his cell, then closed the phone and stuffed it into his pocket. Slinging his bag over his shoulder, he gasped, "Thanks, man. Thanks a lot!" as he ran to the door. He handed the woman the pass and threw one final wave to Walter while she scanned it, then disappeared down the ramp. The agent shut the door behind him.

Grabbing his bag, Walter turned and headed back down the concourse, smiling. He felt proud that something good had come out of this trip after all. But as he neared the main terminal, the sounds of the concourse—the clack of shoes on the tiles, the echoes of the voices around him—seemed to grow dim and muffled as if he were in a bubble that was collapsing around him.

What was he supposed to do now?

The question hit him with such force that he staggered. A passing traveler, no doubt thinking he was drunk or ill, grabbed his arm to steady him. He held him a few moments until Walter assured him that he was fine, really, thank you very much. He told the man that he must have slipped on something on the floor, and dismissed his concern with the promise that if it happened again he would seek medical attention immediately. Seemingly reassured, the man patted his shoulder, wished him well, and moved on.

But where did Walter have to go? The thought truly had not occurred to him when he gave his boarding pass away. And now here he was, stranded in an airport far from home, with nothing to do, nowhere to go, and no plans for the future.

Walter needed to sit down and think this over.

Carrying his garment bag down the escalator, he bought a large cup of coffee and a package of pretzels from a nearby vending machine. Then he sat under a sculpture of a fireman on a ladder rescuing a young girl and tried to figure out what the hell to do.

Certainly, he couldn't go back to Eleanor's house. That option was closed to him forever. Though they'd tried to hide it, they were obviously relieved when it was time for him to leave. Returning to their house unannounced might upset or even frighten them. Hell, they'd probably even call the police. Sadly, the truth of the matter was he wasn't welcome there anymore, and his heart ached.

He supposed he could fly somewhere, travel to another city he'd never seen. True, he didn't have much money left or enough clothes with him, but he could always charge everything if he wanted. But really, what was the point? The best memories were more about the times spent with people than the places visited, and not having anyone to share a trip with seemed futile and depressing. No, that wouldn't work either.

Outside, daylight faded, and the exterior lights brightened as he sat there debating. When Walter finally checked his watch, he saw that his plane would be landing at O'Hare shortly, and that if he hadn't given his boarding pass away, he would have been home soon. And with that he realized he didn't have anywhere *else* to go. Just no particular reason to hurry there.

And so, his decision made, such as it was, Walter grabbed his bag and took the tram to the car rental area. He gave the young woman at the counter his driver's license and VISA card, and she set him up with a white Grand Am that he could drive to O'Hare. His own car was in O'Hare's long-term parking garage, and the woman assured him that he could return the Grand Am there, that people did it all the time. Outside, he tossed his bags into the rental's trunk, then drove the car away from the airport following the map and directions toward Chicago that the rental agency had provided.

But once beyond the Twin Cities and suburbs, he turned off

the interstate and onto older county roads instead. He drove for about an hour until he realized his thoughts were wandering aimlessly, and he grew afraid that his driving might soon do the same. Away from the metropolitan area, the rural roads were dark and isolated.' Occasionally he passed farms with lights on over the barns, and he found their beacons in the night comforting, making him feel less alone.

The sudden headlights of a passing car in the opposite lane momentarily blinded him. The cloudy sky out here was velvety black (unlike the bright lights of Chicago that turned the night clouds orange), and made it feel as if the hour was later than it really was.

Walter rubbed his tired eyes. After stopping for gas, he spotted a sign for the StarKey Motel near the outskirts of a small town. A white-bulbed star and a blue-bulbed key within a red-bulbed arrow pointed toward the lobby entrance, and impressed by the fact that none of the bulbs were missing or burnt out, he decided to pull in for the night. He parked the car in the space nearest the entrance door. There was a restaurant on the other side of the parking lot, and the sound of laughter inside as people entered echoed on the biting night air.

Coming in from the cold, the heat in the motel's lobby made him feel drowsy. The room contained imitation oak tables and matching chairs and a display rack with recent-issue magazines. A young man with a white wand in his hand was standing in front of a television in the room behind the desk. He made an underhanded throwing motion, and the sounds of bowling pins being hit and a cheering crowd erupted from the TV. When he noticed Walter standing there, he set the wand down on a nearby recliner and hurried to the front desk.

"Sorry," he said, smiling sheepishly. He had short blond hair and acne scars on his cheeks, and his nametag identified him as *Ed*. "Those games are addicting. You looking for a room?"

"Just for the night."

Ed nodded solemnly. "On the way to someplace else. Someday that's gonna be me."

He registered Walter in the computer. Ed's shirt was white and pressed, and the tie he wore was imprinted with the design of the motel's sign. After swiping Walter's credit card, he returned the card and handed him a room key.

"How's the restaurant next door?" Walter asked.

"Pretty good, actually. They've got all kinds of stuff on the menu, but most people around here go for the burgers and to hang out."

"Anything I should avoid?"

Ed laughed. "No, you're safe. I always get the meatloaf sandwich. A couple drops of hot sauce and you're good to go. But watch out for the fries if your system has a problem with grease."

Walter thanked him. Room Six was located at the bend of the ten-room, L-shaped complex. Between the motel and the restaurant, the lot was already about a third full.

Parking the Grand Am directly in front of his room, he grabbed his bag from the trunk and went inside. The furniture was the same style as the lobby's, with thick, navy blue comforters on both double beds that matched the cushions on the chairs. The carpet even smelled new. He dumped the garment bag on the first bed and found the TV and remote inside the oak wardrobe near the foot of the bed closest to the bathroom.

After using the restroom, he trotted around a number of plowed asphalt-gray snow piles and crossed the parking lot to the restaurant. The place was decorated in imitation ski lodge, with dark wood tables and a circular stone fireplace in the center. Empty bottles advertising the kinds of beer they stocked lined the shelf above the window into the kitchen, and the room smelled of fried grease. His mouth began to water.

A sign on a metal pole read *Please Be Seated*, so Walter grabbed a booth with red vinyl-covered seats. A few couples and scattered families occupied tables and booths off to the side, but most of the noise in the room was from a large table of men wearing matching bowling shirts and the women seated with them. They appeared to be celebrating their league championship. When he sat down, a waitress disentangled herself from one of the men's laps and came over to him. She wore black slacks and a pink and white shirt with *Janice* sewn into the breast pocket with black thread. Her blond hair was tied back in a ponytail, and Walter half-expected her to blow a bubble with chewing gum.

"Need a menu?"

Walter shook his head. "Ed next door recommended the meatloaf sandwich. That sounds good to me."

"Ed's working tonight?" Her voice sounded surprised and disappointed. She glanced back over her shoulder. "Um, anything to drink with that?"

"Coffee's fine."

Scribbling the order on her pad, she tore the page off and gave it to the cook, then hurried back to the man at the other table. She whispered in his ear. He chugged the rest of his beer and threw Walter a look that said he blamed him for spoiling their plans. Janice noticed, too, and said something that made the man smile and order another beer. Walter was soon forgotten.

His stomach was grumbling by the time his order arrived. The coffee tasted like it'd been left on the burner too long, but it was strong and acidic enough to peel the grease from the fries off his teeth. The meatloaf sandwich, however, came topped with melted cheddar cheese and grilled onions and was as good as Ed promised, even without the hot sauce.

When Janice refilled his coffee, she brought him a thick slice of apple pie.

"I didn't—"

"It's, like, on the house, you know?"

"Got it. Thanks."

Janice smiled with relief and left the check upside down on his table. Poor Ed. He wondered if the day Ed found out about Janice would be the day he finally moved on down the road to someplace else.

Later, back in the room, Walter tossed his dirty clothes into a plastic bag and climbed into the shower. As the hot water loosened his muscles and he relaxed, his confusion and hopelessness surged back with a vengeance, and his thoughts swirled inside his head like the steam around him.

What the hell was he going to do now? Killing Harris was the culmination of all his pent-up rage, and he felt empty and more alone than he ever had before. He knew why he was meandering across the countryside. Why hurry home? He might as well drive around a while. There was nothing waiting for him except an empty house of bitter memories.

Sadness squeezed his heart when he thought about how he could never return to Eleanor's. They were his family, all he had left, but that door was closed to him forever. He had to admit, he was worried about what they thought of him. Would they call the police on him? He wondered if he'd pushed them too far, telling them everything he did. But when did defending your own home become such a crime? He remembered the way they'd looked at him. What were they saying about him right now? Were they glad to be rid of him, afraid he might have turned his rage against them?

Turning the water hotter, he let the piercing spray scald his skin as if he could sear his past away.

Still, he was glad he gave Helen the money. Calling repair

shops on the sly and withdrawing money from an ATM had drained a good deal of his account, but it would have bothered him more if he hadn't done it. He'd taken out a few hundred extra for some unknown reason at the same time and stuffed the bills in his wallet. Maybe subconsciously he'd known all along that he hadn't intended to go straight home, but besides whatever he charged on his VISA, his limited funds would ensure he couldn't meander too long. He had to go home sometime.

He turned the water off and dried himself with one of the motel's over-bleached, scratchy towels. He knew he was being stupid. Not going home was just putting off the inevitable. Whatever was done, was done. He wanted to get a good night's sleep and drive straight home in the morning, but though the shower and his decision finally put his mind at ease, the coffee still had him wired. So he decided to watch TV for a while. Walter put on clean pajamas, but when he propped the pillows from both beds against the headboard, he noticed for the first time the framed copy of "Footprints" mounted on the wall above the bed.

A shiver ran through him. He leaned closer. The illustration was different. This one had a metallic, holographic image of praying hands overlapping the footprints along the sandy beach, and a couple of the words were changed, but it was essentially the same as the one in their bedroom at home.

Walter swallowed the lump in his throat. He closed his eyes, remembering the day Dottie put up their copy. The windows had been open, and a soft breeze carried the scent of lilacs into their bedroom. Dottie stood on her tiptoes, arms raised, hammering the nail into the wall. While Walter stood behind her admiring how the blue silk blouse and tight black slacks hugged the sensual curves of her body, she glanced over her shoulder and caught him looking at her. A smile played at the corner of

her mouth, letting him know that she knew what he was thinking. She hung the framed copy on the nail, then snuggled back
against him and wrapped herself in his arms.

As he'd buried his face in her luxurious raven-colored hair
that was brushed so often it was always as soft as corn silk, she
told him how much the story meant to her, how much it filled
her with hope. Walter had always been skeptical, but Dottie
firmly believed there was someone out there for everyone,
watching over them.

She believed it to her dying day.

Walter squeezed his eyes shut and ground his forehead against
the gritty motel room wall. Every wonderful memory was
tainted by what happened later. What the cancer hadn't eaten in
her body, the chemotherapy eventually destroyed. All of her
beautiful hair had fallen out, and what little came back grew in
sparse and gray and wiry. And where had he been on the night
she'd needed him most? Why hadn't he been there to watch
over her and protect her from that monster Harris?

He pummeled the pillows until his knuckles were red and the
blood pounded in his ears. The memory of the day they'd put
"Footprints" on the wall had always comforted him with hope
and love, but now only filled him with sadness, mocking him,
reminding him of how he much he had failed her.

Sitting heavily on the bed, Walter leaned back into the pillows
and clicked on the TV with the remote. He felt bitter and resent-
ful and more miserable than ever before, and he hoped he could
find something to distract him or bore him to sleep. He soon
found that even with the motel's advertised "Over 200 HD
Channels Available!" there still wasn't much on. Channel-
surfing up and down the stations, he stopped for a few minutes
here and there to watch the Timberwolves game or roll his eyes
at some moronic talk show. Why anyone would want to put his
or her family's personal heartaches on display for public ridicule

was beyond him. Today's torturous reality shows couldn't hold a candle to the shows he'd grown up with, and he wondered how society had degenerated to the point where entertainment meant enjoying watching other people suffer.

An amusing thought struck him: What if he was one of those people who felt he had to put his life on display? Couldn't you just see him on one of those freak-parade, afternoon talk shows? "I Killed Four Burglars In My Home!" And the reactions of the audience! He laughed out loud. What a nightmare that'd be. Except for telling Dottie's relatives, thank God he'd had enough sense to keep things to himself.

Figuring he might as well watch the end of the Timberwolves game, Walter clicked the channel button, searching for the game, and was surprised to come upon one of the local Chicago stations a few minutes into their news broadcast. Video showed a man on a gurney being lifted into the back of an ambulance. The address of the man's house was printed in a colored strip at the bottom of the screen.

". . . saying Vasquez was shot during an attempted home invasion," said the voice-over of the female reporter. "Police speculate the intruders were after a flat-screen TV and gaming equipment he'd recently purchased. Vasquez should be in the hospital for a few days, but is expected to make a full recovery."

Walter was aghast. Now why did they do that? It was like saying to the intruders: "All right, you goofed the first time, but the house will be empty for a couple more days, so go back for a second try." Hell, they even gave the address in case anyone else wanted a go at it.

He sighed. It was getting harder and harder to tell the difference between newscasts and talk shows anymore.

Other stories followed in the same sensationalized format. A drive-by shooting. A rape. An accident on the Dan Ryan Expressway that snarled traffic for hours. Another council member and a city hall official caught in bed—literally—with a developer. And an update on the celebrity scandal of the month: an actor who had filmed his rape of a fan. While the anchorman babbled, Walter studied the famous statue of Justice in an insert on the screen beside the reporter's head. Everyone knew Justice was blind—all you had to do was look at the blindfold to see that—but he wondered what she really weighed on those scales. The evidence? Or which side had more money or fame?

Walter shook his head. He remembered an old saying about every fortune beginning with a crime, and he had to admit, there certainly seemed to be a lot more fortunes nowadays.

When the anchorwoman announced they were going back live to one of their reporters at the scene of the top story of the night, Walter lifted the remote. He wasn't interested in any more stories or what the weather was going to be. He already had enough on his mind, and he needed a good night's sleep for the long drive tomorrow. But when he aimed the remote at the TV, his hand froze mid-air, and an icy chill ran up his spine.

The live broadcast showed an outside view of his house surrounded by the police.

CHAPTER THIRTEEN

Seeing as how Buczyno's house was right off the Tri-State, Riehle knew they'd make great time to O'Hare. He merged into the (relatively speaking) sparse, post-rush-hour traffic and wove his way through the other cars, trucks, and SUVs headed north. A thousand thoughts cascaded through his mind, and concentrating on his driving was the only thing that helped him stay focused.

How the hell did he manage to get a case like this in his first stint as senior partner? Excitement and anxiety coursed through his nerve endings, making the hair along the back of his neck stand up. He gripped the steering wheel tighter. He had prepared for something like this his entire professional career, made fascinated studies of all the famous serial killer cases, and yet, never truly expected to encounter anything like it in their little town of Westbrook. He knew the eyes of his superiors and co-workers, the victims' families, and the media would be all over him, analyzing and judging his every move. And while the excitement of catching the sonofabitch and becoming the glorified hero made him put the pedal to the metal, he was secretly, desperately, afraid he might do something that would screw everything up.

They were making good time. Traffic moved along at a quick enough clip that he didn't need to put the flasher on the dashboard. The car smelled of their sweat. It had been a long day already.

He glanced at his partner. "Got your cell?" When Capparelli took his phone out, Riehle said, "Call the O'Hare CPD and tell them we're going to be on property. Tell them we need security clearance because we want to apprehend Buczyno when he gets off the plane. Give them his description, the airline flight number and arrival gate, and tell them our ETA is ten or fifteen minutes, tops."

Capparelli punched in the number. "I'll give them Buczyno's license plate and have them search the long-term parking garage for his car," he said while he waited for someone to answer. "Post somebody there, too."

"Good idea."

Riehle listened as Capparelli told the O'Hare cops what they needed, trying to think if there was anything he'd forgotten or left out. A jet passed directly overhead, its turbines screaming, as he neared the turnoff for the airport. Riehle thought he heard Capparelli mutter, "Fucking unbelievable," when he put his phone away.

"They give you a hard time?" Riehle said.

"No."

"Then what's the problem?"

Capparelli shifted uncomfortably in his seat. His skin along his collar was red. What was eating him now? The guy seemed to get aggravated easily enough. Riehle wondered if he had a blood pressure problem. Last thing he needed was to be part-nered with a walking time bomb.

"I was talking about Griskel," Capparelli said.

"What's he got to do with anything?"

"How is anyone supposed to take the investigation seriously with a coroner dressed like that?"

Oh, for Christ's sake. Didn't they have enough to worry about already? He wanted to tell him to deal with it, that things didn't always go the way you thought they should. Instead, he said:

"Don't worry about Griskel. He might be an elected official, but I guarantee no one will work harder to help us put this guy away."

Capparelli seemed to struggle with something he didn't want to say. Finally, he exhaled sharply. "Look, I knew one of Gacy's victims, okay? And Griskel looking like that, in my opinion, mocks the victims and their families. It seems disrespectful, that's all."

Riehle shrugged. Whatever. He could see where his partner was coming from and why Griskel's image bothered him so much, and he was glad he hadn't given Capparelli a hard time about something the rest of them took for granted. But he didn't have time to argue about it now. They were already through the gate, and Capparelli directed them to the secure area where the O'Hare CPD had told them to park.

The O'Hare cops were waiting for them. Riehle and Capparelli went through the TSA screening with their credentials, then proceeded through the checkpoint. Three uniforms escorted them as they raced through the terminal.

"Better hurry," a sergeant named Milner said. He was an African American with a shaved head and was built like a linebacker for the Bears. "The flight arrived ten minutes early and is taxiing to the gate."

"Early?" Capparelli said. "At O'Hare?"

Milner shrugged. "It happens."

They hurried. The amplified sounds of flight announcements and boarding instructions over PA systems, the din of hundreds of passengers talking amongst themselves or on cell phones, the rolling wheels of dragged luggage, and the slaps of the five policemen's shoes on the tiles as they ran huffing and puffing and zigzagging around passengers echoed around them.

Turning onto E Concourse, they passed sports bars and bookstores and a VIP lounge, and as Gate E-Thirteen came into view near the end of the concourse past a coffee kiosk, they saw with horror that the passengers were already disembarking.

"I told you to keep 'em on the plane!" Milner shouted at the airline employees. One of the cops ran to block the door, and passengers crowded the jet bridge as the people in front of them suddenly stopped moving.

"What the hell's going on?" someone farther down the ramp yelled. Riehle heard other murmurs of dissent and a number of shouted complaints about connecting flights they needed to make.

"Get someone to baggage claim. He might have gotten off already," Milner said into his radio. "And hold all luggage for the flight." He gave them the number of the arrival from Minneapolis.

"Find out what seat he's in," he told Barnett, one of the other cops who had run with them. Barnett was a white guy with a buzz cut and a clipped brown mustache and hard, deep set eyes. He ran to the podium, and the gate agent started tapping on her computer's keyboard.

A flight attendant stood by the ramp door, and Milner waved her over. He showed her Buczyno's DMV photo. "You recognize this guy?"

"Doesn't look familiar."

"All right. Tell the passengers there's a security problem in the terminal and we need them to return to their seats for a few minutes. Look around, but if you spot him, don't call attention to yourself. The last thing we need is a hostage situation. Act like nothing's wrong and tell us where he's at. We'll take it from there."

"What's he done?"

"Never mind. Just get everyone back on the plane."

Despite the frustrated complaints, the flight attendant relayed the instructions to the crowded passengers with enough of a hint of authority and fear in her voice to get the people to take her seriously, and she slowly made her way back onto the plane as the ramp began to clear. Meanwhile, Barnett signaled that he'd gotten the seat number and quickly followed behind her.

While Capparelli stood in the corridor, scanning for any sign of Buczyno, Riehle waited in the middle of the lounge for Milner's instructions. They were on his turf, and he certainly had more knowledge of how best to handle the situation. Riehle's heart pounded, and he tried to deepen and steady his shallow breaths. His eyes darted between the curious gathering outside the lounge, the cop guarding the ramp door, and Milner.

Riehle's fingers itched with excitement. He leaned forward, his weight on the balls of his feet, ready to head down the ramp and onto the plane at Milner's earliest command. He wondered how they'd handle it. Would they saunter down the aisle, pretending to look everywhere but at Buczyno until they were right on top of him? Or would he realize they were coming for him and try to run for the back, maybe hide in the toilet or force open a rear door? Would he drag a seatmate or child or stewardess away from them, taking someone hostage? Riehle reached inside his open topcoat, his fingers feeling the grip of his gun. Or would they be able to capture him without running the risk of pulling their weapons and having the guns go off? How would they handle the situation without sending everyone into a panic?

Whatever it was, Riehle was ready for it.

Or thought he was.

Emerging from the ramp, Barnett dragged a bewildered-looking soldier by the arm. Barnett's face was dark and angry as he hustled the young man over into a huddle made with Riehle and Milner.

"What the hell is this?" Milner demanded.

"That's what I want to know!" the soldier protested. His

nametag identified him as *Martinez*. He tried to shake Barnett's
hand off, but the officer held him fast. "Listen, I don't know
what's going on, but I'm trying to get to the hospital. My wife's
in labor."

"Buczyno wasn't even on the plane," Barnett informed them.
"This guy took his seat."

Milner spun on Riehle. "The fuck is going on here?"

"I . . . I—" Riehle stammered. Blood drained from his face. A
sinking feeling wrenched his gut as he suddenly realized that his
worst fear had indeed come true: he really *had* screwed up.
Somehow Buczyno never boarded his flight. He felt the hostile
glares of Milner and Barnett and the curious stares of the
onlookers in the concourse around them. His ears burned, and
tunnel vision made him feel as if he were shrinking, the world
ready to chew him up and spit him out for public ridicule.

A major clusterfuck. And he was responsible for it.

"You think this is a fucking *game?*" Milner yelled, loud enough
for everyone to hear. He got right in his face, their noses almost
touching; and Riehle, aware that everyone was watching, tried
not to flinch. He could feel the heat radiating off the cop's
body, and flustered, he couldn't think of anything to say in his
defense.

Then he heard someone running toward them, and Capparelli shoved them apart and stepped between them.

"Hey, back off, pal. What the fuck you think you're doing?"

"What am *I* doing?" Milner said. "Why didn't you check with
the airline first to make sure he got on the plane before you
wasted our time?"

"We were going with the information we had." Capparelli
turned his attention to the soldier. "Let me see your ticket.
How'd you get your seat?"

"I was on standby, but the flight was overbooked," Martinez
said, sounding grateful that someone was finally listening to

him. His words came out in a rush. "Like I said, Carol's in labor with our first child, and if I didn't get this flight, there wouldn't be another one until morning. I *had* to get out of there. And right when the doors were closing, this guy offered me his boarding pass. Think I'm gonna turn it down? No way!"

"What'd the guy look like?"

He shrugged. "I don't know. Short, kind of stocky, balding—"

Capparelli snatched Buczyno's DMV photo out of Milner's hand. "Like this?"

"Yeah, that's him!" Then his face clouded over, and he put his hands up between them. "Hey, wait a minute. What'd this guy do? Listen dude, I never met him before. Honest. He just gave me his boarding pass, and that was it, I swear."

"We've got to call our lieutenant about this," Riehle said, recovered enough to find his voice. "Stay put," he told Martinez, as he and Capparelli stepped off to the side before Milner and Barnett could say anything.

Riehle punched Gavin's number into his cell phone, preparing for the worst. When he told him what happened, Gavin exploded.

"Sonofabitch!" Riehle heard the sound of something banging, as if Gavin had thrown a book down or slapped his palm on his desk. There was a long pause before Gavin finally blew out his breath. "All right. At least you didn't miss him. The media would have been all over that. Think the soldier knows more than he's telling?"

"Not sure."

"Then stick him in a room to make him think long and hard about it. I want to know everything he can remember. Get his statement. While he's doing that, I want you two to find out if Buczyno got bumped to another flight or changed his arrangements all together. You spot him or find any new evidence, you call me immediately. Is that clear? Then get down to the parking garage and examine Buczyno's car. If there's no visible reason for impounding it, we gotta let the O'Hare cops use it as bait. I'll have someone here put in a call to the St. Paul PD and find out if he's still there. Then I want you and Capparelli in my office at seven A.M. with a plan on how to get back on top of this situation. Got it?"

"Yes, sir." Riehle closed his phone.

"Not your fault," Capparelli said.

"Doesn't matter. Shit's gonna hit the fan and the wind's already blowing my way."

Riehle walked back to the other men and pointed at Martinez. "We need to stick him in a room while we check other flights and airlines."

"But my wife's—"

"After wasting our goddamn time, a room is *all* you're getting out of us for the rest of the night." Using his radio, Milner announced they had a false alarm, then told the cop in baggage claim to return to his station.

He turned on Riehle, getting right in his face again. "You got any idea of the chaos you caused? If I hear about any missed flights or we get any complaints and my ass is grass, I'm sure as shit taking you down with me," he said. "We'll post somebody by Buczyno's car, and if we catch him, you'd better believe we're taking credit for the pinch. Maybe you little 'burbs cops got nothing better to do, but this is fucking *O'Hare!*"

Emitting a piercing whistle, Milner gestured to the cop barring the ramp door. "Let 'em go!" The passengers started spilling out, hurrying past them with curious glances, wanting to know what was going on, but not enough so to risk missing a connecting flight or stay any longer than they had to. And as they passed by, Riehle saw the accusations in their eyes.

Milner stabbed a finger against Riehle's chest, pushing him

backwards. "Now get the fuck out of my sight. And you'd better have a signed authorization from the President *and* the Pope before I ever listen to either one of you clowns again." He nodded to Barnett. "Take them to Security."

Riehle and Capparelli followed Barnett as he led Martinez down the concourse. Riehle's hands were clenched into fists and shoved deep in his overcoat pockets. His ears burned with humiliation. Capparelli remained silent, waiting, but Riehle couldn't tell if the flush in his cheeks was anger with him or embarrassment, too.

Riehle cleared his throat. "Looks like we've got a long night ahead of us."

Capparelli just kept walking.

CHAPTER FOURTEEN

Sit down. Get up. Pace the darkened room. Sit on the end of the bed. Turn on the television. Mute the sound. Get up. Peek out the window. Come back. Sit down. Stare at the TV. Heart pounding. Shallow breaths. Water dripping in the shower— sounds like gunshots! Turn off the TV. Did someone see the lights? Sweaty palms. The remote drops to the floor. Get up. Pick it up. Pace the room. Look out the window. Sit down. Get up. Sit down—

Walter ran his fingers through his hair.

Jesus, he was driving himself *crazy*!

It had been more than an hour since he first saw the news coverage of the bodies discovered in his crawlspace, and he simply didn't know what to do. A mind-numbing panic had taken over his central nervous system, incapacitating him to the point that he couldn't think straight, let alone decide upon a course of action he now needed to take. And soon. Very soon. Because they were coming to get him.

Walter paced the darkened room. The heavy curtains were closed tightly over the window. An orange power light on the wall-mounted hair dryer in the bathroom provided him with enough light to prevent him from banging into the furniture. His heart pounded in his throat. The adrenaline had been racing through his system for so long now that he was starting to feel jittery and dizzy. He sank onto the edge of the bed and hung his head, unable to hold back the tears any longer.

He rolled over on the bed and punched the pillows again and again. Why? Why? Why? How could they do this to him? Though the news report said the police had been called to his house because of a broken pipe, it seemed like too much of a co-incidence that they would be waiting for him on the very day he was supposed to arrive home.

Did they really call the police on him? It seemed incomprehensible that Eleanor, Helen, Lorna, or even Henry would do such a thing. But there was no denying that the police had found out. Was that why Dottie's family were avoiding him? Did they decide to report him as soon as he got on the plane? Was that what Helen meant when she told him to make the legal system work for him? Was she trying to warn him?

Why, oh why, did he tell them in the first place? What the hell was he *thinking*?

Walter swallowed a lump in his throat. He wiped the tears away with the back of his hand. The copy of "Footprints" above the bed mocked him with Dottie's beliefs, and he turned away. He just couldn't believe the only people he'd trusted his deepest secret with—the ones who'd professed so strongly that they were his *family*—had turned him in. Maybe it was all too much for them. That they'd suffered too much with Dottie's loss and this was the final straw. Or the trial had forced them to deal with things no one should ever have to endure. Or maybe they'd simply become different people in the time he'd been away.

Whatever it was, he was now as truly alone as he'd always feared he'd be.

On wobbly legs, Walter staggered to the bathroom. He unwrapped the glass from its protective paper, filled it with cold water from the tap, and took a drink. The glass clattered against his teeth, and water spilled down his chin. He gagged and coughed, then quickly grabbed the edge of the countertop as his muscles spasmed, and he vomited into the sink. The smell of onions and acidic coffee stung his eyes, overpowering the sight of partially digested bits of meatloaf, fries, and apple pie coating the bottom of the sink, and his stomach heaved again and again until his sides ached and nothing else came up but bile and sour-tasting spit.

Spent, leaning on his hands while his arms quivered, he looked up at his reflection in the mirror. The light's orange glow cast shadows in the hollows of his cheeks and around his sunken eyes. Was that how everyone saw him? He shuddered. If the police found him now and released his mug shot, his haggard image would only reinforce the public's misinformed fears and hasty judgments.

Walter couldn't believe this was happening to him. Not after everything he'd already been through.

He rinsed out the sink, then filled the glass with water again and sat down on the edge of the bed. He took a couple of tiny sips, making sure they stayed down, then turned on the TV with the remote. The heat kicked on, and Walter inched the volume up slowly until he could barely hear the TV over the sound of the radiator.

His mouth was dry with shock and fear. A burning knot churned his stomach, and he took another sip of water to hold the nausea down. The panic rose in him again as he surfed the channels, finding coverage of him on more and more of the stations. He watched with growing horror how his world had disintegrated and the public was coming along for the ride. He was even on CNN, for God's sake.

There was no denying it anymore. He was a Wanted Man.

Outraged, Walter watched the continuing coverage of his story on another of the later Chicago network news broadcasts. This one discussed how the window under the porch had come loose and a pipe froze. He tried to remember if he had gone back and re-nailed the board over the window and realized he hadn't.

He'd been in such a hurry to get to St. Paul to tell everyone what he'd done that he only did a quick job of cleaning and had forgotten all about the window. As he'd only tamped it back in place the night he killed Harris—and Harris had broken the glass to get into the house, removing any remaining insulation—the board must have come loose in the cold winds, freezing the pipe.

Sweat broke out on his forehead. Damn! How could he have been so stupid? One careless mistake, and his whole world was falling apart.

Still, he couldn't be completely sure Eleanor or Helen hadn't reported him, either. It seemed like too much of a coincidence that the cops were waiting for him today. He understood now that he was in no position to trust *anyone*.

The scene on the television switched to a reporter standing outside Middaugh Hospital. As the station ran video recorded earlier, her voice-over talked about how Benito Salinas had suffered a near-fatal heart attack when he discovered the bodies. The recording showed a shell-shocked Mary being guarded by a plump police woman with over-teased red hair as they threaded their way through a corridor to a safer part of the hospital, while a throng of reporters shouted a barrage of questions at Mary.

Walter's heart ached at the sight of her. Mary's face was drawn and tired, and the hollows of her eyes were more pronounced. She'd lost more weight and hair since the last time he saw her. He knew what she was going through, what the chemicals were doing to her system (even if Benito was in denial), and he felt a pang of guilt when he thought about what this added shock was doing to them. They were his best and oldest friends, and all Benito had been doing was watching over the house like Walter had asked. The realization of the extra hurt he'd brought down on them—that Benito might *die* because of what he'd found—drove a pain-filled wedge through his heart.

Going back live outside the hospital, the newscaster ended her report by suggesting the police might consider additional charges against Walter if Benito died.

Walter buried his face in his hands. Everything was spinning out of control. *Ever since Harris came back into my life*, he realized. Even when he'd killed the other burglars, things had still been fine. But as soon as Harris came back, everything fell apart. Tonight, Walter finally lost all he had left—his house, his friends, his family. Hell, the cops were probably towing his car out of the O'Hare lot right now. Harris, who'd brought so much pain and destruction into his life, somehow continued to do so even after his death.

How could one person wreak so much havoc on so many people's lives?

A different reporter was questioning a man whom the strip at the bottom of the screen identified as Deputy Chief Dennis Volkovitz of the Westbrook Police Department. "Are you at all concerned about the similarities between the Gacy case and this one?" the reporter asked.

Walter exploded off the bed and grabbed the sides of the TV. He wanted to dive into the screen and strangle the man. Gacy? How *dare* he compare him to that monster! All Walter did was kill burglars who invaded his home. Hell, Harris had even come back intending to shoot *him*! He was aghast. How could the reporter insinuate that he was some kind of monster, when all he did was defend his home? How could he get away with accusing him like that?

Volkovitz nodded solemnly to the reporter's question. "It seems incomprehensible that a serial killer could have been operating in our tight-knit community. We're currently following up on a number of leads, and we won't stop until Buczyno is apprehended and brought to justice."

Justice? *Justice?* Walter's hands balled into fists. *I will not go to prison for Harris!*

"I WILL NOT!"

Walter dropped to the floor. Sweat broke out all over his body. Good God, did he actually shout out loud? What if someone heard him?

As if in answer, a door slammed shut outside.

He turned off the TV, hunkered down, and duck-walked to the window. Blood pounded in his ears. His breath whistled in and out of his mouth as he struggled to keep from hyperventilating.

Did someone from the restaurant recognize him? Or had Ed reported him to the police?

With shaking hands, he peered around the edge of the curtain, half expecting the parking lot to be filled with police cars and SWAT team snipers with their rifles aimed at his room. But the lot only contained the same cars that had been there all evening. He heard a car engine start and watched as Ed got out of the car to scrape the windows. As soon as he finished, a woman who didn't look like Janice ran out of a room two doors down from Walter's and climbed into the car. The dome light popped on when she opened the door, and from the look of the kiss Ed gave her, he knew they weren't aware of anyone but themselves. Walter closed the curtains before their headlights came on, and he heard the crunch of their tires over the salt on the asphalt as their car sped out of the parking lot and onto the road beyond.

His back to the wall, Walter slid to the floor, sighing with relief. He had to get a grip. And fast.

But he knew he was far from safe. Just because Ed hadn't seen the news reports yet didn't mean someone else hadn't. He couldn't stay here any longer.

As quietly as possible, he dressed, packed his bags, and loaded them into the car. He turned on the engine and sat low in the seat in case anyone was watching, letting the defrosters clear the windshield and rear window. When he thought he was as safe as he was ever going to be, he shifted the car into gear and cautiously drove out of the parking lot. He didn't even turn on his headlights until he was certain no one was following him.

He was a Wanted Man now. And he was on the run.

CHAPTER FIFTEEN

"Give me one good reason I shouldn't bounce both of you back to patrol!" Gavin roared.

Riehle and Capparelli squirmed in their chairs in the lieutenant's office. Though the door was closed and the blinds shut, Gavin was loud enough that Riehle was sure everyone in the building could hear him. Shirtsleeves rolled up to his elbows, Gavin leaned his forearms on his desk and angrily tapped a gold pen on the blotter. The meeting had begun promptly at seven A.M., and though it wasn't exactly an ass-chewing, they knew Gavin was clearly aggravated about how their blunder made the department look.

"Sir," Capparelli said, "we were going on the information we had. By the time we learned where Buczyno was and what flight he was taking, he'd have already been on the plane. So it wasn't like we could have contacted the St. Paul PD to apprehend him before then."

"Martinez insists everything happened at the last possible moment," Riehle added. "He didn't even know Buczyno existed until the guy offered him the boarding pass. And Martinez was so grateful to get on the flight that he didn't realize until later that he had no idea who the guy was or how to get hold of him afterward to thank him. So there was no way anyone could have predicted what he did."

"You don't think Buczyno planned it?"

"Why would he have gone to all the trouble of checking in

and waiting at the gate? As far as we know, he had every intention of boarding the plane, and only changed his mind on
impulse."

"Martinez have any other information?"

"Not much," Capparelli said. "The color of his coat and that
Buczyno wasn't wearing gloves when he handed him the boarding pass was all Martinez could add. He couldn't even tell us
what Buczyno's carry-on looked like because it was on the floor
on the other side of his seat."

"Sure he wasn't hiding something? Forgetting little details?
Purposely leaving something out?"

Riehle shook his head. "I doubt it. We took his statement and
contact information and gave him our cards in case he
remembered anything else. But I think he wanted to get to the
hospital so badly that he'd have told us anything we wanted just
to get out of there as soon as possible."

Gavin sighed. "All right. Back to Buczyno. What about other
flights or airlines?"

"Nothing we could find. The airline didn't have any record of
Buczyno changing his flight or switching it to another day. We
had them check to see if he came home earlier in the week or
rescheduled his return flight for any time in the next couple of
months. Same with the other airlines. *Nada.* It's like the guy
just disappeared off the map as far as they were concerned."

"We're running the boarding pass through AFIS," Capparelli
said, "to see if Buczyno's fingerprints are registered. But so far
we haven't found anything."

"What about his car?"

"It's still in the long-term parking garage. We couldn't see
any reason to impound it, so we had to leave it there. The
O'Hare cops are watching it."

Gavin scowled. Aware of how it would look in the media, he
obviously didn't want the CPD to get the credit if they ap-

prehended Buczyno when he returned. "Something made him change his plans, though."

"Maybe he went back to his mother-in-law's," Riehle said.

"First thing I checked after your call," Gavin said. "I sent the St. Paul PD a copy of Buczyno's DMV photo, and they went over there."

"Did they find him?"

"No. The sister-in-law claimed she'd dropped him off at the airport hours earlier and seemed genuinely surprised that he hadn't boarded his flight. The mother-in-law let them take a look around the house to prove he wasn't still there, but clammed up when the cops started asking about his visit."

"Think they can lean on her, maybe bring her down to the station to get more out of her?"

"No reason to at this point. And I get the impression that trying to get something out of the mother-in-law would be like wrestling with a pit bull. Let it go for now. It only emphasizes how you screwed up on this end. We can always go after her later."

Riehle bit back a reply.

"The St. Paul cops are interviewing the airport personnel and checking out local hotels and car rental agencies on their end to see where he might have gone instead," Gavin continued. "I had Nielsen put Buczyno's info and photo on NCIC and LEADS." A listing on the National Crime Index Center's computer and Illinois's Law Enforcement Agency Data System essentially meant they'd put out an APB on him.

He sat back in his chair. "So what are you two doing to get back on top of this situation?"

"Like you said last night, we'll do a more thorough search of Buczyno's house to obtain his credit card information and address book and check his e-mails for correspondence," Riehle said. "That way we'll have an electronic trail to follow and alternate destinations where he might have gone."

Gavin's eyebrows shot up. "That's it? How the hell do you expect me to go to the Chief and Deputy Chief with that?"

Riehle ground his teeth. Interviewing Martinez and the various airport personnel, then coming back to the station to write up their reports, the detectives were running on three hours of sleep. His brain was still foggy, and his eyes felt like they had sand in them. Judging by the look of Capparelli's bloodshot eyes, he probably felt the same. Not knowing anything about Buczyno, they had nothing else to go on otherwise until he resurfaced again.

But Riehle understood where he was coming from. Gavin was under a lot of pressure himself. Had he been thinking more clearly last night, Gavin would have sent additional detectives back to Buczyno's house to find the credit card information while they were stuck at O'Hare. Buczyno's not boarding the plane at the last minute had thrown all of them off their game.

Gavin seemed to have similar thoughts. He threw down his pen. "Fine. Then get your asses over to Buczyno's house and don't come back until you find something that tells us where he went."

The detectives stood.

"In the meantime," Gavin added, "all vacations and leaves are canceled until we catch this guy."

"Yes, sir."

They walked out of Gavin's office, leaving the door open behind them. Riehle had his cop face on, hiding the embarrassment and anger and frustration of being humiliated twice in the last twenty-four hours. He felt the other cops' eyes on him as they pretended hard not to pay the slightest attention to what had been going on in Gavin's office. He wondered what they must think of him and how he was handling the case after being O'Connell's straight-laced stooge for so many years. How many laughs behind his back had that cost him? Riehle clenched his fists. He was more determined than ever now to catch Buczyno and prove what a great cop he was and why he deserved to be senior detective.

Detective Tom Nielsen approached them as they put on their coats. He had short blond hair, sharp blue eyes, and a face that had been ravaged by acne. Nielsen handled most of the computer crimes and research in the department. He handed Riehle a pink memo slip. "Some guy named Martinez called. Said they had a baby girl and everybody's fine."

Riehle stuffed the note in his pocket. "At least something good came out of all of this."

"Call me as soon as you get any info, and I'll find out where he went. Pronto."

"Deal."

Nielsen nodded, then scurried back to his desk. Riehle and Capparelli finished buttoning their coats and headed out the door. A cold wind bit their exposed skin, and the sky was heavy with clouds threatening snow. Salt pellets crunched under their shoes in the parking lot.

"Hey, um . . ." Riehle said when they reached the car. Capparelli turned to face him. "Thanks for standing up to Milner last night."

"No problem."

"No, really. I appreciate it. You didn't have to."

"Yeah, I did. It wasn't your fault, and Milner had no right getting in your face like that."

"But he was right about everything he said, about how I'd mishandled the information and wasted their time."

"He was a thousand percent correct, especially when you consider all the security concerns they have to deal with every day." Capparelli shrugged. "But it was an honest mistake, and there was nothing we could have done, so he didn't need to be such a fucking jag-off about it. Besides, I should have considered that alternate scenario and prepared for it. That's my job. And I *would* have if I hadn't been so preoccupied with Griskel's appearance earlier."

Capparelli blew out his breath, a heavy white cloud in the chilly air. "Listen. Everyone's gonna be all over us from now on. Gavin. The media. The public. Everybody's gonna be watching and criticizing every move we make, so the last thing we need is any friction between us. We got off on the wrong foot the other day, and I'd like to start over." He offered his hand. "Ray Capparelli."

"Kevin Riehle," he said, shaking hands. "Nice to meet you, partner."

Capparelli smiled. "Now let's go catch us a bad guy."

But on the way to Buczyno's house, Riehle pulled to the curb and stopped in front of a tan brick ranch house. In the driveway, a woman in a frayed black overcoat was helping a man out of the passenger side of a gray Honda Civic. Her hand behind his back for support, she gave him an aluminum cane when he stood. He shuffled toward the front walk, carefully, as if the inclined driveway were coated with sheets of ice. Great puffs of breath spouted from his mouth in the frigid morning air, showing his exertion. The blue and orange Bears stocking cap only seemed to enhance the vivid purple and yellow contusions on his gaunt face. His left sleeve hung limp at his side, and Riehle could see part of the cast's sling through the open collar of his faded navy blue jacket.

"Gavin'll have our asses . . ." Capparelli warned.

"We'll only be minute," Riehle said, getting out of the car. "Remember the day we met?"

"The accident? Ahhh, man."

Larry Jensen and the woman turned their heads at the sounds

of the detectives approaching. The woman resembled the injured man, and Riehle remembered Jenny Gavin mentioning a sister coming to the hospital. Framed by limp, dirty gray hair, her face bore the lines of someone who worried too much, and her eyes held suspicion and anger and fear. Jensen, however, offered a sad smile.

"Detective." The word was slurred. Noticing the glazed look in his eyes, Riehle wondered what kind of pain medicine he was on and how much it helped him cope emotionally. "Thank you for the flowers."

"You're welcome. Gwen'll be glad to hear you got them. This is my partner, Ray Capparelli."

Capparelli stepped forward. "Nice to meet you. I'm sorry for your loss."

Jensen nodded, seeming to lean a little heavier on his cane. A chill wind whipped between them, and he blinked hard. He didn't bother to introduce his sister, but looked instead at the tiny house as if entering it would unleash his nightmares and confirm his worst fears.

"I can't believe they're really gone." His eyes misted and his gaze turned inward. Riehle could only imagine the devastating mixture of cherished memories and cruel loss his mind was probably torturing him with. "It was nice of you to visit me in the hospital."

"Like I said, if there's anything I can do, you just let me know."

"You can lock up that sonofabitch and throw away the key. That's what you can do."

Riehle cleared his throat. "Mr. Jensen, I guarantee we'll have him prosecuted to the fullest extent of the law."

"What's that supposed to mean?" his sister snapped. Her voice was as shrill and biting as the winter wind, and carried the accusatory tone of a protestor who knew how to read between the lines and wasn't afraid to voice her opinion. "You let him go? He's back on the street?"

Uh-oh. This was getting touchy, and Riehle had to be careful. "He was able to post bond, ma'am. But he'll face charges in court."

"But you let him go?" Jensen's eyes were focused now, the anger sharpening his vision through the pharmaceutical haze.

"We can only hold him for so long. Like I said, he posted bond."

"He kills my wife and daughter, and what? Now you're protecting him?"

Riehle was beginning to regret ever stopping here. He should have waited until after Jensen had been home from the hospital for a while. "Please don't do this."

"When do I have any rights? Or my wife or daughter? I thought we were the victims here?"

Riehle put his hands up between them. "Mr. Jensen, I understand you're in a lot of pain right now, so I'm going to pretend this conversation never occurred. I want you to take care of yourself and get better. But you need to let us do our job the best way we can."

"Baahhh!" He turned away from them and started toward the front door. "Go do your damn job then. My life is over. I have to bury my wife and daughter this afternoon."

With a menacing glance over her shoulder, his sister helped him inside the house, then slammed the door on the detectives without another word. An icicle fell off the gutter and shattered on the driveway. Riehle shoved his hands in his overcoat pockets and wondered if anything was going to go right today.

"It's the grief," he said, as much to himself as to Capparelli. "And the pain medicine talking."

"I know. But I think we'd better keep an eye on him though, don't you?"

Riehle sighed. "I suppose." He fished the keys out of his pocket. "C'mon, let's get to Buczyno's house before Gavin starts looking for us."

CHAPTER SIXTEEN

Riehle parked the car on the street in front of Buczyno's house. A patrol car blocked the end of the driveway, and a heavily bundled officer guarded the front door. Fluttering in the chilly wind, the yellow crime scene tape that stretched around the perimeter of the yard contrasted sharply with the trampled mud and remaining patches of snow. A few of the neighbors peered around curtains at the handful of journalists making their reports for the morning newscasts.

Straight-arming the reporters who shoved microphones in their faces and shouted questions at them, Riehle and Capparelli ducked under the crime scene tape and plodded up the driveway. Kaminsky gratefully accepted the extra large coffee with cream and sugar they'd picked up for him. Being careful not to spill any from their own cups, they wiped their shoes on the mat, went inside, and closed the door behind them.

An eerie silence greeted them. The overcast sky seemed to throw a blanket over the house, muffling the sounds from outside. A diffuse light trickled in through the opened curtains, showing the dried mud, salt, and water stains on the tiled floors, and the air smelled of stale perspiration and decay. Riehle shivered. No matter how many times he revisited a crime scene after the bodies had been removed, he'd never been able to shake the feeling that he was entering a grave.

"Where do you want to start?" Capparelli said.

Riehle took a sip of coffee. "I suppose the second bedroom

where the desk—hang on, what's this?" His finger tapped a wall-mounted touchpad that had been hidden behind the opened door yesterday. "This seem like the kind of house that needs a security system?"

Capparelli peered out the window and looked across the street. "Bunch of houses have them, actually. Most have signs in the windows or propped up in the landscaping advertising what kind they have. A few houses even have burglar bars on the first floor windows." His gaze traced the edge of Buczyno's window. "There's a sensor here."

"I'm betting we'll find it on all the doors and windows. But I didn't see any sign out front."

"Maybe he didn't want anyone to know he had one."

"Why not? You'd think it'd give him more privacy for the things he did in here." Riehle took a closer look. "System looks like it's on, though. Funny, we didn't hear an alarm when we came in. Do you remember any calls from the dispatcher or from a private security firm about a possible break-in when the neighbor entered?"

"Now that you mention it, no."

"Strange." He popped the top off the touchpad. " 'ADAC Security Systems, Inc.' Never heard of them. There's a toll-free phone number in here though, and a serial and model number." He wrote the information in his notebook. "We'll have Nielsen track it down with the other info. Now let's go tear apart that desk."

The second bedroom contained a brass day bed with a faded white- and purple-flowered comforter and matching curtains; a gray, spiral floor rug (Riehle wondered again why the master bedroom was the only room with carpeting); and a cherry wood desk topped with a brass lamp that matched the bed frame. A three-shelved bookcase in the opposite corner contained numerous manuals on woodworking and an eclectic collection of bestsellers from the last few decades, including *The Da Vinci Code* and Michener's *Chesapeake.*

Pulling the drawers all the way out, they checked behind and under the desk to make sure there weren't any hidden panels before settling down to examine the contents. The drawers, however, were filled with nothing but photographs of Walter and a woman they assumed was Dottie—some framed, some in albums, others still in processing envelopes with their negatives—as if Buczyno was trying to hide from his past by tucking his memories away.

The outside wind rattled the window, and a frigid draft slithered along the floor. Though Capparelli held a framed photo of Walter and Dottie, his gaze had drifted inward, filling with sadness and longing. He studied it long enough to make Riehle uncomfortable.

He cleared his throat. "Find something?"

A flash of embarrassment crossed Capparelli's face. "I was just thinking how happy they looked together. It's a shame things don't always work out like you'd hope." He quickly set the photo back in the drawer and brushed his hands against his trousers. "Doesn't look like we're going to find anything here. But you know, my parents used to pay their bills at the kitchen table."

Riehle shrugged. "Worth a try."

Seen better in the light of day and undisturbed by the activity in the basement, the detectives took a closer look at the kitchen. Varnished oak cabinets surrounded twenty-year-old chipped white appliances. An ancient microwave sat on its own stand near a wall-mounted touch-tone phone (also white), its cord hanging to the floor. The beige ceramic floor tiles were still muddy from last night's activities. A second touchpad was mounted on the wall next to the back door.

They set their coffees on the table and started with the three tiny drawers squeezed between the refrigerator and sink. The top was a typical junk drawer filled with, among other things, loose pens, pencils, a stapler, memo pads, and address labels, all of which rattled and slid around when they opened it. The middle drawer, however, contained an address book atop a stack of carryout menus, while the bottom one held a checkbook, calculator, and a stack of envelopes of bills arranged neatly by size, from smallest to largest.

"Bingo."

Riehle took out the contents of the bottom drawer and sat down at the kitchen table. "Why don't you take a look through the address book and see if we can figure out where else he might have gone."

"Sounds good."

Riehle spread the envelopes out on the table. Each envelope contained monthly statements with handwritten notations when the bills were paid, along with the check number and the amount paid. He quickly found the envelopes for Buczyno's VISA statements and bank account and set them aside. The checkbook showed a balance of just over four thousand dollars and a withdrawal of three hundred dollars in cash on the day before he flew to Minneapolis.

"Think I found something here. How 'bout you?"

Capparelli shook his head. "Hard to tell. It's like anybody's address book—names, addresses, phone numbers, some birth dates, but no one's listed specifically as a friend or relative. Quite a few are crossed off though, but whether they're deceased or moved, I can't say. It's not like he put a notation where he was going."

"But he obviously knew enough by heart that he didn't need to take the book with him." Riehle pulled out his cell phone. "Find the ones in the Minneapolis area, and we'll give them to Nielsen, along with what we've already got. We can follow up on the rest when we get back to the station."

Riehle called Nielsen and gave him the information for Buczyno's VISA and bank checking accounts, the numbers for the security system company, and the names and phone numbers of the people in the Minneapolis area.

"Did you check his e-mail?" Nielsen asked.

"He doesn't have a computer," Riehle said, surprised to realize it was true.

"Not even a laptop?"

"Let me check." He riffled through the credit card statements. "We haven't found one yet, though I suppose he could have taken it with him. But I don't see any automatic withdrawals for an Internet service."

"How about a cell? Then we can track him using GPS."

Riehle checked the envelopes. "Nope. Just phone bills for the landline number matching the kitchen phone."

"Damn, what a dinosaur. All right, I'll start the trace on his VISA and bring Gavin up to speed. Call me as soon as you get anything else."

"Thanks." Riehle disconnected the call. "We need to see if he's got a laptop somewhere."

They searched the remainder of the kitchen, dining room, and living room without any success before going into the master bedroom. The room felt much more lived in than the other one. A worn flowered comforter covered the queen-sized bed and a faded afghan lay folded at the foot of the bed. A dresser and vanity mirror took up most of the wall opposite the closet, and the only decorative items in the room were a silver picture frame on the dresser and an old copy of the religious tale "Footprints" mounted on the wall just inside the door. An ancient clock radio sat on the nightstand beside the bed, and Riehle watched as the minute changed and a panel flipped, amazed that the thing still worked after all these years.

While going through the closet and dresser drawers and not finding a laptop or any other evidence related to the crimes, Capparelli remarked how quiet it was. He bounced on his feet. "Feels like there's extra padding under the carpet that absorbs all the sound. Now why the hell would he put in something like that?"

"Hey, I haven't been able to figure *anything* out about this guy yet."

"Sure doesn't seem like your typical serial killer," Capparelli agreed. He picked up the silver picture frame off the dresser. It contained two photos: a studio black and white portrait of Walter and Dottie on their wedding day beside a more recent, grainy snapshot of the two of them. The words *Happy Twenty-fifth!* were printed on the border beneath. They were the only photographs the detectives had found not hidden away in the desk, and the expressions on Walter and Dottie's faces showed their love for one another had only deepened as the years passed.

A look of wistful sadness crossed Capparelli's face when he gently set the frame down. "Say, uh, I met your wife the other day."

". . . Really?"

"She filled my prescription. Didn't she tell you?"

Riehle shook his head, trying to pretend the question hadn't rattled him. He hated when something crossed over into his personal life. What was Capparelli doing? "Gwen's a real stickler for those HIPAA rules."

Capparelli gauged his expression, as if trying to determine whether Riehle was telling the truth or not. Finally, he said, "Rosacea."

"Rose who?"

He laughed and pointed at his face. "Rosacea. It makes the blood vessels on my cheeks and nose flush. My dermatologist prescribes medication for it and checks it periodically for basal cell carcinoma."

Gwen had mentioned his appearance might be due to a medical condition, and Ray already said he wasn't an alcoholic. Riehle felt like a heel.

"I didn't know."

"Well, I'm not saying there aren't times when it can work to your advantage having people think you're a drunk. You'd be surprised what people will tell you when they think you won't remember." He chuckled. "So she really didn't tell you? Seems like quite a lady you've got there."

"She's my best friend."

Capparelli nodded, sadly. "Yeah, that's the way it ought to be." He hesitated a moment before reaching into his wallet and handing Riehle a couple of wrinkled two-by-three photos.

Riehle stared at the pictures. "Damn! I mean, sorry. What I mean is—"

"S'alright. I'm used to it. She was forty-three when the more recent one was taken."

The first was a picture of a young woman in her wedding gown, and the second was the same woman years later. She was easily one of the most beautiful women Riehle had ever seen. Flowing chestnut hair, radiant blue eyes, a slightly upturned nose over a sensual smile, and a hint of cleavage at the edge of the newer photo, she was quite simply breathtaking. Like Sophia Loren or Raquel Welch, she appeared to be one of those women whose striking beauty only seemed to enhance with age.

"My ex-wife, Charlotte," Capparelli said. "And that's only a picture. You oughta see her in person. Bet you're wondering how I ended up with someone like that?"

"No, honest I—"

"Don't worry, you wouldn't be the first. Including me." He returned the photos to his wallet, stuffed it in his back pocket, and patted it dramatically. "Always keep her next to my heart. Listen, about that story Dixie was gonna tell you—"

Riehle held his hands up between them. "Hey, she never told me, and I wouldn't have paid any attention. I don't know how Paul can stand being around her all day."

"Be that as it may, you're gonna hear it anyway. So you might as well hear it from me." Capparelli squared his shoulders. "The story you'll hear is how I walked in on Charlotte and another man."

"Geez, I'm sorry." And he was. Other than something happening to Karen, he couldn't imagine anything worse coming between him and Gwen. The very thought of it drove a knife through his heart. He felt his devastation completely. No wonder Capparelli had reacted so strongly to his toilet bowl story, saying his wife would have acted the same. Here he'd thought he was being funny, sharing a laugh; while Capparelli probably thought Dixie had told him the story of his wife's affair and assumed Riehle was being sarcastic and vindictive. Now he *really* felt like a heel.

"I'd heard rumors every now and then, but I never expected . . ." Capparelli shrugged, letting the words hang in the air. "Anyway, I went a little crazy and beat the crap out of him. That's what she was going to tell you."

Capparelli seemed to be waiting for some kind of reaction, but Riehle didn't know what to say. After a moment, Capparelli finally turned away, possibly embarrassed at having revealed more than he should have. He cleared his throat, and the portraits of Walter and Dottie caught his attention again. "You know, for a couple who appeared so happy together, it's strange that this is the only souvenir Walter kept out."

"Speaking of which," Riehle said, grateful for the opportunity to break away from their personal lives and return to work, "I don't remember finding any souvenirs from Walter's victims, either."

"Let's take another look downstairs."

But once in the living room, Capparelli kneeled down by the fireplace. He ran his fingertips along the grate. "Looks like Walter had a fire recently." He tipped his head toward the dining room table. "And only five chairs instead of six. I'm wondering if he tied his latest victim to a chair while he tortured him, then burned it afterward."

"Sounds reasonable. But why would he put patio furniture with vinyl cushions in the living room?"

"Got me on that one." Capparelli stood, wiping his fingers on his handkerchief. "Maybe it's something as simple as wanting to feel like he'd moved into a rustic cabin after his wife died."

Said like that, Riehle was curious how Capparelli furnished his new place after his divorce. "I'm beginning to wonder if we'll ever figure this guy out."

"Oh, we will," Capparelli said with a hard determination in his voice. "We will."

The basement wasn't much different than how they'd left it the night before. Dug-out graves in the crawlspace, smeared muddy footprints on the concrete floor, and dried blood caked on the ceiling's support beams. A board had been nailed over the broken window, and the room now was as warm as the rest of the house, though the enclosed, almost stifling air was thick with the odors of wet humus, stale perspiration, and decay.

Riehle opened the green metal cabinet where the evidence tech had found the wire and duct tape. The cabinet contained numerous sets of various tools and normal, everyday cleaning supplies used around the house. But at the bottom of one of the toolkits, he found a thick nine-by-twelve manila envelope that rattled when he shook it.

Using the dryer as a tabletop, he undid the clasp and carefully emptied the contents: three men's wallets, two of which still held money; four rings; one watch; three gold chains; two sets of car keys; and a piece of paper with four rectangles drawn on it—three positioned horizontally side by side, and one perpendicular to the others. Inside each a date was written, with two of the dates being identical, and three of the four had names listed.

Capparelli inhaled sharply. "Buried treasure."

"Yep. A map of the exact positions Griskel found the bodies." Riehle checked the wallets for ID and found each matched a name written for a gravesite. Two of the victims, Alan Wilson and Daniel Sanchez, had been Indiana residents.

The one from Illinois, in the position of the most recent victim, was named Franklin Edward Harris.

Back at the station, Capparelli told Gavin what they'd found, while Riehle called Griskel with the possible IDs for three of the four victims. They'd compare the Missing Persons reports of what the victims were last seen wearing with any fabric samples Griskel found around the bodies before contacting the families. Riehle didn't look forward to the news he would have to deliver.

Later, while Riehle and Capparelli were entering the reports, Nielsen told them about his credit card search. Buczyno, for whatever reason, had indeed skipped his flight and rented a car with his destination listed as Chicago and had stayed overnight at the StarKey Motel in a southeastern Minnesota town near the Iowa border. Nielsen posted the car model, make, and license plate number on NCIC and LEADS, and apprised of the situation, the local cops were already at the motel interviewing the staff and checking his room for evidence.

Subsequent activity showed Buczyno had taken a six hundred dollar cash advance at an ATM in St. Paul on the day before he was supposed to leave and where he'd bought gas and other sundries since, and at one location late this afternoon, he'd taken out another two hundred dollar cash advance on his VISA.

"Guy doesn't have a whole lot to his name, and I can't see him getting very far with those sized withdrawals," Nielsen said. "Me, if I was on the run, I'd have emptied my accounts and maxed out the cards before they were frozen. So why didn't he?"

Riehle didn't have an answer. Nothing this guy did made any sense. He plotted the locations from the credit card purchases on a map, and sure enough, the evidence was right there. Buczyno, it seemed, was making a run for it, headed west.

CHAPTER SEVENTEEN

"G'night, daddy."

Karen stood at the top of the stairs leading down to the family room. She wore pink pajamas with the images of animated movie princesses on the front. Her freshly brushed hair was wet from her bath.

"What? Are you too big for a goodnight kiss?"

Her face broke out in a grin, and she ran down the stairs. Cinnamon was curled up on the floor by his feet, and her tags jingled when she jerked her head up. Riehle put his arm around his daughter as she snuggled next to him on the couch. Her hair smelled of blueberry-scented shampoo.

"Aren't you hungry?" she said.

His dinner sat untouched on the TV tray, the slices of reheated pepperoni pizza getting cold while his beer warmed. He'd been channel-surfing with the remote, trying to find something interesting on TV to take his mind off the events of the day. Instead, his thoughts had wandered, fretting over everything he needed to do, and his dinner congealed while he searched aimlessly, unable to remain focused on the broadcasted images. He switched the channel from the local news to *Full House* on Nick at Nite. He knew he couldn't keep Karen in a protective bubble forever, but he didn't want to expose her to too much too soon, either.

"Guess I'm not, sweetie," he said. "I'm sorry we can't go on vacation for a while. But I'll make it up to you, I promise."

"It's okay, daddy," she said, though she wasn't able to hide the disappointment in her voice. She told him about a girl on the bus who'd broken her favorite pencil that day, and Riehle felt even worse for having to spoil her plans.

"But guess what? At gymnastics, I did a cartwheel on the balance beam without falling today."

"That's my big girl."

"Time for bed," Gwen said, coming into the family room. "You've got school tomorrow."

Karen gave him a kiss and a hug. She clapped her hands. "C'mon, Cinnamon. Nigh-night time!" Then she ran past her mother. "Last one there's a rotten egg!" Riehle smiled at the sound of her laughter as her footsteps raced up the stairs and into her bedroom, Cinnamon trudging along behind her.

Gwen frowned when she looked at his plate. "Not eating isn't going to help catch the guy any sooner." She kissed him on the cheek. "I'll be down in a bit."

"Okay."

He took a couple sips of his beer and started channel-surfing again. Neither the Bulls, the Blackhawks, or the Wolves were playing that night, and none of the movies on the premium channels interested him. But a couple of the superstations had older films he hadn't seen in a while. In one, Peter Finch screamed about how mad he was in *Network*, while the other showed Dustin Hoffman going berserk at the end of Peckinpah's *Straw Dogs*. Riehle bounced back and forth between the stations, but unable to stay focused on either movie, he finally switched off the TV and tossed the remote aside.

What made Buczyno do the things he did? he wondered. What could push a seemingly normal guy over the edge? Questions like these had been driving him crazy all day. He wished there was something he could find or see that would clue him in to whatever was going through Buczyno's mind.

143

Yeah, right. Like the answer was just going to pop up in front of him.

He heard the shower shut off. Gwen came down a few minutes later wearing a red flannel nightshirt. Her strawberry-blond hair was brushed to a shine, and she smelled of fresh soap and the perfume she wore when they were first dating.

She curled up next to him on the couch and rested her head on his shoulder. "Karen's asleep already."

"She had a hard day."

"Like someone else I know." Gwen laced her fingers in his. "You'll catch him. I have faith in you."

"I wish the case didn't have to spill over into our personal life. With Gavin canceling all vacations and personal days, we can't go anywhere with Karen or celebrate our anniversary." *And not break the curse of my parents,* he thought.

"That's just the kind of job you have. And we hadn't decided what we were doing yet anyway, so don't worry about it. We'll be fine." She ran her hand over his shoulders. "You're all wound up."

"This case is such a heater. Gavin's all over us. Everyone's watching every move we make. I keep thinking I need to head back to the station, maybe do some paperwork or something—"

"No. You didn't get any sleep last night, and you tossed and turned the couple hours you were home. You won't be doing anyone any good if you don't get some rest." She tugged his sleeve. "C'mon, let me rub the knots out of your muscles. Then you can get a good night's sleep and concentrate better in the morning."

He slid to the floor and leaned his back against the couch between her legs. Her fingers kneaded his neck and shoulders, and he felt the tension seeping away. "How was the Jensen funeral?" he said.

Her fingers paused for a moment. "Awful. The tiny casket

next to the bigger one was heartbreaking. People couldn't stop sobbing." He heard her sniffle behind him. "The priest gave a very touching eulogy and a speaker from MADD talked about how this was another tragic loss from drunk driving. I don't know how much of the service Larry caught, though. He was pretty out of it."

"He looked bad this morning. Ray and I saw him getting home from the hospital." Riehle tried not to imagine what it would be like to lose his own wife and daughter or how he'd deal with it. Would he drown in a pharmaceutical depression? Or take his anger out in other ways? He was a cop, after all, and cops carried guns. He pushed his darker thoughts away and changed the subject. "Ray said he met you the other day."

"Uh-huh. He came into the pharmacy. He seems like a nice guy."

"Yeah, he is. He told me about his rosacea."

Riehle knew she was smiling behind him. "I told you it might be something like that, didn't I? You should know I'm always right."

"You'd think I'd learn by now." He kissed the inside of her knee and ran his hands over her smooth legs. "So what did I ever do to deserve you?"

"You fell in love with me." She wrapped her arms around his neck and kissed the top of his head. "Feeling better?"

"Much."

"Then maybe you can give me a backrub," she whispered.

After turning off the lights and checking the locks on the doors, they held hands going up the stairs. They found Karen sprawled over the tops of her sheets, with Cinnamon asleep on the bunched-up comforter at the foot of the bed. Ignoring Cinnamon's grunting protests, they tucked Karen back in, being especially careful not to wake her. They rubbed Cinnamon behind the ears, blew Karen kisses and closed her door, then quietly closed their own bedroom door behind them. Moonlight shone through the open curtains, and flickering cranberry-scented candles that reminded him of their honeymoon on Cape Cod bathed the room with a warm glow. The flowered comforter had already been turned down.

They took turns undressing each other. He held her to him and closed his eyes, luxuriating in the feel of her breasts against his bare chest and the smell of her skin and perfume, amazed and aroused at how the sight and touch of her still thrilled him. He guided her onto the bed.

He started slowly, his strong fingers gently caressing her neck and shoulders, feeling the heat rising from her skin as he traveled down her back. His fingertips traced over her buttocks and down the back of her legs, and she giggled, warning him not to tickle her. He massaged her feet and ankles, her legs slowly spreading apart as his fingers and kisses made their way up the insides of her calves and knees and thighs, and when his fingers found the wetness at the top her thighs, she rolled over, spreading her legs around him, and she drew him to her.

His heart pounded. He kissed her eyes, her lips, her neck. The scent of her intoxicated him. Their breathing became faster and their kisses grew more urgent. When his tongue circled her areolas and licked the tips of her erect nipples, she moaned, arching her back, and she reached down and guided him inside her. His breath caught in his throat at the glorious sensation of her warm, wet silkiness sliding over him, drawing him in, and their bodies moved together with familiar rhythms.

The candles flickered. In their light, and in the glow of the moon, her shimmering hair spilled over the pillow. Her half-closed eyes gazed up at him. He wanted to tell her how beautiful she was, how much he loved and needed her; to tell her how she brought him comfort and security and gave him the confidence to believe anything was possible. But she pursed her lips together with a "Shhhh," and pulled him closer, whispering, "Me, too." She wrapped her legs around him then, and her hands slid to the small of his back, pushing him deeper inside. Their hearts beat faster as their bodies moved together, their panting breaths coming shorter and quicker until, finally, when he felt her tremble and heard her gasp, he couldn't hold back any longer and burst inside her as she shuddered beneath him.

Later, when their heartbeats slowed and their sweat added to the warmth under the comforter, they blew out the candles and fell asleep in each other's arms, watching the wisps of smoke curl and dissipate in the moonlight.

CHAPTER EIGHTEEN

The sunlight finally woke him.

Walter rolled away from the painful glare, stretched, and sat up in bed, blinking severely into the otherwise darkened room. The motel curtains were parted slightly, and a sliver of sunlight cut directly through them and across the pillow where his head had been. He rubbed the sandy crust from his eyes and squinted at the digital clock on the bedside table. One-thirty in the afternoon.

His head throbbed. Massaging his temples with his fingertips, he tried to remember where the hell he was. A roadside motel someplace, somewhere in northern Iowa or southern Minnesota—he couldn't remember which. His memory was clouded, and his brain felt like dense steel wool scraping the inside of his skull.

Pushing himself out of bed and shivering in the cold air, he found his pants on the floor. He must have been so tired that he'd just climbed into bed without hanging them up first. All he could remember was after having driven for hours and hours on a caffeine, sugar, and adrenaline rush, he could barely think straight by then. Wary of spiders in a strange motel room, he shook his pants out before slipping them on.

A plastic bag sat on the dresser. He felt around inside it. Under the half-eaten box of chocolate cupcakes and fruit pies, extra packets of sugar and creamer, a toothbrush and toothpaste, some deodorant, a couple of flannel shirts with auto racing emblems on them, and a pocket screwdriver kit, Walter found the bottle of aspirin. He popped the top, poured three tablets into his hand, and downed them with a glass of water from the bathroom, noticing his chipped thumbnail when he set the glass down on the stained porcelain sink. He closed the curtains and dropped wearily onto the bed.

Had it only been two days? he wondered. It felt like he'd been driving forever. That first night was a blur of panic and confusion, broken only by stops to buy gas and to purchase the various sundries and sugary detritus that caught his attention when he paid at the counter or that popped into his sleep-deprived brain while he drove around the countryside. He'd stopped, finally, about five in the morning when he caught himself nodding off at the wheel, the sounds of gravel along the shoulder under his tires jerking him awake. He took a room in a sleazy motel next to a run-down bar in some small, unmemorable town, but he slept fitfully and was back on the road a few hours later.

At some point along the way, his fried neurons realized the cops would eventually check his credit card usage and discover that not only had he rented a car—and what its license plate would be—but also the path he was taking based upon his gas station purchases. He'd almost turned himself in then, ready to simply give up, knowing there was no way he could outrun a manhunt when every law enforcement agency was involved.

But, *dammit!*, he still had some cash left and he just needed time to *THINK THINK THINK.*

And that was when he bought the screwdriver kit.

To switch license plates along the way.

It wasn't exactly a brilliant idea. Or even an original one. He'd read it in countless novels and seen it in dozens of movies. But there was no sense in keeping the plates he had and making it any easier for the cops, either. Besides, he couldn't think of anything else to do. Walter supposed rental companies had a specific number or letter at the beginning of the plate number to identify them as rentals, but that was just the chance he'd have to take. What the hell. All he wanted was a little more time to figure out what he was going to do until the other car owner reported that his plates had been switched. It was worth a shot, anyway.

And wouldn't you know it? Right after buying the toolkit late in the afternoon, he spotted a white Grand Am in a VFW parking lot. He smiled. Dottie must have been watching out for him, after all.

Walter pulled into the lot and parked as far away from the streetlight as possible. He waited for over an hour inside the car with its engine off until the sun finally set and darkness settled around him. During that time a number of other cars parked nearby, spilling occupants who hurried quickly inside the crowded hall for some sort of shindig or other. He heard the sounds of a bass guitar and drums whenever the door opened. Bundled in heavy coats, hats, and scarves, their heads down to protect themselves from the biting January wind, not a single person noticed him bent over in the seat or gave a second thought to the windows fogged by his breath.

When no one else arrived for another fifteen minutes, Walter quietly opened his door and crept to the front of the matching car. Hidden between the front ends of the parked cars, he hoped it'd be harder for someone to spot him there. His heart pounding with excitement and fear, he kneeled on the frozen asphalt, pulled the toolkit from his pocket, and selected the correct-sized screwdriver for the license plate screws.

It was slow going in the bitter cold. The rusty screws felt like they were frozen in place. His gloves slid over the screwdriver's handle. He had to take a glove off for a better grip. Alternating back and forth between using his right hand or left, depending on how quickly the exposed skin became numb, he twisted the screwdriver. The screws screeched with every laborious turn. Swollen with cold, his hand muscles soon grew unable to grip the handle, and he found himself shoving his hands under his armpits inside his jacket to warm them more and more frequently.

His frustration grew. The stinging wind whistled between the cars, making his eyes water. He blinked hard to keep them from freezing. How much time did he have before someone spotted him? His knees ached from kneeling on the frozen pavement, and his fingers tingled and burned. Trying to hurry, he pushed too hard and his left hand slipped. The screwdriver bounced on the asphalt and he fell forward, chipping his thumbnail. Luckily, there wasn't any bleeding he could see.

Finally Walter got the screws out of both plates. He slid each one out by tapping their top edges with the screwdriver and scurried over to his car. Thankfully, the rental's screws were easier to remove, and he switched the first set of plates in no time. He huddled inside his car for a few minutes to warm up then, afraid to turn the engine on for fear of someone noticing. But at least it was out of the wind.

When the pain seemed bearable again, he slid out of his car and hurried over to the other one. He'd just gotten the back plate on and had squeezed down in front when a car pulled into the lot. Hunkering down low, Walter carefully peered around the front bumper.

And almost peed his pants when he saw it was a cop.

The patrol car slowly circled the lot, driving up and down the aisles. Walter's heart beat wildly in his throat. He covered his shallow breaths with his gloves and turned away when the cop drove by. He shivered as the sweat in the small of his back froze to his shirt. Thank goodness the lot was plowed, he thought, or the cop would've seen his impressions in the snow.

The cop parked in a vacant space near the back corner of the lot and stepped out of the car. He said something and his radio squawked back. Walter clenched his teeth to keep them from chattering. He heard the officer's shoes scrape the salted asphalt, and almost wept with relief when the cop went inside.

Walter's breath exploded in a giant vapor cloud. He hadn't even realized he'd been holding it. Fighting the urge to drop the damn plate and get the hell out of there, he forced himself to screw it in place. No sense in calling attention to what he'd done any earlier. When it was tightened down, he glanced around the darkened lot, then raced back to his car and drove away, pausing only long enough to scrape a hole in the frost on his windshield for him to see through.

He'd made it! Walter couldn't believe it. It took every ounce of willpower not to floor the accelerator. That'd be all he'd need right now, getting captured because of some stupid speeding ticket. Wasn't that how they caught the Oklahoma City bomber? He needed to remain cautious and careful.

As the defrosters kicked in and the condensation disappeared, Walter saw his way more clearly. The lights of the small town soon faded behind him, and except for the occasional barn or houselights, the darkness of deserted country roads engulfed him. He'd never felt so free. His arms and legs trembled as the tension seeped out, and he struggled to hold onto the steering wheel. He breathed deeply, and a wave that started as a small tickle in his gut burst forth in giant, raucous laughter so spontaneous and uncontrolled that tears rolled down his cheeks.

"I did it! I did it! I did it!"

Eventually, however, the laughter subsided. Walter realized it was only the rush of adrenaline, excitement, and fear that had made him giddy. He wiped his eyes with the back of his hand. Time to get a grip. A solid meal and a good night's sleep were what he needed most if he intended to evade capture a little while longer.

The thought of food made his stomach grumble. Except for coffee and sugar snacks, he hadn't eaten all day. He pulled into a diner in the next town he came to and went inside. A teenage girl, a younger image of the worn, tired-looking woman who sat behind the checkout register, put him in a booth under a framed print of pastel flowers near the back. He ordered country-fried chicken, green beans and mashed potatoes with gravy, a cup of beef barley soup to start, but no pie for dessert—really, thank you, anyway—and a large glass of milk to settle him down. His eyes were probably bigger than his stomach, but he knew if he didn't get something decent in his system soon, he might throw up all over the table. That'd be all he'd need right now, calling attention to himself. As it was, he was still shaking from earlier.

When the food arrived, he forced himself to eat slowly. The first few swallows of soup churned his nervous stomach, but soon the tendrils of warmth calmed his aching muscles and he relaxed. For the first time in two days, the pent-up anxiety began to seep away. Walter yawned, almost in a daze. He hadn't realized how sleepy he was.

Doubts slowly crept into his mind. He kept his head down while he ate. How long did he really think he could avoid getting caught? He only had so much money, and it was just a matter of time before the cops found him, by accident or design. There weren't a lot of places to go, and sooner or later someone was going to recognize him wherever he tried to hide.

He simply didn't know what to do.

His head jerked up when the phone at the register rang. Did the woman's eyes glance his way when she answered? The hairs on the back of his neck rose. Walter quickly looked down at his food and tried to keep his hand from shaking when he took another bite. Had someone seen him switch the plates? Were the cops onto him already, or was he just being paranoid? The food was making him drowsy, but depression and hopelessness began to weigh him down, and if it weren't for the simple fact that he was too tired to move, he might have turned himself in right then and there.

Instead, when the woman ignored him and left to use the restroom, he ordered a large coffee to go, paid the waitress directly with a decent tip (not too big or too small for them to remember him by), and headed back out onto the road.

The new dose of caffeine made his scalp itch, but soon lifted his spirits enough to get him thinking straight again. Knowing he desperately needed cash and the cops were going to trace his credit card purchases, he drove directly west from where he'd switched the license plates. In the next town, he found a twenty-four-hour ATM and took a cash advance on his VISA. Then he drove further west and an hour later used the card one last time to fill his gas tank, hoping the purchases would make it look like he was making a beeline for either South Dakota or Nebraska (he wasn't exactly sure where he was at the moment), before turning south onto a deserted country road.

At first, he thought it was a pretty clever plan. Make the cops think he was headed west. They'd never expect him to circle back. Or would they? He chewed the inside of his cheek. Always that sliver of doubt. The thing was, he just didn't *know*. How could he possibly expect to second-guess the cops? All he did was kill some burglars and the animal who murdered his wife, and for *that* his whole life had to be turned upside down? No. He wasn't a criminal, goddammit, and he sure as hell wasn't going to let them treat him like one.

The problem was he didn't know how to think like one, either.

He headed east at the next major highway. After about a half hour of passing the occasional car or truck and driving through sleeping towns, Walter grew concerned he might be too visible. Did the stoplights in these rural towns have cameras yet? What if one of the cars he passed was a patrol car? He wondered if there was an APB out on him. Were they searching for any white Grand Am, or would some local cop happen upon him because the guy at the VFW noticed his plates were switched?

So he turned onto the first county road he came to and quickly decided that wasn't such a hot idea, either. Out here on deserted, pitch-black roads in godforsaken farm country, a county sheriff might pull over any unfamiliar car for driving around in the middle of the night. So he turned this way and that, choosing roads at random in a hopeless attempt to disappear off the radar screen, all the while never knowing if it was the right thing to do.

He'd never felt so lost in his entire life.

At the next town he came to, Walter spotted a number of cars parked outside a farm equipment outlet. Pulling into the lot, he switched plates with a dark blue Toyota Camry, then headed for the nearest highway. A plate from a car of a different make and color—that should make it harder to find him. Right?

That was the sixty-four-thousand-dollar question.

The more he thought about it, the more his headache worsened. He supposed he could continue switching plates, but would the cops take notice? How often did plates get switched anyway, and would the frequency point to him and the path he was taking? Should he continue driving in erratic patterns? He could only do that for so long and what would he do when he ran out of money?

And now that he thought about it, why the hell didn't he take out more while he had the chance? He'd intended to set up a pattern with the ATM withdrawals and credit card usage, a false trail for the cops to follow, but he'd ended up outsmarting himself instead. He punched the steering wheel. Surely they'd frozen his accounts by now. What the hell was he thinking?

Walter rubbed his throbbing temples. Stop! Stop! Stop! He

had to stop thinking so much and just *do* something.

The question was: What?

Finally, exhaustion made the decision for him. When his head started bobbing toward the steering wheel, Walter pulled into the first roadside motel he came to. Slipping the guy behind the counter a few extra bucks so he could pay in cash and not have to register (not that the guy really seemed to give a shit one way or the other), he unloaded his luggage, peeled off his clothes, and climbed into bed.

Where the sunlight woke him hours later.

Walter ran a hand through his bedraggled hair. The aspirin churned his stomach, and his eyes were dry and itchy. He sneezed and rubbed his nose. Even in the dim light, he could tell the room wasn't vacuumed or dusted very often. Small wonder the guy at the desk had been so happy to take his cash.

But the worse thing was he realized a good night's sleep hadn't provided him with any better answers.

A long, hot shower took some of the stiffness out of his muscles. After dressing in clean clothes, including one of the new flannel shirts, he turned on the TV and settled on the bed for a breakfast of stale fruit pies and a glass of water from the tap. He channel-surfed up and down the dial, but his mind was thick and clouded, and he was unable to find anything to draw his attention away from his inner gloom and depression.

He could get back on the road, but, really, what was the point? He'd just spend another day driving around in circles. Even if he picked a destination and made a run for it, sooner or later the cops would find him. He'd end up barricaded in some motel room, forced to kill himself before the police stormed the premises. And for all that he and Dottie had gone through, what would it have solved?

Walter looked around the dingy room. Hell, maybe he ought to just stay here. It probably wouldn't be any easier for the cops to find him if he stayed in one isolated, out-of-the-way place. But eventually the money would run out. He checked his wallet. Very soon, in fact. If only he could get a little more money without using his credit card, it might give him more time to think, a better chance to figure out what he needed to do.

But where the hell was the money supposed to come from, anyway?

The sounds of bells and people cheering caught his attention. The TV was showing a commercial for an Iowa casino on the Mississippi riverbank, advertising that all the fun of a lifetime was less than an hour away. Slots, poker, games—it seemed like there was a big winner every thirty seconds and the casino couldn't give its money away fast enough. Walter shook his head, unable to believe the gullibility of some people . . . until a flicker of hope made him smile.

What did he have to lose?

CHAPTER NINETEEN

"Looks like we got some hits on those Missing Persons cases," Capparelli said when Riehle entered the squad room.

Riehle was surprised to find his partner in so early. Spooning with Gwen, the warm curves of her body pressed against him and the scent of her skin and hair in his nostrils, it had been hard for Riehle to roll out of bed when the alarm went off that morning. But he knew Gavin wanted an update ASAP, and he'd arrived a few minutes early, hoping to pull up the very information Capparelli had already received.

When he found his partner sitting alone at his desk, hunched over the keyboard to his computer, his sport coat draped over the back of his chair and a half-empty, already-gone-cold mug of coffee beside him, Riehle felt a pang of sadness. He remembered Simmons saying how Capparelli was famous for putting in extra hours on cases, and knowing what he did now about Ray's ex-wife, Riehle understood. Why go home when there was nothing to go home to? He'd bury himself in his work if he lost his wife, too.

"Check this out." Capparelli waved him over and pointed to his screen. "Alan Wilson and Daniel Sanchez had Missing Persons cases filed by the Hobart, Indiana PD back in July of last year. Alan was nineteen and Danny seventeen at the time their families reported them missing. Both had gang affiliations."

"You run criminal histories on them?"

"Yep. Cops in the area knew these guys real well. Both have arrests for a number of gas station robberies and home invasions, and their most recent listings happened about a week before the date we found written on Buczyno's map. Seems their gang crashed a party a rival gang was throwing in a forest preserve near Merrillville. Several members from both gangs had to be taken to area hospitals for knife and gunshot wounds, and a twelve-year-old girl was hit in the shoulder by a stray bullet. Wilson and Sanchez were arrested. They bonded out, but never showed for their court date. Both had warrants out of Merrillville, and the cops figured they'd skipped town."

"Never knowing they were already buried in Buczyno's crawl-space. Doesn't exactly sound like they're going to be heartbroken over our news. Anything on the unidentified body?"

"Not yet. LEADS and NCIC list a number of Missing Persons cases in the Tri-State area around that time, but we'll have to wait for more info from Griskel before we can narrow it down."

"What about Harris? The most recent one that was beaten to a pulp?"

"Another winner. Guy was in juvie for a couple of years, then transferred to Granger County Jail at age eighteen. His record was sealed, but he got out about a year ago when he turned twenty-one. Last known address is his mother's house in Chicago. It didn't say what the conviction was for, but did state the arrest occurred in Westbrook. I wasn't able to pull up the original reports, though."

"Then it probably happened in the unincorporated area along the tollway, which would put it under the Granger County Sheriff's jurisdiction. That section wasn't annexed into town until about two or three years ago, so the county might still have the records. We ought to give them a call, see if they remember anything." Riehle rubbed his chin. "Now that I think about it, Buczyno's house is in that area. You find anything on him?"

"Nothing. The guy never even had a parking ticket as far as I can tell."

"Damn. All right, back to the history checks. None of these guys sound like choirboys. Any mention of the cops picking up Wilson or Sanchez for male prostitution?"

"*Nada.* But that doesn't mean Buczyno didn't meet them in a bar someplace and bring them back to his house."

"True." Riehle blew out his breath. This case was going nowhere fast. The only connection they had between Buczyno and Harris was that Harris's crime from eight years ago *might* have occurred in the formerly unincorporated section of town where Buczyno's house was located. Pretty slim, he had to admit. Possibly lost in the exchange when Westbrook annexed the unincorporated area, they still hadn't found Harris's file yet, and even if they did find a connection, they still didn't have anything tying Wilson and Sanchez to Buczyno. He was about to say as much to Capparelli when his cell phone rang. It was Simmons.

"What's up, Paul?"

"We got a nine-one-one call about a stalker."

"So what's the problem?"

Simmons sighed. "It's your buddy, Jensen."

Riehle pulled to a stop in front of the Metcalf house on Lyman Avenue and turned off the ignition. It was raining hard, a bone-chilling winter rain, and the heavy drops beat on the car's rooftop and splattered the windshield. A marked unit was already parked on the other side of the driveway, officers standing by in case the detectives needed backup.

Like so many other streets in town, Lyman Avenue had changed beyond recognition in the last few years. What had once been a street of family homes where the kids played ball in the street and block parties were held every summer, Lyman Avenue had fallen, domino effect, into a development of cookie-cutter mini-mansions built right on top of one another, with home security signs posted prominently in the front landscaping. Its male residents held pissing contests by displaying their imported cars in the driveways, while the wives parked their SUVs over the line between two parking spaces at nearby shopping malls.

And in the middle of it all, Larry Jensen stood at the end of the Metcalfs' driveway.

Riehle and Capparelli pulled the jacket hoods over their heads and slammed the car doors shut to warn him of their presence before walking up to him.

"What are you doing?" Riehle asked.

Soaked to the skin, Jensen stood there, shivering.

"He killed my family," was all the puppeteer said.

Riehle looked at the house. Two lofty stories of cold, white brick, a steep roof, and an extended room over the imposing three-car garage. Manicured landscaping sculpted into corkscrews, and Malibu-style lights that, at night, would illuminate the cobblestone driveway and front walk like a runway. An immense crystal chandelier hung in the front entryway, as seen from the outside through the arched window above the forest green door inlaid with decorative wrought iron and beveled glass. As Riehle watched, the corners of the upstairs curtains fluttered, and shadows moved behind the front door.

"Larry, you can't stay here like this."

Jensen blinked hard against the rain that slapped his face and ran down his cheeks. He didn't say a word.

The front door flew open. "Get him out of here!" Metcalf yelled from the safety of his home.

Jensen remained where he was. The bruises on his face appeared almost gray in the rainy morning light, and his firmly set lips were blue. Riehle squeezed Jensen's shoulder reassuringly before he ascended the inclined driveway. The air grew colder as he approached the house.

"That's it? You're just going to let him stand there?" Metcalf said when Riehle reached the front stoop. The commodities broker stood in the doorway, his arms crossed and feet planted shoulder-width apart, bathed in the glow of the chandelier from above. Unlike Riehle, who, when he relaxed at home, wore blue jeans and sweatshirts from places his family vacationed, Metcalf wore a cream-colored cashmere sweater over a button-down dress shirt, sharply creased khakis, and penny loafers. "What's it going to take to get him out of here?"

Riehle showed his detective's badge. "What seems to be the problem, sir?"

"Problem? I'll tell you what the goddamn problem is. He's harassing me. I want him arrested. They need a detective to do that?"

Metcalf's house had no outer storm door, most likely because it would hinder the view of their expensive, custom-built door from passersby, and Metcalf stood in the open doorway as if his very stature, on-paper wealth, or self-absorbed arrogance could prevent anything unwanted from entering. The exterior design of the house also lacked any type of shelter or overhang to protect visitors, and the rain poured down on Riehle while Metcalf stayed warm and dry. Metcalf kept his hand on the doorknob and didn't invite him inside.

Riehle tried to keep the growing anger and irritation out of his voice. "Has he threatened you in any way?"

"He's been standing on my driveway all morning scaring my family to death! What the hell else does he have to do?"

As if on cue, Metcalf's wife and twin daughters appeared at the top of the stairs behind him. The wife wore a shiny teal silk blouse and black dress slacks, and the girls wore matching pink and black outfits. All three had straight blond hair, the mother's shorter and more expensively cut. She held her arms protectively around her daughters and looked down her nose at Riehle, while the girls, wide-eyed, stared at him as if he were the villain.

"Do I have to remind you that there are anti-stalking laws in this state?" Metcalf said.

In his pockets, Riehle's hands curled into fists. He knew he ought to show a little professional detachment, but the guy was really beginning to piss him off. So instead, he stepped closer and said through gritted teeth: "You killed his wife and baby daughter. Be a man and go talk to him. Can't you show a little sympathy? Some remorse?"

"My lawyer's handling all that. We're getting a restraining order against Jensen." Metcalf glanced over his shoulder, then lowered his voice. "How *dare* you talk to me like that in front of my family! Now do your goddamned job and get him the hell off my property, or I'm calling your superiors."

Then he slammed the door in Riehle's face.

Capparelli hawked and spit on the lawn when Riehle reached the end of the driveway. "Fuckin' ass-wipe thinks he rules the world."

Riehle put his arm around Jensen and guided him toward their car. "C'mon Larry, you have to go. We'll drive you home. Really, you can't do this anymore."

"He killed my family," Jensen said. "Doesn't he care?"

Only about himself, Riehle wanted to say.

CHAPTER TWENTY

The casino parking lot was overflowing by the time Walter arrived.

He had tried to time it for later in the evening when he thought most of the excitement would be over, when the we're-done-for-the-night patrons would be filing out and heading home, celebrating their meager winnings or mentally fabricating another lame excuse on how they'd lost the rent money again. But as he turned the Grand Am down yet another aisle, he saw how the sodium vapor lights cast their orange glow over rows of salt-smeared vehicles without an empty parking space to be found, and no one drunkenly searching the lot to retrieve their car and open a space for him.

Near the back, Walter turned his car around and threw the gearshift into park. He stared out the windshield. The temperature outside was just above freezing, and a light rain began to fall, creating a halo effect around the overhead lights. He turned the wipers on. Above, through the click-clack of the wipers, he could see attendants pushing wheelchair-bound senior citizens through the lighted, Plexiglas-enclosed walkway over the parking lot that connected the hotel to the new, land-based casino. On the far side of the parking lot and across the road, just barely within the glow of the lights, the old riverboat casino was still docked along the shore of the Mississippi River. Dark and abandoned, it looked as forgotten as a broken toy discarded the day after Christmas.

Walter rubbed his tired, itchy eyes, the irritated membranes watering when he scratched the grit out of the corners with his dirty fingernails. He'd been driving for a couple of hours now, and the interior of the car smelled of nervous sweat and stale coffee. His emotions had pogoed between excitement and fear the entire way. Would he make enough money to stay on the run? Or was he walking into a trap, a place where he'd be spotted and arrested immediately?

Just what the hell did he think he was doing here, anyway?

One of the three charter buses parked in front of the hotel started its engine, and Walter crouched down in his seat. Over the top of the dashboard, he saw the first bus in line pull away from the hotel, wind its way through the parking lot, and turn left onto the road that ran along the shore of the Mississippi. Though it was late, he hadn't seen anyone board the bus to leave. Was there some sort of overnight special with the hotel? Why else would it still be so crowded?

This wasn't going well at all. Walter's fingers massaged his temples, the beginnings of a caffeine-induced anxiety headache making his eyeballs throb. Was it the weekend already? He couldn't remember. The last few days—on the run with little sleep and strung out on coffee and junk food—were a blur to his hazy memory, and he realized he didn't even know what day of the week it was.

Another hotel room light snapped on high up on his side of the parking lot. Between a number of partially closed curtains, he could see that many of the rooms had their lights on. Whether the guests had returned to their rooms for the evening or were still in the casino, though, he couldn't say.

An uneasy feeling crept over him, like a spider crawling up the back of his neck. The original plan was to come to the casino, lose himself in the crowd, and hopefully make a few bucks. But the thought of him trapped in an overflowing crowd, getting pushed and shoved around while the other patrons squeezed closer and closer, made cold sweat burst out on his forehead and trickle down his spine.

It was suddenly more than he could handle. Walter threw the gearshift into drive. Whatever opportunity awaited him, he knew he wouldn't find it here tonight.

At that moment, however, a security vehicle came around the other side of the hotel. Fighting the urge to peel out of there, he slowly drove up and down a couple of aisles, turning his head away from the vehicle as if he were searching for an open space. When he reached the front of the lot, he furtively glanced in the rearview mirror and saw to his relief that the security officer wasn't paying him any attention. His breath came out in a grateful rush. He had to get a grip.

Heart pounding and arms jittery with fear, he turned left onto the road, following the path of the departing bus. Walter's hands clutched the steering wheel so hard his knuckles turned white. Leaning forward to peer out the windshield, he flipped on the defroster to clear the glass. The last thing he needed now was another close call.

Driving north, in the triangle of his headlight beams, Walter saw that one side of the road was bordered by steep hills with winter-bare trees and limestone bluffs; while on the other, the shoreline wove in and out. Sometimes the great river came within feet of the elevated road, but at others it extended out enough to allow a Bed and Breakfast or two to be squeezed in, often at the top of a rise that was bordered by a wall of rocks and boulders to protect against any surge or rise in the water. In the glow of the buildings' lights, he could see a sheet of ice extend from the shoreline out into the river.

Walter pulled into one of the B&B lots, his tires scrunching on the pavement. Between two mounds of asphalt-peppered plowed snow, he saw a rusted metal railing leading down to a private boat dock. He momentarily thought about staying at the B&B for the night, an easy jaunt back to the casino tomorrow; but one glance into the lobby with its large green ferns in polished brass pots and a glass-faced cabinet filled with wine bottles told him he'd stick out like a sore thumb. And judging from some of the activities of the shadows on the thin curtains, a single old man like himself would not be welcome.

A wave of sadness swept over him, enhanced by exhaustion from the adrenaline wearing off. He ran a hand over his stubbled chin. He and Dottie used to go to places like this, little romantic getaways where they'd sip cocktails while watching the sun set over the waters, and make love in four-poster beds with over-stuffed feather pillows after relaxing in the hot tub.

His eyes watered. "I don't belong here," he said, his voice raspy in the lonely darkness. He punched the steering wheel. *Goddamn you, Harris!* Blinking back tears, he spun out of the parking lot and turned back the way he'd come, feeling life always steered him in the wrong direction no matter what way he turned.

The rain began to fall in earnest now, the occasional sleet particle pinging off the glass between the heavy drops splattering the windshield. He turned the wipers on high and shifted uncomfortably in his seat. He needed to take a leak. He thought about stopping at the casino's hotel and running inside to use the restroom, but nixed that idea when he saw the security vehicle was still patrolling the lot. Gritting his teeth, he drove past and continued on.

South of the casino the Mississippi curved, and the road rounded a bend. About a hundred yards beyond, along another rise, Walter spotted about a dozen cars parked haphazardly between the side of the road and the graveled shoreline. Whether they belonged to gambling addicts or those desperate enough to walk all the way back to the casino along an unlighted stretch of highway, he simply didn't care. He grabbed the first open spot, shut off the engine, and ran to the river's edge, his fumbling fingers getting the zipper open just in time. The strong, coffee-concentrated smell of urine wafted up as his bladder gratefully relaxed.

The freezing rain pelted his face. "Could be worse," he said, a harsh laugh escaping his throat, the relief and exhaustion making him chuckle at the memory of the grave-robbing scene from *Young Frankenstein*. But then, zipping his pants up, he realized that no, no it couldn't be. On the run from the police, almost out of money, and taking a piss in the middle of nowhere while the rain soaked him to the skin, Walter knew he was nearing the end of his rope.

How much longer can this go on? His unanswered prayers and hopes washing away in the rain, he felt even Dottie had forsaken him. How much worse could it possibly get?

Not much was the only answer that came to him.

Walter turned and squinted into the darkness. Off to his left, past a few more cars and an empty space large enough for one more, stood a pile of discarded railroad ties and wooden pallets stacked so haphazardly he thought the entire lot might be intended for a bonfire. Across the road, mounds of dirty snow surrounded a pile of rusty I-beams and steel girders. He wondered if the casino had wanted to build another hotel there and either the funding or the interest had dried up in the sagging economy, and the developers decided to abandon everything, leaving it all behind to rot.

Walter filled with despair. He understood how someone could give up in the face of a hopeless situation.

A barge horn sounded out on the waters. He walked to the edge. The wind blew freezing rain in his face, and he shielded his eyes with his hand. The cold was getting to him. His bones ached and his joints felt like they had sand in them. He stood on the brink, looking down. The boulder-strewn embankment dropped twenty feet to a layer of ice that extended out into the dark flowing river. He kicked a loose stone over the edge and watched it bounce on the ice and slide into the unforgiving waters.

He swallowed the lump in his throat. It would be so easy, he thought. One step and it'd all be over. He'd feel the pain of crashing through the ice, the chill of the icy waters soaking his clothes and pulling him under, gagging as the water rushed into his nose and mouth, his lungs freezing as they desperately ached for air, instinctively struggling as he sank deeper and deeper until his chest squeezed tight as the numbness crept in from his fingers and toes, and he floated away in darkness . . .

Yes, it would be so easy. And why not? Life no longer held a purpose for him. Tonight had only served to remind him how the times of romance and laughter and fun were all behind him, his life leading to this very moment, left alone in a place so abandoned that even the casino had given up on it.

The rain ran down his cheeks. Overwhelming sadness, like a hand, reached inside his chest and squeezed his heart as he stared down into the abyss. Maybe it was for the best, he decided. Walter twisted the wedding band on his finger, then lifted his foot, his joints cracking in the cold. A little pain awaited him, but so much less than Dottie had had to endure. He turned himself over to her spirit and guidance. Soon it would all be over and he could be with her again.

Go on. Lift it higher. That's right. Now lean forward, just a little bit more—

A flash of light and the grumble of an engine, and Walter ducked down, his on-the-run instincts automatically kicking in. A car rounded the bend from the casino, heading his way. He scrambled along the ridge and dove behind the pallets and railroad ties. His heart raced as the car approached and came to a stop a few yards away.

Had the security officer spotted him? Did they call the cops?

The car shifted gear and pulled into the vacant space on the other side of the rotting wooden ties and pallets. Walter crawled on his elbows and knees to the riverside edge of the pile. Some of the ties stuck out unevenly, and he could see between the protruding ends that they'd backed the car in. His view was directly lined up with the rear bumper.

The driver killed the engine, and the red taillights winked out. Walter heard the doors open, then close, and two people walked around to the back of the car, their shoes crunching the gravel beneath. They stopped at the top of the embankment. Walter covered his mouth to hide the vapor clouds from his breath as just a few feet away, two men wearing long dark trench coats stared down into the river.

"This is good," he heard one of the men say. "Denny'll like it. Close enough to send a message. Whenever they find it."

"What about the ice?" said the other.

The first one put his foot up against a basketball-sized rock and pushed. Walter heard the rock clacking and bouncing over others on the way down, followed by a groaning thud and sliding sound.

"Well, fuck me."

"Try this one." They both leaned against the largest boulder at the top and were rewarded by a series of cracks and a splash. "Now we're in business. Open the trunk."

Keys jingled. Walter saw the man nearest to him aim the remote at the trunk and the lid popped. The trunk light illuminated the men's faces when they lifted the lid and peered inside. Both men were clean-shaven, but the driver had a square face with a cleft chin and a Roman nose, while the passenger had beady eyes that were too close together and a port-wine stain under his left ear.

"Grab that end," the driver said, and with a couple of grunts and groans, they hefted something out of the trunk. Walter saw it was about six-feet long and wrapped in black landscaping tarp and was heavy enough to sag in the middle between them. A prickling sensation ran up his spine. He clenched his teeth to keep them from chattering.

But as they lowered the bundle, the sagging middle hit the bumper, and Port Wine lost his grip, dropping his end. The bundle landed hard and the tarp fell partially open, exposing a hand and a forearm wearing a white shirt with a black armband.

Walter's blood froze.

"Careful, willya!" the driver snapped. Port Wine quickly closed the tarp and lifted his end, and the men carried their package to the edge of the brink. They swung it back and forth, and on three, let it fly. A heart-wrenching moment later Walter heard a splash below.

"Nothin' but net," the driver said.

Port Wine slammed the trunk shut, then suddenly stood perfectly still. "Hold on. You smell that?" He walked a few feet away and sniffed the air. "Jesus, somebody took a piss out here."

"Animals. Shows you what kind of people they attract. You watch: Denny won't put up with that shit." His keys jingled again. "C'mon, let's get out of here."

The doors slammed and the engine roared to life.

Walter scrambled around the pile. The car hesitated a moment as if the men were debating which way to go, and he got a good look at the license plate before the men turned north, heading back toward the casino. He waited until he could no longer see the taillights, then crawled to the edge and peered over the embankment. A large black hole in the ice showed him where the men's delivery had gone through.

He shivered as the wind blew freezing rain in his face. Any personal thoughts of plunging into the murky depths were gone.

Walter got in his car and drove south, shaking from more than the cold.

CHAPTER TWENTY-ONE

ADAC Security Systems, Inc. was located in a strip mall off Orland Avenue in Glencrest. The door beeped when they entered. Wall-mounted cameras with red recording indicators aimed down at them from the upper corners of the tiny reception area. Off-white, floor-to-ceiling vertical blinds protected the black leather couch and chairs and the glass and chrome coffee and end tables from direct sunlight. Framed posters of home and business security products and glowing reviews from satisfied customers, law enforcement, and techno magazines adorned the walls. Opposite the window, a receptionist sat behind a glassed-in partition, next to which was a locked door leading to the interior of the store. The office smelled of ammonia window cleaner.

"May I help you?" the receptionist said, setting aside the magazine she was reading. When the detectives showed her their shields, she stood, sliding the glass window farther open. "Oh, of course. Mark'll be with you in a minute. He's just finishing up with a client."

She reached out and shook their hands. Her blue manicured nails were painted the same color as her outfit, which also matched the color of her eyes. Her blond hair was frosted and her teeth were bleached, cosmetically hiding her true age somewhere between forty and fifty, but she wore only a hint of makeup and her smile was warm and genuine.

"I'm Ruth. Can I get you some coffee while you wait?"

"No thanks, really. We're fine." Capparelli pointed to a stack of women's magazines on the corner of her desk. "My ex-wife used to read those things religiously. I swear, her mood depended upon whether or not the celebrity couple of the month was happy or not."

"Oh, please," Ruth said. "Like anything they do affects my life." She randomly picked a magazine from the middle of the pile and handed it to Capparelli. "Go on, test me. Pick any article, and we'll see how I do."

"I, um, really don't think . . ."

"C'mon. It'll be fun while we wait."

After he picked an article and glanced through it, she tapped a dramatic finger on her chin and pretended to ponder it seriously.

"Let's see. Our featured star had a difficult childhood and had to overcome some heartbreaking trauma that still haunts her to this very day. But she's tough and she persevered, and except for that embarrassing little incident her publicist made go away, she's never been happier. In fact, she recently met the love of her life, her true soul mate, just in time for the premiere of her new movie. *And*," she added, leaning forward conspiratorially, "there's even talk of children in the future."

Capparelli was impressed. "Hey, you're good."

Ruth waved his words away as if it were nothing, really; but her eyes sparkled with his compliment. "It's always the same. I swear, all they do is change the name every month." Her laugh was bright and infectious.

The door next to them opened suddenly and a man in a black overcoat glanced their way, then pulled on his gloves and exited the store. Riehle grabbed the inner door to keep it from closing, as a deep baritone voice from the intercom at the receptionist's desk said, "Is this chit-chat time or can we get a little work done around here?"

Ruth covered the speaker with her hand, whispering, "His bark is worse than his bite. Honestly, he'd be lost without me." She winked. "Go on in."

"She seems nice," Riehle said, as they made their way down the hall to the owner's office.

His cheeks slightly red, Capparelli grunted. "Yeah, I suppose."

From the gruffness of the voice over the intercom, Riehle half-expected Mark Bernstein to be a pudgy, greasy-haired man in a wife-beater T-shirt, when in fact he turned out to be a tall, skinny computer geek with sandy hair and frameless glasses with rectangular-shaped lenses. He wore a black, long-sleeved shirt buttoned to the neck, designer jeans, and high-top sneakers. His grip was firm when they shook hands, and the pupils of his brown eyes were pinpoints, making Riehle wonder if the man was on amphetamines.

"I appreciate your calling ahead, but can I see some identification first?" Bernstein studied their photo IDs and shields before he took the slip of paper with Walter's name, address, phone number, and security system's serial and model numbers written on it.

"Have a seat," Bernstein said, indicating two client chairs that matched the style of those in his reception area. He sat down at his kidney-shaped glass desk, tapped on his keyboard, and brought Buczyno's account up on the computer screen. "So what do you want to know?"

"Name doesn't ring a bell?" Riehle said. "The house in Westbrook with the bodies buried in the crawlspace?"

"That's him? Really?" Bernstein sat up straighter, his interest piqued. He squinted at the screen and tapped his keyboard. In the reflection off his glasses, Riehle saw an image enlarge. "Man, you'd never guess he was that kind of guy just by looking at him."

"So you remember him?"

"Not by appearance. Let me see what kind of system he had." He chewed a thumbnail while his eyes scanned the specifics in the file. "Says here we installed the system about five years ago, and—oh, wait. Sure, I remember now."

"Something unusual?"

"Most of our clients want something unusual," he said. "That's our niche. You want a few standard package systems with some customized features, you go to the big guys. You want something tweaked, you come to us." His eyes narrowed. "Nothing illegal, detectives. It's just how we survive in a very competitive marketplace."

"We're not suggesting otherwise. All we want to do is understand what kind of system Buczyno had and why he felt the need for it. And anything else you can tell us about him."

Bernstein shrugged. "Why does anyone need a security system? Personally, I think everyone ought to have one."

"It's certainly made our job easier," Riehle agreed, trying to get the guy to open up more. "But what can you tell us about him?"

"Almost nothing. In my job, people tend to look alike after a while. It's the technology that fascinates me."

"Then what made his system so different that you remember it five years later?" Capparelli said.

"Because I had a blast setting it up." Bernstein pulled his chair closer to the monitor. "It was really cool. One of the first I did like this. A very simple, straightforward wireless system. No audible alarms. No local police, fire, or emergency notification or to any private security company. Just a signal transmitted to a remote receiver."

"That didn't strike you as odd?"

"Odd's my business. What do I care why someone wants his system a certain way? That's why they come to me. All he wanted were touch pads for the front and back doors, and sensors on all the windows and doors that set off an alarm in his watch."

Capparelli sat forward. "His what?"

Bernstein smiled. "That was the cool part. It looks like a regular digital sports watch. But I replaced the original face with a new one and added some microchips and a vibrating mechanism to the workings. Now, if someone tries to break into his house, his watch alerts him."

"How so?" Riehle said.

"The sensors transmit two distinct signals. The first is a contact sensor. If anything touches the window or door, a signal is transmitted to the watch, making it vibrate. Pressing the crystal will display a red LED number on the face corresponding to which door or window was touched." He rolled his eyes. "We spent a *lot* of time calibrating the sensors so they wouldn't go off by rain or wind or small animals."

"And the second?"

"Is an intermittent vibration. A broken or opened window or door will transmit that signal, and pushing the crystal here will also tell you where the breach occurred. In other words, it means someone's inside your house."

"You can do that?"

"Are you kidding? You can do almost anything with a couple of microchips. Have you seen the things they're doing with kids' toys lately?"

"So let me get this straight," Riehle said. "You designed a security system that tells a man when someone is breaking into his house while he's still inside it?"

"Or outside."

"Excuse me?"

"The signal transmits outside the house, too."

"How far?" Riehle said sharply, thinking that was how Buczyno knew they'd been in his house and why he'd skipped his flight and made a run for it.

"Not far. Only about a hundred yards. That way if he was on his way home from the store or something, he'd know ahead of time if someone had broken in."

"Or broken out," Capparelli said, his tone low and threatening.

Bernstein's eyes darted back and forth between the detectives, his pupils widening with comprehension. He put his hands up between them. "Whoa, hey. I just made the system the way he wanted it. I didn't know how he was going to use it."

"You didn't think it was a little weird?"

"Weird? You want weird? You oughta see some of the stuff I've designed for people. As far as I could tell, this system was set up to let a guy know if his home had been violated. That's all. What he did with it after that, I had no idea. Honest."

"Then you won't mind explaining to our computer expert exactly how this system was designed." Riehle wrote down Nielsen's name and number, then gave him one of his own cards as well. "And if we have any follow-up questions, you'll cooperate to the fullest. Correct? Because we'd hate to have to get a warrant to examine those other systems."

Bernstein swallowed hard. "No problem, man. Take what you need."

"A complete printout of Buczyno's file will do nicely for a start."

Their next stop was Middaugh Hospital. Dixie had called to tell them that Benito Salinas was out of ICU, and Riehle and Capparelli wanted to talk to him personally. When they arrived, they saw that Mary had pulled the room's only cushioned chair over to the space between the window and Benito's bed, and she sat there holding his hand. Foil "Get Well Soon!" balloons on plastic

posts stuck out of the numerous floral and plant arrangements
that filled the shelves on both sides of the room. The first bed in
the room was empty, and a nurse wearing teddy bear scrubs
stood between the beds with her back to the door, changing his
IV bag.

Riehle knocked on the door, and the detectives introduced
themselves. "We were hoping you'd feel well enough to ask you
a few questions."

The nurse looked like she was about to send them away, but
Mary invited them in. Riehle and Capparelli stood at the foot of
the bed. The TV was off, and the only sounds in the room were
the whoosh of warm air from the heating vents and the weak
and slightly uneven beeps of Benito's heart rhythm pattern on
the monitor. The room smelled of freshly cut flowers and
disinfectant.

After hanging the new IV bag, the nurse turned to the detectives. She held her hand up in front of their faces, the fingers
splayed. "Five minutes," she said, her tone an uncompromising
warning. "He just came down from ICU this morning and isn't
stable yet. Don't you *dare* do anything to upset him." She didn't
leave the room until after they assured her they wouldn't.

Benito lay slightly propped up in the bed, a rumpled sheet
covering him to the middle of his chest. He held Mary's right
hand with his left, while his right rested on top of the sheet, the
back of which was covered with a giant purple bruise around
where the IV needle was inserted. The fluorescent light above
the headboard accented the hollows in his cheeks, and though
his pasty skin draped across his bones as if all the fat in his
body had been sucked out, Mary somehow looked the worse for
wear. Her complexion was pale and sallow, and the sockets
around her red-rimmed eyes were sunken and dark. She looked
as if she hadn't slept or changed her clothes in days. Her thinning hair was a wild mess, as if she kept combing it with her

fingers out of frustration, worry, or simply not knowing what else to do.

Riehle's old fear of hospitals erupted in goose bumps across his shoulders and the back of his neck. He hoped they were monitoring Mary's condition as well.

"What did you want?" Mary asked. Her voice was hoarse from exhaustion and crying, and Riehle regretted disturbing them so soon after Benito's transfer out of ICU. "We already told everything to that redheaded police woman—I'm sorry, I don't remember her name."

"Officer Claudia Dixon. Dixie, for short."

She shook her head as if to clear her thoughts. "I'm not sure what else we can tell you, then."

Riehle shoved his hands in his overcoat pockets, uncertain what to do with them. If he were a patrolman, he'd probably twist his cap in his hands. "We'll make this quick, I promise. We're very sorry for everything you've had to go through. I imagine it was quite a shock."

Benito nodded weakly. "We've lived next door to Walter for more than thirty years." The heart monitor blipped with an irregular beat, and three pairs of eyes darted to the screen. Riehle held his breath until he watched the following beats return to normal. Benito squeezed Mary's hand reassuringly. "We never expected anything like this from him."

"Did you ever notice any changes in his personality?" Capparelli asked softly, as if lowering his voice might somehow cushion the impact of their questions. "Mood swings, things like that?"

"He had a very difficult time after Dottie died," Mary said.

"We understand she had cancer."

Mary nodded. "When it was all over, we tried to get Walter to move to Arizona or Florida, someplace far away. We thought it would be best for him to get away from the things that reminded him of all he'd been through. But he wouldn't hear of it. He said the expenses had drained their savings—bankrupted them, really—and he wouldn't have been able to afford to move even if he'd wanted to."

"He was depressed then."

Benito gave them an odd look. "Well, I should say so."

"What about changes in behavior?" Riehle asked.

"It's hard to say, since he kept to himself for a long time afterward," Mary said. "He practically became a hermit. Stayed indoors, let the yard go to seed, hardly even said hello when he went out to get the paper or take out the garbage. We were very worried. He and Dottie were like family to us. But we thought he just needed time alone to deal with everything that had happened to Dottie."

"It took him about a year to snap out of it," Benito said. "I'd been encouraging him to pick up his woodworking again, anything to get his mind off what they'd been through, and he finally got into it with a real zest. He redid everything in the living and dining rooms. Chopped up and burned the old furniture and handcrafted new ones, painted the rooms—you name it."

"How quickly did you notice this change?"

"Practically overnight," Mary said. "We woke up one morning and he was hauling in new wood. After that, he became more like his old self again. Then he did the same thing again last summer. We asked him why he didn't donate the furniture to a homeless shelter, but he said destroying it helped him deal with his frustrations." She shrugged. "How could we argue with that?"

"What'd he do after destroying that first set of furniture?"

"Started right in on the yard. By the end of the summer, it was the best-looking house in the neighborhood." Benito rubbed his chest. "Almost made it look too good. You can see our houses from the Tri-State, and our neighborhood isn't what it used to be. I kept after him to put bars on the windows or to get an alarm system like everyone else, but he wouldn't hear of it—so you can imagine my surprise when I saw he had one. I'd warned him that we'd been robbed a couple of times, but all he ever said was that a man's home is his castle, and he had a right to protect it any way he wanted."

Benito rubbed his chest again. He rested his head back against the pillow and exhaled deeply. Mary's eyes pleaded with them.

"Just a couple more questions, Mr. and Mrs. Salinas, and then we'll leave. I understand you discovered the first body." Riehle wasn't sure how much they knew, and he wanted to ease them into it.

"Actually, the plumber did." Benito indicated a large philodendron plant in a wicker basket tray. "Tony's been by a few times to see how I'm doing. Poor guy had to deal with that *and* with me."

"Yes, he was quite shaken. So you're aware there were other bodies?"

"Hard not to," he said wearily. "It's been all over the news."

Good point. "Did you ever notice any increase in traffic around Walter's house? Young boys coming to visit?"

Benito's heart rate sped up. "No, no," he insisted. "*Nothing* like that. Walter isn't anything like how the news is trying to portray him." His face winced in pain. "Hasn't Walter suffered enough already? He's a good man, I tell you. A good man." Perspiration broke out on his forehead.

"Mr. Salinas, do the names Alan Wilson, Danny Sanchez, or Franklin Edward Harris mean anything to you?"

His heartbeat spiked, then fluctuated erratically, the green line on the monitor suddenly bouncing all over the place. Mary jumped to her feet, frantically pushing the nurse's call button as Benito leaned forward, clutching his chest. Footsteps slapped in the hall and doctors and nurses rushed in, pushing him back down onto the bed and drawing the curtain closed around his bed, while the nurse with the teddy bear scrubs furiously pushed them out of the room.

"Goddammit! I *told* you not to upset him!" she yelled, slamming the door in their faces.

The detectives stood there, thunderstruck. Riehle's own heart beat wildly in his chest. Angry nurses and curious patients up and down the hallway stared at them.

"What have we done?" Riehle said.

Capparelli's face flushed.

"Nothing, I hope. But I think we'd better get the hell out of here."

They rode back to the station in silence, both of them lost in their shared concerns and fears. When they arrived, the detectives found a message from the coroner waiting for them. Riehle sucked in his breath.

"Griskel confirmed three of the Missing Person files. He wanted to talk to you about them," Nielsen said.

Relieved, Capparelli snatched the memo slip out of his hand. "Fantastic. Thanks, we could use some good news." He looked at his watch and groaned. "Damn, it's after five."

"Can't hurt to give it a try," Riehle said, sitting on the edge of his desk and pushing the phone toward him.

He punched in the number. "Hello, this is Detective Ray Capparelli from the Westbrook PD. Dr. Griskel called while we were out and I'm returning his call—" He made a sour face and dropped his hand down by his side. Riehle heard laughter coming from the other end of the line.

After a moment, Capparelli lifted the receiver back to his ear. "Yes, I'm sure you've been wanting to say that all day . . . Uh-uh

. . . Okay, we'll check it . . . Just leave a message that we'll call him in the morning . . . Thanks."

Capparelli slammed down the phone. Riehle bit his cheek, trying to hold it in; but the look on Capparelli's face, added with the unexpected turn from the stressful events of the day, was too much for him, and the grateful laughter and tension burst out of him like water from a broken dam.

"Elvis already left the building?"

"Am I the only one who didn't see that coming?" Capparelli gruffly pulled his chair away from his desk, sat down, and turned on his computer screen, trying to hide the smirk on his own face. "His secretary says they e-mailed us copies of the preliminary reports."

Back to business, Riehle leaned over his shoulder as Capparelli opened the attachments. "Yeah, here we go." His finger tapped the monitor. "Hair and clothing samples found with the bodies, along with an evaluation of the bones corresponds with the age, gender, and clothing last seen worn by Wilson, Sanchez, and Harris in their Missing Persons reports. He recommends DNA testing to be sure, but we'll have to contact the families either way."

"Anything on the unidentified body?"

Capparelli scanned the report. "Short blond hair, black concert T-shirt, blue jeans. Bones indicate a male, age eighteen to twenty-five. Silver ball stud found in the mouth—probably a tongue piercing. Griskel estimates the body was in the crawl-space about five years or more. He included photos of the silver stud and portions of the T-shirt that still had designs on them."

"Gives us something to go on, at least. We can backtrack through the reports and see what matches up."

While the printer made copies of the report and photos, Riehle said, "I'll notify the Hobart and Merrillville, Indiana PD. Why don't you find the address for Harris's mother and we'll take a trip out there."

"Sure thing. But man, I'm not looking forward to that. Especially after what happened to Benito. Think we ought to call and see how he's doing?"

"Better not. I'll call Jenny Gavin later and find out how he is." Riehle ran a weary hand through his hair. "Let's just get this over with, go see Harris's mother, and call it a day."

"Sounds good. Although . . ."

"What?"

Capparelli tapped his fingers on the desk. "I know it's been a long day, but . . . you up for a stakeout?"

CHAPTER TWENTY-TWO

The casino was less crowded the next night. Walter wandered aimlessly around, searching for something to spark his enthusiasm. Or at least explain what the hell he was doing here. After watching the two men throw the body into the Mississippi River the previous night, anyone else in his right mind would have quickly gotten as far away as possible. Especially when Walter realized the dead man had worked here. Seeing the casino employees in their Wild West–themed white shirts and black armbands—the very outfit the man was wearing—had been a shock. Knowing that any sudden startled movements would only attract attention, it took every ounce of energy not to run right out of there. His mind raced with panicked thoughts. *What if the police caught him here? Would they blame that murder on him too?* But ever since he saw the commercial on TV, and even at the risk of being spotted by security (or worse, the killers themselves), Walter found himself inexplicably drawn here. He needed to know why.

In the far corner away from the main bar stood dispensers for complimentary soft drinks, coffee, and hot chocolate. Walter grabbed a white foam cup off the top of the tower and, tired of all the coffee he'd been having lately, helped himself to some hot chocolate instead. Crossing his arms over his chest and leaning back against the cabinet, he sipped his drink while studying the casino from this particular vantage.

He was surprised at how different it was from what he'd

expected. Oh sure, it looked the same. The dealers, bartenders, and waitresses in their white shirts and armbands, the pit bosses and security in their red velvet Wild West saloon uniforms, the green felt–covered hardwood gaming tables and stools, the wagon wheel chandeliers hanging from the lofty ceiling, and the people sitting around the gaming tables and multicolored slot machines with flashing lights—all of that was just like in the commercial.

What surprised him was how *quiet* it was. Which wasn't to say it was silent. Not by any means. People shouting drink orders or talking among themselves, trying to be heard over the TVs at the bar and those suspended above the gaming tables or the satellite radio tuned to a classic rock station emitting from hidden speakers. However, instead of being brash and loud the noise was more subdued, as if within a bubble. What seemed to be missing was the excitement shown in the commercials.

Walter mentally shrugged. Maybe it was an off night. Or maybe last night held more of what the commercials promised. But he couldn't help noticing the difference in the patrons. The commercials advertised the casino as a hip place where younger groups of couples dressed to the nines or in business casual huddled around the gaming tables or slot machines that gushed coins, young people who jumped and shouted with exuberance whenever someone won every few seconds. In truth, however, most of the people here tonight were Walter's age or older. They sat quietly in front of their favorite games, wearing blue jeans and sweatshirts or faded wool sweaters, and fur-lined boots on their feet. Some in wheelchairs even had blankets folded over their laps as extra protection against chilly winter drafts.

The few younger people in attendance were scattered around, mainly at the slot machines. Most were alone, but a number of couples sat together. They wore clothes similar to their older counterparts, though a few of the women wore T-shirts and many of the unshaven men had ball caps on their heads. Their drinks from the bar rested on the machines, or were held in their left hands while the right fed the one-armed bandits and pulled the levers or pushed the various buttons. Their eyes, red and watery from the alcohol or the smoke rising from the lit cigarettes dangling from their lips, conveyed more hope and desperation than excitement.

Even the slots were different. Instead of the loud bell-ringing, coin-clacking-in-metal-tray noises he expected, the machines emitted glub-glub sounds as if they were all underwater, and whirred as printed receipts issued whatever someone won.

Where was the fun in that?

No, Walter simply didn't understand the attraction to places like this. Still, he couldn't shake the feeling that he needed to be here tonight and was frustrated because he didn't know why. He wasn't sure if it was his own last act of desperation, and a deeper part of him regretted that he hadn't jumped into the river last night, ending all his uncertainty.

An elderly couple approached. A woman with sparse gray hair and wearing thick tortoiseshell glasses sat in a wheelchair being pushed by a tall, stooped man with a shock of white hair. Their coats were folded in her lap, and her arms rested on top of them, trembling slightly. The man brought the wheelchair to a stop in front of the drink dispensers. Walter started to move aside, when out of the corner of his eye he saw a security man looking their way.

He turned to the aging couple. "Here, let me help." After asking what they wanted, Walter poured two cups of hot chocolate for them.

The gentleman took both cups and set them on the counter-top. "Thank you." His voice was soft and hoarse. He cleared his throat and pointed to row of plastic lids and a container of straws. "If you'd be so kind."

Walter watched as the husband slowly and deliberately placed the lids on the cups. He peeled away a perforated opening for one, then poked a straw through the X in the middle of the other and gave it to his wife. Her hand shook when she reached for it. Gently holding her hand, he guided it to the cup and helped her bring the straw to her mouth. She took a sip, then tilted her head back and smiled up at him. Their eyes locked for a moment, and though it was obvious he spent most of his time now taking care of her, the expressions on their faces could only be described as a contented serenity, as if all the promises made on their wedding day for their life together had indeed come true.

Walter felt something wrench inside him.

"Marge. George. How're you doing tonight?" The security man had come up beside them. He stood a few inches taller than Walter. The fabric of his red uniform was stretched over a muscled frame that hinted he might have played football in high school or college. His short brown hair had a severe widow's peak that made Walter think of vampires. The security badge worn around his neck displayed a recent photo and identified him as *Ernie*.

They exchanged pleasantries for a few moments, Ernie asking about an upcoming visit from the grandkids and Marge wanting to know how Ernie's date with the waitress from the restaurant went, before the security man turned to Walter.

"And how about you, sir?"

"Me?"

"Having a good time?"

Walter's hand tensed around the cup. It suddenly occurred to him that he might have been recognized and that Ernie was distracting him while the police moved in behind him, ready to arrest him on the spot. He fought the urge to glance over his shoulder, and it took all of his will to keep his face expressionless and look Ernie straight in the eyes. Sweat rolled down from his armpits.

"Absolutely," he somehow managed to say.

"Good. Y'all take care. Anything you need, just give a holler." Ernie patted Marge on the shoulder. "And little sips now, Marge. We don't want you burning the roof of your mouth again."

Ernie winked at them before moving on, and after George and Marge left for their favorite slots, Walter breathed a sigh of relief. He wiped the cold sweat off his forehead with the back of his hand. He wanted to get the hell out of there, but knew if he headed for the exit right now it would only attract attention. Best to pretend he was having a good time.

But where to go? He finished his hot chocolate and stuffed the empty cup in the trash bin under the countertop; then, trying to give the impression that he was searching for his favorite game, Walter made another tour of the place. Starting at the front, the glass doors to the building opened into a long, wide vestibule. To the left were the gift shop and a fancy restaurant, while an elevator and a set of escalators to the right led up to the landing where the ramp from the hotel emptied out. The remainder of the second floor was filled with a sports bar, a franchise sandwich shop, and a giant ballroom with a concert stage. Walter wondered if the chandeliers swayed when the people danced or jumped up and down to the music.

The main design, however, was to draw patrons into the casino, and just beyond the security guard station and a row of turnstiles, the entryway opened up into a cavernous room filled with every imaginable distraction intended to keep people there as long as possible to continue spending their money. It amazed him how much stuff could be crammed in while still appearing spacious. The gaming tables extended in two rows on either side of the center aisle from just beyond the security guard station to the large cashier's window along the back wall. They had all the expected ones like blackjack, roulette, and Texas Hold'Em, but there were a few surprises as well. Like some of the poker tables. He figured Mississippi Stud and Flop Poker were variations, but what the hell was Pai Gow? Giant flat-screen TVs showing sports events and CNN Headline News were suspended above the gaming tables in quad-box forms that reminded Walter of miniature versions of the scoreboard at the United Center. Several bars were located strategically around the room, but the main peninsula-shaped bar was located at the front. A door behind the bar led into the fancy restaurant on the other side. A large flat-screen TV was centered above the displayed bottles, and several additional smaller TVs hung from the lowered ceiling above the peninsula-extension of the bar. The far walls along the room's perimeter also held numerous TV screens, but these only displayed advertisements for upcoming concerts, their restaurants, and gaming best odds, and photographs of some of the casino's biggest money winners and how much they won. There was also a private VIP lounge, bar, and High Stakes blackjack table; a sushi and buffet room; a snack bar; another fancy restaurant; an open doorway that led to a non-smoking room; restrooms worthy of a five-star hotel; and numerous ATM and ticket redemption machines.

But mostly, the casino was filled with slot machines.

And such variety! In addition to the expected sevens, BARs, and fruits, there were monsters, pharaohs, Arabian princesses, Trojan warriors, wildlife, and mermaids. Some were based on movies, like *Alien* and *The Creature from the Black Lagoon*, even *The Godfather* and *The Wizard of Oz*, while others on TV shows (*The Price is Right* and *Wheel of Fortune* he expected, but *Sex and the City*, *The Monkees*, and, especially, *That Girl* took him by surprise). It seemed anything could be transformed into a slot machine nowadays. All flashing lights and dinging and whirring and glub-glubbing with promises of great rewards.

Walking down the aisles and around the various back-to-back rows and four-machine islands of slots, their rotating screens on top and flashing lights enticing him, Walter felt a compelling urge to choose a machine and play. But which one? There were so many. He glanced surreptitiously at the seated patrons to see what types of slot themes they preferred. Most simply ignored him as if he wasn't there, while a few glared suspiciously at him when he passed, their bleary eyes warning him to stay away from their guarded secrets and impending fortunes.

He finally chose one in the first open row he found. Taking a dollar from his wallet, Walter slid the bill into the machine and, seeing this one didn't have a lever, pushed the button instead. The pictures spun and came to a stop on a combination of three different fruit. He thought he'd lost, but the machine clicked and whirred, and spit out a voucher saying he'd won fifty cents.

Walter stared at the piece of paper. People came from all around for this? It had all the excitement and fanfare of getting a ticket for a parking garage. He put in four more bills, just to be sure he hadn't missed something, and got back a grand total of two dollars and seventy-five cents in winnings. The machine glub-glubbed some more, encouraging him to try again, but he couldn't shake the feeling that it was sticking its tongue out at him whenever it printed his receipt.

He came all the way here for this? Disgusted, Walter got up from his seat. Almost tearing up the vouchers, he thought, what the hell? Money's money. Too embarrassed to present such a small amount to the woman at the cashier's window, though, he slid the vouchers into a nearby ticket redemption machine and collected his meager winnings that way.

Stuffing the change in his pocket, he turned as a sudden commotion arose at the bar. The patrons were leaning forward on their seats, their eyes riveted to the TV screens and shouting at each other to "Shut up already. I'm trying to listen here!" Using the remote, the bartender raised the volume high enough to drown out their voices. People stood, some even leaving their precious slots for a better look. Walter hurried over.

Squeezing into an opening at the back of the crowd, he tapped the shoulder of one of the men sitting at the bar. "What's happening?"

"They're about to announce the verdict."

"For what?"

The man looked at him as if he were crazy. "The Renwick case. Whaddaya think?"

Walter stared at the screen. At that moment CNN switched from a split screen of the anchor and a reporter standing outside the courthouse to a full screen of the defendant, flanked on either side by his lawyers, rising for the verdict. A strip ran across the bottom of the screen reviewing the pertinent, sensational details of the case and announcing that the jury had returned.

When the defendant lifted his head to face the jury, though, it all came back to him. The celebrity trial of the month. The famous young actor accused of raping the overzealous fan. The prosecution's case included positive DNA results, the woman's toxicology reports showing traces of Ecstasy and a blood-alcohol level of twice the legal limit, and a digital video recording a friend of the actor had made during the act (that was later downloaded off the Internet by millions of voyeurs) showing Renwick writing the titles of his movies on the nearly-comatose victim's body with her own lipstick while he thrust himself inside her. The defense had argued that the woman was a deranged stalker who forced herself on him, promising to leave him alone forever if he would only fulfill her fantasy of making love to her; her body, the video, and his semen the ultimate trophies for his most ardent and devoted fan.

Sickened by the audacity of the defense attorney and the cheering fans outside the courtroom who daily wept and prayed for the smug, sadistic heartthrob, Walter remembered first watching a news report about the progress of the trial on the night that Harris returned. How long had it been? Two weeks? Three? It felt like another lifetime.

A hush fell over the crowd. What began as disgusted raspberries soon erupted into angry cursing as the jury foreman announced "Not guilty" on all nine counts. The downtrodden patrons booed and hissed when a smiling Renwick hugged his lawyers. They ordered refills on their drinks and pushed away from the bar as the TV screen filled with the alternating images of an incredulous reporter, cheering crowds, and Renwick's attorneys addressing the media in their ridiculously expensive suits. When an insert of the blindfolded Justice statue appeared in the corner of the screen, Walter knew what had tipped the scales again.

The man sitting next to him gulped the remainder of his drink and slammed the glass down so hard the ice spilled out and bounced over the wooden bar top. He shook his head. " 'Swhat's wrong with America today," he said, before sliding off his stool and shuffling toward his own choice of an unwinnable game.

The bartender scooped up the ice cubes and tossed them into the sink. He wiped the bar with a towel. "Something you need?" he asked Walter.

"Nothing you can get me."

The bartender nodded as if he understood completely.

Walter wandered over to the non-smoking section and plopped down in one of the slot chairs. He rested his forearms on the machine. The metal was cold against his skin. On his way back he'd noticed that the gaming tables had begun to fill with younger couples laughing and drinking and cheering like in the commercials. But the excitement didn't extend to include him, and all he felt was an empty heaviness weighing him down.

He saw Ernie walk past the open doorway. Should he tell him what he saw last night, report a possible homicide? That he saw two men dump a body—one of Ernie's fellow workers—into the Mississippi River? The thought that more criminals were going free churned anger in him that he hadn't felt since Harris returned.

And yet what could he do? Walter could just imagine the confrontation. *What were you doing out there?* Ernie would say. Then he'd ask him his name and take him to the authorities. And then where would he be? They'd probably even blame the murder on him. No, no, that simply wouldn't do.

A feeling of hopelessness washed over him. It was all too much. Walter clasped his hands. Was that why Dottie had brought him here, to a casino? To see how the system protected and rewarded the privileged few? To understand how the overwhelming odds he and Helen and other victims faced were stacked against them? He squeezed his eyes shut and hung his head. Was that what she wanted to tell him? That he'd only been fooling himself? That sooner, rather than later, the cops were going to catch him, and it was only a matter of time?

He opened his eyes. So that was it then. That was what she wanted him to understand. She needed him to be strong, to stop running and take a stand. It was up to him to choose the time and place while he still had the chance. That's why she brought him here, what she wanted him to see. He understood now.

Walter stood tall. Tomorrow then, he decided. He'd have dinner and enjoy his last night's sleep as a free man, then after breakfast, turn himself in. He'd walk into the nearest police station and confess what he'd done. *I killed the burglars who broke into my home and the animal who murdered my wife.* No lawyers, no wimpy deals or plea-bargains—he wasn't a criminal. He'd stand up for what he believed in, take responsibility for his actions, and face the consequences. Be the man Dottie needed him to be.

He slapped the machine. That was it then. That was his final decision.

Walter felt like a giant weight had been lifted off his shoulders.

His legs trembled as he walked back into the main room of the casino. An odd giddiness flooded his nerve endings, a lightness of being that sapped his strength, as if making the decision had freed him. He felt exhausted. And surprisingly hungry. What should he have for his last meal? He didn't know what prison food tasted like, but imagined it somewhere between warm oatmeal and melted plastic. He wanted a dinner filled with taste sensations that he'd never be able to experience again. A medium-rare steak so pink in the middle it still oozed. He'd order it with every kind of steak sauce, Worcestershire, soy, and hot sauce they had. Imagining the look on the waitress's face, he laughed out loud. To hell with what she'd think.

What else? Garlic mashed potatoes with gobs of real melted butter. A salad filled with vegetables and diced red and green peppers and sprinkled with chopped hard-boiled eggs and bacon bits. Down it all with a couple of draft beers. Coffee with dessert, maybe chocolate cake or a crisp cinnamon apple tart with a scoop of vanilla ice cream topped with hot caramel. His mouth was watering by the time he reached the aisle with the gaming tables.

Walter took out his wallet and counted the remaining bills. Let's see: after dinner and a tip, the night's stay at the motel, and a decent breakfast in the morning he still had, oh . . . twenty bucks left. He pulled a twenty-dollar bill out and stuffed the wallet back in his pocket. He knew he'd never see the money again when he turned himself in. No sense in letting the cops have it, though.

But where should he go? Walter had never had a poker night with his buddies. He and Dottie always played euchre with Benito and Mary. So that was out. And he didn't feel like rolling the dice (how cliché would that be anyway?), or want to bother with learning how to play Texas Hold'Em. Guess that left blackjack.

He started for the cashier's window to buy some chips, but at that moment a man at the roulette table next to him walked away. When the dealer said, "Place your bets!" he seemed to be looking right at him.

Roulette? Walter thought. He shrugged. Why not?

He stepped up to the table next to a boisterous young couple who'd obviously had a few drinks. The woman wore a black cocktail dress and a single string of pearls, while the man wore a tuxedo with the bow tie untied. They touched each other so often that Walter wondered if they were on their honeymoon. He handed the dealer the twenty-dollar bill and was given a stack of blue chips in return.

Now where to put them? Fascinated, he watched how the other players positioned their bets on the layout. Some placed their chips on single numbers, while others split the bet between two neighboring numbers by putting chips on the line between them or over the corners, covering four. And some bet on a whole column, or all of red or black, or a section covering a third of the board. Most seemed to have a personal system or to play favorite numbers, but the honeymooners haphazardly placed their bets everywhere. The bride's arms swung wildly about, tossing chips all over the table and laughing at wherever the chip came to a stop, as if each number was a punch line to a joke only she and her new husband understood.

So what should he do?

Then Walter saw the number four was open.

His breath caught in his throat. Dottie's birthday was April fourth. Was *that* why she brought him here? What she'd been trying to tell him all along?

His heart pounded with hope and excitement. He knew she wanted him to trust her, to have faith and to turn himself over to her. His hands trembled as he moved his entire stack of chips. But just as he was about to bet it all on black four, the bride's arm swung wildly, banging into his hands and sending his chips cascading over the table layout, her own chip landing on the very spot he'd wanted.

Walter's jaw dropped. He stood there with his mouth hanging open. Unable to catch his breath, he couldn't make a sound.

"Omigosh!" the woman said. A drunken giggle escaped the splayed fingers covering her mouth. "I'm like soooo sorry!"

Apologizing the entire time, the young couple quickly gathered his scattered chips. Walter simply stood there, leaning his weight against the side of the table, confused and disoriented as if he'd been rudely woken from a dream. When the honeymooners placed the chips in his open hands, his fingers were numb. His head felt as if it were stuffed with cotton, and he didn't realize someone was talking to him until the husband put his hand on his shoulder.

"Are you all right, man?"

Walter nodded dumbly.

"Last chance!" the dealer called. "Place your bets!" Without thinking, Walter set his chips on the first open number he saw, and the dealer waved his hand over the table. "No more bets!"

Slowly, his mind emerged from the fog. It wasn't until the dealer spun the wheel and Walter heard the ball clatter that he realized what he'd done.

He'd put all his blue chips on green zero.

Blue. And on *zero*. The shock of what he'd done hit him like a slap in the face. Blue and zero. *Depressed,* he'd bet everything on *nothing.*

His eyes welled with tears. Dottie had indeed been trying to tell him something after all. She was telling him that his luck had finally run out.

Somewhere in the back of his mind Walter heard the ball bounce and clatter to a stop, but he wasn't listening any longer. He felt as if his soul had been ripped out. His appetite was gone. Maybe he ought to just turn himself in right now, he thought. Knees wobbling beneath him, Walter began to stagger away when a hand grabbed his arm and roughly pulled him back to the table.

"Where the hell are you going?" the young husband demanded. When Walter stared at him, uncomprehending, he pointed to the ball on the wheel and the marker on the table.

"You won, man!"

CHAPTER TWENTY-THREE

"I swear I can't figure this guy out," Capparelli said.

The detectives' car was parked on the street across from the Buczyno house. It was after nine P.M., and the low-hanging cloud cover reflected the beams of the streetlights and the head- and taillights of the cars whizzing by on the Tri-State below, silhouetting the Buczyno property with an eerie orange glow. A mild breeze fluttered the yellow crime scene tape stretched between the winter-bare trees along the parkway, and a faint rain misted the windshield with an occasional sleet particle pinging off the glass.

Riehle and Capparelli had been sitting there for a couple of hours now, not knowing what they might expect or find. The interior of the car smelled of stale coffee and the tang of leftover Chinese takeout. Every so often a car would pass them coming off the ramp, the headlights momentarily blinding them in the darkness. Next door, the Salinas's house remained dark and empty, weighing Riehle down with guilt and sadness every time he looked at it. Periodically the other neighbors would peer out the windows at them, hands cupping their eyes as they pressed their faces to the glass, their gazes always going from the detectives' car to the Buczyno house before they retreated back within the safety of their own homes. From Riehle's viewpoint, the other houses on the block almost seemed to lean away from the tainted Buczyno property as if it were a cancer that threatened to infect the entire neighborhood.

Riehle turned to him. "What's to figure out? Buczyno murdered four young boys and now he's on the run."

"You've been inside his house. Did we find any toys? Any photos or souvenirs besides the wallets and grave map? Notes? Crazy writings? Manifestos? Anything to suggest the guy had a darker side?"

"Besides the bodies rotting in his basement?" It was the same discussion they'd been having for the past two hours, tackling the argument from every conceivable angle until the futility of the situation made them frustrated and edgy. "Maybe he didn't need anything else. Maybe he's into torture. Don't forget the garrote wire and duct tape. Could be he was just into flesh wounds and watching the blood run down the floor drain."

"That *would* explain why Griskel didn't find any broken bones on the previous three's remains," Capparelli admitted grudgingly. "But what set him off with Harris then?"

"Who knows? Maybe Harris did or said something or tried to escape and Buczyno went berserk. Until we find a connection between the two—if any exists—we may never know. And chances are Buczyno won't tell us anything when we do catch him."

"Yeah, that's been bugging me. If there was a connection, why doesn't anyone remember it?"

"I've been stuck on the same thing. Buczyno's never even had a parking ticket as far as we know, and Harris's records were sealed. No one at the sheriff's department recognized either name when we called—although they admit there's been a lot of personnel changes lately because of budget cuts. So it's possible that if someone had a run-in with them he's no longer with the department." He shrugged. "And except for the Salinases, the neighborhood's completely changed over the years, and nobody really knew him." When they'd interviewed the other neighbors, a few said they'd heard rumors that *something* had happened in Buczyno's house, everything from meth labs to gun-running to child pornography (which had definitely piqued the detectives' interest), but no one could provide them with any specific or corroborating details, and Nielsen hadn't been able to find any departmental or media references to substantiate any of the wild claims, or even a mention of them in the local newspapers.

Capparelli said, "First thing tomorrow then, we'll push harder to find Harris's file—both in our department and county's. Hopefully we can find it and that'll tell us what we're missing."

"Gotta try something." Riehle drained the last of his cold coffee and crumpled the cup. "You know, I was thinking. Another thing we could do is check the local gay bars. Show Buczyno's picture around and see if anyone recognizes him. See if he was prowling for victims there."

"Already done."

"*What?* When?"

"Last night after you went home. I wanted to get a jump on things before anyone's memory got confused with seeing his face on the news."

"Whoa, what are you saying? That you're—"

"No, *I'm* not."

"Then how would you know where the bars are? You just moved here. I—wait a minute. Dixie, right?"

Capparelli nodded.

"Of course. But she's not . . . I mean, what are you saying? That there's someone in the department?" He put a hand up between them. "Never mind, I don't want to know."

Capparelli cleared his throat. "All I'll say is that woman is a wealth of information—better than any street informant I ever had—and I'd recommend staying on her good side, if you know what I mean."

Thinking about all the comments he'd made to Simmons

about Dixie, Riehle hoped to God Paul had kept his mouth shut. "So the bars," he said, getting back on track. "Did you find anything?"

"*Nada*. Nobody'd seen him before. Of course, Buczyno's other victims were from Indiana. We could always call the Hobart and Merrillville PDs and have them check the bars in their area."

And let more departments do the legwork for them again? No. Riehle felt like all they were doing was sitting around waiting for something to happen. Or worse, letting another law enforcement agency apprehend Buczyno and steal their thunder like the O'Hare cops wanted to do. He knew that was a sore spot with Gavin, too. No, there had to be something they could do, something they were missing right here.

Unfortunately, their meeting with Harris's mother hadn't yielded any answers. In fact, it'd left them more confused and frustrated than ever. During his time as a police officer, Riehle had encountered all kinds of reactions from grieving parents when he'd had to deliver horrible, life-altering news: everything from fainting and numbness to wailing grief and angrily striking out at the messengers of their devastating news.

But Harris's mother became far more verbally abusive with them than any normal anger could justify. Refusing to allow the detectives into her home, she'd made them stand outside on her crumbling concrete stoop under the dim glow of her yellow-bulbed porch light, watching them shiver in the cold, drizzling rain while she screamed at them through the partially opened door, literally blaming them for her son's death; how they should have seen it coming and protected him, and accusing them of everything from neglect to police brutality and favoritism. The woman's vicious, unrelenting tirade had seared their already frayed nerve endings, leaving them shell-shocked and dazed after an already long, agonizing day.

Sapped of all of their energy and nearly at their wits' end, the detectives were no closer to understanding and capturing Buczyno after their visit with Harris's mother than they were before. And after two hours of sitting in this damned car, Riehle wondered if he and Capparelli shouldn't have gone to a bar instead. A couple of beers might have sparked their synapses and given them the proper insight into what direction to go next, which the coffee and Chinese takeout had failed to provide.

"So what should we do? Re-interview the neighbors?" he said, grasping at straws. He suddenly remembered the image of Benito in the hospital and wished he hadn't said anything.

Capparelli winced, too. "Any news on Benito?"

"Yeah. Sorry, I forgot to tell you. I called Jenny Gavin when you went in to pick up dinner. His condition's stabilized and they think he'll be okay, but she said in no uncertain terms that you and I are officially *personae non gratae* around the hospital."

"Can't say as I blame them." He gave a weary sigh and ran a hand through his hair. "Hmmm, re-interview the neighbors? No, I wouldn't go there just yet." He sat up straighter in his seat. "See, that's the other thing that's bugging me. Nobody's said anything bad about Buczyno, except for those wild rumors a few said they'd heard. Sure, most haven't lived here very long and didn't really know him, but there wasn't any 'you know, I always had an uneasy feeling about him' or anything like that. In fact, they're all defending him. Everyone feels sorry for him, saying he never recovered after the death of his wife."

"Maybe that was the turning point. Something inside him snapped."

"But *why*? His wife died of cancer. That doesn't turn a man into a serial killer. The worst thing anyone can say about him is that he became a recluse in his mourning. But he'd started to come out of it lately. Hell, he was even part of the neighborhood watch program and nobody there picked up any bad vibes on him."

"Neither did the people who worked with Ted Bundy on that rape-prevention escort service," Riehle argued. "And working the neighborhood watch could be a great way to know if anyone had any suspicions about him."

"Or to watch for potential victims." Capparelli chewed his lower lip. "True. But chances are pretty slim that Buczyno could spot someone somewhere, get off the watch, and grab the victim before he had a chance to move from the location where he was originally spotted without Buczyno calling attention to himself." He shook his head. "The timing's just not there to grab the intended victim."

"Or without anybody else seeing a thing or becoming suspicious about his actions."

"Exactly. And there's nothing in his past that indicates those predilections or any tendency toward violent behavior." Capparelli lifted a white cardboard container and opened the top. "See what I mean? He doesn't follow any of the profiling rules. That's why I can't get a handle on this guy. No cop's instinct, no gut feeling, no *nothing*. And it's driving me crazy."

He picked at his leftover fried rice with a clear plastic spork, his eyes staring out the windshield at the surrounding neighborhood. "I can't tell you how many times I sat outside some asshole's house or apartment in Chicago just to get a feel for the guy. Call it intuition, but I always got something from the neighborhood, the way people moved around the house or avoided it on the street. People in the area always knew more than they'd ever tell us."

Riehle grinned. "So what'd you think? We'd catch him trying to sneak back into his own house?"

"Stranger things have happened. But we've been inside this guy's house and sitting here for God knows how long, and I don't know about you, but I'm drawing blanks."

He took a bite of fried rice, then pointed the spork at Riehle, emphasizing his words as if it were a lecture wand. "You know, if this were one of those formula serial killer novels, right about now there'd be the obligatory chapter where the villain murders another victim in a way so horrendous that the police—when they find the body—and the readers think: 'We gotta catch this guy *before he kills again*!' "

"Don't forget the maniacal laughter," Riehle added, "as the killer savagely satisfies his increasing bloodlust. But in his near-godlike image of himself, he carelessly leaves behind the final clue needed to solve the crime and bring the villain to justice."

"Goes without saying," Capparelli agreed. But the grin dropped from his face as his expression soured. Even in the dim streetlight, Riehle could see a deep flush suddenly rise up his partner's neck, and Capparelli jerked as if he were about to throw the rice container out the window, visibly bringing himself under control just in time. Frustrated, he crushed the container instead, some of the rice spilling over the top like escaping maggots, and stuffed it into the restaurant's takeout paper bag.

"Yeah. Too bad it ain't one of those formula novels."

But it wasn't. Nor was it a TV show or a movie with a happy ending. Four people were brutally murdered in his suburban hometown, and it was up to Riehle to find the guy and bring him in. And other than waiting around for some other law enforcement agency to catch him, he had no idea what to do next. The greasy, uneasy feeling in his stomach reminded him that everyone was watching him fail.

A car passed by, momentarily blinding them. Capparelli rubbed his tired eyes. "How much longer you want to stay?"

"Doesn't matter. Karen's in bed, and chances are Gwen already fell asleep on the couch watching TV. I can stay a while longer." Riehle tilted his head side to side, working the kinks out of his neck. "Word is you used to go on a lot of these stakeouts. Did you really catch that many guys?"

"Absolutely. Sometimes all you had to do was wait the guy out. Other times . . ." He shrugged, looking away. "Other times, it was just an excuse not to go home."

A silence descended over them, hanging like a heavy pall. Capparelli cleared his throat. "Sorry, I didn't mean to go off on that track."

"It's all right."

"I just never thought it'd turn out the way it did, you know? I used to worship the ground that woman walked on. How'd you and Gwen meet?"

"Got set up on a blind date. I was at the academy while she was in pharmacy school at UIC."

"So some blind dates really do work out, then."

"So far, so good."

Capparelli smiled, and nodded a little sadly. "Charlotte and I went together all through high school, got married right after. There wasn't anything I wouldn't do for her."

He looked out the window, but his eyes were far away. His jaw muscles worked. "Problem is, a woman that beautiful gets used to the extra attention. Guys always wanting to do things for her, flirting, you name it. They'd be practically falling all over her even when I was standing right there."

His eyes searched Riehle's face for judgment. "She'd come into the station and the other guys would whistle and wink. She really got off on that. Then it was, like, up to me to prove I deserved her, like it was some kind of competition or something."

Riehle shifted uncomfortably. He was a typical cop, not real big on heartfelt confessions unless it had to do with solving a crime, and he still felt a little uncomfortable about Capparelli admitting his wife had been unfaithful. But he didn't want to be rude, either.

"Was she always like that?" he asked politely.

"Not at first. But I should have seen it coming. Her mother was the same way. Divorced three times. Held onto the guys long enough to drain their bank accounts, then dumped 'em when she got bored. You get along with your mother-in-law?"

Riehle raspberried. "To this day, Gwen's parents still believe that by marrying a cop she married beneath her."

"Then you know what I mean. When Charlotte's mother died, I sucked on a helium balloon and started singing and dancing like the Munchkins when Dorothy's house landed in Oz." Capparelli shrugged. "But even though the die was already cast, I was bound and determined not to let it happen to us. Someone winked at her, I bought her a new necklace. Somebody whistled, I took her to the best restaurant in town. Started requesting a lot of overtime to pay for everything she wanted, tolerating all her mood swings until one night it finally hit me: she wasn't doing a goddamned thing for me. And I thought, why am I the only one who's trying?"

He blew out his breath. "After that, we were just going through the motions. I'd work overtime just to stay away from her. Then when I caught her with that other guy, well, that was the final straw."

Simmons had mentioned Capparelli was known for working late, but obviously no one had guessed the real reason he wasn't going home. "Maybe you'll find someone new," Riehle offered, trying to be positive. "You know, if you found the right person . . ."

"No, I'm done with relationships. No more 'Yes, dear,' 'No, dear,' 'I-swear-to-God-I-won't-do-it-again-if-you-just-tell-me-what-the-fuck-I-did, dear.' I mean, seriously, why would I want to put myself through all that again?" He held up a hand. "Thanks anyway, but I'm doing fine. Frankly, I like going home to a house where you don't have to walk on eggshells."

"Gotta do what's right for you," was all Riehle could think to say. "Me, I can't imagine my life without Gwen and Karen."

"Speaking of which, I hear you're trying to get away for your anniversary."

" 'Trying' is the operative word, all right. But Gwen wants us to take Karen to Disney World instead."

"So what's the problem?"

"My parents never made it to their tenth anniversary."

Capparelli slowly shook his head. "Sorry, you lost me."

Now it was Riehle's turn to look away. He ran a hand over his chin, the rough, uneven bristles of a long hard day scratching his fingers.

"My father had ALS. Lou Gehrig's Disease. He killed himself right before their anniversary."

"Jesus. I'm sorry."

The interior of the car suddenly felt smaller, and the air inside was thick and stifling. He squirmed in his seat.

"My mother was really looking forward to it. They were going on a Caribbean cruise, the first one they'd ever been on. Dad had a little shoe repair shop, and Mom worked as a cashier in a grocery store. The trip was going to cost them a fortune, but I remember Dad insisting he wanted to pay for all of it." Riehle glanced at his partner. "He was like that. We never had a lot of money, but he was a proud man. Very proud. He always worried about how other people saw him."

"He wanted everyone to know that he could take care of you and your mother."

"Yeah, exactly. But I think Mom was looking forward to it because she realized it was their last chance to spend time together before the disease made it impossible for him to get around. He'd already fallen several times by then, and I think they were worried it was progressing faster than the doctors had predicted and he wasn't going to be able to make it."

"So what happened?"

Riehle sighed. "Hell, I don't know. I was only eight years old. It's still a blur to me. I remember something about my mother getting to his store a few minutes late and Dad had fallen while a customer was there, and that they had a really big argument about it later after I'd gone to bed.

"What I do remember, though, was waking up in the middle of the night because my mother was screaming, and running into the living room and seeing my dad lying on the floor, vomit all over his face and the carpet, and a vial of pills and a half-empty bottle of vodka on the coffee table." He rubbed his forehead. "Then it's all a blur again. I hardly even remember the funeral. I just remember being numb."

Outside the mist turned to a light rain, and the droplets ran down the windshield.

"You never asked your mom about it?"

"Oh, hell no."

"Why not?"

"You don't know what it was like for her. She was devastated. Talking about it was just too hard on her. It would have been like rubbing salt in her wounds. I didn't want to cause her any more pain."

"But surely by now, after all this time—"

"No, you don't get it. You didn't see her, the look on her face . . ." Riehle blinked quickly as the memories came rushing back. He swallowed the lump in his throat.

"It was a couple days after the funeral," he began, "and I was still walking around in a fog. I just couldn't believe my dad was really gone, you know? I was looking for something that reminded me of him, something I could hold onto that would make me believe he hadn't left us forever. So I went into his den."

He looked at Capparelli. "It was really just the spare bedroom

210

my parents had converted into an office. It had a couple of chairs and a desk where my parents paid the bills, and Dad could work on paperwork he brought home from the shop." He wiped his palms on his trousers.

"Anyway, I was standing there looking at all his stuff when I noticed the time on their new ceramic anniversary clock was wrong. Dad died in the fall, right after Daylight Savings Time ended, and the clock hadn't been changed. So I started to correct it when all of a sudden I heard this gasp behind me, and I spun around. My hand hit the edge of the desk and I dropped the clock, and it shattered on the floor."

Riehle breathed deeply. "Mom was leaning against the doorjamb. I thought she was going to faint. Her hands were covering her mouth, trying to stifle this awful, heart-wrenching sob that seemed to burst right out of her. And the way she was looking at me . . ."

In his mind, he could still see and hear her as if it had happened yesterday, still see the broken ruins of their clock on the floor, its hands stopped forever. A thin sheen of sweat broke out on his forehead. "I'd never seen her like that before. Even at the funeral. And I realized she was upset because I'd broken the last thing Dad had given her. It was like I was forcing her to confront all the pain and shock and loss she'd been going through that I knew she wanted to protect me from. So I panicked and ran out of the room and never talked about him again in front of her."

"But you've discussed it since then."

"How could I? You didn't see what it did to her, what kind of life she's had to live. I had to grow up knowing I was the one who hurt her the most. So I changed the subject every time she brought it up."

"But what does this have to do with your anniversary?"

"Don't you get it?" He shook his head as if Capparelli were

too dense to understand. "It's my way of making it up to her. By going on our anniversary, it'll be breaking my parents' curse, like she and Dad really got to go on their trip after all. Then it wouldn't be such a burden to her anymore."

"A burden? What are you talking about? If you want her to feel like she went on the trip, then why don't you just take your mom with you?"

"On our anniversary? Don't be stupid. That's like Gwen wanting to take Karen along. This is my way of breaking my parents' jinx and keeping Gwen from having to go through a life like my mother had."

"Then what about Karen? We're cops, you know. Something could happen to us before your trip. How would she feel?"

"She'd be fine, just like I was," he insisted. "What's your point?"

"I'm just saying, are you sure this is really about your mom? Or Gwen or Karen, for that matter?"

His nostrils flared. "What's that supposed to mean?"

Capparelli put his hands up between them. "Hey, nothing, man. Just trying to help."

Riehle turned away. Goddammit, why did he even bother? Nobody ever listened to him. Everyone always thought they knew better.

Outside the wind kicked up, turning colder. They sat there a while longer in silence. The darkness encroached as a number of surrounding houses turned their lights off for the night. Riehle drummed his fingers on the steering wheel, stewing, feeling the heat in his cheeks. All their waiting and talking hadn't provided them with any answers, it seemed.

"Ready to get the hell out of here?" Capparelli said.

"Sure, why not." He threw the engine in gear and made a three-point turn to head back to the station, noticing a few remaining backlit curtains flutter along the street as they drove away. "Maybe a good night's sleep will help us think better in the morning."

"You really gonna get any sleep tonight?"

Riehle thought a moment. "Probably not," he admitted. "Gwen says I toss and turn a lot when there's something on my mind. I'll probably end up keeping her awake all night because of it."

Capparelli nodded. "I hear you. Charlotte always said I snored whenever something got stuck in my craw." His fingers flexed wide, then closed into a tightly clenched fist. "I swear, something like this gets me so frustrated I just wanna—ah hell, there's that damned graffiti again."

They had just turned onto Maple Avenue and were driving under the overpass for Route Eighty-three where FREDS RULE was spray-painted on the concrete. "Why the hell does that bug you so much?" Riehle asked.

"I don't know. There's something about it that's just so *wrong.*"

Riehle laughed, his anger over their earlier dispute beginning to dissipate. He pulled to a stop at a red light at the next intersection. Up ahead was a strip mall with most of its stores still open and a brightly lit gas station minimart on the opposite corner.

"That reminds me. I promised Gwen I'd pick up a gallon of milk on the way home."

"And I need to get a lottery ticket. It's up to twenty-three million this week."

"Are you serious? Why waste your money? Do you have any idea what the odds are against winning?"

"Hey, I gotta find some way to pay for gas." He tapped his window. "Pull over to that hardware store for a minute, willya? I need to get something."

"Can't it wait until after work?"

"It already *is* after work," he reminded him. "C'mon, I'll only be a sec."

"Whatever." Riehle parked in front of the store and Capparelli hurried inside. A frigid breeze flooded the interior of the car when he opened the door. The temperature had dropped, and outside the misting rain had frozen to tiny ice pellets pinging off the windshield. He turned the intermittent wipers on as Capparelli raced out of the store, collar up and head bent down, clutching his purchase in a brown paper bag against his overcoat.

He slammed the door when he got in. "Head back the way we came."

The hair along Riehle's neck rose. As Capparelli fastened his seatbelt, Riehle heard the unmistakable tocking sound of a ball inside a metal container in the crumpled paper bag.

He grew uneasy. "Ummm, I don't know about this . . ."

"Just do it, willya? C'mon, hurry up."

Riehle retraced their route until his partner told him to stop alongside the graffiti. Capparelli opened the door, popped the plastic cap off the aerosol can, and started shaking it.

Riehle panicked. "Are you crazy? What if we get caught?"

"Relax. No one's gonna be out on a night like this. I gotta do something to blow off steam or I'm gonna go crazy. Just keep your eyes peeled and I'll be right back." He slammed the door and hurried over to the concrete wall.

Riehle fidgeted. Sure enough, much to his horror, Capparelli began spray-painting the wall. Riehle bounced in his seat, trying to look out all the windows to see if anyone was watching them. His heart banged in his chest, and his breath came out in such short ragged gasps that he had to wipe the windows off with his coat sleeve to clear the condensation away.

Was Capparelli out of his mind? Gavin'll have their asses when he finds out about this!

Riehle looked over and found that, much to his surprise, Capparelli wasn't painting over the old graffiti at all. Instead, under

FREDS RULE

he wrote:

BUT CLAUDE RAINS

in large black letters. Then, with a satisfied smirk on his face, he raced back to the car and climbed in.

His stunned brain not knowing what else to do, Riehle hunkered down in his seat and did his best not to burn rubber speeding out of there.

"You're showing your age, you know," was all he could think to say.

"Just shut up and drive."

CHAPTER TWENTY-FOUR

Mack Reynolds knew what he wanted. He wanted to be head of security for a major Las Vegas casino.

He told himself that every morning when his alarm went off at exactly nine A.M. after only six hours of sleep; when he showered and shaved and splashed on cologne; when he dressed in crisp shirts, tailored suits, and polished shoes; when he ate breakfast while watching CNN; and when he drove to the casino, parked his car in the employee lot, and said hello to everyone from Sarah (who made his morning coffee) to Ian (the morning pit boss), making sure to ask each and every one of them about an update on some current event in their personal lives that they'd previously shared with him.

Mack knew that getting ahead was in paying attention to the details.

Sure, working security in an Iowa casino was a long way from the desert. But many of the investors in casinos on The Strip had passed through, and Mack made sure they were well taken care of. And he'd made sure they remembered him. Cards and private cell numbers were exchanged, and Mack followed up on every invitation. Favors given, favors returned. Vacations in Vegas were a whirlwind of VIP treatments with rooms, parties, women, clubs, and booze. They told him they liked what they saw, how he handled himself, and he wanted *more*. The only thing they didn't offer was a job. The implication was there all right, but they wanted Mack to prove himself first, to justify their belief that he could make the leap from Triple-A to The Show.

Mack knew he needed something big. And he had every intention of finding it.

Sipping the coffee Sarah brewed especially for him (French vanilla roast with a sprinkle of cinnamon), he walked around the casino. Mack liked to get a feel for the action before heading to the security room. Today was starting off slow even for a weekday, he noticed. Most of the regulars were already there, spread about at their favorite stations. Though they probably knew each other by sight, they rarely intermingled, preferring instead to remain in their own private worlds, oblivious to the other sights and sounds around them. And with the newer gaming regulations, the staff knew to keep a close eye on them. The last thing management needed was a lawsuit charging that the casino catered to those with gambling addictions.

Mack made his way up and down the aisles, around the numerous slot clusters and past the gaming tables, nodding good morning to the dealers and pit bosses and receiving greetings in return. Admittedly, he'd originally been disappointed when management had replaced the High Stakes Poker room with a non-smoking section filled with more slot machines; but truth be told, action had been rare at those tables and the casino made most of its money on slots anyway, especially after the economy tanked. Mack understood. Business was business, and you did what you had to do to survive. Satellite radio was tuned to an oldies station this morning, and the flat-screen TVs suspended above the gaming tables showed a rebroadcast of the previous night's Bulls and Lakers game and CNN Headline News.

He sipped his coffee. Life in the casino always fascinated him. Even when it was slow like this, he loved to watch the spectacle. How the staff in their Wild West saloon uniforms hovered over the green felt–covered hardwood tables and stools, and worked hard to exude an air of excitement while the bedraggled patrons shuffled between their favorite games. He knew many regulars were down on their luck and should be spending their money elsewhere—but hey, who was he to tell them how to live?

Sometimes during these morning walk-throughs, though, Mack found himself missing the old riverboat. Sure, the new land-based casino had all the bells and whistles and was far more spacious than the cramped, tri-level boat—not to mention the greater ease of surveillance in keeping all the gaming on a single floor—but the boat was his first job right out of college. He'd flourished there, found his niche and risen quickly through the ranks. His fondest memories, however, were the quiet moments alone on the second floor landing, resting his forearms on the imitation wooden railing and looking down on the gaming tables below. He'd felt like his own eye-in-the-sky. Standing there apart from the rows of noisy, light-flashing slots and their silent, drab worshippers around him, he'd loved watching the drama unfold, and the sense of being above it all.

Nope, no doubt about it. Whether it was the old riverboat or the flashy new casino, the job here was a rush. But he'd trade it in a heartbeat for the high-rolling, money-flashing, fancy-dressed action of life on The Strip. He just needed the right ticket.

Making his last pass around the outer perimeter, Mack glanced inside the VIP lounge, and the coffee turned to bile in the pit of his stomach. Ah hell. It looked like it wasn't going to be his day, after all. Denny LaMotta sat on the High Stakes Blackjack table's center stool like he was perched on a throne. Wearing a four-thousand-dollar gray pin-striped suit, black Italian leather shoes, diamond rings on his pinkie fingers, and sporting a two-hundred-dollar haircut that highlighted his graying temples, LaMotta was surrounded by his henchmen, playing his hand and scooping up mounds of chips, laughing as everything went his way. Which it always did.

Mack ground his teeth. Like a dirty finger probing an open sore, Denny LaMotta's entire existence was a flagrant reminder of all that prevented Mack from achieving his goals. LaMotta was mobbed up, he was sure of it. Just as he was sure that La-Motta was trying to muscle his way in and seize control of the casino. But he'd never been able to prove a goddamnned thing, and no matter how many times he warned management or the Department of Criminal Investigation, he was always shot down. *How* dare *he make ridiculous accusations against such an upstanding member of the community*! It infuriated him that they wouldn't even listen to him anymore. And trying the FBI had only netted him a grumbled, "We'll look into it."

LaMotta turned and grinned at him. Mack's blood boiled. The sonofabitch somehow always knew he was there. Mack wanted to put his fist through those pearly whites, but kept his poker face on instead. LaMotta knew about Mack's accusations and took great pleasure in rubbing his nose in the fact that Mack couldn't get anything on him.

Like what happened to John McGinnis. The Texas Hold'Em dealer had been missing for three days now. John's ex-wife was frantic with worry. She called incessantly, hounding him and the police for any new information, insisting it wasn't like John to up and leave like that.

Mack agreed. He was certain LaMotta had something to do with the disappearance. Mack had no proof, of course, but the night before he disappeared, John was seen arguing with Scott Pryor, a guy with a port wine birthmark, who was one of La-Motta's closest hotheaded, needle-dick pissants. A gut-wrenching feeling told him he was right, that LaMotta was involved, even if he didn't have any proof. Yet.

As if reading his thoughts, LaMotta winked at him before returning his attention to the game. Laughter arose from the table. No longer hiding the scowl on his face, Mack threw the cold remains of his coffee in a trash receptacle and stormed to the security room. His photo ID badge bounced off his chest as he moved.

Goddammit! He'd give anything, *anything*, to nail that sonofabitch. LaMotta still held the cards for now, but Mack vowed that somehow, someway he'd force him to ante up.

Mack swiped his badge in the lock and pushed his way into the security room. Davis and Mansfield were already there, seated at their consoles. Banks of ten-inch black and white closed-circuit monitors, interspersed with larger screens for color playback, glowed brightly from their positions in the black-paneled walls. The images shifted constantly as Davis and Mansfield tapped their keypads to bring up whatever camera angle they wanted. The room smelled of stale coffee and leftover French fries.

Davis swiveled his chair around. An unlit cigarette dangled from his lips, his most recent attempt to quit smoking. The sleeves of his white shirt were rolled halfway to his elbows. He clasped his hands behind his head.

"You're gonna give yourself an ulcer over LaMotta, you know."

"Whatever." Davis was supposed to be reviewing the previous night's security videos, but Mack knew they'd watched the whole exchange. They were the only ones who reluctantly agreed he might be onto something, no matter what management claimed, and he knew they were covering his back. Still, he hated having his frustrations on display.

He changed the subject. "Anything happen last night?"

"Nah. It was pretty slow."

"What about you?" he said to Mansfield.

"I got nothing." Mansfield was the hairiest guy Mack had ever met. He trimmed his curly black locks once a week, shaved to his collarbone, and self-consciously wore long-sleeved shirts no matter what the weather was to hide his furry forearms from view. "All we had were a couple of pickpockets and that church group from Des Moines you like so much."

"That was about it," Davis agreed. "About the only other thing that happened was Slater got in again."

Mack groaned. A registered gambling addict, Louis Slater had an uncanny way of blending in with groups at the front door. Slater was a nice old guy that everybody liked. For all Mack knew, getting inside was his only remaining thrill. It was his daughter-in-law, Tina, who was the real pain in the ass. She blamed the casino for his addiction and waged a battle in the media against their right to do business, and they needed to be on the constant lookout for him to avoid getting sued.

Mack rubbed his temples. Tina had visited his office so often that the memory of her shrill voice automatically bounced around the inside of his skull like a small caliber bullet. "Please tell me nobody let him play."

"Nope, you'd be proud. Everyone was as friendly as pie, but no one let him even touch a table. And the slot attendants kept his hands full with free soft drinks."

"Remind me to give everyone a great evaluation. He didn't try to pull a fast one on anyone new? What about Claire, who's filling in for John?"

Davis swung back to his console. "Here, I'll show you." He pulled up the image of Slater at the Texas Hold'Em table. Mack watched how Slater stood behind the players, sipping his drink and congratulating a winner or clapping a conciliatory hand on the shoulder of a loser at the end of every round. But when a stool opened up and Slater tried to slide onto it, Claire placed her hand on the table in front of him and shook her head. Slater

221

offered the seat to a lady standing behind him and waved to the other players, and Claire didn't resume play until after Slater had stepped back from the table.

"Not bad," Mack said. "She handled it nicely without embarrassing him in front of the others. And *they'll* remember how we treated him." He nodded. "Good PR."

He was about to turn away when a man in the background caught his attention. He tapped the monitor. "Zoom in on this guy right here."

"Something wrong?" Davis said.

"Just get me a better picture."

When the image enlarged, Mack felt a tingle at the base of his skull. He knew he was onto something, that indescribable sixth sense that had guided him this far in his career. But he couldn't remember where he'd seen the guy before. "Show me where he went."

Davis pulled back for an overhead wide angle view of the floor and ran the video forward until the guy passed behind Slater and stopped at the roulette table. They watched as he bought a stack of chips, then got his hand knocked aside by the honeymoon couple staying in room five-twelve as he went to place his bet, spilling his chips all over the layout.

"Switch to camera three," Mack said. The new angle gave them a straight-on shot of the guy standing at the table. "See what he does." He held his breath as the young executive and his stunning (though obviously drunk) wife scooped up his chips while the guy stood there as if he'd just received the shock of his life.

"Pause?"

"Not yet. I want to see what happens."

Mack leaned toward the screen, almost wishing he could climb through the glass portal back in time to the moment everything occurred. His heart beat wildly as he watched the dazed man put his entire stack on zero, then began to stagger away before being pulled back by the executive and shown he'd won.

"Freeze. Give me a head shot. Enhance," Mack said, hearing the growing excitement in his voice. "Print it."

Davis pulled the sheet from the printer and handed it to him. The digital image was as clear as if the guy had posed in a photographer's studio.

"So? Who is he?" Davis said. He and Mansfield studied the picture over Mack's shoulder, trying to figure out what all the excitement was about. "Is he in the Griffin Book or something?"

Mack knew. He felt the tingling sensation crawl over his shoulders and down his arms. He tried to keep his hands from shaking. He'd verify everything first with face recognition software before going to DCI, but it was him, all right. That serial killer from Chicago who was on the run. Mack had seen his photo on CNN that morning, and he held the proof that the guy was in his casino last night.

"Run the videos and follow his every movement through the casino," Mack said. "Then check the lot recordings. Find out if he's staying at the hotel. If he arrived by bus, check with the line, see what tour he's on. And if he drove, get me the car's description and plate number."

"What's going on—?"

"Just make it your top priority. *Now*. I need to catch this guy."

Damn right, he did. Catching him was Mack's ticket out of here.

CHAPTER TWENTY-FIVE

Riehle knocked on the door and stuck his head inside the office. "You wanted to see us, lieu?"

Gavin looked up from his desk. "Detectives. Yes, come in." He set his pen down and leaned back in his chair. His suit jacket was still on, and his tie was perfectly knotted. Everything on his desk was neatly organized, and the face that greeted them seemed devoid of all emotion. The hairs along the back of Riehle's neck rose.

"And close the door behind you."

Riehle glanced at his partner. Capparelli hadn't been there long enough to recognize the signs, and Riehle had no way of warning him now.

"Have a seat," Gavin said when they'd closed the door.

It was rumored that Gavin originally wanted to be a prosecutor, but had dropped out after the first year of law school because all the research and nit-picky memorization of obscure cases drove him crazy. He wanted something more immediate and hands-on, and his intelligence had quickened his rise through the ranks. But he never lost his sharp eye for detail and was known for weaving traps around anyone who thought he was dealing with a simple-minded, overweight bully with a gun.

Gavin offered a tight smile. "How's the Buczyno case coming?"

The highest profile case to ever hit their department, and Gavin was *asking* how it was going? Gavin didn't ask, he *deman-*

ded. He demanded end-of-the-day reports, updated plans at morning meetings, and to be brought up to speed on any new information as soon as it was found in case the deputy chief had to talk to the media. Gavin already knew as much as they did.

Oh man, they were in deep shit about something.

Capparelli, however, appeared completely unfazed. Though he straightened in his chair, his mannerisms were relaxed and at ease. Was he oblivious to the brewing storm? Or was he ignoring it altogether? Riehle remembered Simmons warning him that Capparelli had a problem with authority, and he prayed that his partner wasn't choosing this moment to push the envelope.

Hoping to defuse the situation, Riehle said, "Griskel positively identified three of the four victims with Missing Persons cases. We've interviewed their family members, but can't find any connection to Buczyno. We've followed up on sightings at a couple of motels in Minnesota and Iowa and places where Nielsen found he'd used his credit card to buy gas, but even with postings on LEADS and NCIC, local law enforcement hasn't spotted him yet."

"And besides a few unsubstantiated rumors," Capparelli said, "all we got out of the neighbors is that Buczyno's a real stand-up guy who fell apart after his wife died."

Gavin acknowledged what he already knew with a firm nod. "I heard you were doing surveillance on Buczyno's house last night. Find anything *outside* the scene of the crimes?"

A red flush rose up Capparelli's skin from under his shirt collar. "Nothing, sir," Riehle said quickly.

"So basically, you've been sitting around on your asses while everyone else does your work."

Capparelli's eyes hardened. "It was after our shift. Sir. I was trying to get a feel for Buczyno and his neighborhood, trying to figure out what made him tick or pushed him over the edge. I used to do it all the time in Chicago, and sometimes it helped. But we didn't put in for overtime. We were doing it on our own time."

"This is a murder investigation. As far as I'm concerned, you're *always* on the clock." Gavin's jaw muscles clenched so hard Riehle heard his teeth grind. "Speaking of which, while you two Sherlocks were sitting out there, a witness reported seeing some jackass spray-painting graffiti under the Route Eighty-three overpass while his partner sat in the car. Know anything about it?"

"Absolutely not, sir," Capparelli said, his voice tight as the snare closed around his neck. "But I promise as soon as we capture Buczyno, we'll put all our efforts into catching the guys."

Gavin shot up so fast his chair flew backwards, slamming into the bookcase and knocking the family photo onto its glass face.

"You think this is a fucking joke?" The way Gavin leaned over the desk, his eyes wild with fury, he reminded Riehle of a rabid Doberman straining at the end of its leash. He even had white spit in the corners of his mouth. His face was purple with rage.

"Think I'm fucking playing with you?" Gavin pulled a DVD in a clear plastic case out of his desk drawer and threw it onto the desktop. "You're goddamned lucky the hardware store's owner is a friend of mine. He gave me the security disc."

"Sir, I—"

"STOP! Do you have any idea what the media would have done if they'd gotten hold of this? Showing our senior detectives screwing around while they're supposed to be catching a serial killer who's on the loose? They'd make us look like we put Inspector Clouseau's demented cousins on the case, and I will not—repeat, *NOT*—let you make fools out of this department."

The veins on Gavin's forehead stood out so prominently they looked like they were about to burst. "I don't know what kind of shit you pulled in the city, but it's going to stop right here, *right now.*"

"Yes, sir."

Someone knocked on the door, but Gavin ignored it. He aimed his finger at the detectives. "I swear to God, if I can prove you did this or if you EVER pull this kind of shit again, I'm gonna transfer both of you to Brookfield and make you crossing guards in the children's petting zoo. Am I making myself perfectly clear?"

The knock came again.

"What is it?" Gavin yelled.

Dixie opened the door and hesitantly stepped inside. She glanced at Riehle and Capparelli before handing Gavin the pink memo slip. Dixie ran out of the office.

Gavin read the note. Some of the anger drained from his face, refilling with disgust. "Great. Another one of your goddamned problems, Riehle. This is turning into a real red-letter day for you. I swear my life was easier when O'Connell was around." Gavin threw the note at him. "Now get the hell out of my sight and take care of this."

The detectives left the office fast before Gavin changed his mind and suspended or fired them on the spot.

"What's going on?" Capparelli said.

Riehle handed him the memo without saying a word, still too embarrassed and angry over their ass-chewing and the dig about O'Connell.

Capparelli read the note, then crumpled it and threw it away. "Man, what a day this is turning out to be."

Riehle drove around the cops blocking the street and pulled to a stop in front of the tan brick ranch house. The garage door was up, and the gray Honda Civic inside had its trunk open, its light a misty glow in the cloud-covered early morning air. Jensen's sister stood on the driveway with a couple of uniformed cops. He noticed the media wasn't there yet, but knew they would be soon enough. They loved the gruesome stuff.

"Hold on a sec." Capparelli turned to face him, simultaneously blocking the view of the cops who were looking to see who'd arrived. "About what Gavin said, I owe you an apology. I didn't mean to hang you out to dry for something I did."

"I know that."

"No, I'm serious. Hear me out. It was a stupid thing I did last night, and Gavin had every right to come down on me like that. But I'm sorry he went after you, too. I was frustrated and just trying to blow off some steam. This Buczyno guy, I mean, I can't . . ." Capparelli's fingers grasped at empty air as if he were trying to get a handle on more than just the right words. "I can't figure this guy out and it's driving me crazy, okay? I do and say stupid things when I'm angry. But I wouldn't let anything come down on you."

"I know."

"And I *need* you to know that. I know you put up with a lot of crap with O'Connell, and I'm not going to be like that for you. Now personally, I think Gavin can't prove anything and was on a fishing trip because he's under a lot of pressure." He held up his hand. "Understandably. But all he's got is a vague description of someone writing graffiti in the dark and video of me buying spray paint the same night—which I'll say is for a project at home. No big deal. But if it ever came down to it and push came to shove, I want you to know I wouldn't do anything to put you in harm's way, career or otherwise. I wouldn't do that to my partner."

Riehle caught the slight inflection and wondered what else Capparelli was trying to tell him. "Don't worry. I trust you."

Capparelli replied with a simple nod, but Riehle noticed the tenseness in his jaw relaxed. He glanced over his shoulder. "C'mon, we'd better get out there before they wonder what the hell we're doing."

The detectives walked up the driveway. When Jensen's sister saw who it was, she broke away from the officers and ran to them. She grabbed Riehle's arms, sobbing hysterically, the tracks of earlier tears still wet on her face.

"Oh, please, please, please, he doesn't know what he's doing, he's in so much pain, I just don't know what to do and I'm afraid he might hurt himself, can't you see? I only want to protect him, please, you have to help him, you're his friend, you don't know what it's been like for him, oh please, just try to understand—"

Riehle peeled her claws off his sleeves and handed her, protesting, over to one of the officers, then took the other aside.

"Take her to the station and get her statement. Now. Before the media arrives."

"Right away."

The detectives ignored her cries and pleas for help as the officers practically dragged the near-delirious woman to the patrol car. They turned away and walked up to the house. In the garage, Riehle saw a pick and four muddy shovels, one with a broken handle, inside the Honda's trunk. There were dirt clods on the floor of the trunk and on the rear bumper, and fresh wooden splinters on the pavement directly beneath. The driveway and front walk were smeared in a pattern that suggested something heavy had been dropped and dragged to the door.

"I swear, the world keeps getting weirder," Capparelli said.

Riehle stepped up to the front door. "You ready for this?"

"Ready as I'm ever gonna be." Capparelli opened his coat. "Let's get this over with."

He took a deep breath, then knocked on the door to the home of the grieving puppeteer.

The door creaked on its hinges. "Mr. Jensen?" Riehle pushed it all the way open, and the detectives stepped inside the house. "Larry? It's Kevin Riehle. With the Westbrook police. We need to ask you some questions."

The tiny home was quiet and still. To their right, mountains of still-wrapped presents buried the living room furniture and spilled over onto the beige carpeting. A banner proclaiming "Welcome Home, Kaitlin!" in six-inch-high, green foil letters was thumb-tacked against the far wall. Muddy footprints made a path down a hallway to their left.

Capparelli moved past him, then waved him into the kitchen. "Take a look at this." A collection of crushed beer cans and a cardboard pizza box littered the countertops. The trashcan was pulled out from the cabinet under the sink, and atop the days-old refuse was a sawn-off, muddy arm cast.

Riehle pushed aside the remains of a half-eaten pizza and found an open prescription bottle. Three white tablets clattered at the bottom of the orange plastic vial. The label told him that Jensen had filled his codeine prescription for forty pills three days earlier.

"People in pain do some really weird shit," Capparelli said, as the sound of a man's voice began to drone from the far end of the house.

Riehle reached inside his overcoat, his hand gripping his weapon. He nodded to Capparelli. Slowly, they made their way down the hallway. The walls were covered with framed photographs of a smiling Jensen at numerous schools and community events, mementos of a happier time. Riehle's heart pounded within his chest. The air was thick and heavy, and he felt as if he were moving underwater. The slurring voice grew louder as they approached.

They stopped outside a tiny bedroom at the end of the hall and looked inside. Near the window a mobile suspended white and blue bunnies above an unfinished oak crib. The sheets on the mattress appeared crisp and clean. Squeeze bottles of lotions and ointments stood neatly arranged on a nearby changing table, and a hanging cloth bag was stuffed with disposable diapers. Ceramic bookends atop the dresser held a small collection of multicolored Dr. Seuss and Winnie-the-Pooh volumes. The room smelled of cherry wood chips, dank earth, and decay.

Riehle's gaze dropped to the floor. He nudged his partner. The footprints led to a muddy casket in front of the closet doors. Fresh wooden splinters, an abandoned crowbar, and Jensen's sweaty, mud-stained jacket littered the carpeting around it. The coffin was open and empty except for the pink satin lining.

The call from Jensen's overwrought sister had come in at almost the same time as that of the graveyard caretaker.

"But Rosamond pricked her finger, and she fell into a deep, deep sleep."

The detectives turned toward the thick, scratchy voice. A box stage with black curtains at the edges had been set up in the far corner of the bedroom. Jensen stood behind its black velvet background, his pasty arm in a sling. The fingers of his right hand guided the strings that gently laid the marionette beside the tiny loom. A bassinet rested on the far side of the stage, and the strings for the figure inside it were attached to a wooden cross secured to the top of the backdrop.

Riehle had read *Sleeping Beauty* to Karen many times. "Larry," he said softly. "We need to talk." In the dim morning light, he saw the purple and yellow contusions on Jensen's face, severe bruises for the many wounds that might never heal. His eyes were red and swollen. Dirt encrusted his hands and fingernails.

"Rosamond slept for a hundred years, until a handsome prince entered the castle and beheld the most beautiful woman he had ever seen." On the stage, the marionette bent to kiss the sleeping girl. Jensen manipulated both control wands with his uninjured hand, and Rosamond awkwardly woke and hugged her prince. Tears ran down the puppeteer's face.

"That was always the children's favorite." Riehle realized with a start that Jensen was talking to him now. "*Rumpelstiltskin, Rapunzel, Hansel and Gretel, Little Red Riding Hood*—I've played them all for the schools, at church meetings, for the kids in the neighborhood. But they always liked *Sleeping Beauty* the best. Everything ends happily ever after." The crosses slipped from his fingers, and the marionettes slumped to the stage. His lip quivered. "And I never got to perform it for my own daughter."

Capparelli moved closer and visibly paled when he looked down onto the stage. His eyes flicked toward the opened casket. Jensen's dirt-smeared red flannel shirt was plastered to his skin, and the smell of his sweat hung heavily in the air. His eyes burned with fever, and Riehle saw the man was shivering.

Though it had rained a couple of times since the funeral and the temperature hadn't dipped below freezing, it was still January. The ground at night had to be hard as rock. Fueled by prescription drugs, alcohol, and overwhelming grief, Jensen's determination and strength must have been almost inhuman. Riehle couldn't imagine the toll it had taken on him.

"This isn't the way," he said.

"She didn't even get to see her room," Jensen insisted, his teeth chattering around the words. He lifted the control wand for the figure in the bassinet. "We hoped she'd like everything we did for her." The strings, tied to the figure's tiny wrists, clapped the hands together. Riehle noticed the dimpled knuckles in the parched skin. The puppeteer's shoulders heaved uncontrollably.

A chill slithered up Riehle's spine as if the cold had followed him inside. He peered onto the stage and swallowed hard against the lump in his throat.

"My sleeping beauty." Jensen's voice cracked and his face twisted in pain. His hand shook when he tenderly placed the wooden cross upon the chest of the child who would never awaken.

Riehle draped his coat over the broken man's shoulders.

"I miss them so much," Jensen sobbed, as the detectives led him away.

"I know," Riehle said. "I know."

CHAPTER TWENTY-SIX

Walter turned into the motel and parked his car in the lot. He leaned back against the headrest, letting the motor idle.

What a day! He still couldn't believe it. Winning at roulette had been a revelation. It wasn't the amount he'd won—seven hundred dollars wasn't exactly a fortune—but it *was* an affirmation that he was doing the right thing. Here he'd been at his lowest point, ready to give up and turn himself in; and the next thing he knew, he had money in his hands and was on the road again. It was as if Dottie was really watching out for him, guiding him, reaffirming that his life had a purpose. She was telling him that he was doing the right thing, that he *should* stay on the run, and that something even better was waiting for him down the road.

Walter could hardly contain all the emotions that swelled within him and threatened to burst from his very skin. The fact that Dottie was here, *really here*, guiding and watching over him, was a feeling so joyously overwhelming he almost couldn't handle it.

He was the happiest he'd been in a very long time.

Shutting off the engine, he got out of the car and opened the trunk with his keys. A frigid breeze whistled past his ears. It was colder out today. Sunset was less than an hour away, and the darkening late afternoon sky was heavy with thick gray clouds threatening snow. Even now, a few scattered flakes drifted down on the wind. He had taken the rental through a car wash earlier in the day, and the water drops that froze along the edge stung his bare fingertips when he raised the trunk lid. He was in such a good mood, though, he hardly noticed.

He pulled his suitcase and several shopping bags out of the trunk and slammed the lid closed. After leaving the casino with his winnings, Walter had driven south along the river until he found another motel where he'd registered, paid two nights' stay in cash, and climbed into bed. Excited as he was, he surprisingly fell asleep as soon as his head hit the pillow and didn't wake until almost noon, enjoying the most restful night he'd had since his flight to Minneapolis.

In the morning, after a celebratory breakfast at the diner adjacent to the motel, Walter went into town and left the Grand Am at the car wash while he cleaned his clothes at a nearby laundromat. He really only wanted the inside of the car cleaned to get rid of the coffee and fast-food smells and the remnants of body odor, but thought it might seem suspicious if he didn't get the outside washed as well. Then, in anticipation of the long road trip ahead of him, he bought some new shirts, socks, underwear, and jeans, filled the tank with gas, and had an early dinner before heading back to the motel. He was looking forward to a relaxing night of mindless television and going to bed early before hitting the road again tomorrow.

Thinking how wonderful a hot shower would feel, Walter grabbed the suitcase and shopping bags and thumbed the auto-lock on his key chain before realizing what he'd done. The headlights flashed and the horn honked once as the lock engaged.

His heart skipped a beat as old instincts kicked in. The last thing he wanted now was to call attention to himself. His eyes scanned the parking lot and saw he was the only one around. Relieved, his breath whooshed out in a giant white vapor cloud as the motel clerk, the phone to his ear, came to the window and peered outside. Sheepishly, Walter nodded and lifted the bags higher in an apologetic greeting.

The clerk's mouth opened. He lowered the phone and, after a moment's hesitation, offered a tentative wave with his free hand as if uncertain what to do. Walter almost laughed at the surprised expression on the man's face. Poor guy probably wasn't used to people waving to him. He'd have to make sure to leave the guy a decent tip.

The clerk waved a few seconds longer as Walter headed toward his room, then turned quickly away from the window, and resumed his phone conversation.

Inside the room, Walter locked the door and tossed the suitcase and shopping bags onto the spare bed. The sudden warmth of the room brought beads of sweat to his forehead. He draped his coat over the back of the desk chair, set his boots beside the door, and adjusted the thermostat.

Rummaging through his suitcase, he found a well-worn pair of jeans, his softest flannel shirt, and favorite wool socks. Opening a new package, he pulled out a fresh pair of underwear, then set the whole bundle of clothes on the edge of the vanity. He peeled off his dirty clothes, stuffed them in a plastic bag and climbed into the shower.

Thirty minutes later Walter sat on the bed, dressed in his most comfortable clothes. He leaned back against the headrest, sipping from a plastic bottle of lemonade he'd gotten out of a vending machine at the laundromat, and surfed the TV channels with the remote, searching for something interesting to watch. In the pauses between stations, he heard a car door shut outside.

Walter stretched. After a heavy meal and a relaxing shower, he knew he should feel sleepy, but felt rejuvenated and alive instead. Excitement coursed through his body. The thrill of knowing that Dottie was here with him and watching out for him tingled his nerve endings. He found himself frequently glancing to the side, secretly hoping to catch glimpse of her spirit nearby.

He could hardly sit still. Walter shifted about, making a mess of the bedspread. He tried to find a comfortable position and something on TV to take his mind off the revelation so he could get a good night's sleep, but finally gave up. It was impossible. He was antsy and anxious and, truth be told, he couldn't wait to get back on the road again to find whatever Dottie had in store for him.

No time like the present, then. Leaving the TV on for background noise, Walter flipped the suitcase open and dumped the contents of the shopping bags onto the bed. The cellophane crinkled when he removed the remaining underwear and shirts from their wrappings.

So where should he go? His hands rearranged his laundered clothes to accommodate the new purchases while he considered the question. Where *could* he go? Head south to Arkansas or Oklahoma? Or lose himself in the wild mountains of Wyoming or Montana? It wasn't like he had any specific destination in mind.

Or even had a lot of options. Anyone he knew would have seen him on TV by now. They'd be afraid to harbor a fugitive—or worry what he might do if they did. Like Eleanor and Helen. Surely they'd warned his brother-in-law Karl that he might be coming, and no doubt the police were watching his Seattle home in case he did. He realized he didn't have anyone to turn to.

Which he, oddly enough, found comforting. Without a targeted destination, the cops would be completely lost not knowing where he went.

Walter smiled. Maybe that's what Dottie had in mind.

He retrieved his shaving kit from the bathroom, stuffed it

into the side compartment with his shoes, and was about to zip-per the suitcase shut when he thought he heard another car pull into the motel lot. Walter pointed the remote and shut off the TV, then sat quietly on the edge of the bed. Outside, he heard two men talking.

His hands felt clammy and cold. More people in the tiny motel created a better chance of getting spotted. Maybe that's what Dottie was trying to tell him, why he felt so anxious to move on. He'd learned to trust his inner feelings and the mes-sages Dottie sent.

A few moments later, he heard a door close and all was quiet again.

Walter blew out his breath, almost laughing. Good God, he was getting paranoid. He felt ridiculous. Dottie would take care of him. It was probably just the clerk helping a new guest with something in his room.

Speaking of which, he owed the guy a tip. He pulled out his wallet and counted the bills. A little under five hundred dollars remained after the day's expenses. Not much, but enough to carry him to whatever Dottie had in store. Last night he'd thought briefly about letting his winnings ride at the roulette table, but was afraid he'd lose everything. Or worse, attract at-tention if he kept winning. So, ignoring the other players' encouragement to keep going, he'd cashed his chips at the table—slipping the dealer a fifty-dollar tip—and left the casino, watching carefully to make sure he wasn't followed.

No, he decided, Dottie's gift and message came with that single win. It was her way of saying she was watching out for him. Walter anchored a twenty for the desk clerk under the telephone on the nightstand between the beds. He hoped the maid wouldn't pocket it instead.

Time to go. He wiped his hands on his jeans, shoved his feet into his boots, and donned his jacket. It would have been nice to have gotten a good night's sleep, but he was ready to move on. Walter smiled. He checked the room once more to make sure he hadn't left anything behind, then opened the door—

To a parking lot full of cops standing behind their squad cars, their rifles aimed right at him.

CHAPTER TWENTY-SEVEN

This was the guy they'd been searching for?

Riehle leaned back against the closed door of the Westbrook PD interview room, feeling the cold metal chill the skin between his shoulder blades under his shirt. He was tired and frustrated, and a tightness at his temples warned him a serious headache was coming on. He massaged his forehead with his fingertips.

Something didn't feel right.

Waiving extradition before an Iowa judge, Walter Buczyno was transferred back to Westbrook, arriving late last night amid a flurry of media coverage. Uniformed officers held the press back while the transfer vehicle snaked its way through a barrage of flashbulbs and minicam lights to the ramp leading down to the station's underground loading bays. After completing the necessary paperwork, they unceremoniously dumped him in a holding cell, where he spent the remainder of the long, lonely night.

Riehle checked his watch. He and Capparelli had started in on Buczyno early that morning and had been going at it for several hours now. Aside from the three men's voices, the only other sounds in the light gray–painted room were the soft whir of air from the vents and the occasional scrape of Buczyno's chair on the floor. Their superiors watched and audio- and video-recorded everything from behind the one-way mirror to his left, and Riehle did his best to hide his aggravation and growing uneasiness from them.

Crossing his arms over his chest, he stared down at the man seated before him.

Short, slightly heavyset, and balding, Walter Buczyno sat in his orange DOC jumpsuit with his hands clasped together and his forearms resting on the wooden table, answering their questions and never once complaining or demanding a lawyer. The most he'd done was ask for something to drink, and the water he'd requested sat half-empty in the paper cup on the heavily scarred table near a ballpoint pen and the pad of Voluntary Statement forms provided for him. He never raised his voice or acted violently in any way, claiming that he killed the four boys because they'd broken into his house, threatened him, and tried to rob him. The expression on his face had remained impassive throughout the detectives' questioning. His eyes, however, conveyed a resigned look, though who he'd made his peace with—his fate, the legal system, his god, or his personal demons—Riehle couldn't say.

It seemed almost impossible to believe that this was the same guy who'd cleverly eluded an out-and-out manhunt in six states for so long, caught, finally, from tips by a casino security manager and an observant motel clerk.

Something didn't feel right.

He couldn't quite put his finger on it. Riehle knew it was downright stupid—*dangerous* even, especially in his profession—to judge anyone by his appearance. But though he already knew what Buczyno looked like, Riehle found he had a hard time matching the man before him with the image he'd built up in his mind. His answers to their questions were short and direct; not the single thread of truth woven within a fabric of lies that hardened criminals often used, nor the rambling confessions of a haunted amateur who had gotten in over his head. Riehle couldn't help feeling there was something missing, some single element that would tie everything together. And it troubled him.

Capparelli, however, didn't have that problem. Antsy as a wild animal that smelled raw meat outside its cage, Capparelli paced back and forth, angrily snarling questions at Buczyno as if he were the monstrous Gacy who'd stolen his boyhood friend away. Capparelli barely held himself in check at times, possibly by the knowledge that their superiors were watching through the mirror. To his credit, Buczyno never flinched when Capparelli got right in his face, which only seemed to infuriate his partner even more.

"So you just expect us to believe that these four boys were all burglars breaking into your home? That you were only defending yourself?" Capparelli said for the millionth time.

"That's what I'm saying."

"Then why does everyone want to break into your house? How do you explain that? Three home invasions is a hellava lot. What do you have that's so valuable? Drugs? Stolen merchandise? Stacks of cash?"

"No! No! Nothing like that! How many times do I have to tell you?"

"Then what do you have that's so damned important?"

Buczyno hung his head. "I don't have anything anymore."

Round and round it went. They'd spent most of the morning covering the same ground, going over it again and again, trying to poke holes in his story. But Buczyno remained steadfast the entire time.

Riehle pinched the bridge of his nose. He had to admit he was getting frustrated himself. Frankly, he wanted to throttle the guy, and vaguely wondered what would happen if he let Capparelli have a go at him. While he didn't condone police brutality or torture, he knew the public often had a hard time grasping the fact that criminals weren't about to spill their guts just because you were being nice to them. Not gonna happen.

And yet, that's exactly what Buczyno was doing.

242

Something wasn't right.

Riehle knew he could have stopped hours ago. They had the evidence, their man, his confession. Any thick-headed cop wanting the easy way out would have said, "Case closed, I'm outta here" a long time ago. And yet, doubt gnawed his intestines like a hungry dog. Call it cop's instinct, call it what you will. But something wasn't adding up, and Riehle needed to know *why*.

Pushing off the door, he approached the table. "All right. Let's try this again." He could almost hear the exasperated groans of his superiors in the adjacent room. But Riehle knew the only way to break someone's story was to go over it again and again until a discrepancy arose, allowing the detectives a chink in the armor to penetrate and probe until they discovered what really happened.

"Just to be clear, are you sure you don't want an attorney present?"

Buczyno nodded. "Lawyers only make things worse."

"At least we're in agreement there," Capparelli said.

Riehle ignored his partner. "Stating again for the record, I want to remind you that everything is being audio- and video-recorded, and that you were previously read your rights, you waived your right to an attorney, and you voluntarily signed the Miranda waiver form." When Walter agreed, he unfolded a copy of the map they'd found in Buczyno's basement cabinet and set it on the table. Riehle's finger tapped the drawing of the grave with the earliest date.

"Tell us again about the boy in the concert T-shirt."

Buczyno's shoulders sagged. "It was about a year after my wife died." He paused, his eyes searching Riehle's face. Moments later, his right hand briefly clenched into a fist.

Riehle frowned. He'd noticed he did that periodically. Buczyno had remained steadfastly unremorseful throughout their questioning. The occasional, seemingly unconscious clenched fist was the only outward sign of emotion he'd shown all morning. And he always looked at them before he did it.

What was Buczyno looking for? It was almost as if he were seeking some kind of acknowledgment from them.

Before he could ask him, Buczyno continued.

"The house and yard were a complete mess. Pretty much everything in my life had gone to hell by then and I didn't care. With Dottie gone, I figured why bother taking care of anything if it was all going to be taken away?"

He sighed. "I was having trouble sleeping. I hid a baseball bat under my bed because I kept having nightmares. I'd wake at any little sound." He turned the gold wedding band on his finger, and Riehle observed his flat-edged fingernails, as if Buczyno trimmed them with straight scissors. "But that night, I really did hear someone. There was this horrible crash. I jumped out of bed, grabbed the bat, and ran into the kitchen. And there was this kid breaking down my back door with a crowbar.

"And I mean *breaking* down the door. The idiot was swinging the crowbar all over the place, shattering the glass panes, wrenching the door out of the frame, splinters flying everywhere," he said. Buczyno made eye contact with the detectives. "It was a couple of years before Mary and Benito built the extension onto the back of their house, but I swear to God I still don't know how they slept through it all. That kid was so wild he must have been on drugs. His eyes were little pinpoints and his face was cut and bleeding and he didn't even notice. But when he saw me, he *charged*."

Buczyno's gaze focused inward on the memory as if it were playing out again right before his eyes. "He chased me into the living room. At first, I tried to defend myself by putting the furniture between us to keep him out of reach until I could get to the phone and call the police. But he just kept coming at me, swinging the crowbar and missing me, and taking big chunks out of the furniture.

"And I found myself getting madder and madder. Who the hell did this guy think he was, coming into my home and attacking me? So finally, when he missed one time, I swung the bat as hard as I could and hit him over the head. He went down like a sack of potatoes."

"Was he dead then?" Riehle asked.

"Oh, hell no. That's why I think he was on drugs. He kept getting back up. The stupid jerk wouldn't stay down, and he wouldn't listen to me when I tried to get him to calm down, so I just kept hitting him over and over until he finally died. Must've taken only about five minutes or so, but it was the longest five minutes of my life."

Riehle pulled up a chair, turned it around, and sat down, resting his arms along the backrest. Up until now Buczyno's story had been too pat, too well-rehearsed, as if he had been telling the story by rote. His story remained the same, but now the anger was seeping through, and Riehle wanted to keep him talking.

"What'd you do next?"

"What could I do? When I finally stopped shaking, I started cleaning things up. There was a lot of blood."

"Why didn't you call the police?"

"Are you kidding? How would it have looked?"

"If he'd been on drugs, toxicology reports would have corroborated your story. We'd have listened."

"Like hell. I trusted you before and what did that get me?" His fist clenched. "No. We've created a society where lawyers get rich, criminals become celebrities, and victims are expected to feel lucky if they're portrayed in a made-for-TV movie." He shook his head. "So I took care of the problem myself."

He told them how he'd wrapped the body in a sheet and dragged it into the basement, then dug a grave in the crawlspace and buried him.

"But the living room and kitchen were a complete disaster. So I stayed up the rest of the night, breaking apart the back door and furniture and burning them in the fireplace, sweeping up pieces of glass and wood splinters, and scrubbing and bleaching the walls and floor tiles and anything else that was contaminated by his blood."

He ran a weary hand over his face. Riehle could almost picture the man's exhaustion the next morning.

"The whole time, I kept expecting the cops to come barging in and arrest me. I jumped at every little sound. I knew the bleach wasn't going to clean everything completely and that I'd have to paint the walls to cover the stains and get something to hide the smell of the body." He shrugged. "Besides, I needed a new door. So right after the stores opened, I went out to buy everything I needed, like a door, wood, paint, and lime."

"And that's when Mary and Benito saw you."

Buczyno nodded. "I gave them a story about needing to get on with my life, that redecorating and working with my hands would help me make a fresh start. I felt terrible lying to my best friends like that, but from the way they acted, you'd have thought I'd answered all their prayers," he said. "Anyway, after installing the new door, I started repainting the walls, stripping and refinishing the tiles, making new furniture—even cleaning the yard. Then when the cops didn't come by after a few days to arrest me, I stopped being afraid. I took control of my life again."

"Where'd the kid come from?"

"No idea. Honestly. He didn't have any ID on him and I never found a car or heard about any missing kids from the neighborhood. There was never anything about him on the news, either. It was almost as if the kid had never existed."

Riehle chewed his lower lip. Much as he hated to admit it, the kid sounded like a runaway, and it saddened him to realize they might never know who he was.

"What about the boys from Indiana?" Capparelli said.

"Couple of tattoo-covered gangbangers. Not exactly a lot of hope for the future of mankind."

"What happened, Walter?" Riehle said, steering him back on track.

Buczyno took a sip of water. "After I got the house fixed up and was sure no one could smell anything funny, I had a security system installed. I knew I couldn't trust some outside agency or the police to come into my house if it ever went off, so I had it customized to set off a silent vibration, like a pager, on my wristwatch to warn me if anyone ever tried to break into the house again. A number would light up on the watch's face that indicated which door or window was touched or opened that tripped the alarm. That way, I'd know what direction they were coming from. And I had my bedroom carpeted so they wouldn't hear me waiting."

Buczyno's description confirmed what Mark Bernstein from ADAC Security Systems had told them about his set-up, and what he and Capparelli had surmised in the house. Riehle nodded for him to continue.

"I didn't want all that bloodshed if it ever happened again, so I kept a roll of wire next to the bat under my bed." He shook his head, disgusted. "Sure enough, about eleven o'clock one night last summer, I heard glass break in one of the back door panes and the sound of the bolt being turned. So I got out of bed, grabbed the bat and wire, and waited for the intruder by the bedroom door. And when he came into the hallway, I hit him in the stomach, knocking the wind out if him. That gave me enough time to drop the bat, wrap the wire around his neck, and strangle him."

"Until you heard his friend."

"Right. The punk took a shot at me, then tried to make a run for it. I grabbed the bat and chased him into the living room, and when he turned around to shoot again, I hit him in the wrist and knocked the gun out of his hand.

"And would you believe it? He started swearing at me like *I* was robbing *him*," Buczyno said. "Made me so damned mad I hit him in the face with the bat. He landed on the couch, then rolled onto the floor to get away from me, but I sat on his chest and pressed the bat against his throat until his Adam's apple collapsed and he stopped breathing."

Goosebumps rose on Riehle's forearms. It was the same story he'd heard all morning, but it still gave him chills.

"But he'd bled all over the new cushions. So I had to burn another set of furniture and make new ones again. Only this time I used vinyl-covered cushions in case it ever happened again. Easier to clean. Smartest thing I ever did."

That explained the patio furniture in the living room. Practical, Riehle had to admit, in a twisted sort of way. "What'd you do next?" he said.

"Made sure the first one was dead."

Capparelli rolled his eyes. "No. *After* you killed them."

Buczyno shrugged. "Pretty much the same thing. Dragged their bodies downstairs, dug holes, covered them with lime and buried them in the crawlspace. Only this time, one of them had car keys. I found the car about a block away. Not real hard to find with the Indiana license plates," he said. "I parked it along the outer edge of a grocery store parking lot in case there were any cameras, wiped everything down, and walked home. Part of me kept thinking you'd identify me by some hairs or DNA I'd left behind, but after a few days, they just towed the car away and no one ever came for me."

Riehle didn't bother explaining that it wasn't as easy as it looked on TV. They wouldn't have matched him because he didn't have a prior record and sample on file. "What'd you do with the gun?" he said instead.

"Tossed it in the Des Plaines River."

Though they'd already discussed this detail earlier, Riehle nodded as if it were the only answer that made sense. "We found a manila envelope containing this map," he said, tapping the drawing of the graves, "and the boys' personal effects. Why didn't you throw them away?"

Buczyno sighed. "I'm not completely heartless," he said, directing his remarks at Capparelli. "I knew those boys had families. I figured someone would find them after I died, and it would give their families some closure. So I labeled the gravesites and put all their stuff in there. I didn't even take the cash out of their wallets. I'm not a thief, you know."

"Just a murderer."

Buczyno's eyes hardened. "Are they my victims because I killed them?" he said angrily. "Or am I the victim of unsuccessful robberies?"

"That's walking a mighty fine line there, Walter," Capparelli said. "You know what I think? I think the more you did it, the more you enjoyed it. And you got bolder because you never got caught. It became a thrill for you. Hell, you probably even went out looking for victims, figuring no one could catch you."

"No! They all came into my house!"

"And why, Walter? Why? That's what I don't understand. What do you have that everyone wants?" Capparelli pressed harder. "I think you enjoy it. I think you get off on it. This last time you got off on it so much you beat the guy to a bloody pulp—"

"No," Riehle said. Shocked into silence, Capparelli had a confused look on his face. Buczyno's expression grew wary, and Riehle's skin tingled. He was onto something here. He could feel it.

"No, your story's different when it comes to Harris. He wasn't just another random burglar, was he? You already knew him." Riehle pushed the chair away and leaned forward until Buczyno was forced to look at him. "Time to come clean. Who was he? And what did he do that made you go berserk?"

Buczyno's eye twitched, and Riehle knew he had him.

"Tell me, Walter! *Who was Franklin Edward Harris?*"

CHAPTER TWENTY-EIGHT

Stick to the story!

Walter knew he was slipping. The detectives saw him flinch when they pushed him on Harris this time. But he was tired. He'd hardly slept a wink last night in that cold, brightly-lit holding cell, and they'd been going at him since early that morning. He desperately wanted to rub the grit from his eyes, but was afraid of showing any sign of weakness. Cops were like vultures when they smelled dead meat.

Stick to the story.

It was a simple plan he'd come up with on the trip back from Iowa: Own up to the fact that he'd killed four burglars who'd broken into his home. He was only defending himself, he'd confess honestly. It was nothing personal, but now that they'd caught him, he was ready to act like a man and accept responsibility for his actions. Remain unemotional and straightforward throughout the whole thing, keeping his answers short and to the point. Don't offer up any additional information, least of all about Harris. Either they already knew about his connection to him and Dottie, or his record was truly sealed and they had no idea. No sense in giving them extra material to use against him.

At first, Walter was surprised by how unremorseful he'd sounded. But then he realized that he'd been expecting to be arrested for so long and had gone over his confession so many times in his head that he'd drained all of the emotion out of it.

Coupled with the fact that he honestly believed the four intruders had gotten what they deserved, he was simply telling the detectives what really happened.

Tell the truth and stick to the story. Seemed simple enough.

But the cops had other ideas.

Walter got the impression that the only way the detectives—especially the older one—could understand his actions was if they could prove he was a crazed, serial-killing lunatic. The concept of a man taking care of his own problems because the legal system had already let him down seemed beyond their grasp. And so they badgered and harassed him, going over his story again and again, trying to break his defenses down until he became so frustrated and angry that he lost control of his emotions, providing them with the few desired seconds of video and sound bites to be played *ad nauseam* throughout the news and tabloid programs that would prove to the public that he had indeed been a ferocious danger to his community all along.

Walter wasn't going to let that happen.

And yet they kept after him.

Riehle, the younger detective with the short brown hair, said: "Franklin Edward Harris. That name mean anything to you?"

"Should it? You tell me." The sarcasm in his voice was loud enough for all of them to hear. He didn't know if they'd read Harris's file or not, but he wasn't about to let them turn his actions into some sort of *Death Wish* vengeance scenario. Walter clenched his fist. Harris had returned to his house intending to kill *him*, and all Walter did was what should have been done in the first place. He wasn't going to let the cops twist things around for their convenience.

Capparelli slapped his palm on the table. "Answer the question, goddammit!"

Annoyed, Walter bit back a reply. The detectives had started in with their good cop/bad cop routine first thing that morning, and he'd quickly grown tired of it. The older one with the longer, graying hair and goatee, Capparelli, seemed like a typical old-school cop, the kind of hard-nosed bully who believed there were only two types of people in the world: cops and criminals. For whatever reason, Capparelli appeared to have a personal edge to his anger and had spent most of the morning trying to provoke Walter into an emotional outburst that would prove he was some kind of dangerous monster or freak.

But it was the younger one, Riehle, that worried him. Riehle held back, studying him, analyzing Walter's every movement and word. And when he leaned closer, forcing Walter to look into his eyes, it almost felt as if the detective were reaching an invisible, psychic hand inside his skull, its fingers probing the folds of his brain like he was riffling through a file cabinet, searching for the specific memory or event that would provide him with the information he needed. It gave him the creeps.

He didn't trust either one of them.

"Walter?"

Trying to intimidate him, Riehle was close enough now that Walter could smell eggs and coffee on his breath. A sheen of sweat broke out on Walter's forehead. He reached for the cup of water, using the opportunity to break eye contact. Thirsty as he was, Walter was careful how much he drank. He'd heard how cops wouldn't let you go to the bathroom, making you squirm until you finally pissed your pants and confessed to anything out of humiliation and shame.

Not gonna happen here. Though he'd already lost everything else, he damn sure wasn't going to let the cops steal his dignity too.

Still looking away, Walter took a small sip and set the cup down, his hand surprisingly steady. Truth of the matter was he was tired and miserable and wanted it all to end. His heart felt heavier than it had when he'd stared into the dark, cold waters of the Mississippi River, and it took all of his remaining energy to hold onto his failing composure.

He became aware of a snapping sound. Out of the corner of his eye, he saw Capparelli's left hand balled into a fist, while his right snapped the fingers faintly and steadily like a time bomb ticking, ready to go off at any moment. The logical part of Walter's brain warned him that the detective was only trying to provoke him, but the sound in the tiny room grated his already frayed nerve endings.

How could Dottie do this to him? That was what upset him the most. He couldn't believe she'd brought him all this way just to end up having him spend the rest of his life in prison for murdering the man who'd killed her. Was she punishing him for not protecting her that night? How many sleepless nights had he spent tossing and turning, agonizing over that very thing?

Hadn't he suffered enough already?

Walter swallowed the lump in his throat. His heart ached. He felt guilty that he was questioning her, but he had his doubts. He'd put his faith in her, trusted her to guide him, and he felt like she'd abandoned him in his time of need.

Whatever happened now . . . did it matter anymore?

He blinked hard, desperately trying to hold back the tears. "Harris," Walter heard himself say before he could stop himself. "It's all because of Harris."

Riehle's body jerked, interested, intent. "What is?"

But Walter merely shook his head.

"Admit it, Walter. You knew him, didn't you? Was he the guy who found those other boys for you?"

"No, no. Nothing like that," he said angrily. "I already told you what happened."

"Sure, that was it," Riehle said, ignoring him, baiting him. "He got your victims for you. But then what happened? Did he threaten you? Threaten to turn you in?"

"No, I said!"

"Is that why you beat him to death? To keep him from talking? Was he going to the police?"

"You don't know what you're talking about!" Walter clenched his fist. He was willing to accept his fate, but he wasn't about to let them twist it into something it wasn't.

Keep it together. Don't let them rattle you.

Stick to the story.

"No, you knew him, all right. You knew him real well." Capparelli's face and neck flushed red. "It's sickos like you and Gacy who prey on young boys—"

"*Gacy?* Is that what you think? You're disgusting."

"I'm not the one who's been making it with little boys." His fingers snapped louder and faster, and his left hand slowly rose as if he was getting ready to hit him. "I think you and Harris had something going. I think you liked it rough and dangerous and things got way out of hand—"

"Stop it! Stop it! That's not what happened! Haven't you been listening?" Walter turned to the mirror. "Any of you?"

"But you knew him," Riehle said, pushing. "You tried to hide it from us. You knew who he was all along, didn't you? So tell us, Walter. Tell us who he was right now!"

Sparks popped in his field of vision. His heart pounded against his ribs and his breath came in short, ragged gasps. He gripped the edges of the table with both hands, trying desperately to hold on.

The detectives crowded him, getting right in his face.

"Who was he, Walter? Who was Franklin Edward Harris?"

Walter exploded from his chair. "The bastard who raped and killed my wife!"

Chapter Twenty-Nine

Everything went still, the moment frozen in time. The air was thick and heavy, pausing as if everyone in the entire building suddenly held their breath. Riehle could almost hear his superiors moving closer behind the one-way mirror.

"What did you say?" Riehle asked, his voice barely a whisper. Stunned, his peripheral vision collapsed into a focused tunnel, the world condensing to the three of them in that tiny, sweaty, stagnant room. The hairs along the back of his neck rose.

Buczyno frowned. His eyes searched their faces, the anger subsiding as a confused look—no doubt matching their own—took over. Then his momentum turned like a train switching tracks, and his rage came roaring back with a vengeance.

"I knew it! I *knew* it! It's always about protecting the criminal, isn't it?" Walter said. "You never once thought about what he did to me or my wife."

"What are you talking about?"

"I *told* Helen you didn't care! I knew I couldn't trust the police. That you don't care about people like me. Like us. Protect and serve, my ass. Do you have any idea what we went through? Suffered through? That's why people like us have to take things into our own hands."

Capparelli moved as if he was about to strike him. "Now you listen to me—"

Riehle pushed the two men apart. "Whoa! Back off. Both of you." He ran his fingers through his hair. What the hell just happened? "Everybody calm down. All right?" He pressed his hand firmly against Buczyno's shoulder trying to sit him back down, but Walter shrugged it off.

"No! I will *not* calm down. I'm tired of being treated without any respect. I worked my whole damned life, paying my taxes and bills and being the best person I could be. And then when Dottie got sick and became a victim, they took everything away from us." He slapped his hands flat on the table, the sound an angry blast in the tiny room. "All you cared about was protecting a criminal."

"You're the only criminal I see here," Capparelli said. "What the hell are you talking about?"

"Harris. Harris Harris Harris! Who do you think we're talking about?" Buczyno aimed his finger at them. "He raped and killed my wife. It's all in his record. Didn't you read the file?"

"How could we? Harris's juvenile record was sealed," Riehle said, backpedaling quickly. The lie was easier than admitting the damned file was lost.

The play of emotions across Buczyno's face was painful to behold. Anger, resentment, agony, exasperation—his expressions conveyed the look of a man pushed beyond his limits. His eyes grew unfocused. His hand went to his chest and his breathing became short and shallow. The table legs scraped the tiles as he tottered against it. Riehle caught him before he fell and helped him into the chair.

Riehle looked at the mirror, trying to project a sense of urgency. Should they call for medical assistance? He handed Buczyno a cup of water. "Here, take a drink."

Buczyno took a small sip, then pushed the cup away. He shook his head sadly, as if the weight of his realization was too much to bear.

"You never understood. I can't believe it. All this time, you're still protecting him after everything he did."

Riehle set the cup down and held the man by his shoulders, steadying him. Capparelli stood ready in case Buczyno tried something, the expression on his face clearly indicating that he hoped he would.

When it finally looked like Buczyno was going to be okay, Riehle said, "We want to understand. Really, we do. But you have to help us. Tell us what happened, Walter. Tell us what's in the file."

Walter closed his eyes. A tiny tear squeezed out of one corner but refused to drop. His temple muscles twitched. Riehle wasn't sure if it was anguish or anger that possessed him now.

Buczyno took a deep breath and exhaled sharply. He wiped his eyes and looked at them, his jaw set in a firm resolve.

"You have to understand," he said. "My wife was everything to me. We were never blessed with children, so we only had each other to depend on. But then she got sick. The cancer, the *treatments* . . . tore apart the woman I loved, and I couldn't do anything about it. I've never felt more helpless in my life."

He ran a weary hand over his grief-stricken face. "Finally, when we knew she wasn't going to make it, I brought her home. She didn't want . . . she didn't want to die in a hospital," he said, swallowing a catch in his voice. Then it got a hard edge to it. "But the insurance company refused to pay for her hospice care, and I had to sell my business to get the money we needed. I would have done anything for her."

He squeezed his eyes shut. "Dottie was so frail. A nurse came by twice a day to administer her medications and change her oxygen tanks. She'd lost all of her beautiful hair and weighed only ninety pounds. She could barely move, but she wanted to die with dignity."

"Tell us what happened," Riehle said.

A haunted look washed over Buczyno. He turned his wedding ring around and around on his finger. "I'd been down in the basement most of the day. Dottie wanted to be buried with some photographs and mementos of our life together, and I was making a special box for her to put them in. I was going to surprise her with it."

Riehle thought about all the woodworking equipment in Buczyno's basement and the quality of the workmanship he'd seen in the living and dining room furniture. He could only imagine the love and intricate detail Walter had carved into the last gift he would ever give his wife.

"It'd rained earlier that day," Buczyno said, "and when I opened the basement windows to air the sawdust out, I remember how fresh it smelled. Dottie wanted to watch a movie that night, so I went to out to pick one up. I was only gone about a half hour or so. But I'd left the windows open while I was gone."

Buczyno's hands trembled, and a mixture of rage and agony crossed his face. Riehle wondered in how many nightmares and tortured memories Walter had revisited this scene.

Riehle remained quiet, waiting.

"When I got home," Buczyno began a long moment later, "I noticed the basement window screen was broken out of its frame. At first, I thought maybe I hadn't secured it right when I'd opened it earlier and it had fallen to the floor." He shuddered. "But then I saw the muddy footprints."

He turned the ring on his finger. "The cops said later I dropped the movie right there." He shrugged. "I can't say. I don't know. I just remember running into the house, screaming Dottie's name. And when I got to the bedroom, there was this . . . there was this kid—"

Buczyno faltered, seemingly unable to find the words he needed to say. He clenched his jaw so tightly the muscles bunched like cords along the side of his face. An agonized whimper escaped his lips.

"He was on top of her," he said, his voice shaking with pain and misery. The tears began to flow. "*Raping* her. Raping the love of my life while she lay dying in a hospice gurney hooked up to an IV."

There was anger in his eyes now when he glared at Capparelli. "And *you*. All morning long I've had to listen to you calling *me* a sicko. But you never saw what Harris, that . . . *animal*, did to my frail, ninety-pound, skin-and-bones wife. How *dare* you call me sick after what he did to her!"

"What did you do?" Riehle said quickly.

"I pulled him off her and beat him unconscious, then called the police and an ambulance," he said. "But she never recovered. She'd already been in so much pain, and what he did to her . . ." Buczyno sobbed into his hands. "He broke her hip and three ribs and tore her so badly it took the doctors almost an hour to stop the bleeding."

Riehle offered him a tissue, and he wiped his eyes. "Dottie went into a coma and never came out of it. She died three days later. I never even got to say goodbye."

The room fell silent except for the sound of Walter crying. The detectives sat down, giving the man time to collect himself. Inwardly, Riehle had to admit the story affected him. He glanced at his partner, but if there was any sympathy for Buczyno, Capparelli didn't show it. Though his complexion had returned to normal, his expression was still one of guarded suspicion.

"And then the lawyers started in." Buczyno wiped the snot from his nose. "They made me use words like 'alleged.' Like what I *allegedly* saw him doing," he said, the disgust clear as a bell in his voice. "Meanwhile, while Dottie was in a coma from her injuries, Harris got an ivory tower attorney to defend him *pro bono*. You ever hear of Melissa Thorne?"

Riehle nodded, and a low growl emanated from Capparelli's

throat. A total media hound, the woman sucked up to any reporter she could snare, getting as much air-time as possible. She made her living insinuating police and prosecutors falsely accused and harassed her clients, using the regional and national exposure of the poor ones to file claims of police beatings, torture, and false imprisonment to then attract as clients the CEOs and CFOs who could pay for her extravagant lifestyle.

"Real piece of work, that one." Buczyno clenched his fist. "An hour after my wife died, Thorne threatened to sue me for bodily harm for injuries Harris sustained when I hit him and held him down until the cops arrived. Then she got the judge to ignore his prior arrest record and hired a medical examiner to testify that Harris hadn't killed her, that the cancer would have done it anyway. She argued that Dottie had merely been in the wrong place at the wrong time—as if being in a hospice gurney in her own home was her fault!—and Harris shouldn't be held responsible. Because of that, he was sentenced for only six years until he became twenty-one." Buczyno slammed his fist on the table. "*Six years!* For killing my wife!"

"That must have been hard for you to accept," Riehle said.

"I don't know what was worse: the things he did to her, or what her family and I and all our friends had to endure afterward." Buczyno wiped his eyes with the back of his hand. "The fact that my wonderful, beautiful wife was gone forever in such a brutal way, and that an animal like him was allowed to live his life with a clean slate after he got out was hard enough. But the way Thorne talked about her, and the things Harris said after his sentencing—" His hands shook with rage.

"I'm sure your attorney objected and the judge threatened to hold them in contempt," Capparelli said. "And most of it was stricken from the official record."

"But it didn't stop them from *saying* those things!" Buczyno argued. "It was bad enough having to listen to everything he did to her and the humiliation of the courtroom seeing her private parts when they showed photos of her injuries. But the way Thorne talked about her in the trial, and how Harris said in the hallway after his sentencing that Dottie's last words were that he was the best fuck she'd ever had—it was like she was being raped all over again in front of everyone and we were being raped along with her."

He glared at Capparelli. "So what if it wasn't in the transcripts? You can't erase what we heard or wipe those soiled images from our memories. We—her family, our friends, and I—all have to live with that for the rest of our lives. How could they let him do that? Don't *we* have any rights?"

"When the police arrest someone," Riehle said, "we do our best to make sure that the person is prosecuted to the fullest extent of the law."

"But do the *victims* have any rights? You read the criminal his rights as soon as you arrest him. So why can't you tell the victims and their families that they have the right to be treated with dignity, the right not to be shamed and humiliated and victimized by the criminals and their attorneys all over again?"

"We can't do that."

"Why not?" Walter argued. "Why not?"

"The legal system isn't designed that way."

"Then maybe that's the problem."

"So your answer was to become a serial killer?" Capparelli said. "To go out and find Harris after he was released so you could kill him because the court system didn't?"

"Haven't you been listening?" He turned to the mirror again. "Any of you? He came to my house to kill *me*. He was such an animal that he believed the only reason he was convicted was because I testified against him, *not* because of what he did to Dottie.

"You should have heard the things he said while I was beating him with the bat," Buczyno continued. "How it was my fault for ruining his life, how Dottie had never had it so good with a real man before, and how he'd waited a whole year after his release before coming to get me to throw the cops off. If there was ever anyone who deserved to die, it was him."

"Sounds like a whole lot of smoke and mirrors to me," Capparelli said. "All I'm hearing is a weak rationalization for your twisted sense of justice."

"Twisted? *Twisted?* I killed the man who raped and murdered my wife and had returned to kill me," Buczyno argued. "Meanwhile, a politician, who was later convicted in his own corruption scandal, took someone off Death Row who had cut a baby out of a woman's body while she was still alive. And you're saying *I* have a twisted sense of justice?"

"I don't give a damn what some politician did," Capparelli said, his face flushed with anger. "We're here to talk about what you did. And all I'm seeing is a man who murdered four people in cold blood, who made up a bullshit story about burglaries and tried to get away with it. Well, I for one don't buy any of it, and I will *personally* see to it that you're put away for the rest of your life."

"You think I give a damn about what happens to me now? I've lost everything. But I still have my dignity, and I'll proudly go to my grave knowing I avenged the love of my life."

Buczyno rose from his chair and met Capparelli's glare with a challenge of his own. "A man is supposed to protect what belongs to him. What kind of man does nothing?"

Riehle moved quickly, expecting a fight to break out. But instead of seeing his partner attack the man, Capparelli merely stood there, tottering and ashen, the blood completely drained from his face and wearing an expression of extreme surprise and pain.

He looked like he'd been kicked in the balls.

Before Buczyno could register any change in the detectives, Riehle shoved Walter back down into his chair and pushed the pen and pad of Voluntary Statement forms toward him.

"Write down everything you told us. Then we'll review it for the record and take it to the lieutenant."

Then he grabbed his partner's arm and hustled him out of the room, thinking: *What the hell just happened here?*

Something wasn't right.

Chapter Thirty

"I don't give a rat's ass about any mitigating crap!" Gavin roared. "He killed four people in this town, and I'll be goddamned if I'm gonna let him go free!"

Gavin held court in his office. The blinds were shut and the door was closed, but Riehle had no doubt that everyone in the entire building could hear him. Riehle and Capparelli were sitting in the chairs in front of Gavin's desk as if they were in the hot seats, while State's Attorney Evan Sandoval and FBI Special Agent Phillip Kleisner leaned against the filing cabinets behind them. Gavin had pushed his swivel chair out of the way, and he alternated between angrily pacing back and forth behind his desk and leaning over the desktop on his knuckles. His fists were clenched either way.

"No one said anything about letting him go," Riehle said. They'd been on his case ever since they'd gotten to Gavin's office. Gavin wanted everything neat and tidy. Everything Riehle had said and done during Buczyno's interview had been picked apart, and it irritated the living shit out of him. He chose his words carefully though, as Gavin was his superior officer. "I'm just saying there are additional circumstances to consider."

"Like hell there are," Sandoval said. Even if Riehle hadn't seen him enter the room, he would have known he was there. The muscle-bound, fastidiously dressed state's attorney with gelled-back hair wore enough cologne to fill an entire stadium. He tapped his pinkie ring against the metal filing cabinet when he spoke. "I can't believe you're buying into it. Cut through the bullshit and look at the facts."

"And the facts agree that Buczyno was telling the truth," Riehle argued. Harris's missing file had finally been found. It had gotten mixed in with a DUI file during the jurisdictional transfer from the county sheriff's office to the Westbrook PD when the town annexed the unincorporated area. Though juvenile records were considered sealed, the truth was they were only sealed from the public; cops and prosecutors could access them whenever necessary, and they'd gone over everything as soon as it was found. Harris's rap sheet listed multiple arrests for home invasion, attempted robbery, and gang affiliations between the ages of eleven and fourteen, and at age fifteen, the rape of one hospice-bound Dorothy "Dottie" Buczyno for which he was remanded to a juvenile home until age eighteen, then transferred to Granger County Jail to serve out the remainder of his sentence until age twenty-one. Everything Walter said was confirmed by the police report and notes taken during the trial.

It also explained why they'd never been able to find any newspaper or online references to the case. Though her injuries had probably contributed toward her death (and why Walter felt Harris had murdered her), Harris had only been officially charged with and convicted of aggravated criminal sexual assault, and the identities of rape victims were rarely released to the media.

"The truth as far as *he* sees it. But that isn't necessarily how the legal system views it."

"Let's not forget what he did to those other boys," FBI Special Agent Kleisner said. "There isn't a single piece of evidence to corroborate his story about what happened to them. For all we know, he fabricated the entire thing. Remember: Serial killers are narcissistic, morally deficient, psychopathic liars who get away with the things they do because they *are* so convincing."

Riehle shifted uncomfortably. The very presence of the lanky, redheaded agent in the room made him uneasy. The FBI's jurisdiction extended well beyond that of their little suburban town, and because two of the boys were from Indiana, the feds could steal the case away from them at any time.

But even more than that, Riehle was worried about his partner. Capparelli had been oddly quiet, almost subdued, since leaving the interview. Something Buczyno said had struck a deep, personal nerve, and Riehle didn't know what was involved, much less what to do about it.

"First, let's make one thing perfectly clear," Sandoval said. "The state would never consider dropping or reducing the charges. A defense attorney might be able to convince a brain-dead jury that Buczyno wasn't guilty by reason of whatever cockamamie excuses they'll use. But there is no way the state will not, and should not, pursue this matter to the fullest. So if you're trying to convince me otherwise, forget it."

"I never said—" Riehle began.

"And second, have you thought about the ramifications of what would happen if we did? The media has already built this guy up in the public's eyes as the latest Gacy. Can you imagine the outcry if we even considered letting him go? Everything from being called soft on crime to social and political outrage. Every group with an agenda would be up in arms and shoving it back in our faces, and the global media would eat it up. You want to want to see yourself on everything from CNN and Comedy Central to *Saturday Night Live* and YouTube for the next ten years? They'd mock us mercilessly. Hasn't Illinois suffered enough scandals already? You really want more?"

"There's also the concern about Buczyno's safety," Kleisner added. "Putting him back on the street would be signing his death warrant. Think about what all those vigilantes went through, like the New York subway guy. This would be a hundred times worse. Every weekend warrior, gangbanger, gun nut, and psycho-fanatic would use him as target practice, trying to make a name for himself. And then he'd claim that he was only doing what the legal system should have done anyway. And so on and so on."

"You really want to open up that can of worms?" Sandoval said. "Neither do I."

Gavin exhaled sharply. He rubbed the back of his neck. "This whole clusterfuck is my fault. I should have formed a task force right from the get-go. But no, I thought we already knew who did it, how hard could it be to find the guy? Serves me right for putting Starsky and Hutch in charge."

Riehle bristled. "Hey! We found him."

"No, *you* didn't. A sharp-eyed motel clerk and the head of security at an Iowa casino did. You only questioned him after he was transferred back." Gavin leaned over the desk. "And then you went soft on him and got swayed by his story. Your job was to get the facts and his confession. Period. Then hand it over to the lawyers to sort out the complications."

"What complications?" Sandoval said. "He killed four people. The state doesn't care if his victims were saints or sinners, it's still first degree murder. Then there's the other charges of kidnapping, concealing of a homicide, dismembering of a human body—"

"Don't forget crossing state lines if he grabbed those boys in Indiana," Kleisner added.

"We're only just beginning to scratch the surface of what he did here," Sandoval agreed. He crossed his arms over his chest. "Face it: We've got this guy by the short hairs. No matter what he says, he's going down. You ask me, this whole burglar-killing story is nothing more than an elaborate smoke and mirrors cover for old-fashioned revenge."

"Now hold on a minute," Riehle argued, on firmer ground here. He turned around in his chair to confront the state's attorney. "If they were truly revenge killings, why wouldn't he have gone after Melissa Thorne, Harris's defense attorney? Or the judge? Or anyone else involved in the case?"

"Maybe he just hadn't gotten around to it. Or the opportunity hadn't presented itself yet. We don't know what else this guy might have done. All we can do is nail him with the evidence for the crimes we know he committed."

"Exactly. For what we *know* he did," Riehle said. "And yet you're willing to stand here and accuse him of plotting to murder a defense attorney and judge. Just like you're willing to accuse him of stalking and kidnapping those boys before he murdered them, when there's no evidence to indicate that anything happened any differently than what Buczyno said."

"All right, say for argument's sake that he didn't go out looking for any of his victims," Sandoval said. "Why'd those boys come all the way from Indiana?"

"Happens all the time," Riehle said. "Boys looking for some action and they spot Buczyno's house from the Tri-State, right by the exit ramp. It's a nice house that appears unprotected in a crumbling neighborhood. Whether they're looking to fence something in the city or want to blow off steam on the way home, they figure to get in and out and back on the tollway before anyone's the wiser. Only the house isn't the easy target they think it is."

"Sounds like Buczyno was trying to entice potential victims," Gavin said.

Sandoval shook his head. "That's like saying a woman deserves to be raped because of the way she dresses."

"Then he's like that guy on the New York subway."

"Not at all," Riehle said. "Buczyno never left his house. They all came to him."

"*Allegedly*," Sandoval argued.

"What I don't understand is why did Harris go back?" Gavin said.

Riehle shrugged. "You know how the world works today. Spill coffee on yourself and it's the restaurant's fault. Murder someone and accuse the arresting officer of racism. Nobody's responsible for his own actions anymore—it's who's ever accountable. And the deeper the pockets, the better." He sat forward. "Harris figured he did time not because he raped a sick old woman, but because Buczyno testified against him. And the whole time he was away, he planned on getting even."

"Except Buczyno was ready for him."

"Right. Harris even waited a year after his release to throw off any suspicion, for all the good it did," Riehle said. "When Buczyno realized who'd broken into his home this last time, he took out all his frustration on the man who'd made his life a living hell. Then he swabbed the basement, threw the broken chair and baseball bat into the fireplace, and caught the first available flight to St. Paul to tell his wife's family that he'd finally avenged Dottie's murder. It was only sheer coincidence that the pipe fitting burst while he was away. Otherwise we might never have discovered any of this."

"So you're agreeing he was still a threat? That he would have continued doing what he did if we hadn't caught him?"

"Only if someone else broke into his house," Riehle stressed. "Remember, we never found a single witness who ever saw him hanging around bars or any other public place, and so as far as we know, he never went out looking for victims. So the question we need to ask ourselves is this: Is a man really a serial killer if he only kills the burglars who break into his home?"

"Are you trying to be his defense attorney?" Sandoval said. "Because it sure sounds like you've got the whole thing worked out for him. Even if the murders-as-self-defense angle was justified, he's still guilty of all the other charges, because he didn't call the cops and he tried to destroy the evidence."

"Absolutely." Riehle put his palms up between them. "I'm just reminding you that a man has the right to defend himself in his own home, especially when you consider everything that happened to his wife."

Surprisingly, it was Capparelli who said, "Because a man's home is his castle."

They all looked at him as if he'd woken from a coma.

"Nice of you to join us," Gavin said sarcastically. "Then let's hope it's only one man's castle, gentlemen, because I don't need a whole town of vigilantes."

"Or an opportunity to widen the legal loophole defense attorneys already abuse," Sandoval said. "Thanks, but no thanks. I've got enough headaches as it is."

"All I'm saying is there must be some other way," Riehle said.

"If there was only one body, sure, I could understand self-defense or diminished capacity, maybe later agree to reduce the charges to involuntary manslaughter. But four? No way. It looks too premeditated."

"But—"

"I understand your point, detective. But I'm sorry. There's simply no way around it."

There was a soft knock at the door.

"Who is it?" Gavin yelled. When Dixie opened the door and stuck her head in, he said, "We're in a meeting here. Can't it wait?"

"No, sir." Her eyes met Riehle's. "There's a situation involving your friend Jensen."

"I thought he was still in the hospital under guard?" Capparelli said.

"Another one of your goddamned problems." Gavin's face

flooded with disgust. "Go take care of it and get the hell out of my sight."

As the detectives stood, Special Agent Kleisner said he'd have a go at Buczyno. Riehle clenched his fists in frustration and pushed his way out the door, knowing that the case had probably just been taken out of their hands.

CHAPTER THIRTY-ONE

"You've certainly made things interesting for us this morning, Walter."

Expecting the detectives to return after leaving him alone to stew a while, Walter was surprised when a different man entered instead. He took a seat opposite him at the interrogation table and drummed his fingers on the tabletop a few moments before introducing himself as FBI Special Agent Phillip Kleisner. The man's reddish-blond hair was parted on the right, his pale skin freckled, and the bridge of his nose was severely pinched as if he had until recently worn thick, heavy glasses. His suit and tie were regulation G-man, though they hung loosely on his tall, lanky frame, and he reminded Walter more of an emaciated former basketball player than the hard-bodied agents so often portrayed in the movies.

That he took his profession seriously, however, was never in any doubt.

Kleisner reminded him that everything was still being audio- and video-recorded and confirmed that Walter had previously waived his rights before reaching for the pad of Voluntary Statement forms. He pulled a gold pen from his suit's inner breast pocket and clicked it continuously while he read Walter's written statement. When he finished, he tossed the pad on the table and threw Walter a skeptical glance with his glacial blue eyes.

"That's quite a story you've got there," he said.

Here we go again. "I'm only telling the truth."

"Right. Like I haven't heard that one before."

Walter ground his teeth. "Harris was trying to kill me, and the other boys were burglarizing my home."

"And you were only defending yourself because you were the victim. Yeah, I heard your little speech about criminals having all the rights," Kleisner said. "But let me tell you something: No matter what you've managed to convince yourself to justify your actions, a month into your sentence when someone shivs you in the shower or a trustee lets some of the homeboys into your cell after lights-out, we'll see how many rights you think you have then."

Leaning forward, he rested on his forearms. "Now. Doesn't mean I'm not interested in talking with you, though." He tapped his pen on the tabletop. "Frankly, this is one of the more unique situations I've run across. Extenuating circumstances and all that. Suffice to say, maybe there's something we can work out between us."

A chill pierced the back of Walter's neck as if someone had nicked the base of his skull with an icicle. Every instinct warned him not to trust the guy. "What are you saying?" he asked cautiously.

Kleisner opened his hands as if to show he had nothing to hide, his mocking expression wondering how anyone could suggest otherwise, though his eyes were hard and flat.

"Time to face the music, Walter. The state's attorney assigned to your case is Evan Sandoval. I've known the guy for years, and I sure as hell wouldn't want to be in your shoes. You might think you have a great defense now, but once Sandoval gets hold of you, you're toast. He's brought guys with iron-clad alibis down in flames. So you'd better believe I'm your last chance."

"Meaning?"

"Cut the bullshit and tell me what really happened."

Walter sighed. "The one boy was whacked out on drugs, and Harris and the Indiana boys had guns. If I hadn't defended myself, I'd be the one who was dead. End of story. What else do you want me to say?"

"Then where are the guns?"

He gestured at the statement pad. "I already told you. I dumped one in the Des Plaines River and the other in the Cal Sag Channel. What'd you think? I was going to keep those nasty things around my house?"

"I just find it interesting that you don't possess a single piece of evidence to support your claim, and anyone who could refute your story is dead." Kleisner shrugged dramatically. "Maybe it's me, but some people might think you're a clever, predatory serial killer who's making the whole 'defending yourself' thing up."

Walter refused to be goaded. "So you'd rather I was dead? Better to let the real criminals go free?" He shook his finger at him. "Everything happened exactly as I wrote it, just like I told the detectives, and I'd do it again if I was put in the same situation."

"That's the thing. You are *never* going to be in that situation again, because you're looking at spending the rest of your life behind bars unless you can give me something right here, right now, that will convince me otherwise."

"You want me to plea bargain? With what? I told the truth. Only criminals who are trying to get away with something cop a plea. I'm willing to stand up for what I did."

"Excuse me, I didn't realize you were so principled."

Walter ignored him. "If there was any justice, you'd let me go. I only did to Harris what should have been done in the first place."

"Let you go? Puh-leeze. If it was only Harris, that'd be one thing. But what about the other boys? Or were you hoping we'd

275

forget about them? You're looking at a slew of charges: first degree murder, kidnapping, dismembering a human body, concealing of a homicide," the FBI agent said, counting the charges on his fingers, "and a dozen others I can think of off the top of my head, multiplied by four bodies. You want me to go on? Sandoval's got enough right there to lock you away forever."

"And justice? Gimme a break." Kleisner held up his hands between them. "Let's make this perfectly clear. On one hand we've got justice, while the other has the legal system." Walter noticed the man's hands barely touched. "And the way things work around here is *you* don't have the right to be judge, jury, and executioner."

Walter felt the screw tightening, but was unable to suppress his anger any longer. "Gee. Sorry. I forgot who has all the rights."

"Better lose the attitude, pal. Don't forget who's holding your fate in his hands."

"I never said I didn't kill them. I'm willing to be responsible and pay the price for my actions."

"Good for you. Pleading guilty—I like that. Then you'll be the only one in prison who actually committed the crimes he was sentenced for," Kleisner said, his tone heavy with sarcasm. "They'll lock you up, Sandoval will keep his high conviction record, maybe even run for office on the notoriety of the case, and the public will go back to the illusion that their streets are safe and nothing like this could ever happen to them." He tapped the table with his pen. "Wake up, pal. This is your one and only chance. Fuck with me and it's over."

Walter looked away. At that moment, for some unknown reason, the image of the man in the casino saying, "You won, man!" popped into his mind. Only now he didn't feel like a winner. How could he? He felt like the most lonely, abandoned soul that had ever lived. Maybe he'd heard the man wrong. Maybe the guy had said: "You're one man." Sure, that had to be it. *You're one man,* all right. *One man against the legal system.*

And what was he supposed to do about it?

He thought about the statue of the fireman rescuing the little girl in the Minneapolis-St. Paul airport. Poised on the brink of being consumed by the hell-fires of the prison system, Walter wondered if anyone was going to rescue him. Then again, he believed in what he'd done, that Harris deserved everything he got. Walter felt that plea bargaining was something a sleazy criminal did when he was guilty, and while he *had* committed a criminal act, he didn't believe he truly was a criminal. Copping a plea would mean having to see himself as a criminal and not just as a man defending his home.

So he had to ask himself: Did he even want to be rescued?

Then again, why should he have to go to prison for killing the man who'd murdered his wife and had returned to kill him?

Back and forth, back and forth, Walter struggled with the conflicting turmoil within him.

"What do you want?" he asked finally.

"The truth. *All* of it. I think you're holding out on something and I want to know what it is. Tell me, and I'll talk to the detectives and state's attorney about considering the extenuating circumstances, maybe see about reducing the charges and work something out. Otherwise, you're history."

And there it was. Walter felt his world crashing down around him. Kleisner hadn't been listening to him at all. The cops, state's attorney, and even the FBI still believed that there was some sort of lurid connection between him and Harris and the other boys, and they were trying to entice the information out of him with empty promises. They'd never believed him. Not once. It was all a ploy. Just like when everything had happened to Dottie, the insurance companies, Melissa Thorne, and the judge had had their own agendas, never once caring what happened to them. Only now the authorities wanted to lock him in a cage and throw away the key, all for protecting his home and doing to Harris what should have been done in the first place.

Walter's eyes swam and he buried his face in his hands, refusing to allow the tears to fall. How could it have ever come to this? All he'd ever tried to do was protect himself and his wife from the horrors of the outside world, and he'd failed miserably. Dottie was dead, long gone and buried, and now he was about to spend the rest of his life in prison for defending himself against the man who'd killed her.

His heart ached as it never had before, and it took every remaining ounce of energy to keep from sobbing uncontrollably. Standing on the precipice, facing the abyss of the prison system, he felt more alone and abandoned than he had when he'd stood on the brink of the Mississippi River contemplating ending it all in the dark, cold waters of the unforgiving river.

And he wondered: Rather than endure this inevitable fate, why *hadn't* he jumped when he still had the chance? What had kept him from doing so? Surely this wasn't what Dottie intended for him. It wasn't like her to be so vindictive, to punish him for his very human mistakes, so unforgiving as to abandon him in his time of need. Her promises of love were for forever. He believed that. He believed it with all of his heart, and he realized that not putting his trust and faith in her was his greatest sin. She had always brought out the best in him, and he truly believed that she meant for him to find something better.

But what?

Kleisner leaned back in his chair, crossing one leg over the other knee, trying to appear casual but only succeeding in projecting his growing anger. "From where I'm sitting, I don't see many options. Give us the finger and you go away for the rest of your life. Cooperate," he said, pointing his pen at him, "tell me what I want to hear, and I'll see about making some kind of deal. But you'd better make up your mind, Walter. I'm not a very patient man and you're running out of time. Quickly. So what's it gonna be?"

Walter knew he couldn't lie to Kleisner, fabricate something that would later make things worse for him. He wanted to tell the truth. But what did he have? His mind frantically searched his memories for something, *anything* the FBI might want or need, but he couldn't think of a single thing.

Sweat beaded on his forehead. What could he possibly have that they wanted?

"Clock's ticking . . ."

Helen's parting words echoed inside his mind: *Make the legal system work for you.*

And just how was he supposed to do that? He was only one man. What could he possibly do?

Walter wiped his forehead with the back of his hand. Think! Think! Think! His heart pounded against his ribcage. He'd heard that the keys to someone's success often lay within that person's grasp without him or her ever knowing it. He truly believed Dottie had a purpose for him if only he was willing to find it, and he trusted that she had a reason for bringing him here.

But what was it?

You won, man!

You're one man.

One man against the legal system.

"Last chance . . ."

And like the statue of the girl clinging to the fireman who carried her to safety, Walter felt himself reaching for Dottie, understanding now how she'd been there all along, waiting patiently for him to cast aside his doubts so she could save him.

Make the legal system work for you.

279

Then suddenly, he knew what to say.

Kleisner slapped his palm on the table. "Time's up."

"Wait!"

"Too late. You had your chance." Kleisner pushed away from the table, his chair legs scraping on the tile. He banged on the door and a uniformed officer opened it. "Maybe I'll see you at the arraignment—"

"Don't you want to know about a body dumped in the Mississippi River near a casino?"

His long arm shot out, slamming the door shut in the startled officer's face. But the FBI special agent didn't care. His attention was focused completely on Walter.

"I'm listening," he said.

CHAPTER THIRTY-TWO

Though the early afternoon sun was unobscured by clouds, all of the warmth had been drained from the sky.

Riehle and Capparelli pulled to the curb, parking their car down the street from the Metcalf house. Most of Lyman Avenue was cordoned off with wooden sawhorses as a dozen uniformed officers held its evacuated residents and the surrounding streets' residents at bay. News of the hostage situation had drawn additional curious bystanders and the media like flies. The glare from the overhead sun and a cold, bitter, whistling wind forced the detectives to keep their heads down, though it didn't prevent an angry cluster of women, led by Metcalf's wife, from spotting them.

"There he is! That's the one who threatened us!" she yelled, pointing at Riehle. Minicams and microphones swung in his direction. "It's his fault that evil man is inside our house!"

Ignoring her and the barrage of questions shouted by reporters, the detectives headed straight for the police sharpshooter and the hostage negotiator who were positioned behind the squad car blocking the end of Metcalf's driveway. The sharpshooter had his eye to the rifle's scope and his head was turned away, so Riehle couldn't tell who it was. But there was no mistaking Lippencott, the negotiator. With his dark brown curls, aviator sunglasses, bushy mustache, and perpetual salon tan, he seemed to feel the dress code was determined more by the TV show *CHiPs* than departmental regulations. The media loved him, however, and with his actor's looks, there was no denying that in a crisis situation the people in trouble preferred talking to him over any buzz-cut, uniformed officer. Riehle wondered why Lippencott even needed him today.

"I oughta tell that uppity bitch in front of everyone that Jensen wouldn't be here if her drunken husband hadn't killed his family in the first place," Riehle said when they reached them.

"Forget it," Lippencott said. "You really want to let the media chop up what you say? Angry cop yelling at the defenseless wife of a man being held hostage at gunpoint? Not smart. Now, how about we focus on getting both of them out of there alive and worry about your personal issues later."

Riehle exhaled sharply. "Right. So what do we know?"

Lippencott told them what they'd been able to find out so far. "Jensen's been in the hospital under psych watch with a police guard outside his door ever since that little incident when he dug up his daughter's corpse. This morning started out like usual with a visit from his sister."

"Sheila."

"Right. Only this time they had a huge argument and she stormed out of the room. According to eyewitnesses, they were still yelling at each other as she went down the hallway. At one point she turned around and acted like she was about to go back, but then changed her mind, spun around, and barreled right into a tray of instruments and medications for other patients on the floor. Made a hell of a noise, I understand. Then she slipped on the pills, fell to the floor, and started screaming at the nurses, who all came running. Including the cop outside Jensen's door."

"Uh-oh."

"You got it. Jensen, who apparently was already dressed in his street clothes under the bedcovers, snuck out during the disturbance to a rental car waiting in the parking lot. We figure Shelia gave him the keys and told him its location before the charade started."

"Creating a diversion for his escape," Riehle said, disgusted. "That woman has a real attitude about cops."

"So I gather. Then she disappeared in all the commotion when they realized her brother was missing."

Capparelli fumed. "I swear, if I ever get my hands on her—"

"Not our concern," Lippencott said. "Our problem right now is that Jensen is holding Metcalf hostage at gunpoint inside the house."

"Where'd he get the gun?" Riehle sighed. "Let me guess: Sheila had it stashed in the car for him."

"That's the scenario we're going with."

"Goddammit!" Capparelli said. He had a sudden thought. "Where're the kids?"

"In school. And they don't know anything about it. We found the rental parked on the street the next block over. We're not sure if Jensen hid and waited until he saw the wife and kids leave or if he simply timed it right, but when Metcalf answered the door, Jensen pushed his way inside. The two men have been alone in there ever since."

"Sure about that?"

"Far as we know. That's one of the things we need to find out."

"So why are we here?" Riehle said.

"Because you're the only one Jensen will talk to. The first thing he did was have Metcalf call his wife on her cell, tell her what was going on, and specifically request to talk to you. Jensen hasn't answered any of our calls since because he's been waiting for you."

"Great. So now she really thinks I'm in cahoots with him."

"You're the man."

"Hold on," Capparelli said. "I've been involved in hostage situations before. Shouldn't you be—"

"Don't tell me what to do. I agree this isn't going according to protocol, but right now my job is to defuse the situation so nobody gets hurt. Jensen threatened us with a time limit saying he won't agree to any terms until after he's talked to you, and we haven't heard a goddamn thing from them since. So that's all I have to go with."

Lippencott punched the number into his cell and handed Riehle the phone. "Nice and easy now."

He waited through two rings and Metcalf's politician-sincere message before the beep. "Mr. Jensen?" Riehle didn't know if the men were near the answering machine or in a completely different room, but he wanted Jensen to hear him clearly. "This is Detective Kevin Riehle. My partner and I are outside the house and we'd like to—"

"Come inside," Jensen said. Then he broke the connection.

Riehle closed the phone and gave it back. "He wants us to come in."

"Both of you?" Lippencott said.

"He didn't say otherwise."

Capparelli shook his head. "Something doesn't feel right. Think Metcalf's already dead?"

"That's what we need you to find out. But I'm not letting him ambush you, either." Lippencott had them unbutton their jackets. "Got your Kevlar vests on? Good. Keep your coats open and your weapons ready."

He told Riehle to give him his cell, then he called the number, opened it on the first ring, and stuffed it in Riehle's front pocket.

"Leave the line open. Keep talking. I want to know what's going on at all times. Tell us what room you're in. We've got architectural plans of the house. Question Jensen about what he did to Metcalf so we know what condition he's in. Keep Jensen talking. Separate once you get in there so you won't be an easy target. Try to position yourselves so Jensen is between you. He won't be able to watch both of you at the same time and it'll throw off his concentration. Keep him relaxed. Just a nice little chat between friends."

Lippencott indicated a number of locations. "SWAT team's on the way. We'll position the snipers all around the house. If Metcalf is dead and you feel threatened in any way, get the hell out of there. If force is needed and you're in a situation where you can't subdue him by yourselves or get out safely, concussion grenades are ready if you think we can take him alive. Keep in mind that you'll be impaired too, so don't leave yourselves in a compromised position in case Jensen comes out of it first. The curtains are drawn and we can't shoot blindly, so you'll have to be very specific on what window you're nearest. Then get down and stay the hell out of the way. Any questions?"

When the detectives said no, Lippencott reviewed the code words for the various emergency situations, made sure the safeties were off on their weapons, and told them to get going. "I want four *live* bodies when this is over."

"Roger that," Riehle said.

The detectives slowly made their way up the driveway. Riehle was peripherally aware of the shouting in the background and the other officers and the media watching and judging them. The cold wind whipped the hair on their heads and numbed their skin. Riehle had never felt so exposed.

They stopped at the front door. Riehle remembered standing there in the rain when Metcalf wouldn't allow him inside, a barrier to the outside world that Metcalf felt he could personally control. He could only imagine Metcalf's surprise when Jensen forced his way into his private sanctum. Riehle had an eerie vision of Jensen maneuvering a dead Metcalf like a marionette:

tongue hanging out, head lolling to the side while Jensen manipulated the strings, making Metcalf dance in a way he never could while the man who had destroyed his family was still alive.

"Ready for this?" Capparelli said.

"Ready as I'll ever be." They waited until a news helicopter passed overhead before drawing their weapons. "I'll cover you."

"Got it."

Positioning themselves on either side of the door, Riehle knocked, then turned the knob and pushed the door open a few inches. "Mr. Jensen?" he shouted. "It's Detective Riehle." When he didn't hear any response or movement on the other side, he added: "We just want to talk."

Still nothing. Riehle readied his weapon, nodded to Capparelli, then took a deep breath and kicked the door open wide. Capparelli went in low and to the left while Riehle moved to the right in a shooter's stance, looking down the barrel as he swung his gun back and forth, searching.

They were in the tiled foyer. Capparelli crouched at the foot of the stairs leading to the second floor while Riehle checked the adjacent living room, both of them moving to the sides farthest away from the long corridor that extended from the front door to the kitchen at the back of the house.

Nothing moved. Everything was as still as a graveyard at dawn.

Riehle spotted another doorway leading from the living room into the dining room and around to the far side of the kitchen. Signaling where he was going, he gestured for Capparelli to hang back until he was in position.

Taking a quick glance down the corridor, Capparelli mouthed *Go*.

Pistol extended before him, Riehle scurried through the living room, stopped, checked to make sure all was clear, then hurried through the dining room to the doorway leading into the kitchen. He hung back, just inside the doorway, his back pressed against the wall, trying to control his breathing. Blood pulsed in his ears.

After raising his eyes to the ceiling in an unvoiced prayer, he risked a quick glance around the corner. The ultra-modern kitchen had a center island with a touchpad range, stainless steel appliances, granite countertops, and glass cabinets with recessed lighting that showed off the china patterns and crystal glassware. So perfect was everything in placement and cleanliness that Riehle fleetingly wondered if dinners were ever made there, or if everything was takeout and reservations. A guilty pang shot through him. Riehle's house had squeaky wooden cabinets hiding plastic tumblers and mismatched vacation coffee mugs, and the contrast was a stark reminder of how people like Metcalf sometimes made him feel inadequate as a provider for his own family. The kitchen smelled of stale cappuccino.

And in the family room beyond, an armed Jensen stood over a kneeling, disheveled Metcalf.

Riehle took a calming breath, getting his head back in the game. Both were still alive. So far so good. He swallowed hard, then called out: "Mr. Jensen? It's Detective Riehle. I'm in the dining room. I'm coming into the kitchen. Everything's nice and easy now, okay? I just want to talk."

"Please come in, detective," Jensen answered. "I've been waiting for you."

Carefully, Riehle rounded the corner, weapon held waist-high with both hands. Jensen had moved closer to the fireplace so that the kneeling man was between them, though he wasn't using him as a shield. Instead of the fevered man he'd last seen, Jensen appeared strangely calm. A look of relief flashed across his face when he saw Riehle, filling the detective with hope that everything was going to be all right, before Jensen replaced it with an angry mask. Riehle involuntarily tightened his grip on his gun.

Capparelli saw the change, too. He came out of the hallway then, his own weapon extended, and moved quickly into the family room along the farthest wall away from them while Riehle simultaneously stepped to his right, placing the cooking island between them.

If Jensen was bothered or upset by Capparelli's presence, he didn't show it.

Riehle felt a buzzing inside the back of his skull. The smell of cappuccino, the sharpness of the surrounding details, the crackling of the wood in the fireplace all came into focus. His cop sense warned him that everything wasn't what it seemed.

"We just want to talk," Riehle reassured him. Then remembering the phone was on, he said, "How are you feeling, Mr. Metcalf?" for Lippencott's sake and anyone else who was listening.

Metcalf mumbled an inaudible response.

"Are you uncomfortable by the fireplace?" he asked, trying not to sound too obvious. He didn't voice out loud his observation that Metcalf was hunched in an execution-style pose, wrists and ankles bound with duct tape, because he didn't want to alarm anyone. Jensen wasn't aiming his gun at the back of the man's head, and Riehle didn't want any panic or sudden storming of the house. Right now, his demeanor was relatively nonviolent and Riehle intended to use that to defuse the situation.

Metcalf merely shook his head in answer to his question.

Keeping his right hand on the gun, Riehle held up his left hand, palm open, fingers splayed, showing he wasn't trying to hide anything. "We just want to talk, right? Just like you asked. But it's hard to hear you all the way over here in the kitchen, so I'm going to come closer now. Okay?"

Riehle took a careful step forward, then another, slowly,

watching Jensen closely and gauging his reactions. No quick or threatening moves. His mouth was suddenly dry.

When Riehle reached the family room carpet, Jensen pointed the gun at Metcalf. "Stop."

Riehle's heart hammered against his ribcage. He felt almost dizzy from the rush of overloaded senses: the lingering aroma of cappuccino, the thick, smoky air, the warmth of the crackling fire that made his cheeks flush, and the nearness of the other two men whose lives hung in the balance.

"Sure. Okay, then," he said, trying to appear calm and relaxed. "This is good."

Metcalf bowed his head. Here in this meticulously designed room with its plush leather couches, beveled glass tables and ceramic lamps, silk plants, thick carpeting, artsy knickknacks and books most likely never intended to be read, the disheveled man appeared small and hopelessly out of place.

Jensen sniffled. He wiped his moist eyes with the back of his free hand. His gun hand trembled slightly and his lower lip quivered. Sweat soaked his shirt along the collar and under his armpits. From a distance Jensen had appeared calm and collected, but up close Riehle could tell the man was barely holding himself together.

"Don't do this," Riehle said softly.

It was the wrong thing to say.

"Don't do this?" Jensen said. Anger flared in the troubled man's eyes. "Don't *do* this? That's all anyone keeps telling me." He prodded the back of Metcalf's head with the gun barrel and Metcalf flinched. "But what about him? He's the one who killed my family. Why didn't anyone say that to him?"

The hair rose on the back of Riehle's neck. The stifling air around them felt as charged and volatile as a lightning storm over an oil refinery. He held up a placating hand. "You're right, I'm sorry. That's not what I meant."

"What you meant? Why do you think we're here?"

"Okay, okay. Let's just calm down a minute. No one wants to get hurt."

"*Hurt?* He killed my family! The only thing that's ever mattered to me, and all anyone's done since then is tell me what *I* can't do."

A flicker of light caught Riehle's attention. From where he stood, the way the firelight reflected off the beveled glass coffee table with the fireplace positioned behind him made it look as if Jensen was surrounded by flames.

"Larry . . ."

"He. Killed. My. Family!" Jensen spat out the bitter words. A log popped in the fireplace and Metcalf twitched. "And you've been treating *me* like a criminal ever since. Putting out a restraining order, sticking me in a hospital—*he's* the one who killed my family! Why doesn't anyone do anything to him?"

The resentment, anger, frustration, and depression started bubbling over. "Why are you protecting him? Don't I have any rights? My family was everything to me, my whole reason for living. Everything I did was for them and he took them away from me. Forever. I wanted him to understand what he did, but he didn't care. All this time, he's never even said he was sorry!"

"All right, all right already," Metcalf sputtered. He tentatively glanced over his shoulder. "I'm sorry. There, I said it. Are you happy now? Now let me go and I won't press charges."

Riehle wanted to slap him. All of this was his fault. In his fancy house with its plush furniture and expensive appliances, the man appeared to have everything except an ounce of decency or compassion. Riehle reminded himself that he was here to protect and serve and to get everyone out safely. But looking down at the man who had caused so much pain, Riehle was ashamed and disgusted with himself for allowing someone like Metcalf to make him feel inferior.

"See? *That's* what I mean. Do you see how he treats me?" Jensen began to tremble violently. "He still has *his* family. But I have nothing. Nothing!"

Capparelli moved slightly to the side, putting more distance between them, and Jensen's wild eyes went back and forth between the detectives. Capparelli lowered his weapon slightly as Riehle said, "Relax. Everything's going to be fine."

"He left me no choice."

"There are always choices."

"I just can't deal with it anymore."

Sweat rolled down under Riehle's shirt. He extended his hand. "Then let me help. This can all end peacefully."

"No," Jensen said. His voice was filled with sad resolution as he placed the barrel of the gun against Metcalf's head. "No, it's just gonna end."

Time shifted into slow motion then. Metcalf hunched his shoulders and squeezed his eyes shut, preparing for the fatal shot even as Riehle raised his arms and brought his hands together to grip his weapon, his reflexes kicking in while his muscles struggled as if he were underwater with lead weights attached to his limbs. Capparelli took a step forward, and Jensen moved his gun away from Metcalf's head and aimed it at Capparelli before his partner could bring his own weapon up in time. Riehle watched in horror as Jensen lifted the gun toward Capparelli's unprotected face; and Riehle aimed his weapon, his finger tightening on the trigger as Jensen, seeing Riehle was about to fire, suddenly swung his gun arm out into the open air between the detectives and turned his body toward Riehle. A voice inside Riehle's head screamed "Don't! Don't! Don't!" even as his instincts and training took control, his finger squeezing the trigger and the gun going *BLAM! BLAM! BLAM!* before Riehle could stop himself; and he watched helplessly as Jensen's chest exploded with three gaping red holes as the man flew backward, his arms flailing wildly and his feet up in the air, crashing into the glass end table and knocking the ceramic lamp to the floor and finally coming to rest on top of the potted silk plant beside the fireplace.

Everything suddenly went still.

Riehle's ears rang from the shots. His head throbbed and his palms were wet. The smell of cordite filled the room. A wave of sadness unlike any he'd ever felt before washed over him as he looked down at the man who'd lost everything that was dear to him and now had nothing left at all. Riehle wasn't sure if the gun in his trembling hand or the pressure in his heart was heavier, but the horror of the terrible moment and the growing realization of what had really happened seemed almost too much for him to bear.

His nose crinkled at the sudden odor of urine and feces. Riehle noticed the stain on Metcalf's pants and the widening puddle beneath him.

Metcalf glanced over his shoulder at the dead man and the blood splattered on the walls and fake plants, before turning on the detectives.

"Look what you did!" he shouted, his face flushed with indignation. "You almost got me killed!"

CHAPTER THIRTY-THREE

". . . Walter Buczyno, the alleged Westbrook serial killer, was discovered hanging in his cell early this morning prior to his intended transfer to the Granger County Jail," the television reporter announced in her indignant, politically correct tone. She stood so the viewer could see the Westbrook Police Department sign over her right shoulder and was positioned so the wind would enhance the fullness of her hairstyle. The word LIVE and the station's logo appeared in the screen's lower left corner without obstructing her outfit. "Westbrook officials refuse to comment about the possibility of foul play at this time. Melissa Thorne, the prominent attorney, will be joining us shortly to discuss the hotly debated issue of prison security and the rights and mistreatment of inmates—"

"Ah Christ, not her again," Capparelli said. It was early afternoon, and the detectives sat in recliners in the living room of Capparelli's townhouse watching the news and weather reports on his wall-mounted, flat-screen TV. Dressed in jeans and a faded Ozarks sweatshirt, Riehle was on suspended leave with pay during the investigation of Jensen's shooting, while Capparelli, wearing khaki slacks and a denim shirt rolled up to his elbows, was taking a few "strongly encouraged" vacation days. Gavin had used the pretext that he wanted them away from the media spotlight, but the detectives figured he simply wanted them out of his hair. "Media whore! She's been on every station so far."

"Want to change the channel?" Riehle said. "Or turn the whole thing off?"

"Nah, we'd better keep it on. Just in case. You never know what they might come up with." Using the remote, he muted the sound when Melissa Thorne started in on another one of her famous rants. "Doesn't mean we gotta listen to her crap, though."

Riehle finished his beer, set the empty green bottle on the table between them, and settled in the chair, allowing his eyes to wander around the room. A large cabinet entertainment center filling the entire wall around the television held Capparelli's DVR and DVD player, stereo components, and a massive collection of CDs and DVDs. The mismatched couch, recliners, lamps, coffee and end tables (one holding a pathetic-looking cactus), and a desk with a computer, monitor, and printer on top filled the room with an eclectic mix of country comfort and discount electronics. Though the décor screamed "Male, suddenly on his own," the furnishings felt oddly comfortable, in an ESPN sort of way.

Outside, the first flakes of the huge, end of January storm began tapping against the window.

On the television screen, Melissa Thorne was replaced with a previously run clip of uniformed officers and coroner's officials wheeling a gurney carrying Buczyno in a body bag out of the Westbrook PD station.

"*Straw Dogs*," Riehle mumbled.

"How's that?"

"Nothing," he said, surprised that he'd spoken out loud. "It was just something I saw on TV when the case first started. You remember *Network*? And *Straw Dogs*?"

"Sure. Peter Finch so mad he wasn't going to take it anymore, and Dustin Hoffman going berserk because his wife was raped and people were breaking into his . . . ah man, I see where you're going. Don't do that to yourself."

Riehle shrugged. "Both movies were on the same night right after we started the case. Part of me wonders if I'd only thought more about it, or put two and two together—"

"What? Like it was some cosmic clue to help you solve the case? Forget it. You couldn't have seen the connection. Besides, the universe doesn't work that way, and you'll only drive yourself crazy pretending it does."

"But if we'd only done things differently—"

"Would it have made any difference? Really? Even if we'd known what had happened in that house, we still would have had to go after him. Buczyno's fate was already determined before we ever came on the scene."

Grudgingly, Riehle had to agree. Still, he privately wondered how may other things he'd missed during his life that had been right in front of him all along.

He stared at Buczyno's DMV photo on the TV screen. "I keep thinking about what he said about taking care of his own problems. Do you think that's why people are so fascinated with shows like *The Godfather* and *The Sopranos*? That people nowadays feel so victimized and preyed upon by society that they're fascinated by anyone who takes care of his own problems, for good or bad?"

Capparelli took a long swallow of his beer. "That's a little deep for me. Personally, I just want to make it through the day in one piece, one day at a time, knowing at the end of the day that I did the best I could and leaving it alone at that."

"Then you think we did the right thing?"

"We did the only thing we could," Capparelli replied. "Doesn't matter anyway now. The case is out of our hands, and honestly, I'm glad to be rid of it. Time to move on. Speaking of which," he said, getting out of his chair, "let's put on some music. This whole thing depresses the hell out of me."

"Sounds good."

Perusing his CD collection, Riehle was surprised to find the complete collections of R.E.M. and U2 among the expected classic rock and jazz selections. "I thought you didn't listen to anything recorded after nineteen-eighty?"

"No, I said I didn't listen to people with purple and green hair." Capparelli grinned. "Seriously though, music has always been an important part of my life. Hell, I've even picked out two songs I want played at my funeral."

"Really? Which ones? C'mon, you can tell me."

Capparelli hesitated. " 'Knockin' On Heaven's Door.' "

"Dylan. Sure. What's the other?"

" 'I Hear You Knocking.' "

Riehle laughed. "Some people might not find that so amusing, though."

"Screw 'em. I'm the one who'll be dead."

"Not yet."

"Nope, not yet. Thanks to you." He cleared his throat. "Anyway, what about you? Any songs you want played?"

"Never really thought about it. I don't know. Buddy Holly's 'It Doesn't Matter Anymore,' I guess."

"Sure, that'll work," Capparelli said, though not sounding particularly impressed. He pulled a Miles Davis CD out of the stack. "Ever hear *Kind of Blue*?" When Riehle shook his head, he popped the CD into the stereo and adjusted the volume. "I like to think of it as the Rosetta Stone of jazz for those of us raised on rock and roll."

Riehle listened for several minutes, appreciating the music. "You know, when I close my eyes, I can almost imagine myself in New York in the Fifties, looking out my apartment window at a rainy day." Then he barked an embarrassed laugh. "Geez, will you listen to me? Always putting pictures to music. Too many years of watching MTV, I guess."

"Look at the bright side: What if MTV was invented a decade earlier? Can you imagine having to sit through the videos for 'Billy, Don't Be A Hero' and 'Heartbeat, It's A Lovebeat'?"

"Only at gunpoint," he admitted.

"Take a seat and enjoy the music, while I get us some salsa and chips and a couple more beers."

"Best idea I've heard all day."

Riehle offered a smile as Capparelli went into the kitchen. He knew Ray was trying hard to cheer him up, inviting him over for the afternoon while Gwen took Karen to gymnastics after school. But the truth of the matter was he'd been pensive and moody ever since the shooting. Visions of Jensen plagued him throughout the day, haunting images of the desperate man purposely turning toward him, making himself a target. And at night he woke in sweat-soaked sheets, trembling uncontrollably, almost feeling Gwen's hand on his shoulder and vaguely aware of her loving reassurances; but lost, instead, inside a nightmare moment whose intense sights and sounds and smells had yet to diminish within his troubled mind.

Suicide by cop.

It was all so easy to see now that he tortured himself with a single, unanswerable question: *Why couldn't I stop in time?*

Riehle rubbed a weary hand over his forehead. So many mistakes he'd made. For all the shenanigans O'Connell had pulled, he never once did anything like this. If Riehle hadn't always been in such a hurry to judge his former partner's conduct, he might have learned something that could have prevented the mistakes on this case. Hard lessons learned at the cost of a good man's life.

No wonder Gavin wanted him out of his sight.

Holding a bowl of salsa inside a larger bowl of chips in one hand and gripping two beer bottles by the necks in the other, Capparelli reentered the room and set everything down on the end table between the two recliners before noticing Riehle's expression.

"Don't go there, partner."

"He *used* me," Riehle said, spitting out all his hurt and self-incrimination in that single phrase.

"No, he *needed* you."

Capparelli took a seat and indicated Riehle should do the same. He handed Riehle a beer when he was settled, then took the other for himself. "Jensen was in pain, the kind of pain that eats you alive, and you were the only one he could depend on to make it all go away."

"But why? Why did it have to come down to that?"

"He told you. He couldn't live without his family. And when Metcalf took them away, his life wasn't worth living anymore."

Recalling the look of relief on Jensen's face when they'd confronted him in Metcalf's house, Riehle felt ashamed that he had interpreted it as a sign of hope, when in fact Jensen had other plans in mind. He knew his suffering was almost over.

"Why couldn't I have seen what he was doing?"

"Because you can never know what's going on in someone else's head," Capparelli said. "Besides, he wasn't thinking clearly by then. He was in too much pain."

"Do you think he would have harmed Metcalf?"

"Sure, it's possible. I mean, you've got to admit that digging up his daughter's grave wasn't exactly the sanest thing to do. He . . ."

Capparelli sighed. Sensing Riehle needed the truth, he said, "No, probably not. I doubt Jensen could have hurt a fly. Even at the end, he couldn't bring himself to harm Metcalf, the one person who'd taken everything away from him. That's why he needed you, because he couldn't even hurt himself."

Riehle nodded. Though his partner's words reaffirmed his own suspicions, it didn't ease his burden. Jensen was dead because of his actions. He took a sip of beer, but the brew tasted as bitter as his mood.

A flash of anger rose within him. Instead of being grateful for saving his life, Metcalf, embarrassed that he'd shit and pissed his pants, had retaliated by publicly threatening to sue Riehle, Capparelli, and the entire Westbrook Police Department for reckless endangerment, harassment, and any other trumped-up charges he and his slimy ambulance chaser could come up with. As it was, his lawyer had already petitioned the court to drop all charges related to the accident because of the mental anguish Metcalf had suffered at Jensen's hand during the hostage ordeal.

Riehle swallowed the sour bile that rose in his throat. In his darkest moments, in a place so deep within himself he didn't want to admit existed, Riehle wished that Jensen had killed Metcalf before the detectives arrived.

"So the financial guy who destroyed an entire family, he, what? Gets away with everything?"

"Isn't that the way it always works?" Capparelli said. "Me? The one I want to get my hands on is Jensen's sister."

Last seen at the hospital on the day of Larry's escape, Sheila was nowhere to be found. The detectives had put out an APB on her, but it appeared the woman had gone underground. Studying her past history and rap sheets listing numerous arrests for unlawful protesting, public disturbances, and civil disobedience, they discovered many gaps in the woman's recorded existence and realized she knew what she was doing and how to accomplish it for an extended period of time. Frustrated, they knew the only thing they could do was wait her out until she eventually resurfaced again.

"Okay, so maybe I took Jensen out of his misery. But it doesn't make it any easier on me. He still used me."

"No, he needed you," Capparelli repeated. He looked down at his beer bottle, then added so softly that Riehle almost didn't hear: "Like I did."

Riehle frowned. "But you said he never would have harmed anyone. You were never in any real danger."

"No, that's not what I'm saying at all."

A hush fell over the room. The CD had already played through, and the only sounds remaining were the faint whistle of heated air rushing through the vents and the tapping of snowflakes blown against the windowpanes.

Curious, Riehle held his tongue. Capparelli obviously had something important on his mind, something he needed to share. Riehle pushed aside his own frustrations, wanting to help.

"Remember the story about how I beat up the guy I caught in bed with my wife?" Capparelli said after a long moment. "Well, um, that's not the way it really happened."

Riehle didn't know what to say.

"Everything was great in the beginning. Charlotte was so amazingly beautiful that I was willing to overlook things for a long time." He swallowed hard. "Probably too long."

Unable to meet Riehle's eye, Capparelli stared down at his beer bottle. Starting at one corner, he began peeling off the foil label. The *tink*ing of his thumbnail against the glass was the loudest sound in the room.

"Looking back," he continued, "I realized I'd been in denial for years. The way the other guys at the station all hovered around her at bars or the station house picnics, or the way they'd suddenly stop talking when I came into the room. Nothing too obvious, at first. I just chalked it up to jealousy, you know, like they were envious of me being with such a babe. That is, until the night I found a photo of my wife on the locker room floor."

Riehle was unable to hide the surprise on his face.

"It was a picture I'd never seen before. She was in bed, under the sheets, and though it didn't show anything, her hair was messed up and you could tell what she'd been doing." His nostrils flared when he exhaled sharply. "Thing is, her hairstyle was one she'd had ten years earlier."

"Was the photo sticking out of someone's locker?"

He shook his head. "No, I found it under a sink near the trash can, so I couldn't tell who it belonged to. I don't know if it was left out by mistake or on purpose, but I went nuts when I found it. All these thoughts started rushing through my head. How long had this been circulating? How many of the guys had seen it? Were there any other pictures of her? Who else had she been with? How long was everyone fucking my wife and laughing at me behind my back?"

Grabbing what he'd been able to lift up so far, Capparelli ripped the label off the bottle, crumpled it in his fist, and threw it across the room. "I was angry and hurt and embarrassed, and I took out my rage on the trash can and mirrors and toilet seats."

"Did you confront her about it?"

"Of course, but she denied everything. Said it was probably a photo I didn't remember taking. Yeah, right. But I knew, and after that, everything started to add up. The times she wasn't home when I got off shift, the way the bed hadn't been made since morning, the odd smells, how she always flirted and the way the other guys acted around her . . . until the night I came home early and caught her in the act."

Clenching his teeth, his jaw muscles visibly tightened along the sides of his face. "I thought it'd be one of the guys from the station, and I was ready to beat the shit out of him. But when I saw it was our new neighbor, a guy who'd moved in only a few weeks before, I saw Charlotte for what she really was and realized she wasn't worth it." Capparelli's head bobbed, like a condemned man accepting his fate. "So I just closed the door and walked away."

Stunned, Riehle said, "Then Dixie's story . . . ?"

"Was a lie. We made it all up, Charlotte and I. For all the crappy things she did, she claimed she understood how important my image was and wanted to prove she still cared about me. A cop is a man of action, a hero on the streets. Anything less shows weakness. So we agreed on the story that I beat the guy up to save face."

Capparelli stared into his beer as if the answers to all his inner turmoil floated within. "But not long after, even before our divorce was finalized, the guys were smirking and openly mocking me, and I knew she'd lied to me again." He rolled his eyes. "Surprise, surprise. Pretty soon I felt like everyone knew that I was the guy who'd done nothing at all."

Now Riehle understood why Capparelli had reacted so strongly to Buczyno's question: *What kind of a man does nothing?* It had speared him to the very heart of his insecurities. Doubtless he thought Buczyno (and possibly everyone watching through the one-way mirror) was mocking him. Riehle felt for him. No wonder he looked like he'd been kicked in the balls.

"I thought I could deal with it, at first. Everything was out in the open, so fine, it's done, it's over, time to move on and be grown-ups about it." Capparelli shook his head. "But my fellow detectives and officers had other ideas. No one wanted to be partners with a guy who didn't stand up for himself. Too risky. But I fought back. I had seniority, I'd worked too damn hard to get to my position and I wasn't going to give up without a fight. And I thought things were finally starting to get better until the night we raided the meth lab . . ."

His hands tightened around the bottle, and his eyes took on a hard glint.

"It was supposed to go by the book. The meth lab was located in the basement of a three-flat on a crowded, run-down street. Most of the guys were going in behind the battering ram, but the commander ordered two of us to cover the alley. That way we'd be in position in case they tried to escape out the back."

He glanced sideways at Riehle. "That was the plan, anyway. But the guy assigned to me, Dominic, was one of the guys who always gave me the hardest time about Charlotte. We were supposed to cover each other. I went in first, but he didn't arrive until a minute later."

An angry red flush rose up his neck and cheeks. "When we got back to the station, I laid into that sonofabitch until the other guys finally broke us up. Dominic claimed he was late because he thought he heard someone call him from the side yard. And the commander believed him."

Capparelli put up his hand. "Now I know what you're thinking. It was an accident, a freak coincidence, maybe I'm being a little paranoid. Sure, sure, I know. Cops look out for their own, right? The Brotherhood of the Badge, the Wall of Blue, and all that shit. But let me tell you something: Things are different when money or a woman is involved."

He took a long breath and slowly released it. "I gotta tell you though, that was the longest minute of my life. A lot of things went through my mind. Standing in that darkened alley, streetlights busted out and open windows all around me—any one of which could have had a sniper waiting—and I felt like I'd been set up and was going down." He shrugged. "Okay, so nothing happened then, but who's to say it wouldn't the next time? Or the time after that? And then I realized I couldn't trust them anymore.

"So the next morning I put in for my transfer."

Riehle nodded, understanding. Gavin had told him on their first day that Capparelli had transferred for personal reasons. Betrayed by both his wife and his fellow officers—it didn't get any more personal than that.

Capparelli tipped his beer toward him. "And then I met you.

And the very first time we were in danger you were there for me."

Riehle started to protest, but Capparelli stopped him. "Sure, we know now that Jensen was just forcing your hand. He probably wouldn't have fired. But you never hesitated, not even for a second." He shifted in his seat. "What I'm trying to say is that with my wife, my neighbors, my so-called friends and colleagues . . . it's been a long time since I've known anyone I could trust."

He looked him straight in the eye then. "And that means more to me than anything else I can imagine. I want you to know that I'll always have your back. You can depend on me."

Riehle tipped his bottle toward him. "Never doubted it for a second, partner."

They talked a while longer until they had nothing left to say, then sat comfortably in silence, enjoying each other's company, flipping back and forth between the various news and sports stations until it became apparent that the storm outside was growing worse and it was time for Riehle to leave. He finished his beer and set the bottle on the end table. "Better hit the road."

"Glad you came over." Capparelli walked him to the front door. He opened the hall closet and reached inside for Riehle's jacket. But their coats were tangled and when he shook them apart, a CD fell out of Capparelli's overcoat pocket and bounced to the floor at Riehle's feet.

He picked it up. "*The Best of Spandau Ballet?*"

Capparelli snatched it out of his hand. "Nothing. Just forget it. I mean . . ." He sighed. "Ah hell, it's for my dinner with Ruth tomorrow night, okay?"

"Who?"

"Ruth. The receptionist at ADAC Security Systems?" His face flushed with embarrassment. "She seemed kinda nice, you know? So I went back to ask her out, and 'True' was playing on the radio and she was, like, singing along at her desk when I walked in, so I thought, well, you know, it might be nice to play it in the car on the way over to the restaurant and—what are you grinning at?"

"Not a thing, buddy," Riehle said, biting the inside of his cheek. "Not a thing."

Capparelli looked down at the CD cover. "You won't tell anyone at the station, will you?"

"I wouldn't dare." Riehle put on his jacket. "So what made you decide to ask her out?"

He shrugged. "Guess I realized that being alone wasn't all it's cracked up to be." He waved the CD at him. "Seriously. You won't tell anyone about this?"

"You can count on me."

Capparelli smiled. "Thanks, partner."

Riehle opened the door. Outside the wind was beginning to pick up, and several inches of snow had already accumulated. He shook his head. A few days ago they were wearing windbreakers and now, this. Chicago weather, gotta love it. It was funny how nature had a way of throwing things at you.

He spun around and snapped his fingers. " 'Nature's Way.' "

"What is?"

"No, no. The song by Spirit. Can't you hear that opening line playing at a funeral?"

Capparelli thought for a moment, then threw his head back and laughed. His laugh was so warm and big and genuine that Riehle knew that their partnership, and yes, even their friendship, was going to work out just fine.

It was snowing even harder by the time Riehle cleaned off his car and drove away. The flakes were large and heavy and coming down at an angle as a fierce wind began to build. Soon everything would be covered under a blanket of whiteness, hiding the dirt, and making the world appear fresh and clean and pure. For a while, anyway.

Riehle breathed deeply. The windshield wipers swept back and forth while the defroster blew warm air across his face. On the radio the broadcaster described numerous accidents, lane closures, and dangerous whiteout conditions. The much-anticipated snowstorm with heavy accumulations that always followed a January warm-up had finally arrived with a vengeance.

He headed home. Though the snow was falling steadily, it had yet to reach the intensity that was currently pounding the northwest suburbs, and Riehle's thoughts turned inward as he navigated the winding streets.

What was it Capparelli had said that first day as they were driving away from the Jensen accident? Something about how people dealt with the loss of their loved ones?

Yes, that was it. Death. An inevitable and undeniable part of life, and he could no more protect his loved ones from it than he could prevent it for himself. But like a veil that had been lifted from his eyes, he saw more clearly now how much it was all around him, acutely reminding him of the frailty of human life and the precious, scant time spent on this earth. And how the decisions made and actions taken based upon the impact of death affected the remainder of that limited time, not always for the best.

Buczyno's obsession with the unfairness of the legal system as the anger within him eroded his soul. Jensen's inability to recover from shock, and his physical and emotional tailspin after the drunken accident that robbed him of his family. Griskel mocking the Grim Reaper himself with his rock star costumes in order to deal with the untimely death of his wife, the Alzheimer's disease that had stolen his mother away, and the horrible and mundane deaths he faced daily as coroner. Even Capparelli's divorce reflected the death of their relationship. Every person dealt with it in their own way. Some accepted their fate and moved on; others compartmentalized their anger and sorrow and subdued their pain by immersing themselves in spirituality or denial, or filling their void with drugs, alcohol, and/or other destructive behaviors; while still others dwelt upon the circumstances of their loss to the point of letting it define their remaining existence, allowing their grief to consume and, ultimately, destroy them.

Riehle felt the tires slide beneath him, and he tightened his grip on the steering wheel. The storm was coming down heavier now, the intensity reducing visibility like a white glove closing around him. He blinked hard, refocusing his attention on the road, noticing other motorists sitting up straighter in their vehicles and slowing down, taking the storm more seriously now as well.

Gwen and Karen were supposed to be attending a double session of Karen's gymnastics that afternoon. Riehle pulled over and tried calling them on his cell phone, but he could only reach voice mail on both their home and Gwen's cell numbers. He left messages on each, warning them about the hazardous conditions and to be extra careful, and telling them that he loved them.

A few more blocks and he'd be home. Riehle had just turned onto Maple Avenue when a car up ahead swerved onto the shoulder just beyond the underpass for Route Eighty-three and cut the engine. He was about to see if the motorist needed help when the driver suddenly jumped out of his car, ran toward the spray-painted graffiti, and started throwing snowballs at the words that Capparelli had written.

Riehle held back and pulled onto the shoulder. He powered the passenger side window down, and even from that distance he could hear the man swearing. As Riehle watched the man retrieve an aerosol can from the trunk of his car and begin spraying black paint over BUT CLAUDE RAINS, a woman pushed open her door and let loose an angry barrage in a tone so loud and piercing that it hurt Riehle's eardrums to hear it. His shoulders hunched, the man continued painting over Capparelli's words as he tried to ignore his wife's verbal onslaught while she publicly berated him.

Unable to hide a grin, Riehle made a note of the plate, but doubted he'd do anything with it. Then he powered the window up and drove past. He thought about charging the man with defacing of public property (selectively choosing to ignore any knowledge of Capparelli's actions, of course), but he knew that whatever happened to this man at home was far worse punishment than anything Riehle could do to him. The wife slapped the man's arms and shoulders and the back of his head as she tried to steal the spray paint can away from him, her shrill voice penetrating the window glass, and Riehle realized sadly that the only place this Fred ruled was in his own mind.

Poor guy. Riehle wondered if the man ever stopped to consider how his life had turned out this way, ever wondered what might have been if he'd only taken another path instead, wishing he could turn back time—

Riehle's hands jerked and the car fishtailed, the wheels losing traction and banging up over the curb, the car sliding, barely missing a yellow-painted fire hydrant and finally coming to a sudden stop along someone's parkway. His head bobbed forward. His hands clutched the steering wheel so tightly that his knuckles turned white and the tendons in his forearms quivered. His chest pounded and the blood sang in his ears. The windshield fogged over as his breath came in such short, ragged gasps that he was almost hyperventilating.

Was that all it was? He buried his face in his sweating palms, squeezing his eyes shut to hold back the tears. All these years he'd been hurting himself and the ones he loved without ever realizing it.

Could it really be that simple?

He shifted the car into reverse, the tires thankfully finding traction, and merged into the sparse traffic. He took a deep, calming breath. Home was only a couple of blocks away, but he turned the car around instead and headed back into the storm.

CHAPTER THIRTY-FOUR

"So the great detective finally figured it out," Ellen Riehle said.

"You don't have to rub it in, Mom."

She gestured to the kitchen table. "Have a seat, hon. Want some hot chocolate? WGN says it's going to be a pretty big storm."

"No thanks." Riehle didn't think the cocoa would sit too well with the salsa, chips, and beer. What he needed was caffeine, something to settle his uneasy stomach. "How about some hot tea instead?"

"Coming right up."

Ellen filled the kettle with water from the tap and turned on the stove. He heard the *tic-tic-tic* and whoosh as the gas ignited. "The news was talking about how that serial killer hung himself this morning."

"That's what they're saying."

Ellen gave him an odd look over her shoulder, but he knew she wouldn't press the issue. She set the kettle on the burner and pulled two tea bags from a white ceramic jar on the countertop. "English Breakfast okay?"

"Sure."

Outside, the wind picked up and blew the snow against the sliding glass door. Several inches had fallen already, and the forecasters were predicting that a foot or more might come down. At the edge of the now-buried flagstone patio, a birch tree, barely visible through the almost whiteout conditions, bent sideways in the storm.

The kettle whistled. Ellen poured the boiling water over the tea bags in the mugs on the counter. Her shoulders were hunched from osteoporosis, and he watched as she bent over the mugs, removing the wet bags and stirring in teaspoons of honey. He wondered about all she'd weathered in her lifetime to care for him, and he realized, finally, how he'd ended up making everything far more difficult than it ever needed to be. Being rigid in his interpretations and justifying to himself that he'd been protecting her, he had, in fact, been hurting her all along, often pushing her to the breaking point through his unwillingness to see anything other than his own twisted viewpoint. He felt something tear inside him.

Ellen set the mugs and paper napkins on the table and sat down. "Oh no, you don't."

"What?"

"You've got that look in your eye again. But I'm not letting you out of it this time. We're going to talk. We *need* to talk."

"I know."

She lifted the steaming mug to her lips and blew across the top, cooling things down. "I was beginning to wonder if you'd ever want to talk about the night your father died. You can't carry that kind of guilt around with you for the rest of your life. I know I can't." She set the mug down. "Did you know I wrote everything down in my will in case you never gave me the chance to tell you?"

The birch tree bent in the wind. He shook his head. "I'm sorry."

"For what?"

"For thinking I was protecting you, thinking I had to be the man of the house."

She patted his hand. "You *were* the man of the house. I'm

just sorry you had to grow up so fast. I'm sure your father never intended it that way."

But that's how it ended up. "So what really happened that night?" he said.

Ellen's face sagged, as if the weight of letting go after so long was the only thing that had been holding her together. "Little things. Such little things that changed our lives forever."

"Mom?"

She traced a finger around the rim of her mug, the ringing sound a faint echo of the howling wind outside. Her eyes were moist when she looked at him.

"Do you have any idea how many times I've thought about that night? Thinking that if I could go back and change just *one* thing, everything would have turned out differently?"

"He had ALS," Riehle said, reminding her as gently as possible that his father was going to die anyway. "There was nothing you or I could have done."

"We could have taken care of him. Made him more comfortable. Spent more time with him. Had a chance to say goodbye."

"His pride wouldn't have let us do anything more."

Anger flashed in her eyes. "Oooh, that damn pride of his. That'd be the first thing I'd change."

"Mom, what happened?"

Her eyes got a distant look in them, of a place she visited far too often. Knowing she'd been preparing for this moment for most of his life, he remained silent, giving her the space she needed.

"Remember how I got to your dad's shop a little later than I'd planned?" She waited until he nodded, making sure he really wanted her to continue. "I knew your father was expecting me, but I ran into a couple of friends at the store and we visited for a few minutes. It didn't seem like such a big deal then. But by the time I got to the shop, he'd already fallen and a customer had arrived before I got there."

"I know that, Mom."

"But you *don't* know how I found him," she said. "And I'm sure he's staring down at us right now, angry that I'm about to tell you this, but, Kevin, your father urinated on himself when he fell."

Riehle's muscles tensed. "What are you saying? That the other man insulted him?"

"No, no, no! Nothing like that. He was a nice man, a regular customer. He was trying to help him. He'd gotten your father some paper towels from the restroom and was helping him sit up when I got there."

"Thennnn . . . I'm not following."

"Remember we had a big argument after you went to bed?"

Riehle nodded. "I was still awake, but couldn't hear what you were saying."

"He wasn't mad I was late," she said. "He was upset by the man's expression when he found him."

She stared down at her mug and ran her finger along the rim.

"That's all he kept talking about. Over and over. About how he couldn't take it, how he didn't want to spend the rest of his life seeing people looking at him with pity in their eyes, doing things that would embarrass us and filling our lives with shame. I told him to stop it, just *stop* it, no one looked at him that way. But he just kept going on and on about how he couldn't do that to us, how he didn't want us going through all that, and that we deserved better than what he could give us now."

Outside, the birch tree fought against the wind, bending almost to the breaking point.

"By the time he finally calmed down, I thought it was over. That it didn't matter I was a few minutes late and it was just a bad case of shame that'd be gone in the morning." Ellen took a deep breath. "But I should have known your father better. How his stupid pride would get the best of him. And when I woke up later and saw the living room light was still on . . ."

She bit her lip to hold back the tears. "I don't even remember the funeral. All I kept thinking about was how different things might have been if I hadn't stopped to talk to my friends. Or arrived before the other man. Or didn't go to bed thinking everything was all right."

Riehle felt the tumblers in his head fall into place. "Then when you caught me holding Dad's clock," he said, "you weren't mad because I was touching his things. Daylight Savings Time had ended and I was simply moving the hands back one hour. But you saw me turning back time."

She swallowed hard, nodding. "And wishing I could go back and change something, anything that might have kept your father from doing what he did."

Riehle put his head in his hands. How could he have been so wrong? He felt his breath come rushing out.

"So, all this time, you were never mad at me? Not even for breaking the clock?"

"Not at first. It was about me and the mistakes *I'd* made," she said. "I always wanted you to know about your father, so you'd remember all the good things. And there were many, believe me. But somehow you built it up in your mind that by not talking about him you were protecting me."

Ellen took his hands down from his face and clasped them in her own. She waited until their eyes met. "At first, I thought it was just your way of dealing with it. A little boy's wall to seal off the pain. But you kept at it, year after year, until you created this fabrication that it was all about me, never realizing what you were doing to yourself and your family."

Riehle bristled. "What do you mean?"

Ellen exhaled sharply. "I swear, sometimes you're as stubborn and pigheaded as your father."

"Mom!"

"You just don't get it, do you? I wouldn't have gotten so mad if it was only about your father and me. But you started carrying it over into every aspect of your life. Dividing and putting everything into their own separate categories and never allowing anything to overlap or interfere with the other. Work and home. Friends and co-workers. Gwen and me." She shook her head. "Honey, life doesn't work that way. Everything overlaps. But when you started denying that Karen needed you, thinking she didn't need time with you because you've been denying your own feelings about your dad, I couldn't take it any more."

Sweat broke out on his forehead as her words sunk in and their meaning became clear.

"If Gwen wasn't able to knock some sense into your head by your anniversary, I'd have given you a good talking to. But you saved me the trouble by coming here today." She took a sip of her cold tea. "I'm sorry, honey, but I can't let you do this to yourself any longer. And I won't let you do it to Karen. She needs you."

The realization of what he'd done struck him like an electric jolt to the heart. Riehle wiped his hands on his pants. My God, he *had* been treating Karen the way he'd always treated himself, pretending that he was worried about Gwen and his mother's welfare when all along he'd been denying his need for his father's presence and love, and expecting Karen to do the same. Capparelli had said as much on their stakeout, and even Simmons mentioned he had tunnel vision when it came to his personal life. Riehle had been so quick to judge others, so busy analyzing how death and loss affected everyone else that he'd never seen what it had done to him.

He shuddered. Sometimes the hardest person to know was yourself.

Riehle looked across the table. Under the worry lines etched deeply into her face and the osteoporosis that bent her shoulders, he saw her true strength for the first time, the burdened woman who had never broken. And she was right. He couldn't do that to her anymore. Or to Gwen or Karen. He'd never realized how much he'd been hurting the ones he loved the most.

Ellen sniffled. She'd been carrying her burden for a long time. The thing Riehle heard most at funerals was how people missed the opportunity to ask the most important questions because they assumed the person would always be there. He didn't know how much more time he'd have with his mother, but he knew there were things she wanted to share with him. And there was so much he wanted to ask, so much he needed to know.

"The snow's getting deep," she said, looking out the window. "You'd better get going before it's too late."

"No, it'll be all right now." Outside, the snow continued to fall, but the fierce wind lessened and the birch tree eased back to its full height, swaying gently in the breeze. He wiped his forehead on his shirtsleeve, then took both their mugs, got up from the table, and turned on the stove.

"Why don't I stay a while longer and you can tell me about Dad. Really, I want you to tell me all about him."

Riehle was online when his family got home.

"Where are you at?" Gwen called out.

"I'm downstairs on the computer." He typed in another few items and hit PRINT as Karen bounded down the carpeted steps with her boots still on, while Gwen followed behind, unwrapping a scarf from around her neck. Giant snowflakes dusted their hair. Cinnamon was curled up near his feet, and her tags tinkled when Karen bent down to pet her.

"I was getting worried about you out in the storm," Riehle

said. "They're saying we could get a foot and a half tonight."

"*Some*body didn't want to miss gymnastics."

Karen grinned. "I can do a one-handed cartwheel now, Daddy. Wanna see?"

"After you take off your boots and warm up with some hot chocolate first. Okey-dokey?"

"Okey-dokey, hokey-pokey."

"What'd you do all day?" Gwen asked.

"Went over to Ray's house for a while. Then I had a long talk with Mom."

Gwen's brow creased. "Everything all right?"

"Yeah. Never better. Really, I'll tell you all about it later."

Karen pulled a thick stack of paper from the printer. "What's this?"

"*That's* a surprise I've got for the two most wonderful girls in my life."

She studied the words on the top page, frowning. "What's a Bed and Breakfast?"

Riehle took the papers from her. "It's a place where mommies and daddies go when they want to spend some time together." He looked at Gwen. "Remember where we stayed in Galena before Karen was born? As long as I'm on suspended leave for a few weeks, I booked us for next weekend so we could celebrate our tenth anniversary a little early. Mom said she'd watch Karen and Cinnamon, and Diane already said she'd cover your hours at the pharmacy."

Gwen offered a lips-only smile. "Sounds nice."

Melted snow dripped from Karen's hair. "Yeah, nice," she said, unable to hide the disappointment in her voice.

"Hey, you don't think I'd forget my favorite princess, do you?" He leafed through the pages, pulling out an e-ticket with her name on it. "What's this say?"

She looked confused. "Where's Or-land-o?" Over her

shoulder, Riehle saw Gwen's face brighten with a huge smile, and her beautiful green eyes welled with tears.

"Why . . ." he said, showing her another sheet with a picture of a hotel printed on it, "it's right here."

Karen gasped. She jumped up and down, her eyes wide as saucers. "Mommy! Mommy! We're going to Disney World!" She snatched the paper out of his hands to show her mother.

"We're all set to go on spring break," he said. "That way you can go on some rides with Emma like you wanted."

She jumped into his lap and threw her arms around him, giving him the biggest hug he could ever remember.

"Oh Daddy, you're the best!"

He held his precious daughter tightly. "No, I'm not, sweetie," Riehle whispered softly into her hair. "But I'm trying."

EPILOGUE

The heavyset man stepped out of his new, white stucco town-house in the gated retirement community and into the Arizona sunshine. The midmorning temperature was already over ninety degrees, and everything indicated it would be as hot and dry as the television weatherman said it'd be. He stooped to pick up the newspaper at the bottom of his driveway.

"Hey, Steadman!"

It took him a moment to react to the name, and by the time the man glanced up and squinted through the brightness, his neighbor had already crossed the short walk between their shared cactus- and gravel-landscaped front yard. Large, blocky sunglasses and a golfing cap with a green visor protected his neighbor's eyes as he extended a liver-spotted hand.

"Roland Segal. Welcome to the neighborhood. How you like things so far, Neil?"

Neil Steadman. It was going to take him a while to get used to that one. Steadman. Like in*stead* of his real name. Walter hoped the protected witness program had used more imagination when they covered his disappearance.

"So where are you from, Neil?" Roland said, after they shook hands. Like most other retirees, he wore a V-neck sweater over a short sleeve dress shirt and khaki slacks. Walter felt sweat bead under his arms and roll down the sides under his Arizona Wildcats T-shirt.

"St. Paul."

319

Roland nodded. "Me and the missus are from Buffalo. We sure don't miss the weather—or the crime. It's real safe around here. You can practically leave your doors open. You up for a round of golf?"

"Thanks, but I've still got a lot of unpacking to do."

"Suit yourself. Maybe we'll have you over later for a drink."

"That'd be nice."

Walter waved when his neighbor drove off to pick up the others for their golf game. He stood at the end of his driveway and looked up and down his street at the endless, identical townhouses. "Behind every great fortune there is a crime," Balzac had written centuries ago. Using a search engine, Walter had found the quote with his new computer last night, and he realized those words still rang true. The little townhouse contained all that remained to him now. It wasn't a great fortune, he knew, but it was his. His only regret was that Dottie wasn't alive to share it with him.

Not that he was going to be there all the time. At times in the future Walter knew he'd be squirreled away in some hotel room or other, awaiting his turn to testify against the men he saw dumping the body of the dead casino dealer into the Mississippi River and implicating their boss in the process. That was part of the deal. Walter had no problem with that.

After he'd told the FBI agent what he'd seen along the river's edge, the FBI brought in Mack Reynolds, head of security at the casino where the dealer had worked. Reynolds had listened to him intently, grinning like a cat with a canary in its mouth while Walter talked about the two men and what they did. He was especially pleased when Walter described the man with the port-wine stain under his left ear and that he remembered the license plate number on the car they drove. But when he told Reynolds about how he actually *heard* the men refer to a man named Denny, and how Denny would be pleased with their actions, Reynolds suddenly looked at Walter as if he'd become the goose who'd laid the golden egg.

"Make a deal with this guy!" Reynolds had said, jumping to his feet. The FBI agent had looked like he was about to argue with him, but Reynolds cut him off. "I don't care what it takes, just make sure he gets what he wants. I'll back anything as long as he testifies for me."

Unable to hide his excitement, Reynolds started for the door. "Where the hell do you think you're going?" the FBI agent called after him.

"Vegas, baby," Reynolds had replied. "I'm going to Vegas."

Walter stood in his new driveway now, the air around him continuing to heat in the morning sun, his insides churning with a confused mix of anger and joy. Anger that the legal system reinforced his opinion that he had rights and options only *after* they'd considered him a criminal, and that as a victim he was little more than a statistic or inconvenience.

Yet at the same time, his whole being was flooded with joy at the knowledge that, spiritually, Dottie was truly here with him and had been the whole time. Closing his eyes, he could almost feel her body next to him, with his arms around her and his face buried in her raven hair while the scent of lilacs wafted on the breeze around them. Putting his trust in her, she had guided him every step of the way toward the path of salvation Mack Reynolds and the FBI were able to provide.

But more than that, he finally understood what Dottie had been trying to tell him all along. She had taken him on a journey to show him that he couldn't stay home waiting for something to happen. He needed to go out and experience everything life had to offer, to find a purpose and his place in the world around him, and to experience life in all its joys and sorrows while he still could. And in those times when he looked into the abyss and felt he couldn't go on any longer, as long as he had faith in her, she, like in her favorite story "Footprints," would carry him on to something greater. All he had to do was believe.

Down the street, another neighbor pulled out of his driveway and drove away, leaving the garage door open. Walter shook his head. He thought about what Roland said about the neighborhood. Safe, he'd said.

Walter nodded. He'd make sure of it.

ABOUT THE AUTHOR

J. Michael Major is a member of the Mystery Writers of America and the Horror Writers Association. His three dozen stories have been published in such anthologies as *DeathGrip 3: It Came From the Cinema, New Traditions in Terror,* and *Tales of Masks & Mayhem, Vol. III,* and such magazines as *Hardboiled, Bare Bone, Pirate Writings, Into the Darkness, Rictus, Outer Darkness, Crossroads,* and *The Sterling Web* (now *The Silver Web.*) **One Man's Castle** is his first novel.